TO

T0066343

“[An] author w

the innate ability to tell a compelling story.”

Tampa Tribune

“John le Carré with a witty, ironic edge.”

Jack Higgins

THE TEHRAN CONVICTION

“Renegade CIA agent Jack Teller is back on the scene in the perilous cauldron of the Iranian Revolution. No character in fiction better embodies the harrowing contradictions of ‘the Company’—and no American writer explores the shadows of our recent history more brilliantly than Tom Gabbay.”

Frank Viviano,
Former Chief Middle Eastern Correspondent,
San Francisco Chronicle

“Told against the background of a real-life CIA coup, *The Tehran Conviction* mixes historical fact with vivid storytelling in ways that will delight readers of both.”

Stephen Kinzer, *New York Times* bestselling author of *All the Shah’s Men*

“Required reading.”

New York Post

“Fans of the previous Teller novels will definitely want to pick this one up.”

Booklist

By Tom Gabbay

THE TEHRAN CONVICTION
THE LISBON CROSSING
THE BERLIN CONSPIRACY

ATTENTION: ORGANIZATIONS AND CORPORATIONS
Most Harper paperbacks are available at special quantity discounts for bulk purchases for sales promotions, premiums, or fund raising. For information, please call or write:

Special Markets Department, HarperCollins Publishers,
10 East 53rd Street, New York, New York 10022-5299.
Telephone: (212) 207-7528. Fax: (212) 207-7222.

TOM GABBAY

An Imprint of HarperCollins*Publishers*

This book was originally published in hardcover June 2009 by William Morrow, an Imprint of HarperCollins Publishers.

This is a work of fiction. Names, characters, places, and incidents are products of the author's imagination or are used fictitiously and are not to be construed as real. Any resemblance to actual events, locales, organizations, or persons, living or dead, is entirely coincidental.

HARPER

An Imprint of HarperCollins*Publishers*
10 East 53rd Street
New York, New York 10022-5299

Copyright © 2009 by Tom Gabbay
ISBN 978-0-06-118860-2

All rights reserved. No part of this book may be used or reproduced in any manner whatsoever without written permission, except in the case of brief quotations embodied in critical articles and reviews. For information address Harper paperbacks, an Imprint of HarperCollins Publishers.

First Harper paperback printing: April 2010
First William Morrow hardcover printing: June 2009

HarperCollins ® and Harper ® are registered trademarks of HarperCollins Publishers.

Printed in the United States of America

Visit Harper paperbacks on the World Wide Web at
www.harpercollins.com

10 9 8 7 6 5 4 3 2 1

If you purchased this book without a cover, you should be aware that this book is stolen property. It was reported as "unsold and destroyed" to the publisher, and neither the author nor the publisher has received any payment for this "stripped book."

Chapter 14

Tetovo is one hundred twenty-five kilometers from the Bulgarian border. I crossed the border an hour before dawn in the locked trunk of a small gray two-door sedan that had been imperfectly manufactured in Czechoslovakia in 1959. In the front seat of the car were two IMRO members from Skopje. They crossed the border frequently and anticipated little trouble. The Bulgars, whatever their official position, had always been sympathetic to Macedonian separatism. The driver, a thickset, neckless man with two stainless steel teeth, insisted that our car would get only a cursory check at the border.

The other passenger was not so confident. The revolt, though history by then, would have put everybody on edge, he said, and the border officials would almost certainly insist on opening the trunk. He wanted me to ride beneath the rear seat, but I simply would not fit into that small space. So I wound up sitting in the trunk with a Sten gun across my knees, ready to start firing the minute the trunk opened.

When we stopped, a guard tapped on the trunk experimentally, then tried to open it. The driver gave him the key, but we had broken one of the teeth, and it didn't work. I heard two of the guards arguing. One insisted that they ought to shoot the lock off or at the very least pop the trunk open with a crowbar. The other, older and evidently more tired, said that he knew the driver, knew there was nothing in the trunk, and was not about to shoot up a man's car. For a while it looked as though the younger guard would get his way, and my finger was right on the trigger, but finally they sent us on through.

We stopped a few miles from the border. The driver had a spare trunk key in reserve and let me out. I left him the Sten gun. We each had a drink of brandy, and he told me to take the flask along with me. I closed it and tucked it away in my leather satchel.

"You know where to go now, brother?"

"Yes."

"Good. Do not concern yourself for Annalya. She is safe, and we shall see that she is kept safe."

"Yes."

"And do not blame yourself for what has happened. Is that what you have been thinking? That it was your arrival that began the rising?"

"Perhaps."

"It would have come regardless. The time was right. Todor knew you brought no help from America. He used you, you see. Your coming was a sign, like a comet in the heavens. It fired the people and put steel in their courage. But there would have been a rising without you, although it would not have been so great a success."

"A success? We . . . your people . . . were butchered."

"Did you expect us to win?"

"No. Of course not."

"And did you think we were such fools that *we* expected victory?"

"But—"

"The reprisals will not be great. The Belgrade government is not that stupid. There will be concessions to us: perhaps a bit more autonomy, the removal of some of the more objectionable Serb ministers in Macedonia. That is one gain. And the other good result is just that action has been taken, that men have stood up and fought and died. A movement feeds on its own blood. Without nourishment it withers and dies. This has been a night of triumph, brother. We fought bravely, and you fought bravely with us. You are safe in Bulgaria?"

"Yes."

"You know the country?"

"I can get around well enough."

"Good. You are sure you do not wish the Sten gun?"

"It might be hard to explain if I get arrested."

"True. But handy in a corner, no? God protect you, brother. It was a good fight."

"It was."

I went eastward on foot, walking toward the emerging sun. The night had been very cold, but the morning was warm in the sunlight, the air very clean and fresh. The hillside was green, but a deeper and much darker green than the fields of Ireland. I was in no hurry and had no special fear of being noticed. My clothes were the same peasant gear worn by the men I saw working in their fields or walking along the road. I knew that they wanted me in Yugoslavia—the last moments in Tetovo, when Annalya and I had huddled together in the storm cellar waiting for a car to spirit us out of town, the army loud-speakers kept demanding that the villagers turn in the American spy. The Yugoslavs wanted me, and by now they might have a fair idea I had gone to Bulgaria, but I couldn't honestly believe they were on my trail. And the morning was too beautiful and the countryside too calming for me to be worried.

It was already growing difficult to believe that the revolution had really happened, that I had been in it and of it. For years I had read avidly of rebellions and coups and risings, of barricades in the streets and gunfire from the rooftops and homemade bombs and savagery and heroism and gutters awash with blood. I read contemporary accounts. I caught the flavor of what happened and what it was like. But it had always been something of which one read.

A girl I once knew took a trip to California and stopped to look at the Grand Canyon. Telling me of it, she said, "My God, Evan, you wouldn't believe it, it looks just like a movie." That, perhaps, is our framework of reference in today's world, our touch point for reality. Life is most lifelike when it best imitates art. The rising in Tetovo had been like a book or a movie, and already it was beginning to feel like something I had read or something I had watched upon a screen. Before that night I had fired guns only in the shooting gallery on Times Square. Now I had shot men and watched my bullets strike them and seen them die. There had, wondrously, been no sense of wonder at the time. And now I could barely believe what had occurred.

The major government assault on Tetovo had crushed our main force of defense and left Todor and a few dozen others dead at the onset. Then there was a stretch of time lost to memory, a confused and hectic bit of fearful scurrying. It never occurred to me to attempt to escape—not, I think, because of a profound emotional commitment to our now-lost cause, but because I was too involved in the mechanics of the fighting, the regrouping of forces, the gunplay, the few pitiful defensive tactics of which we were still capable. It was Annalya who decided that I had to escape and who dragged me away from the fighting, brought me and my leather satchel to relative safety in the cellar, and finally got us a ride south and east of Tetovo.

"You wanted to make sure your brother was killed," I said. "Why are you making sure that I get away?"

"For the same reason."

"I don't understand."

"Todor had to die in battle," she said. "And you must escape. It would be bad for us if the enemy captured you. This way you are our American, mysterious, romantic. The government will know you were here with us and will be unable to lay hands on you. And our people will know you will return some day and resume the fight. So you must escape."

She accompanied me to the farmhouse but refused to go to Bulgaria with me. She felt she would be safe where she was and that she could not leave her people. Her place, she said, was with them. And, in that farmhouse, while other men drank bitter coffee in the kitchen, she asked me to go upstairs with her and make love to her. In a passionless voice she at once offered herself and insisted that her offer be accepted.

It was both loving and loveless—and better than I had thought it would be. Until the moment our bodies joined, it was impossible to think of the act, let alone experience anything resembling desire. But then I was astonished by the urgency of it all. And I was more astonished yet at her cries at a moment of what might have been passion. "A son! Give me a son for Macedonia!"

I did my best.

It took quite a while to reach Sofia, but the city held refuge for me. My host, a priest in the Greek Orthodox Church, lived on the Street of the Tanners, appropriately enough. I did not point out this coincidence to him since I did not tell him my name. I was sent to him by an IMRO member who was also a member of an organization called the Society of the Left Hand. I had heard of this group before but knew very little about it. It seemed to be a quasi-mystic band organized centuries ago to preserve Christianity in the Ottoman Empire. For a time, in the late nineteenth century, they may have engaged in terrorism for profit. I had read that the group had long since ceased to exist, but one learns to disregard such incidental intelligence. Like Mark Twain's obituary, the death notices of extremist groups are often somewhat premature.

And yet, my lack of knowledge of the Society of the Left Hand greatly inhibited conversation. I dared not espouse any particular political viewpoint lest it should develop that Father Gregor did not happen to be in sympathy with that point of view. My IMRO friend had scheduled an eight-hour stay at Father Gregor's for me, after which time I would be able to ride south toward the Turkish border with another friend of his. The first hours passed easily enough. Father Gregor's housekeeper produced an excellent shashlik, and his cellar yielded up a commendable bottle of Tokay. Afterward we sat in his parlor and played chess. His game was better than mine, so much so that we stopped after three games; it was clearly no contest.

As he returned the chessmen to their box he asked if I by any chance spoke English. "I would welcome the chance to speak that language," he said. "One requires frequent practice to remain fluent in a tongue, and I have little opportunity to practice English."

"I have some English, Father Gregor, and would be pleased to converse with you in English."

"Ah, it is good. More wine?" He refilled our glasses. "In an hour we shall have a treat. Or perhaps I should say that you will share my daily treat, if it is your pleasure. At nine o'clock there is a broadcast of Radio Free Europe. Do you often hear it?"

"No."

"For my part, I never miss it. And just as that program concludes there is a broadcast of Radio Moscow, also beamed to Sofia. This is another program I always enjoy hearing. Do you listen to Radio Moscow?"

"Not often."

"Ah. Then, I think it shall be a treat for you. The juxtaposition of these two radio programs is a delight to me. One is dashed from one world to another, and neither of the two worlds reflected has much in common with the world one sees from Sofia. Is this your first visit to Sofia?"

"Yes."

"It is a pity you cannot spend more time here. The city has charms, you know. One thinks of Bulgaria as a crude simple nation of peasants milking their goats and eating their yogurt and living a hundred years or more. One never calls to mind the striking architecture of Sofia or the busy commercial life in the city. I was born on a farm not ten miles from this city and have spent most of my life here. But I have traveled a bit. During the war it was wise to travel. One perhaps was better off if one did not spend all one's time in one place. Do you have difficulty understanding my English?"

"No. You speak very well."

"I was in London for a time. Also in Paris and for a short time in Antwerp. When the time seemed propitious I returned to Sofia. Many of my closest associates have questioned my decision to return here. Why, they wondered, would I elect to spend the remainder of my life in a solemn and often joyless Balkan city? Perhaps you ask yourself the same question."

I attempted something noncommittal.

"One discovers," he said, "that one place is rather like another. And that one's own home, one's ancestral home, has something special to recommend it. You go to Turkey from here, is that correct?"

"Yes."

"To any particular city?"

"Ankara."

"Ah, yes. I was there once many years ago, but I remember very little of the city. My own position then was similar to yours now in Sofia. I had the opportunity to visit the city but lacked the chance to tour it, to see something of its sights. It is unfortunate, I would say, that the involved man has no time for sightseeing. While the tourist, on the other hand, can examine areas at his leisure but cannot relate them to himself because they are not truly involved in his pattern of life. Would you agree?"

I agreed. And I thought specifically of my tour of Andorra, traversing the tiny republic beneath a load of hay. *The involved man—*

By the time we were ready to listen to Radio Free Europe, I still had learned no more of the nature of the Society of the Left Hand. We sat in his library, surrounded by four walls of books, while he fiddled with the dials of an antiquated short-wave radio. I thought of the U.S. television commercials, peasant families huddled together in the darkness, the radio pitched low, the listeners keeping one ear on the voice of freedom and the other ear tuned in anticipation of a knock on the door, a visit from the secret police, a beating, a forced confession, a bullet fired point-blank into the back of the neck. In our comfortable chairs, sipping our large glasses of Tokay, that particular commercial seemed violently unreal.

Throughout the program Father Gregor kept giving vent to peals of unrestrained laughter. He was a tall man, a heavy man, and when he laughed, the walls shook. "Marvelous," he would roar. "Extraordinary," he would explode. And the room would rock with his laughter.

Two news items, both delivered fairly late in the hour, were of special interest to me.

The first was a straightforward report on the revolution in Macedonia. "Do not despair, freedom-lovers of Bulgaria," said the intense voice of a young woman. "The spirit of independence cannot be ground out beneath the heel of communism. Last night patriots in Macedonia rose up in open rebellion against the so-called People's Republic of Yugoslavia. Fighting with sticks and stones, men and women and children stood up on their feet and cast off their chains, fighting against insuperable odds to free themselves from the shackles of economic slavery." The voice dropped an octave. "And once more the brute force of the tyrant crushed the spark of rebellion. Once more the Beast of Budapest trampled on the hope of a people. Once more blood ran red in the streets of yet another country wedged in the shadow of the Russian bear." The voice reasserted itself. "Europeans, Free Europeans, take heart from the example of these Macedonian heroes!

The soil of liberty is fertilized anew by their blood! They have not died in vain! Your day—the day of all mankind—shall come!"

Father Gregor laughed and laughed.

Later in the same program I heard my own name mentioned. I almost dropped my wine glass. This time the speaker was male.

"Yet another act of Russian provocation has threatened the peace of the world," the announcer proclaimed. "This time the crime is espionage, a black art that seems to have been invented in Moscow. The criminal band operates under the leadership of Evan Michael Tanner, an American citizen corrupted by the communist lies and tainted by communist bribery. Through stealth and subterfuge this traitor to the peace of the world managed to get hold of the complete dossier of the British air and coastal defenses. The key defense secrets of this gallant European nation are even this minute moving behind the Iron Curtain toward the tyrant's home base in Moscow.

"Yet there is still hope for mankind. Tanner, it has been learned, is on his way to a small city in northwestern Turkey, there to make contact with his superiors. Will he be intercepted? Free men everywhere, peace-loving men throughout the world, can only pray that he will . . ."

There was a further denunciation of Russian espionage, but I barely heard it. My head was spinning, my palms dotted with sweat. I stole a look at Father Gregor. He seemed too absorbed in the program to pay any attention to me. He was laughing frequently now.

British air and coastal defenses—but how could they have been stolen in Ireland? And if they had been stolen in England, why on earth would the tall man have run to Ireland with them? And for whom had he been working? And why? And—

Gradually, as the announcer shifted to another point, I managed to work out at least a part of it. The only way it made any sense was that the Irish themselves had stolen the British plans. Then the tall man or some other member of his gang had filched the plans a second time in Dublin. That would explain why it was the gardai rather than some branch of British Intelligence that had picked up the tall man's trail, arrested him, and eventually shot him dead.

Who he might be and who might be his employers were still unanswerable questions. But they did not matter tremendously. What did matter was that I seemed to have a load of dynamite in my little leather satchel. It scarcely concerned me where the plans had come from or where they were supposed to be going. But the whole world now knew that I had those plans and the whole world also knew, somehow, that I was on my way to Balikesir, and this was a matter of considerable concern.

How they had found out was another good question. Any of several persons could have told them—Kitty, the Dolans, even Esteban, although I couldn't recall mentioning my precise destination to him. For that matter, I had left a map of Turkey in my apartment, with Balikesir circled in bright blue ink. By now it was reasonable to assume that my apartment had been searched a dozen times over, and the bright blue circle on my map would certainly have been noticed by someone. I didn't think Kitty would have talked and I couldn't picture the Dolans as informers, but of course if Esteban had known anything I'm sure he would have run off at the mouth to the first person who caught hold of him.

The Radio Moscow program had an added kicker. Nothing about the British plans this time, nothing at all. But there was a brief report that went something like this:

"Continuing their program of harassment, agents of the American Central Intelligence Agency once again launched a desperate attempt to undermine the security of one of the peace-loving socialist republics of Eastern Europe. This time our sister nation of Yugoslavia was the victim. Playing on racial friction and decadent economic drives, CIA operatives under the direction of Ivan Mikhail Tanner sparked an abortive fascist coup in the Province of Macedonia. With tons of smuggled weapons and the tactics of Washington-trained terrorists, these social fascists were able to overcome the efforts of the fine people of several Macedonian villages. Through the efforts of people in the surrounding territory, and with the aid of crack government troops from Belgrade, the Washington-inspired uprising was quickly brought under control and the wave of terror ended forever."

I poured myself a fresh glass of wine. It was beginning to look as though there would be quite a delegation waiting for me in Balikesir. The British, the Irish, the Russians, the Turks, the Americans—and, of course, the nameless band that had stolen those plans in the first place.

Why, I was finally beginning to wonder, hadn't I stayed home where I belonged?

"Perhaps I am overly fond of those two programs," Father Gregor commented. "Each, as you can see, is a source of great amusement to me. You noticed, for example, the two rather divergent views of last night's trouble in Macedonia? I wonder which came closest to the truth."

We were drinking thick, bitter coffee in small cups. The radio was silent now. I had trouble paying attention to Father Gregor. My mind was grimly occupied with two problems—the impossibility of entering Turkey and the equal impossibility of leaving Turkey.

"I noticed, too, that one man was mentioned on both programs, though in different contexts. A Mr. Tanner. Did you notice that?"

"Yes."

"Do you find this amusing?"

"I—"

He smiled gently. "May we halt this masquerade? Unless I am very much mistaken, which, I admit, is of course a possibility, I believe that you are the Evan Michael Tanner of whom they speak. Is that correct?"

I didn't say anything.

His eyes glinted brightly. "The infinite variety of life, Mr. Tanner. Once, shortly after the war, I had two alternative courses of action. I could continue to lead a very fast-paced absorbing life. Or I could, so to speak, retire to Sofia. I selected the latter course. As I've mentioned, many persons questioned this decision. That American song—how does it go? About the difficulty of keeping boys on the farm after they've been to France. Do I have it right?"

"More or less."

"Good. At any rate, I made my decision. The precise reasons for it are unimportant. A combination, perhaps, of self-preservation and the conservatism that comes with years. I have noticed, though, that life does not pass one by. When one lives in Sofia, excitement comes to Sofia."

He picked up his coffee, studied it, then set the cup down untasted. "I suspected your identity from the first, if you are interested. You were referred by a member of IMRO, and of course that made me think of Macedonia, and I had heard of you in connection with the uprising. And we spoke in English. That was a test of mine, you see. Your Bulgar is better than my own English, actually. Quite unaccented. But your English has an American accent. This led me to the rather obvious conclusion that you were an American. And during the program I observed your reactions to the various reports upon your activities. But you do not really want to hear me boast of my prowess as a detective, do you? Hardly. At any rate, I know that you are you. Are you really going to Ankara? Or was the report correct?"

"I'm going to a small town. As they said."

"Ah. You have friends there?"

"No."

"None at all?"

"None."

He stroked his chin. "I trust you have a very important reason for going there?"

"Yes."

"May I ask you a delicate question?"

"Of course."

"You need not answer it, and I need not add that you have the option to answer it untruthfully. Is there, perhaps, the opportunity for you of financial profit in Turkey?"

I hesitated for some time. He waited in respectful silence. Finally I said that there was an opportunity for financial profit.

"Substantial profit?"

"Quite."

"So I suspected. I presume you would prefer not to tell me your precise destination in Turkey?"

Did it matter? The rest of the world already seemed to know. I said, "Balikesir."

"I do not know it. In the northwest?"

"Yes."

He took an atlas from a shelf, thumbed through it, located a map of Turkey, studied it, then looked up at me and nodded. "Balikesir," he said.

"Yes."

Father Gregor got to his feet and walked to the window. While looking out it he said, "In your position, Mr. Tanner, I would have a great advantage. I am, as you no doubt know, of the Left Hand. I would be able to enlist the aid of other members of the Left Hand. If I were attempting to bring something into Turkey, they might help me. If, on the other hand, I were bringing something out of Turkey, they again might be of assistance."

I said nothing. I sipped my coffee. It was cold.

"Of course, there is a custom in the Society. I would be expected to give to the Left Hand a tithe of the proceeds of the venture. A tenth part of whatever gain I realized."

"I see."

"What sort of profit do you anticipate?"

"Perhaps a great deal if my information is correct. Perhaps none at all."

"How large a sum if your information is right?"

I named a figure.

"A tenth part of that," said Father Gregor, "would be a substantial sum. Sufficient, I am sure, to interest the Left Hand."

I said nothing.

"But perhaps you would not care to part with a tithe?"

"That would depend."

"On whether you need assistance? And on whether it can be supplied?"

"More or less."

"Ah." He put his hands together. "It would be possible to assemble a dozen very skillful men in Balikesir at whatever time you might designate. It would be possible to supply the materials you might need for a proper escape. It would be possible—"

"A plane?"

"Not without extreme difficulty. Would a boat do?"

"Yes."

"A boat is easily arranged. How powerful a boat would you require?"

"One that could reach Lebanon."

"Ah. It is gold, then?"

"How did—"

"What else does one sell in Lebanon? For many items Lebanon is where one buys. But if one has gold to sell, one sells it in Lebanon. One does not get the four hundred Swiss francs per ounce one might realize in Macao, but neither does one get the one hundred thirty francs one would obtain at the official rate. I suspect you might realize two hundred fifty Swiss francs an ounce for your gold. Is that what you had anticipated?"

"For a priest," I said, "you're rather worldly."

He laughed happily. "There is only one thing."

"Yes."

"It would be necessary for you to join the Society of the Left Hand."

"I would have to become a member?"

"Yes. You are willing?"

"I know nothing about the Society."

He considered this for a few moments. "What must you know?"

"Its political aims."

"The Left Hand is above politics."

"Its general aims, then?"

"The good of its members."

"Its nature?"

"Secret."

"Its numerical strength?"

"Unknown."

"The nature of its membership?"

"Diverse and scattered throughout the earth. Largely in the Balkans, but everywhere. Listen," he said, "you wish to know what you are joining. This is understandable. But you have no . . . what is the expression? Ah. You have no need to know. Perhaps I can tell you simply that my membership in the Left Hand enables me, a simple priest, to live quite nicely in a city where priests rarely live too well. Enough? And I might add that I have only been a priest for a handful of years at that. And that I have few priestly duties. You would be astonished to learn how long it has been since I have seen the inside of a church."

We sat looking at each other.

"You wish to join?"

"Yes."

"That is good." He went to another bookshelf, brought down a Bible, a ceremonial knife, and a piece of plain white cloth. I covered my head with the white cloth, gripped the knife in my right hand, and rested that hand atop the Bible.

"Now," said Father Gregor, "raise your left hand . . ."

Chapter 15

I entered Balikesir three days later on the back of a toothless donkey. From the time I had left Father Gregor, my journey had been an unceasing span of perilous monotony. The trip from Sofia to the Turkish border was uneventful. The crossing of the border, the most singularly dangerous border I had passed, was managed with harrowing ease. With the British air and coastal defense plans between my skin and my shirt, with the leather satchel abandoned in Bulgaria, with my face unshaven and my hair uncombed and my body unwashed, and with Mustafa Ibn Ali's passport clenched in my sweaty hand, I passed through Bulgarian exit inspection, Turkish entrance inspection, and on into Turkey. As I took my first steps onto Turkish soil a whistle sounded to my rear, and someone began shouting. I very nearly broke into a run. It was well that I did not. The whistle and shouting were not for me, after all, but for some fool who had walked away without his suitcase.

After I had bought the donkey, I had just a handful of change left for food. The donkey and I worked our way south and west past Gallipoli and crossed the Dardanelles on the ferry *Kilitbahir* to Canakkale. Then we proceeded southeast to Balikesir. I had to stop from time to time to feed the poor animal and let him get some sleep. As we moved closer to our destination I had to stop even more often because one can ride a donkey only so long before one begins to yearn for a less punishing mode of transportation.

But such details are unimportant, even less exciting in the retelling than in the actual occurrence. I reached Balikesir in the early afternoon, hungry and nearly penniless. I sold the donkey for about a third of what I had paid for him and parted from him with the sincere wish that his next owner would use him more kindly and appreciate him more fully. I walked slowly but surely into the center of the city and knew at last how it felt to be at the eye of a hurricane.

For the remainder of the afternoon I wandered slowly through the downtown section. There could not possibly have been as many agents of various powers as I fancied I saw, but it certainly seemed as though the city was swarming with spies and secret agents of one sort or another. I heard men speaking Turkish in a wide variety of accents and tentatively identified three British operatives, two Irish, a batch of Americans, at least three Russians, and a slew of others whom I included in a broad category headed Spies—Allegiance Unknown.

I had to dodge them all. No one had taken the slightest notice of me yet, and I felt I could remain undetected indefinitely as long as I didn't do anything. But I also had to slip in and out of the streets of the city until I found that house high on a hill at the edge of town, the big house with the huge porch that Kitty Bazerian's grandmother may or may not have recalled correctly. Then I had to break into the porch, remove the gold, accept help from the Society of the Left Hand, and, hardest of all, manage to avoid having the Left Hand walk off with every last cent of the proceeds.

Because I did not trust them an inch.

We had many grand plans, Father Gregor and I. A group of men were already finding their separate ways to Balikesir. We would meet there, according to his plans, and they would help me get the gold from Balikesir to a nearby port, probably Burhaniye. There a boat would lie at anchor, ready to take us on to Lebanon.

I believed this much. But I did not believe my brothers of the Left Hand would be content with a tenth portion. And I did not know how I could get to Beirut without their help, nor did I know how to accept their assistance without getting conned out of the whole treasure.

First things first. If I didn't find the house or if the house held no gold beneath its ample porch, I could forget the whole thing.

I almost hoped it would turn out that way.

There was a moon three-quarters full that night. Around nine I began hunting for the house, and it took me until an hour before dawn to find it. My mistake, at first, was in looking for a house near the edge of the city. What had been the edge of the city forty-odd years ago was the edge of the city no longer. I wasted a great deal of time learning this, then switched tactics and walked along the railroad bed looking for a house overlooking the tracks. It took time, a good deal of time, but it was there, and I found it.

Kitty's grandmother had given me a perfect description. The house was precisely as I had pictured it, large, towering over the houses on either side, with a huge porch with concrete sides. The rest of the house seemed an appendage of that porch, but that was no doubt attributable to my particular point of view.

The house needed painting badly. Some of its windows were broken, a few boards loose on its sides. I approached it very cautiously and came close enough for a quick examination of the porch. As far as I could tell, it had not been remodeled since 1922. The floorboards seemed to have remained undisturbed for a long period of time, and the concrete sides were uniformly black with age. There was one part where the porch might have been broken and recemented years ago—perhaps when the gold was originally hidden away there, or perhaps later when someone else had beaten me to the punch and removed the treasure. There was only one sure way to find out, and it was too close to dawn for me to make the attempt.

I drifted downtown again. I wasted the day wandering through the markets, killing time in a filthy movie house, sitting over cups of inky coffee in dark cafés. At night I returned to the house. I had purchased a crowbar at the market and had walked around all day with it hidden in the folds of my clothing. It would have been better in some ways to break in through the concrete, but I couldn't risk the noise and was afraid I would be unable to camouflage a hole in the concrete afterward.

I waited in the darkness until the last light went out in the huge old house. After another half hour, I went up onto the porch and worked at the boards with a crowbar. It was hellish work—I had to be silent, I had to be fast, and I had to be prepared to melt into the shadows at the approach of a car or a pedestrian. I pried loose boards in a corner of the porch where I hoped no one would be apt to step and finally cleared out a large enough area so that a man could slip through. I looked inside.

Naturally I couldn't see a thing. It was pitch dark within, and I hadn't had the sense to bring a torch.

The temptation to lower myself beneath the porch was overpowering. But it was already too late for safety, and I would have to figure out a way to close the hole after me if I wanted to go inside. I reached down, swung the crowbar down inside and touched nothing. If I just went inside for a moment or two—

Not without a light, I decided. I replaced the boards and fitted nails into enough of them so that no one would crash through, but left things sufficiently loose so that I could open up the hole again in a few minutes instead of a few hours.

Then I went back downtown to kill another day.

By the following night I had traded my crowbar for a small flashlight. I went back to the house—it felt like my home by now—and opened up the hole in the porch again. I had it open when I heard a car approach and I barely dropped from the porch and around the side of the house in time. The car was a police vehicle with a spotlight mounted on the fender. It slowed at the house, and the spotlight swung around onto the porch, and I believe I came very close to fainting. But they saw nothing but a few loose boards, and that was evidently not what they were looking for.

The car passed. I hurried back onto the porch, snapped on my pencil flash and aimed it down the hole in the floorboards into the dark area below the porch.

The beam it cast was weak. But it was enough. I was looking—wide-eyed, suddenly breathless—at the gold of Smyrna!

Chapter 16

I spent the rest of the night beneath the porch. After I dropped through the opening, I arranged the floorboards carefully in place above me. I had to be reasonably quiet. A slight noise, even if heard, might be regarded as the movement of a rat, but repeated loud noises would be sure to attract attention. It was difficult to be silent at the beginning, however. I wanted to throw back my head and howl like a hyena. I had found the gold, and there was a hell of a lot of it, and it made a beautiful sight.

There were sacks and boxes and little leather purses, and everything was stuffed with gold coins. The great majority were British sovereigns with the head of Queen Victoria, but there was a scattering of Turkish pieces and a handful of pieces in each lot from other nations. Counting this treasure was out of the question. Instead, I incorporated the small bags inside the larger gunny sacks and tried to calculate the total weight of the treasure.

My guess placed it somewhere between 500 and 600 pounds. I tried to work out the value of the lot, but my mind would not behave properly. I got hung up on such points as whether to use the troy pound of twelve ounces or the avoirdupois pound of sixteen, whether to estimate on the basis of the official $35 per ounce or the $60-rate I was likely to get in Beirut. I decided ultimately that the whole question was academic. I was sitting in the exhilarating presence of somewhere around a quarter of a million dollars in gold. That was all I really had to know.

But how to get it out?

I hated the idea of a boat. The boat that Father Gregor's cohorts might supply would probably be capable of only twenty knots or so, and a trip from the west coast of Turkey all the way around to Lebanon would take days on end. Even a fast boat would be in the sitting-duck category, easy prey to the Turks whenever they got around to realizing who was on that boat.

A plane would simplify things. If the Society of the Left Hand were such a powerful organization, a plane should be obtainable. But I was beginning to feel more and more convinced that the Society of the Left Hand was very little more than the name of an elaborate confidence game and that the boat was going to take the gold right straight back to Bulgaria where Father Gregor would devise at his leisure a way to convey the gold to Lebanon, or to Macao, or wherever he happened to want it.

It might be best to avoid the Left Hand group entirely. But could I manage to get the gold out on my own? No, I could never bring it off. I had to use the Left Hand. And I also had to keep them from knowing what the right hand was doing.

The Society of the Left Hand made contact in the market a day later. A furtive little man with smallpox scars on his chin flashed me one of the secret signs—a particular arrangement of the fingers of the left hand that Father Gregor had taught me. I could have ignored him, as he did not seem all that confident that the ragged peasant before him was really the man he sought, but I knew I would need him, and it seemed pointless to be dodging everyone in Balikesir at once. I returned the sign. He nodded for me to follow him, and I did.

When we were clear of the crowd, he slowed down and permitted me to catch up with him. He gave me another sign, perhaps for insurance, and I made the appropriate countersign. Then he asked me who my father was. I said I had a father named Gregor. He smiled briefly and led me up one street and down another until we reached a large old house in the Arab section.

"We have rented this house," he said. "You will come inside?"

I went inside and met my four companions. There were three others, I was told. One waited in the harbor at Burhaniye with the boat they planned to use. Two others had left to make arrangements for a car. Had I found the gold? I said I had. Would we be able to get it out? I said we would.

They were all delighted.

"We will help you," the scarred one said. His name was Odon; the others had not volunteered their names. "And we will be content with a tenth of the proceeds."

He was the least convincing liar I had ever met in my life. If I had entertained any doubts as to their intentions—and in my wildly optimistic moments I had willed myself to believe Father Gregor's story—they were forever dispelled. There was now only one point that was unclear. I was unsure whether or not they would kill me after appropriating the gold for themselves.

"Where is the gold?"

I explained its approximate location.

"And how much is there?"

I told him my estimate.

"We will go tonight," Odon said. "There is no time to waste. We will go tonight in the car our men are obtaining. We will—"

"A stolen car?"

"We will purchase a car. One of our men has a Turkish driver's license and a passport to match it. There is no chance we will be questioned. We will go to the house and load the gold into metal strongboxes. You understand? We have the boxes in the garage. Come, I will show you."

There were two dozen steel strongboxes in the garage on top of a huge workbench. The bench overflowed with rusted hardware and tools—long rattail files, rusted padlocks, nuts, bolts, washers. Amid this sea of rusted metal the strongboxes gleamed brightly.

"Have we enough boxes?"

I calculated quickly. "Yes. They'll hold the gold."

"Good. We will fill them at the house. You understand? Or, for safety's sake, you will go beneath the porch and fill them. Then, when you are ready, the car will return for them, and we will all go at once to Burhaniye. Before dawn we will all be on our way." As an afterthought, and as further confirmation of the ship's true destination, he added, "To Beirut, of course. We will sail at once to Beirut."

A dismal liar.

That night clouds concealed the face of the moon. It was a bit of good luck. After midnight we drove to the house. Odon stayed in the car with two of the others. Another pair remained at the house—we were to stop for them before making the run to Burhaniye. I scurried onto the porch, opened up my little rabbit hole, and dropped down into my burrow. Another man passed the strongboxes down to me one at a time.

"Shall I wait with you?"

"No," I said. "Go back to the car. It will take me a while. Drive around or return to the house. Come for me in an hour."

He looked dubious. "I could come down there with you. It would go faster."

"We might be heard."

He went away. Eventually the car pulled off. I doubt that they all were in it. I'm fairly certain one stayed behind to make sure I did not attempt to get away with the gold.

I filled all twenty-four of the boxes. They were very heavy, but one could lift them without a great deal of trouble. I estimated each one weighed twenty-five or thirty pounds, which fitted with my original guess at the total weight of the treasure. I had finished packing the boxes by the time the car returned. Odon came to me from the car and suggested that I hand them up one at a time, and he would trek them back to the car.

That would make it a little too easy. I hopped out of my burrow. "I'm too exhausted to lift another thing," I said. "Send one of the other men to do the lifting. I'll wait in the car."

After all, there was no point in making it easy for them. I could picture them quite clearly, taking the last box from me, loading it into the trunk, and driving merrily away while I struggled out of the porch to wave bye-bye at them. No, I wouldn't be taken quite that easily.

I waited in the car. They brought the boxes out quickly enough, one man handing them up, two others relaying them to the car, Odon placing them in the trunk, but they made enough noise to wake corpses.

Lights went on in the house across the way. I had visions of the whole thing going to hell in a handcar. I called to them to hurry, and they hurried, and they hurried, and lights went on in the house whose porch we were robbing. My head ached dully. My mouth was dry. We loaded the last box, and the men piled into the car. In the distance a siren howled. Police? Probably.

Odon started the engine. It didn't catch at first, and I was certain the idiot had flooded the motor. It caught the second time, and we got the hell out of there. He drove well, at least. He put the gas pedal on the floor, and we were back at home base in no time at all.

Odon stuck the car in the garage. "Get the others," he told one of the men. "And hurry. We have to be on that boat before dawn. There's no time."

I got out of the car. I passed the hardware bench, scooped off a curved linoleum knife. As I walked around the car I stuck the knife into the left rear tire, pulled it out fast, and pocketed it. The tire did not blow but went down fast, almost instantaneously. I let one of the others discover it. He pointed it out to Odon.

Odon cursed rather colorfully. Someone remembered that there was a spare in the trunk. He opened the trunk. The spare tire was wedged in behind the strongboxes. Three of us wrestled it out, and in the process I got in a few good licks with the linoleum knife. No one noticed these at first. They thought the tire merely needed to be inflated, and Odon discovered an air pump in the rear of the garage. The damned garage had everything. They tried to pump up the tire, but it wouldn't inflate, and then the one who had passed me the strongboxes spotted the cuts in the tire and showed them to Odon, and Odon went out of his mind. He cursed the two who had purchased the car, cursed the fates for giving him fools for companions and threw in a few words that were not part of my command of Bulgarian.

He was obviously not at all pleased. "We have to get another car," he said. "Damn it to hell, somebody go out and steal a car. We have to—"

An argument developed. Two of the men utterly refused to make the trip in a stolen car. Another pointed out that they could get a tire in the morning and they could use some sleep for the time being.

"And if in the meanwhile someone runs off with the gold?"

"None but us know of it."

"And if one of us does so?"

"How? In a car with a flat tire?"

The wait-until-tomorrow crowd carried the day. Odon locked the trunk and closed the garage door. We all trooped inside the dingy house. A cupboard yielded up a bottle of rather poor brandy. We all drank, and Odon's spirits began to improve with drink. We drank and sang and drank and danced and drank, and one by one we dropped off to sleep until at last all of us were sleeping peacefully.

All but one of us.

When they were asleep, when it was as safe as it was likely to get, I slipped out of the house and into the garage. With such an abundant supply of tools around, the locked trunk was not much of an obstacle. I was very busy for almost an hour. Then I slipped back into the house. They were all still asleep.

I suppose the most intelligent move would have been to murder them in their beds. I cannot honestly say that the thought did not occur to me. It did, and I felt foolish rejecting it out of hand, but I could not possibly have done otherwise.

I had killed men in Macedonia. I told myself as much, reminded myself that I had quite fiercely gunned down men who had done absolutely nothing to me, while I was now unable to kill a group of unpleasant men who intended to rob me blind. This did not seem to make any difference. The men I had killed in Macedonia had been gunned down in the heat of real or imagined revolutionary passion. It was quite a different matter to slash half a dozen throats in the dark of night. I was evidently incapable of it. And, actually, I was more than a little pleased by the discovery.

But I did not suspect my fellows shared my reservations regarding the murder of sleeping men. And so I contrived to be obviously awake before them. Odon sent a man out to buy a tire. He came back with it and put it on the car. There was another argument: Should we or should we not wait for darkness? We decided not to wait. Around two in the afternoon we all piled into the car and headed for Burhaniye.

It was an easy drive. The ship, a trim little cutter, lay at anchor, with a thickset man on board. He came down to greet us. The harbor officials were taken care of, he reported. They would look the other way. We need only load the ship and be off.

Odon took me aside. He handed me a sack full of padlocks. "You must lock the strongboxes," he said. "It is only fitting, as you are the man who will receive the greater share of the gold and you must be assured that we do not try to cheat you. If the boxes are not locked, we might take more than our share during the voyage. Do you understand?"

"But I trust you, Odon."

He very nearly blushed. "No matter," he said. "You take the boxes from the trunk. Inspect their contents, if you wish, and lock them. Then pass them to us, and we will relay them into the boat. And then we will all get on board and be off. For Beirut."

I could not avoid the feeling that he had never told a lie before meeting me. I went to the trunk and Odon opened it with his key. I locked each box in turn and handed the boxes one by one to Odon's men, who carried them to the ship and came back for more. By the time I was handing over the final box, all of the men had managed to work their way onto the boat. Only Odon was left, and just as I passed him the final box, a man called his name from the ship.

"Ah," he said, "there seems to be trouble on board. Wait right here, I'll be back in a moment."

"I'll go with you."

"Oh, it's not necessary. Ah, what's that down there?"

I looked where he pointed. He had picked up the tire wrench and he telegraphed the blow so completely that it took a certain amount of effort to let him hit me at all. But he got me—going away, just a glancing blow on the side of the head. It hurt and it staggered me, and I followed through and sprawled in the sand.

It occurred to me as I lay there that there was a glaring flaw in my plan. Suppose he hit me a second time while I lay there like a lump? Suppose he very neatly caved in the back of my skull?

A glaring error. But, after all, I was new at this sort of thing. In any case, Odon didn't try for a second shot. Perhaps he was as unused to hitting people as he was to lying. He dropped the tire iron, tucked the strongbox under his arm, and ran to the ship.

I did not move an inch until the ship was out of sight.

Chapter 17

I got into the car, a Chevrolet about ten years old, and I understood it well enough. They had been kind enough to leave the keys in the ignition. I turned the car around and drove back to Balikesir, found the house, pulled into the garage, and closed the door. I had work to do. Fortunately I had plenty of time to do it.

Because they would not open those strongboxes until they reached their destination, which would take a day at the least. They wouldn't open the boxes because they would not trust one another well enough. As long as the locks were unimpaired no one would be able to remove some of the gold before they got back to Sofia and split it into their unrightful shares.

I could see them all, gathered in Father Gregor's comfortable house, ceremoniously unlocking or breaking open the padlocks, lifting the lids of each box in turn, and finding nuts and bolts and files and weights and nails and screws and rusty hardware of all sorts. Some six hundred pounds of rusty hardware, by my own admittedly rough estimate. Six hundred pounds of scrap metal, some of it lying loose, some of it neatly wrapped in ancient cloth bags and leather pouches. But all of it junk, and all of it theirs, and not a scrap of gold anywhere.

I had presented my unofficial resignation from the

Society of the Left Hand. It bothered me in a way—it was, as well as I could remember, the only organization from which I had ever resigned.

But it did not bother me very much.

The gold was where I had left it, piled under a tarpaulin in the farthest corner of the garage. I used a variety of tools to open up the door panels of the Chevy and packed the door solid with gold coins. I stowed more of them under the seats, inside the cushions, under the trunk lining, and on top of the hood liner. It took several hours to pack the car properly. I did not want anything to rattle too obviously. A certain amount of rattling was perhaps inevitable, but one expected rattles in a ten-year-old automobile. I used newspaper and rags to muffle the more obvious rattles, tightened the car up again, patted the fender gently, and went back into the house.

I found a razor and some soap. I got out of my clothes, bathed, shaved, and put my filthy clothes on again. I would have preferred clothes that looked as though they might normally be worn by someone prosperous enough to own a car. I thought of buying some clothes before I left. There would be time for that later, I decided, when I was well out of Balikesir. In some other city, where police were not schooled to be on the lookout for Evan Tanner, I could more safely prepare for the rigor of a border examination.

I went back to the car. The Turkish passport and the Turkish driver's license were in the glove compartment. Odon had no further need of them, just as he had no further need of the car or of me, and so he had abandoned us all together. I drove out of Balikesir. I drove south and east and south and east and I kept driving for a very long period of time. The roads were bad, and the car would not go over forty miles an hour without the front end shimmying madly. I stopped every fifty miles for oil. From time to time I grabbed a sandwich or a cup of coffee, then got behind the wheel and went on driving endlessly south and endlessly east.

According to the speedometer, I logged about eight hundred miles all told. I drove nonstop for almost two full days. In Antakya, in the southeast corner of Turkey, I finally purchased some decent clothes. I paid for them with gold pieces, which occasioned a certain amount of interest, but gold is apt to circulate in that corner of the world, and the merchant was more interested in cheating me than in calling the gold to the attention of the authorities.

I had no trouble at the border. I did not particularly resemble my passport photograph, but no one particularly resembles his passport photograph, and I drove from Turkey to Syria with little difficulty. I headed due south through Syria, hugging the coast, and had even less trouble passing from Syria into Lebanon. The Customs guards checked my car well enough, but they had no particular reason to take the doors apart, so they didn't. They looked in the spare tire, they rummaged through the glove compartment, and they let me go.

They missed the gold, the secret documents, and the fact that I was not the person whose passport I carried. Aside from that they didn't miss a trick.

I stayed at a good hotel in Beirut and put my car in the hotel garage. I told the bellhop that I was interested in finding a reliable gold merchant, and I tipped him a sovereign. Within an hour a young Chinese came to me. Did I have gold to sell? I said that I did. Would I accept fifty dollars an ounce? I said that I would not.

"How much, sir?"

"Sixty."

"That is high."

"It is low. You would pay sixty-five if I insisted. Tell your boss that I do not bargain. Tell him sixty dollars an ounce."

"How much gold, sir?"

"Six hundred pounds."

"Six hundred pounds sterling?"

"Six hundred pounds of gold," I said.

He did not wink, he did not blink, he remained wholly inscrutable. He left, he returned. "Sixty dollars an ounce is acceptable," he said.

"May I meet your boss?"

"If you will come with me."

I went to a very modern office in a very modern downtown building. A Chinese in a London suit sat across the desk from me and worked out the details with me. I was a very difficult bargainer at first. After the fun and games in Turkey I had given up trusting anyone. But we worked out the arrangements. Several of the Swiss banks maintained major branches in Beirut. I need only open an account in one of them, a numbered account, and the Chinese would deposit funds in my account equal to sixty dollars an ounce for my total consignment of gold. His company had a warehouse where we would have sufficient privacy. I drove the car there, and several of his employees unloaded the gold from the car according to my directions. It was all weighed and tallied before my eyes. I have been unable to decide whether or not the scales were dishonest. On the one hand, the gold merchant seems to have been exceptionally honest, ethical, and scrupulous. But, at the same time, any man's honesty seems apt to bend when the stakes reach sufficient height.

It made no difference. He could cheat me an ounce on the pound, and it would still make no difference. Because the gold weighed out at five hundred seventy-three pounds and four ounces troy weight or 6,880 troy ounces.

"I will allow an average of .900 fine for the gold," he told me. "It is coin gold. Some is finer, some not so fine. Some no doubt is counterfeit. Neither of us has the time to check each piece, is it not so? It will be checked before it is sold, and my firm will either gain or lose depending upon the assay. If you insist, we will assay it before paying you, but it would force you to remain in Beirut for another week at the very least. For this reason—"

"Your terms are satisfactory," I said.

"You wish payment in Swiss francs?"

"Will the bank accept dollar deposits?"

"Of course."

"Is it convenient for you to pay in dollars?"

"Of course."

"I would prefer dollars."

"Of course."

The rest was mechanics. I fully expected someone to attempt to cheat me out of the whole bundle, but no one did. We went to the Beirut offices of the Bank Leu. I opened a numbered account and received a very involved explanation of the precise manner in which the numbered accounts operated. No one, I was assured, would ever know of the existence of the account or the balance in it without my express permission. No government on earth could obtain such information. I and only I could make withdrawals from the account. I would, however, be paid no interest. He wanted me to realize that I would be paid no interest.

That, I said, was quite all right with me.

We concluded the transaction. The Chinese merchant took all the gold away—he would eventually realize approximately fifty percent over and above expenses on his investment. I did not begrudge him the profit. The bank would also make out handsomely, carrying a huge account and paying no interest on it. I did not begrudge the bank their gain, either.

I had on deposit precisely $371,520.

I took a hundred dollars of this incredible sum in cash. I went back to my excellent hotel. In the clothing shop downstairs I bought a suit of clothes, a shirt, a suit of underwear, a pair of socks, and a pair of shoes. I added a tie, cuff links, and a belt. I went upstairs and bathed and dressed and had a huge and excellent dinner in the hotel restaurant.

There was only one thing left to do. After dinner, and after I had spent about an hour resting as completely as possible on my most comfortable bed, I left the hotel and took a taxi a few blocks farther down the street. I got out of the cab in front of the American Embassy. It was late in the afternoon, almost time for the Embassy to close for the day.

I walked up the steps. The late afternoon sun was hot. I opened the door and stepped into the utter luxury of genuine American air-conditioning. It made me more honestly homesick than I could have imagined possible.

A young man sat behind a large desk in the hallway. I stood in front of his desk for several minutes before he raised his neat head from the pile of papers in front of him.

He asked if he could help me.

"I hope so," I said. "You see, I've lost my passport."

"Oh, *have* you?" He rolled his eyes, signaling his great irritation at stupid tourists who lost their passports.

"I suppose this happens rather often," I said.

"Too often. *Far* too often, to be frank. The absolute importance of keeping one's passport handy . . ."

I let him go on for quite a while. It was not an unpleasant lecture. I wish I could remember all of it.

Finally he found the appropriate form, poised a pen, and looked up at me.

"I don't suppose you remember the number?"

"I'm afraid not."

"No, naturally you don't. It never occurs to anyone to jot down their passport number. Not sufficiently important." He sniffed. "Your name?"

I paused, perhaps for dramatic effect.

"Oh, come now," he said. He was really incredibly snotty. "Now, don't tell me you've forgotten your name as well?"

"My name is Evan Michael Tanner," I said. "If you've forgotten it, I don't think you have much of a future with the State Department. I suggest you get off your ass and tell your boss the name of the stupid tourist who's been taking up your time. Evan Michael Tanner. You go tell him Evan Michael Tanner is here, and you see what he says."

But he remembered the name. It was delicious to watch his face mold itself into one expression after another. He reached for a buzzer and rang for the guards. We waited for them to come for me.

It didn't get at all rough until they got me back to Washington. The guards kept me under surveillance until the snotty kid could report to someone higher up, and eventually some men more important than he came to interrogate me. They assured themselves that I was really Evan Tanner, found out that I was, and conducted me to a windowless room on the second floor. A guard made sure that I was not carrying a weapon. I was not. Then two of them stood in front of me while I sat in a swivel chair.

"There's a report that you had the British plans," one said.

"I do."

"You have them with you?"

"Yes."

"At this moment?"

"Yes."

"Care to turn them over?"

"If you'll show me CIA identification."

"I'm not CIA."

"Then get someone who is."

They got someone who was, and I solemnly took off my jacket, unbuttoned my shirt, loosened my undershirt, and came up with the packet of papers the tall man had passed on to me in Dublin. The CIA man checked them out.

One of the State Department men asked if everything was there.

"I don't know," the CIA man said. "I have to use a phone."

He went away. I sat with the two men. They offered me cigarettes, and I said I didn't smoke and finally I remembered to tuck in my shirt and button it up and put the jacket on again.

The CIA man came back and said that as far as he could tell everything was there.

"I don't know how the guard missed it. He frisked him for a gun."

"Well, it wasn't a gun," the CIA man said.

"Still, he should have found it."

"Forget it." The CIA man turned to me. "Of course, those could have been copied," he said.

"True."

"Were they?"

"No."

"Why the hell did you come here, Tanner? I don't get it. Who are you working for?"

I didn't say anything.

"What do you expect, a pat on the head and a ticket home? Did you know that you started six international incidents all by yourself?"

"I know."

"I was just on the phone to Washington. They want you sent there in a private plane under a quadruple guard. Today, they said. We can't get hold of a private plane today."

"When, then?"

"Christ, I don't know. Maybe tonight, maybe tomorrow morning. Who knows? Tanner, you honest to God amaze me, you really do. How in hell did you wind up in Beirut? I wish I knew more about you. I know you're hotter than a grenade with the pin out and I know part of where you've been, but I don't know the rest of it. Why don't you tell me about it?"

"No."

"They'll ask the same questions in Washington. Make it easy for me. Brighten my day."

"I can't."

"Did you really start a revolution?"

I didn't answer that or any of the other questions he

asked me. The whole business was very frustrating for him. He knew that I would be sent to CIA headquarters in Washington and that he would never find out the answers to any of his questions. The agency might keep him busy, but evidently he didn't often run into anything as exciting as me and he was all curiosity, and I wasn't helping him a bit.

They eventually locked me into the room with a double guard. The guards were decent enough fellows. The three of us played hearts. I won about seventy cents, but I refused to take the money. It didn't seem right, somehow. After a few hours the CIA man came back with a few other men, and they handcuffed me rather elaborately and drove me to the Beirut airport. There was a smallish jet waiting at the runway. They loaded me into it along with four guards and the CIA man, and we took off for Washington.

No one had brought anything to read. Anyway, with the handcuffs on I couldn't have turned the pages. It was a very boring trip.

Chapter 18

The jail cell in the basement of CIA headquarters in Washington was far more comfortable than the dank dark room in Istanbul. It was well lighted and very clean. There was a bed, a small dresser, and a shelf of paperback books. The books were mostly spy novels, I discovered. This struck me as very funny at first, but after I'd read them one after the other as one day followed another I lost sight of the humor of it all. It began to get to me after a while. I read the same spy novel twice and didn't realize it until I was within twenty pages of the end.

The meals were good. Actually, there was no single dish that was as good as the pilaff I had had in Istanbul, but there was a great deal of variety in the cooking, and I'm sure the diet was more nutritious than toast and pilaff and pilaff. The only aspect of the two weeks I spent there that became absolutely unbearable was the endless routine of questioning. It went on and on, and they seemed determined to keep it up forever. It was the complete reverse of Istanbul—there I had been ignored, left entirely alone for days on end, and here I was questioned morning and noon and night, questioned endlessly, and over and over, until I was certain that the next session would be the one to break me.

"Who are you working for, Tanner?"

"I can't tell you."

"Why?"

"Those are my instructions."

"We're more important than your instructions, Tanner."

"No, you're not."

"We're the U.S. Government."

"I'm working for the Government."

"Oh, you are? That's very interesting, Tanner. You're working for the CIA?"

"No."

"For whom, then?"

"I can't tell you."

"The U.S. Government?"

"Yes."

"I think you're crazy, Tanner."

"That's your privilege."

"I think you're full of shit, Tanner."

"That's your privilege."

"You say you're working for the U.S. Government?"

"Yes."

"What department?"

"I can't tell you."

"Why? Because you don't know?"

"I can't tell you."

"Who's your boss?"

"I can't tell you that, either."

"Tell me something about this agency, Tanner. Is it like CIA?"

"In a way."

"You can't tell us the name?"

"No."

"Can you tell us somebody who works for it?"

"No."

"Suppose we give you a phone. You call somebody and make contact, okay? And then they can come and spring you, and we'll all be happy. How does that sound, Tanner?"

"No."

"No? Why the hell not?"

"I was instructed not to make contact."

"So what the hell are you going to do? Sit here forever?"

"Sooner or later I'll be contacted."

"How? By voices talking to you in the night?"

"No."

"Then, how, Tanner? Nobody knows you're here. Nobody's going to know unless you tell them. There were no leaks in Beirut. You came here on a hushed-up flight, and the CIA alone knows you're in Washington. Now, how in hell is anybody going to get in touch with you?"

"They will."

"How?"

"I can't tell you."

"I can't tell you, I can't tell you, I can't tell you. Like a broken record. Tanner, you son of a bitch, that's the whole trouble, you bastard, you can't tell us a thing. Who gave you those papers?"

"I can't—"

"Shut up. Why did you turn them over to us?"

"Those were my instructions."

"Really? I thought you couldn't give us a thing, Tanner."

"I was told to deliver the papers to the CIA if I could find no other alternative. It would have been better to deliver them to my superiors, but I could find no way to get into the country except through the American Embassy, and that meant delivering the papers to you. I was supposed to do it only if there was no other choice open and I couldn't contact my own group or get to the States under my own power, so I gave the papers to you."

"Were they copied?"

"Not while I had them."

"Where did you take them?"

"I can't tell you."

"Were you on other business? Or were you just cruising around Europe with the papers in your pocket for a couple of weeks?"

"I can't tell you."

"You're a son of a bitch, Tanner. I don't believe a word you're saying. We'll keep you here until hell freezes, do you know that? Take him back to his cell. God, he gives me a pain—"

Well, what else could I do? I know they didn't believe me. If they had swallowed my story, I would have doubted their competence. It was, admittedly, an absurd story.

But what else could I do? I had to get back to the States. It was my home, for one thing, and for another I was finding it increasingly exhausting to be on the run. I could not endure being a hunted man forever. Obviously I had to go back home and had to straighten everything out, somehow.

And so the story. I was working for a governmental agency, it was secret, it was important, and the CIA didn't know about it. I couldn't make contact, I couldn't give out information, I couldn't do much of anything but sit on my cot and read spy novels or sit on my chair and say "I can't tell you" until everybody got sick of listening to it. I had no idea what would happen eventually. I did not particularly want to think about it. It seemed impossible that they would let me go, and it was even less likely that they would release me to another country, or bring me to trial, or—

I couldn't imagine what they would do to me. Unless they would merely keep me in my cell forever, and that did not seem very likely. Sooner or later they would tire of questioning me. And then what? Would they release me?

They might. Not in a matter of weeks, perhaps not in a matter of months, but sooner or later they would tire of housing me and realize that I was not going to tell them anything more than I had already told them. Their attempts to trap me in questioning sessions were getting nowhere. Whenever I was asked anything remotely tricky, I merely announced that I could not tell them the answer. It was an umbrella for every possible sort of storm. They couldn't trap me. They couldn't get anything out of me. They couldn't do a thing.

Once I made a mistake. I asked one of them when they would let me go.

He grinned. "Tanner," he said, "I can't tell you."

I laughed. Actually, I figured I had it coming.

"Tanner, would you like to know something? I'll tell you something—we almost believe you. Almost. Why don't you help us out?"

"How?"

"Give us one name. That's all, one name. Just one person we can call up and find out if you're really you. Just one little name, Tanner, and maybe you'll be able to get out of here."

"I can't."

"A phone number, then."

"No."

"Tanner, I realize that you're gung ho. I realize you're loaded up to your old wazoo with esprit de corps and all that. We're very tall on those commodities around here, as far as that goes. God bless the agency, and long may she wave. And you probably feel the same way about your own group, right?"

"So?"

"What I'm getting at, Tanner, is we're all of us willing to die for our country. And we're even willing to go through hell for CIA. But there are certain contingencies, Tanner, that are not covered in the rule book. You don't want to spend the rest of your life rotting in a stinking cell when your own people are a few blocks away and all you got to do is holler. You know something? They're probably desperate for you to get in touch. They're probably beginning to worry about you. Why not let me call them for you?"

"No."

"Give me the initials, Tanner. Just the initials."

"No."

"It's all a big lie, isn't it? You a communist, Tanner? Or just a nut?"

"No."

"I don't believe a word of it, Tanner. Not a word."

"That's your privilege."

"You'll stay here the rest of your life. The rest of your goddam life. Is that what you want?"

"No."

"Well, how the hell will you get out?"

"My superiors will have me released."

"How will they find you?"

"They'll find me."

And they did.

* * *

They found me after breakfast. I had been in the jail cell for over three weeks, and by then I was past the point of wondering how long I could hold up under questioning. I knew by then that I could hold up forever. The questioning had tapered off now. Sometimes two or three days would go by without a session, and the sessions themselves were getting shorter and less vicious.

Until one morning after breakfast a guard came and turned the key in my cell door. One of the CIA men was with him. "They've come for you, Tanner. Get your things."

What things? All I had were the clothes I was wearing.

"And follow me. They found out you were here, finally. God knows how. I guess we've got a leak we don't know about. You come with me. You know something, Tanner? I didn't believe they'd ever come for you. I didn't believe there was anybody to come. I thought you'd sit in that cell forever."

"So did I."

"You can't blame us, you know. Put yourself in our position, you'd have done the same thing. Am I right?"

"You're right."

"So you don't blame us?"

"Of course not."

"Some of the things we said—"

"Just part of the interrogation. Forget it."

"Well, okay, Tanner. You're all right, Tanner."

Two men in dark suits were waiting in the front lobby. One of them said, "Phil Martin," and extended a hand. I shook it. The other said, "Klausner, Joe Klausner," and I shook his hand.

"The Chief just heard about you," Martin said. "It took us a long time. You've been here three weeks?"

"About that."

"Christ."

"It wasn't so bad."

"I'll bet," Martin said. "The car's out front. The Chief wants to see you right away. There's a bottle in the car if you want a drink first. You look as though you could use it."

There was a half pint of blended whiskey in the glove compartment. I took a long drink, capped it, and put it back. The three of us sat in the front of the car with me in the middle. Phil was driving. Joe turned in his seat as soon as we had pulled away from the curb. He stared out the back window.

After a few blocks he said, "Yeah, they're following us. Two cars double-teaming our play. A brown Pontiac and a light gray Ford. See 'em?"

"Uh-huh."

"Goddam CIA. Tell you the truth, I'm happy to see 'em there. If they're tailing us, it means they still don't know where our offices are. Which is just as well. Lose 'em, Phil."

"There would have to be two of them. Those boys don't even go to the john by themselves."

"So just lose 'em."

Phil lost them. He went around blocks, dashed the wrong way on one-way streets, and shook both our tails in less than ten minutes. "It's a hell of a thing," he said, "when you have to worry more about your friends than your enemies. The Chief is very anxious to see you, Tanner. He didn't know you were one of ours. He suspected it when we got rumbles about the bit in Macedonia. Dallmann had contacts in Macedonia. Dallmann's dead, you know."

"I know."

"Well," Phil said.

We rode the rest of the way in silence. Phil dropped us in front of a shoe-repair shop in a Negro slum. Joe and I entered a building by the door to the right of the shop and climbed three flights of squeaking stairs to the apartment on the top floor. He knocked. A deep voice invited us inside. Joe opened the door, and we went in.

Joe said, "Here's Tanner, Chief."

"Good. Any trouble with CIA?"

"None there. They followed us, but Phil outran them. He's good at that."

"Yes," the Chief said. "He's a good man."

"You want me to stick around?"

"No, that's all, Joe."

"Check."

Joe left and closed the door. The Chief was a round-faced man, bald on top, with fleshy hands that remained in perfect repose on the desk in front of him. The desk was empty of papers. There was a box labeled IN and another labeled OUT. Both were empty. There was a globe on the desk and a map of the world on the wall behind him.

"Evan Michael Tanner," the Chief said. "It's a pleasure to meet you, Tanner."

We shook hands. He motioned me to a chair, and I sat down.

"Dallmann's dead," he said. "I suppose you knew?"

"Yes."

"Shot down in Dublin, ironically enough. It must have happened just after he passed the papers to you."

I nodded.

"I suspected you might be Dallmann's man when we first began to get reports on you. We're not like the boys at the Central Intelligence Agency, you know. I don't believe in teamwork. I never have. It may be useful in some types of operations, but not in our type. Do you follow me, Tanner?"

"Yes," I said.

"I encourage my men to develop their own operatives. Keep them secret, don't let me know about them. When one of our men goes out on something, he goes alone. If he's in trouble, he can't call for help. If he's caught, I don't know him. So I didn't know you were one of Dallmann's group. I suspected it, as I said, but I wasn't sure. I became somewhat more certain when we received reports of the incident in Macedonia." He smiled for the first time. "That was excellent work, Tanner. That was one of the neatest bits of work in years."

"Thank you, sir."

"It may well turn out to have been the biggest wedge driven in Yugoslav hegemony since the end of the war. They were astonished when that revolt broke out. Astonished. The last thing anyone expected was a blowup in Macedonia. I know Dallmann had things planned in that area. I suppose that was why you made your first trip to Istanbul?"

"That's right."

"And of course that fell in. Brilliant work of yours, picking up Dallmann in Dublin afterward. And then having the nerve to carry through with the Macedonian plans. Most men would have settled for the British papers and brought them straight home. Dallmann would be proud of you, Tanner."

I didn't say anything. Dallmann—the tall man—must have guessed I was on his team from the Istanbul fiasco.

The Chief looked down at his hands. "Strange situation in Ireland," he said. "The Irish filched that set of plans out of London as neat as anything. The British didn't even know who had them. But we knew and we couldn't let them stay in Irish hands. Irish security isn't the best in the world, you know. And those plans were fairly vital. Dallmann took them away in a matter of days. Another power could have done the same thing. We had to do the job first for two reasons. To get them away from the Irish and to teach Downing Street an important lesson in security. First nonsexual security scandal they've had in some time. Ought to keep them on their toes, don't you think?"

We both got a good laugh out of that one.

"The CIA give you a hard time, Tanner?"

"It wasn't too bad."

"You don't sleep, do you? Got that from your records. That must come in handy."

"It does."

"Um-hum. Imagine it would. Sorry I had to put you through three weeks of CIA interrogation. Understand you didn't tell them a thing."

"I had to give them the plans."

"Well, that was all right. Couldn't be helped." He chuckled. "You must have given them the willies. You know their standard interrogation procedure? Nothing fancy, just let a man fall asleep, then wake him up and question him, then let him drift off to sleep again, then more questioning. They hit you at your weakest point that way. But they couldn't do that to you, could they?"

"No."

"Very handy. Never thought of insomnia as a survival mechanism. Very interesting."

"Yes, sir."

He got to his feet. "You have contacts with fringe groups and nut groups throughout the world, don't you? Professional? Or a sideline?"

"Just a hobby."

"Valuable one, isn't it? You do much work for Dallmann?"

"No. Just incidental work before this job. Nothing important."

"Suspected as much. And yet you maintained discipline all the way, didn't you? And handled yourself like a professional. Very interesting."

For a long moment neither of us said anything. Then he came around the desk, and I got to my feet, and we shook hands again.

"What are your plans now, Tanner?"

"I'll go back to New York."

"Back to business as usual, eh?"

"Yes."

"Good. Very good." He thought for a moment. "We might have a piece of work for you now and then."

"All right."

"We're hell to work for. I don't know exactly what sort of arrangement you had with Dallmann. Doesn't much matter now, does it? But we're very hard masters. We give you an assignment and that's all. We give you no contacts. We don't smooth the way for you a bit. But at the same time, we don't ask for reports in triplicate. We don't want to know what you did or how you did it. We just expect you to deliver the goods. If you get caught somewhere, we never heard of you and you never heard of us. We can't even fix a parking ticket for you. And if you get killed, we drink a toast to your memory and that's all. No group insurance. No full-dress funeral with burial in Arlington. Understand?"

"Yes, sir."

"So you might hear from us some time. If something comes up. Sound good to you?"

"Yes, sir."

"I like your style, Tanner. Especially in Macedonia. That was quite a performance." He smiled again briefly, then turned aside. "You'll find your own way out. Walk a few blocks before you catch a cab. Might as well go straight back to New York. Don't ever try to contact me. I suppose you know that much, but I'll say it anyway. All right?"

"All right."

"How are you fixed for money?"

"I could use plane fare. I'm out of ready cash."

"Besides that."

"I'm all right." I thought for a moment. "I managed to . . . uh . . . pick up a little for myself this trip."

He laughed aloud. "Just like Dallmann," he said. "He never even put in for expenses. Said he made a neater profit than we could ever pay him in salary. I like to encourage that sort of thing. Teaches a man to think on his feet. You'll fit in fine with us, Tanner."

He gave me two hundred dollars for the plane and incidental expenses. We shook hands a third and final time, and I let myself out.

Afterword

Evan Michael Tanner was conceived in the summer of 1956, in New York's Washington Square Park. But his gestation period ran to a decade.

That summer was my first stay in New York, and what a wonder it was. After a year at Antioch College, I was spending three months in the mailroom at Pines Publications, as part of the school's work–study program. I shared an apartment on Barrow Street with a couple of other students, and I spent all my time—except for the forty weekly hours my job claimed—hanging out in the Village. Every Sunday afternoon I went to Washington Square, where a couple of hundred people gathered to sing folk songs around the fountain. I spent evenings in coffeehouses, or at somebody's apartment.

What an astonishing variety of people I met! Back home in Buffalo, people had run the gamut from A to B. (The ones I knew, that is. Buffalo, I found out later, was a pretty rich human landscape, but I didn't have a clue at the time.)

But in the Village I met socialists and monarchists and Welsh nationalists and Catholic anarchists and, oh, no end of exotics. I met people who worked and people who found other ways of making a living, some of them legal. And I soaked all this up for three months and went back to school, and a year later I started selling stories and dropped out of college to take a job at a literary agency. Then I went back to school and then I dropped out again, and ever since I've been writing books, which is to say I've found a legal way of making a living without working.

Where's Tanner in all this?

Hovering, I suspect, somewhere on the edge of thought. And then in 1962, I was back in Buffalo with a wife and a daughter and another daughter on the way, and two facts, apparently unrelated, came to my attention, one right after the other.

Fact One: It is apparently possible for certain rare individuals to live without sleep.

Fact Two: Two hundred fifty years after the death of Queen Anne, the last reigning monarch of the House of Stuart, there was still (in the unlikely person of a German princeling) a Stuart pretender to the English throne.

I picked up the first fact in an article on sleep in *Time* magazine, the second while browsing the Encyclopedia Britannica. They seemed to go together, and I found myself thinking of a character whose sleep center had been destroyed, and who consequently had an extra eight hours in the day to contend with. What would he do with the extra time? Well, he could learn languages. And what passion would drive him? Why, he'd be plotting and scheming to oust Betty Battenberg, the Hanoverian usurper, and restore the Stuarts to their rightful place on the throne of England.

I put the idea on the back burner, and then I must have unplugged the stove, because it was a couple of more years before Tanner was ready to be born. By then a Stuart restoration was just one of his disparate passions. He was to be a champion of lost causes and irredentist movements, and I was to write eight books about him.

The Thief Who Couldn't Sleep was Tanner's debut, and it might never have happened if I hadn't brought home a dinner guest one evening in 1965. The fellow's name was Lincoln W. Higgie—Bill to his friends—and he'd recently returned from Turkey, where he'd spent a couple of years earning a precarious living smuggling rare coins and antiquities out of the country. (Precarious because it was illegal; if the authorities caught you they might sentence you to death, which was bad, or throw you into prison, which was demonstrably worse.)

Bill Higgle was a numismatist—if you Google him, you'll find he wrote a book on the coinage, tokens, and paper money of the Virgin Islands—and I was editing a numismatic magazine at the time. He showed up at the office, I brought him home to dinner, he brought a bottle of Bushmill's as a hostess gift, we sat up late and drank it, and he told me a story of a horde of gold coins hidden in a house in Balekesir, and of the too-late efforts of a couple of free spirits from Aramco to recover it.

Remarkably, I recalled our conversation the next day. And, more remarkably, I remembered the as-yet unemployed fellow with the damaged sleep center and the passion for lost causes. I put the two together and, well, I hope you've enjoyed the result.

Lawrence Block
Greenwich Village

Enter the World of Lawrence Block's Evan Tanner

Lawrence Block is widely acknowledged by both fans and reviewers to be one of the best mystery writers working today. He is also one of the most prolific, and his varied series—from the lighthearted romps of Bernie the Burglar, to the angst-ridden travails of Matthew Scudder the ex-cop, to the cool musings of Keller the Hit Man—have impressed readers with their versatility. He is a Mystery Writers of America Grand Master and a multiple winner of the Edgar® and Shamus awards.

But before the Burglar, Scudder, and the Hit Man, there was Evan Tanner—the most unusual spy who ever lived! Tanner hasn't slept a wink since a piece of shrapnel destroyed the sleep center in his brain, allowing him to get up to all sorts of trouble. BookPage *calls the series "lighthearted . . . reminiscent of the tongue-in-cheek novels of Donald Hamilton (the Matt Helm series) or even Ian Fleming's classic James Bond stories," while the* Rocky Mountain News *says, "Block is a true pro at coming up with offbeat adventures and peopling them with fascinating characters."*

Read on, and enter Tanner's world! . . .

The Thief Who Couldn't Sleep

A wake-up call is the last thing that Evan Tanner needs. Champion of lost causes and beautiful women, Tanner hasn't slept a wink since the sleep center of his brain was destroyed. And with the FBI keeping tabs on him, the CIA tapping his phone, and a super secret intelligence agency wanting to recruit him, keeping wide awake is definitely a smart choice.

An alarming cause is the last thing Evan Tanner needs. But when he hears about a fortune in gold that's just waiting for him to liberate it, he's off. Getting across international borders, though, proves to be a difficult chore, especially when there's all that loot to carry as well. Not to mention the law, which is one step behind him and quickly catching up.

The Canceled Czech

Edgar® Award-winning author Lawrence Block delivers the second suspenseful romp featuring one of his most popular characters: Evan Tanner. With a shocking array of talents and no need to sleep, Tanner poses as the perfect secret agent—to treat a Nazi war criminal to an early withdrawal.

Janos Kotacek has been imprisoned by the Czech government and will no doubt be tried and hanged for his crimes. But to the super-secret intelligence agency that Tanner occasionally works for, Kotacek is worth more alive than dead. Tanner's orders are simple: go to Prague . . . storm a castle . . . free a criminal. That, of course, is the easy part. Keeping himself and his captive alive will take all of Tanner's waking hours. Good thing he's got some to spare.

Tanner's Twelve Swingers

Globe-trotting spy Evan Tanner has just accepted a daunting assignment: He's agreed to find a heartsick friend's long-lost love—and smuggle her out of Russia.

Everyone Evan meets on his trek across Eastern Europe is desperate for a one-way ticket to America—and for many of those people, he's the only hope. There's a subversive Yugoslavian author, a six-year-old future queen of Lithuania, and the beautiful woman Evan's been sent to rescue—a sexy Latvian gymnast who wants to bring her eleven swinging teammates along for the ride.

Now Evan has to find a way to get his unruly brood of political refugees safely onto U.S. soil. Some might say it's an impossible task, but Evan always finishes what he's started—even when his own life is on the line. . . .

The Scoreless Thai

Would you believe Evan Tanner in the guise of a slightly batty butterfly collector?

Trotting through the woods, flailing his net?

You would? So did nearly everyone else.

Everybody except the band of guerilla bandits who decided it was safer and saner to snare Tanner than to let Tanner snare butterflies. They stripped him, stuffed him into a cage and told him: "Upon the rising of the sun, we will lead you to the chopping block and sever your head by driving the blade of an axe through your neck. . . ."

Tanner's Tiger

Minna might be heiress to the Lithuanian throne, but she was still a little girl—one who was just thrilled about going to the World's Fair in Montreal. How could Evan Tanner know that this innocent outing would lead him and Minna into the middle of a terrorist plot? And not just any terrorist plot, but the most daring, most dastardly plot of all time . . . to blow up the Queen of England!

Tanner's Virgin

Evan Tanner loves lost causes and beautiful women. The FBI has a thick file on him, the CIA taps his phone, and a super-secret intelligence agency wants him to be their man! How can Evan Tanner turn down the urgent plea of a mother in distress—especially when the mother has a daughter as beautiful as Phaedra Harrow? Phaedra has disappeared into the hands of white slave traders somewhere in the Afghan wilderness. And Tanner, it appears, has no choice but to find her. . . .

Me Tanner, You Jane

Superspy Evan Tanner's newest assignment is to bring back alive the missing ruler of a new African nation . . . and the state treasury that's missing with him. But waiting in the heart of Africa is Sheena, a missionary's renegade daughter with an appetite for men and power, a taste that puts Tanner in the lovely arms of this deadly lady and lands him in hot water—the kind that can turn a spy into a cooked goose.

Tanner on Ice

Once, Evan Tanner was known as the thief who couldn't sleep, carrying out his dangerous duties for a super-secret intelligence agency. Then someone put him on ice—for about twenty-five years. Returning to the world (and trying to catch up with a quarter century's worth of current events), Tanner is about to embark on a new covert assignment that will take him to the exotic Far East, where mystery and menace are a way of life. . . .

Now, whether he's dodging double crosses or disguising himself as a monk, Tanner is learning that when it comes to power games, pretty women, and political wrangling, some things never change. And he's making up for lost time—with a vengeance.

To my father, Jacob

Conviction (n.)

1. A fixed or strongly held belief.

2. The act of being found or proved guilty.

Funny how the future always seems to come down to the past.

ONE

October 1979
New York

As far as I could remember, it was the first time I'd held the dead man's hand. I knew a guy once who was so superstitious that he'd fold the infamous aces and eights whenever he saw them, but not me. I sat back and waited for the action. It had been a long night of busted flushes and gut-shot straights going nowhere and this might be my last chance to pull something back. Of course Wild Bill Hickok was probably thinking along the same lines as he contemplated the hand, unaware that a Colt Peacemaker was about to blow a .45-caliber hole in his luck. Funny. You'd think an old gunslinger like Wild Bill would know to sit with his back to the wall. I certainly did.

I glanced around the table. It was the usual Friday-night collection of postmodernist bohemians, New Wave cokeheads, and weekend refugees from Wall Street. I knew the faces and some of the names, but not much else. It was one of the things I liked about Barnabus Rex. Nobody tried to sell you their life story. If they didn't come for the backroom cards, it was for the eight ball, or to feed the old Rock-Ola jukebox, which at the moment was blaring out Blondie's "Heart of Glass" for the umpteenth time.

Four and a half years had passed since the fall of Saigon. It had been the end of a chapter for me, but like a lot of other people, I was having trouble turning the page. Don't get me wrong. I wasn't in any sort of desperate straits, but Vietnam left its mark on anyone who spent time there, and I was no exception. It was a tough place to leave behind, and I'd hung on to the bitter end, not realizing until that last chopper was lifting off the embassy roof that I'd stayed because I had no idea where else to go.

New York was the closest thing I had to a home, and as good a place as any to get lost for a while, so I caught a flight from Manila, and two days later I was ensconced in a top-floor loft at the corner of West Broadway and Grand. It wasn't elegant—or legal, for that matter—but it was cheap, and it had space, which was what I needed more than anything at that point. Once I'd cleaned the place up, put some plumbing in, and declared victory over the rats, it wasn't half bad, either. There was even a view, looking south onto the newly built twin towers of the World Trade Center.

A guy with long, tangled hair and cocaine eyes decided he'd try to steal the pot for ten bucks. I should've given him some rope, let him hang himself, but I couldn't resist the urge to wipe the silly grin off his face, so I raised back. He folded his bullshit, and that was enough for me. I called it a night.

A light October rain was falling as I stepped onto Duane Street and headed uptown, lingering through the no-man's-land of dark warehouses and hidden sweatshops that I still thought of as the Washington Market, even though everyone else had taken to calling it Tribeca. There was something invigorating about the city at this hour, especially down here. The streets were empty and still, but there was this vibration in the air—a charge in the atmosphere that went right through you, quickening the heart with a dose of adrenaline and arousing the senses. It made you feel alive, ready for anything.

I picked up the early edition of the *Times* from a box on Canal, then made my way home as the day's first gray light crept onto the horizon. As I approached the graffiti-covered industrial door that I called home, an uneasy feeling came over me—a distinct sensation that I was being watched. It wasn't the first time I'd felt that way in recent days, but a quick glance over my shoulder confirmed that no bogeyman was lurking, so I pushed the door open and stepped into the building's dark, musty-scented entranceway. I guess old habits die hard, I thought as I stepped into the freight elevator and made the slow ascent to the fourth floor.

Sleep was out of the question, so I headed into the darkroom, where there were still a couple of unprocessed rolls from the Andy Warhol shoot I'd done for *Esquire* the previous day. It had been an interesting afternoon at The Factory, which was what the artist called his studio overlooking Union Square. The session had ended in disaster when Warhol demanded that I hand over my undeveloped film so he could "edit the shit out." I thought he was joking at first, but when I realized he wasn't, I laughed and told him to go fuck himself. His face went the color of one of his Campbell soup cans, and in a hilarious attempt to intimidate me, he called in security, which appeared in the form of a large transvestite who called himself "The Sugar Plum Fairy." I'm sure the guy was tough enough, but, hell, he was wearing hot pants and black silk stockings. I had a good chuckle and walked out with my film intact, but my career in deep shit. *Esquire*'s photo editor—a guy named Brad—called that evening to spit blood down the line. He promised at the top of his lungs that I'd never work again, so I said "fine" and hung up on him.

"That was clever," Lenni said.

"He's an asshole."

"So are you, Jack."

"Yes, but I'm a lovable one." I flashed her a smile.

"Debatable."

She picked up the phone and soon had Brad back on the line. After a bit of back-and-forth about what an insufferable jerk I was, she went on to say that it was a shame, because I had some fantastic shots. Prizewinning stuff. The fact that she hadn't seen any of it didn't make her any less convincing, and it piqued Brad's curiosity. When she wondered out loud how he'd break it to his publisher that the Warhol article would have to be delayed because there were no photos, he finally figured out that he was stuck with me.

"Tomorrow afternoon, four o'clock, his office," Lenni said as she hung up. "I hope you've got something good to show him."

"Tomorrow's Saturday," I noted.

"Oh, right, I forgot. You'll be in temple all day."

I shrugged and went back to the *Rolling Stone* article I'd been reading about the Blues Brothers. "He's a jerk," I grumbled.

"Maybe so," Lenni said, defeating my attempt to get the last word in. "But he's a jerk who pays well."

I couldn't argue with that. Photographing celebrities for a living certainly had its drawbacks—Andy Warhol wasn't the worst I'd come across—but it paid the bills. And everybody's got bills to pay.

Lenni Summers was a Pulitzer Prize–winning journalist, but she'd been no more than a fresh-faced novice when I first laid eyes on her, in the back of a Huey in January of '68. It was the first day of the Tet Offensive, and we were both hitching a ride up country to Danang, where the action was. Amid all that chaos, something clicked, and we got together that night. We'd been on and off ever since, more on than off lately. Lenni hadn't exactly moved in—at least not officially—but she was more or less full-time now. We were an easy kind of close, the kind that doesn't involve having to tell all your deep, dark secrets. And Lord knows, I had a few.

After what happened in Berlin, it was pretty clear that I'd have to disappear for a while. I knew too much, and certain people knew I knew too much. So I headed south, to warmer waters, landing in a spot that was as close to paradise on earth as you can imagine. White sandy beach, palm trees gently swaying in a warm tropical breeze, and plenty of native girls to crack your coconuts. It took me all of six weeks to figure out that paradise on earth is just about as boring as it gets. I stuck it out for another two long years, until one afternoon, while swinging in my hammock and listening to the faint signal I'd managed to get out of Miami by building a forty-foot radio tower, "Monday, Monday" by the Mamas and the Papas came on the radio. I started wondering if they were playing it because it was actually Monday, and then I realized that I didn't even know what month it was. It was time to get out of paradise, before I lost track of the years.

The next morning I packed a bag and headed for Mexico City, where I knew a guy who could arrange for papers. Sitting in a bar with a Dos Equis in one hand and a newspaper in the other, I caught up with the world and decided there was only one place to be. Forty-eight hours later, I was in Hong Kong, buying a Minolta SR-T 101, and I landed in Saigon the following day as Jack Monday, freelance photojournalist. The fact that I barely knew how to load film didn't faze me, and somehow it all worked out. The next nine years were a long way from paradise, but they were a long way from boring, too.

* * *

I woke up feeling pretty good, considering I'd only managed three hours sleep, and I was building up to a good mood when I remembered my four o'clock groveling act with Brad. I got out of bed, made some strong coffee, and was in the process of gathering the Warhol shots when the doorbell rang. Strange, I thought. The doorbell never rings.

"Yeah?"

There was a long silence on the other end of the intercom, but I knew someone was there. I could hear breathing.

I tried again. "Who's there?"

A woman's voice, halting and anxious, finally came over the speaker. "I . . . I have something for you . . ." She spoke with a foreign accent that I couldn't quite place.

"What is it?"

"A message."

"What kind of message?"

"It's . . . May I come inside?"

Probably working some kind of scam, I thought. Checking to see if anybody's home before her boyfriend goes up the fire escape and through a window to grab the TV and stereo. "I'll come down," I said.

Slipping into my jacket, I grabbed my portfolio and made the descent to the ground floor. She was facing the street when I opened the door, with her back to me, but I could see that she wasn't at all what I'd been expecting. Middle-aged and elegant, she wore a cream-colored raincoat, expensive black boots, leather gloves, and a pink-and-green flowered silk kerchief tied around her head. My appearance seemed to startle her. She spun around, took a step backward, and had a long look at me through the designer sunglasses that covered much of her face.

"It *is* you," she whispered. "I . . . I thought it was, but I couldn't be sure."

It took a minute to sink in.

"Zahra . . . ?" I gasped.

"You remember me."

All I could do was laugh. Not because it was funny, but because it was so goddamned impossible. It was like a shadow coming to life, or a character from some long-forgotten dream suddenly appearing. We'd existed in another world, another life, and it was jarring to see her standing there, flesh and blood, looking me in the eye.

"May I come in?" she asked nervously.

"Sure . . . Sure, come in."

I stepped aside to let her pass, then closed the door. I was speechless, unsure which question to ask first. What was she doing here? How did she find me? What did she want? I didn't have to ask the last question because the answer was pretty clear when Zahra reached into her purse and produced a Smith & Wesson .38 snub nose, which she pointed at my chest.

"If the idea is to shoot me," I said, "you should go ahead and do it now. Because the longer you wait, the harder it'll get."

"I suppose you have a lot of experience with that."

"Not a lot, but some. It's not a good idea to talk to the person you're planning to kill, either. In fact, the best method is to sneak up from behind and shoot them in the back of the head. It's tough to kill someone while they're looking you in the eye."

"Perhaps not so difficult when you feel so much hatred."

"Depends on the kind of person you are, I guess."

"And how much you hate."

Zahra pushed her sunglasses up onto the top of her head, allowing me to get a better look at her face. The flush of youth was gone, of course, but the years had done little to diminish her exotic beauty. The jet-black hair with eyes to match, the finely sculpted features, the clear olive skin. Time had added a few character lines, and a streak of silver gray, but other than that, she could have walked straight out of the past. The real change was internal, of course. There was a weariness about her now, a melancholy that she wore like a suit of armor.

"How long have you been following me?" I asked.

"Five days."

"How did you find me?"

She paused, unsure if she should be allowing this cross-examination, but decided there was no harm in it. "It was by chance. You passed me on the street one day. I wasn't sure it was you, so I followed."

"And decided to kill me."

Her finger tugged at the trigger. "It's what you deserve."

"Naturally, I don't see it that way. But you're the one with the gun."

Zahra didn't move—not a muscle. It was as though she was locked in the moment, stuck between the unalterable past and two very different futures. I was pretty sure that she didn't have it in her to gun me down in cold blood, but there was always the possibility that I was wrong. As we stood there, both of us waiting to see which way she'd go, I thought about the last time I'd seen her. It might as well have been another lifetime, but the memory came through fresh and sharp and clear, as though days had passed and not years.

TWO

August 1953
Tehran

The streets weren't safe. I'd already slipped by one patrol, and I was hearing the occasional rattle of automatic gunfire in the distance. Sticking to the back roads, I drove cautiously, stopping at each intersection to listen for the low rumble of approaching tanks.

Operation Ajax lay in ruins. It had been a complete and utter disaster. Couldn't have gone worse. Colonel Nasiri, who was supposed to have arrested the prime minister, had been arrested himself; General Zahedi had disappeared, presumably gone into hiding; and military units loyal to the government had fanned out across the city, arresting anyone who looked out of place. The first ever CIA-directed coup of a foreign government had ended in a fiasco.

The evening had begun well, with spirits high and vodka flowing. We'd all gathered at the safe house, located in a quiet district in the northern suburbs of Tehran, to await news of the military takeover we'd been planning for four months. Somebody had brought along their record collection and by midnight we were belting out a rousing rendition of "Luck Be a Lady" from the musical *Guys and Dolls*, proclaiming it, on the fifth or sixth round, the official theme song of the operation. But the victory celebration had been premature, and it had nothing to do with Lady Luck.

One of the Khasardian brothers had turned up at around 3 A.M. with the news. When Colonel Nasiri and his troops had arrived at the prime minister's residence, they'd been ambushed by officers loyal to the government. While Nasiri was being arrested and driven off in a jeep, most of the other officers we'd recruited were suffering the same fate. There could be only one conclusion. We'd been betrayed.

I made a left turn and hit the brakes hard, screeching to a stop just short of the hulking Mk III Crusader tank that was blocking the road. The gunner swung his 8mm machine gun around and I shoved my hands out the window, hoping like hell he'd see they were empty. One nervous tug on the trigger at this range and they'd be washing me off the street for days.

"Doost!" I called out, using the Farsi word for "friend." I was quickly surrounded by a half-dozen Iranian soldiers. Each was armed with a bolt-action combat rifle, and each had it pointed at me. *"Doost!"* I repeated, louder this time.

The unit's commander, a young sergeant, stepped forward and indicated with a wave of his pistol that he wanted me to get out. Making slow, deliberate moves, I opened the door and stepped onto the pavement.

"Gozarname!" he barked, demanding to see my passport. I didn't have it, or any other identification for that matter, but I wasn't about to tell him that. Anyway, I had a better idea.

"Dar M'shin . . ." I said, pointing toward the car. In the car.

A cursory nod of his head indicated that I should get it, so I lowered myself into the driver's seat, reached across to the passenger side, and popped the glove compartment. I handed him the thick envelope without explanation, but he knew very well that he wasn't getting a passport. He gave me a look, told his men to retreat back to the tank, then peeked inside.

"Dollars," I said in English. "Lots of them. Thirty thousand to be exact. You can count it if you want." Of course he had no idea what I was saying, but I felt it was a good idea to keep talking. "Let me through and it's all yours," I said.

He looked up and narrowed his eyes at me. There was no question of handing it back. The guy was just sizing me up, speculating about who the hell I was and what could be so important that I'd pay this kind of money to get past him. Bribes were nothing new to him, but this was more money than he could ever have imagined holding in his hand, let alone putting in his pocket. He must've known that he was betraying something pretty big, but like they say, everything has its price. For me, it was a bargain.

A smile crossed the sergeant's lips, but it was short-lived. He started waving his arms and yelling orders across to his men. I couldn't follow the specifics, but it wasn't necessary. Someone scrambled into the belly of the tank and a moment later the beast was huffing and puffing as it rumbled backward, crushing someone's beautifully manicured front lawn so I could get through. It would've been easier for me to go around, of course, but I guess for thirty grand he thought it only polite that he be the one to move.

I left the car on the street and climbed the stone steps, passing under the old fig tree, to the big wooden doors. It was a relatively modern villa, dating from the midthirties, of little architectural interest. The unimposing facade masked a deceptively large building, housing several apartments that were inhabited by various members of the family. There was also an expansive courtyard and garden in the rear, which, in good weather, was where most of the living and entertaining took place.

Yari answered the bell himself. He wasn't surprised to see me. In fact, he seemed to be expecting me. Dawn was just breaking, yet he was decked out in a smart business suit. The bruises on his face were all but healed, but he'd carry the scars from the brutal beating he'd received three weeks earlier for the rest of his life.

"You've heard the news?" he said, stepping aside for me to enter. I gave him a look. He knew damn well I'd heard the news. "Well . . ." He shrugged. "These things are bound to be unpredictable."

"Let's not play games," I said.

"Oh?" He shot me a look. "But I thought you enjoyed games. You play them so well."

"You're smarter than this, Yari. We had an understanding."

"The understanding was based on the idea that you would win. That doesn't seem to be the case."

"It's not over."

"Yes, Jack," he said quietly. "It is over, and you have lost."

We faced each other across the tile floor. The house was quiet and still—not like the first time I'd been here, when I'd been greeted with smiles and hugs from what seemed like half of Tehran. Yari's mother and father, aunts and uncles, friends, brothers, sisters, cousins, nephews, nieces. They'd all welcomed me into their home. I'd made my first miscalculation about Yari that night. I'd underestimated him, misread his idealism as weakness. But that was done. We were where we were, and raking over past mistakes wouldn't change anything.

"Why did you come here?" Yari finally said.

"To tell you what you have to do to make this right."

He shook his head. "You're no different than the rest of them," he said. "I had hopes—"

"I don't give a damn about your hopes," I said flatly, surprised at how empty my own voice sounded. Yari made no attempt to disguise his contempt.

"Well, then. It seems that you've made a dangerous trip for no reason."

"No," I said. "I have a reason."

I raised the manila envelope I'd been gripping in my hand, held it out for him to take. If I'd given it to him three weeks earlier, when I'd first received it, things wouldn't have gone like this.

Yari studied the envelope. He couldn't have known what was inside, but he seemed to understand that, whatever it was, it would change things. He looked up at me and I suddenly felt sick to my stomach. It didn't help that I hadn't eaten or slept in I don't know how many hours, but I wasn't gonna kid myself. I knew where the pain in my gut was coming from.

"I'm sorry," I said, breaking the promise I'd made to myself. "But you've given me no choice."

Yari hesitated, then stepped forward. He was about to take the envelope when his sister's voice rang out.

"Yari!" she called out in Farsi. *"Yari, where are you?"*

She stopped short when she saw me, quickly ducked back behind the door. As modern as she liked to see herself, Zahra still had many of the old-fashioned modesties that had been instilled in her, and her natural reaction was to hide rather than show herself in dressing gown and slippers. Keeping the door between us, she stuck her head out and smiled charmingly.

"Jack? Why are you here so early?" Her face dropped when she saw our expressions. "What's happened?"

"Nothing. Everything is fine," Yari said. "Go back inside."

"I can see that something has happened," she persisted. "What is it?"

Yari sighed. He knew he wouldn't shake her without some

sort of explanation. "There's been an attempt to overthrow the government," he said. Zahra gasped, and Yari quickly continued. "A small group of army officers tried to arrest Mossadegh, but they were unsuccessful. They've all been arrested themselves."

"Thank God," she said, then looked to me. "The British are behind it, aren't they?"

I hesitated, but she waited for a response. "Hard to say," I mumbled.

"When will they understand that those days are over?" She was prepared to continue, but Yari cut her off.

"Go inside now," he said sternly. Yari often spoke to his sister as if he were her father. He was my age, thirty-eight, but his position in the government had made him de facto patriarch of the family. I'd even seen his father defer to him. "Please, Zahra," he added in a softer tone. "Go inside and turn on the radio. Mossadegh will speak soon. I'll be there in a moment. Jack and I have things we must discuss."

Zahra nodded, then turned to me and smiled as she withdrew back into the house. It was no more than an innocent parting glance, of no particular significance, but it was enough to sink my heart. She had no idea that my visit would turn her life upside down. It wasn't fair—I knew it wasn't fair—but the stakes were too high for that to matter. I'd made that mistake once already.

Yari took the envelope, slowly unwound its string closure, and removed the contents. He stood there, perfectly still, for what seemed like an eternity, staring at the first grainy image. Then he looked at the second photograph, and the third. When he came to the final shot, he gasped, rocked back on his heels, and slumped against the wall. His face had gone as white as a sheet.

THREE

October 1979
New York

Zahra didn't say a word, but I could see it in her eyes. Murder wasn't in them. She lowered the gun and let it slip through her fingers, onto the wooden floor. I wasn't sure what to do next, but before I could do anything, she'd spun around and made a headlong exit out the door and onto the street. I caught up with her as she was frantically trying to get a key into the door of the rented getaway car she'd parked around the corner. I stopped a few feet short and waited.

She shook her head and sniffed back the tears. "I thought I could do it . . . I wanted to do it . . ."

The early morning rain had dissipated, leaving behind a gloriously sunny autumn afternoon, the kind that brings the world into crisp, clear focus. I suggested we walk and led Zahra north, across Houston Street to Greenwich Village, then into the bustle of Washington Square. We found an empty bench in a far corner and sat quietly for several minutes. I could see that Zahra had things to say, but I let her come to it in her own time.

"Do you have a cigarette?" she finally asked.

"I quit. Two years ago."

"Oh." She looked genuinely surprised. "You used to smoke all the time."

"I still miss it."

She nodded vacantly, then looked away, toward a crowd that had gathered around a gas-guzzling, fire-breathing street performer. You couldn't see the star of the show from our vantage point, but every few seconds a great cloud of flames would explode into the air above the group, eliciting an admiring gasp of approval. I don't think Zahra was even aware of what she was watching.

"Last week, on the day before I saw you," she said, turning back toward me, "I received a telephone call from a stranger. He was Iranian, an old man who'd managed to escape. He had just arrived in the United States. The reason for his call, he said, was to deliver a message from a mutual acquaintance in Tehran—an old friend who I hadn't heard from in years. He told me . . ." Zahra paused to tamp down her emotions. "He told me that Yari had been arrested."

The news shouldn't have surprised me. Many of Iran's former government officials had been detained since the overthrow of the Shah back in January, and I'd wondered a couple of times about Yari's fate. Still, hearing it like this wasn't the same as speculating about it over an article in *Newsweek.*

"Do you know who's holding him?" I asked. It was an important question because political prisoners were being held by both sides of the power struggle that was taking place between the more moderate, secular forces, who had formed a new government, and the Islamic clergy, led by Ayatollah

Khomeini. Yari's best hope—maybe his only hope—was to be under the control of the fledgling government.

"He is in Qasr," she said. "Do you know what it means?"

I nodded. Qasr prison was where the Islamic Court was holding individuals they intended to put on trial. And by trial they meant an opportunity to read out a list of the defendant's supposed crimes before he was taken out to the courtyard to be summarily executed. The proceedings, which usually lasted no more than a couple of hours, took place in secret, without any advance warning. Once the execution had been carried out, an announcement would appear in an Islamic newspaper, giving the name of the latest victim and the nature of his offense, which was usually something like "Crimes Against Islam" or "Injustices Committed Against the People of Iran." Several hundred trials had already taken place, and there were another three to five thousand prisoners in Qasr awaiting their judgment day.

"I'm sorry," I said, causing Zahra to frown.

"People always say this. If you are ill, they are sorry, or if they have crashed into your car, it's the same. *I'm sorry.* What does it mean?"

"It's just something to say."

"Yes, you're right. It's just something to say."

She looked away again. The pyrotechnics had come to an end and the crowd was drifting away as the street performer desperately passed the hat.

"Yari became a different man after you left," Zahra said wistfully. "He stopped speaking to me. We haven't been in touch at all since I came here, twenty years ago. Still, he's my brother. I can't stand to think what those bastards will do with him."

"The situation could change," I said lamely. She gave me a look, but rightly ignored the empty offering.

"Do you believe in fate, Jack?"

"I haven't given it much thought."

"There must be a reason why things happen the way they do. Even if we don't understand what it is."

"I wish I could believe that."

"For me to look up, at precisely the right moment, and to see you walking by. Of all the people on the earth, on the day after I learned that Yari is in prison. It can't be a coincidence. There *must* be a purpose!"

The sun was dipping down below the tree line now, casting us into shadow. The thin October air had captured none of the day's warmth, and the evening's chill came on quickly. Zahra absentmindedly pulled her coat closer and folded her arms over each other.

"I was too angry," she said. "I wanted to strike out, to punish you, so I didn't understand. I couldn't see it."

"See what?"

"The reason I was supposed to find you."

"What do you think the reason was?" I asked, not believing for a moment that there was one.

"You're meant to help him," she said. "You're meant to rescue Yari."

I guess I should have seen it coming, but I didn't. I tried to formulate a response, but all that came out was an uncomfortable laugh.

"Zahra . . ."

"You can do it," she said firmly. "You and your CIA."

"Zahra, I'm—"

"Don't try to deny it," she said, fixing me with a dark look. "We were innocent enough to believe the lies back then, but not now."

"Even if I was in the CIA—which I'm not—what makes you think I could help Yari, let alone rescue him?"

Zahra shook her head and looked at me like I was either a liar or a fool. "Everyone knows the CIA can do as they like," she said reproachfully.

There it was. The myth.

The myth of the great and powerful Central Intelligence

Agency. All-seeing, all-knowing, invincible, invulnerable, and unassailable. More powerful than a locomotive, and able to leap tall buildings in a single bound. Imbued with unlimited power, with a sinister hand in every assassination, every coup, and every political upheaval on the planet! *Everyone knows the CIA can do as they like.* Surprising how many people believed that, particularly outside the United States. The Company had acquired legendary status, and was regarded with a bewildering mix of disdain, admiration, and fear, but most of all, with a completely unrealistic idea of what it was actually capable of doing.

And Zahra was no exception. No matter how many times I tried to tell her that even the mighty CIA wouldn't be able to rescue Yari from a maximum-security prison in a country that the United States had next to no diplomatic relations with, she wouldn't buy it. In her mind, it was just more lies, more cover-up, more evidence of the long betrayal that she and her people had suffered at the hands of American imperialism. There was nothing I could say that would have convinced her otherwise.

It was dark by the time we left the park. I put Zahra into a cab on Sixth Avenue and started to walk. I had no destination in mind, not even a direction, but I had to be moving. I was sorry that Zahra had become so bitter. She was anything but the first time I met her. I couldn't help smiling when I thought about it. Dancing the tango. She was full of confidence, full of optimism, full of hope. Young, in other words. Young and naive. I guess I'd been naive, too, in my own way. Hell, we all were back then.

Yari trusted you, Jack. We all trusted you. And when you betrayed us, we lost everything.

I tried to ignore Zahra's parting words to me, but they kept coming back, like an echo of the past they conjured up. I'd been responsible for a lot of shit in my time, both in and out of the agency, and I certainly wasn't proud of it all. But I never saw the point of rummaging around to find something to feel guilty about. I wished that it had turned out better for Yari, but—

That's it, isn't it? That's the excuse. When we need someplace to hide and it isn't working, we always have that little piece of rhetorical comfort to fall back on.

What the hell am I supposed to do about it?

FOUR

"Going somewhere?"

Lenni was leaning against the door frame, watching me pack. I wasn't sure how long she'd been standing there.

"Yeah." I tried my best to smile. "Just a day or two."

"Get a job?"

It was a loaded question, because I hadn't seen her since Saturday night, when I'd confessed to skipping the *Esquire* meeting. She'd been cool about it—in every sense of the word—and I was well aware that she'd disappeared for a couple of days in order to avoid a blowup. I was also aware that she had come back with something to say.

"I've got to see someone," I said, leaving it at that. I knew Lenni wouldn't call me on it, and she didn't. She just stood there, arms gently crossed, with a slightly bemused look on her face.

"You're going to have to talk to me at some point," she said. "More than just hello and good-bye."

There was no use pretending that I didn't know what she

meant. I was well aware that Lenni had been cutting me a lot of slack for a lot of years, and I also knew that she was running out of rope. I couldn't really complain. For Christ's sake, we'd known each other for eleven years and she still thought my name was Jack Monday.

"We'll talk when I get back," I said.

"Okay."

"You can stay here," I added lamely. She knew she could stay, I didn't have to say it.

"No . . ." She shook her head. "You know where to find me. Give me a call when you're ready."

"A couple of days," I repeated.

She surprised me with a smile—a warm, genuine smile, like I'd said something endearing. "Don't look so worried, Jack. I don't need to know everything. Just something."

I nodded. Lenni shook her head, smiled again, then slipped out of the room. I heard the front door gently close behind her.

The Eastern shuttle out of La Guardia landed at Washington National just after four o'clock. I picked up a nondescript Ford at the Hertz counter, bought a map in the bookshop, and was on the road by four-thirty. Not wanting to spring my surprise until after dark, I decided to take a spin around the capital, which I hadn't seen since the days of Ike and Mamie Eisenhower. Twenty years. Christ, how could two decades slip by so easily?

On the surface, nothing had changed. Jefferson and Lincoln maintained their silent vigils from the banks of the Potomac, looking inward toward the White House and Capitol dome, where the men of the day wielded power with an eye toward holding on to it. At the capital's fulcrum, the Washington Monument rose above it all, marking the intersection of history and power, where great ideas came up against the realities of the day. The balance had been strained in the years since my last visit. Assassination, war, civil strife, and political scandal had put Jefferson and Lincoln to the test, and shaken the country to its core. The effect was to make it wary, unsure of the way forward. For the first time in its history, America had doubts about itself.

Maybe a little self-examination isn't such a bad thing, I thought as I strolled up the National Mall and along the Reflecting Pool. Know your opponents' weaknesses, but know your own better. Didn't someone say that? Maybe not. Jimmy Carter had even given it a name: "The National Malaise." Well, as comfortable, and maybe even as healing as a malaise might be, there comes a time when you have to put it aside, and get back into the game.

Woodside Lake was one of the more upscale neighborhoods in Fairfax County, and being just a few miles west of Langley, it was home to any number of high-and-mighty spooks. I found Toby's place at the end of Sunny Side Lane, a two-story newly built brick monster, set back from the road in a heavily wooded area. The drapes were drawn, but I could see that the lights were burning behind several of the thirteen front-facing windows.

If anything could be done for Yari, Toby Walters was in a position to do it. Enlisting him was probably a long shot, but it was the only shot I could think of. He might be deputy director of operations now, mixing with all the grand pooh-bahs, but we'd been friends at one time. Okay, maybe "friends" was an exaggeration. Toby and I had never really seen eye to eye, but then I didn't see eye to eye with very many people, particularly agency people. Still, we'd worked side by side, in the early days, when the Company wasn't much more than a collection of guys with a common purpose. We were the original brotherhood, before the cynicism set in and the corporation took over. We'd laid the foundation for that myth.

I'd spent Sunday afternoon thinking through how I wanted the conversation to go. Once he'd gotten over the shock of seeing me, and asked where the hell I'd been for the last two decades, I'd get to the point. Toby wasn't the type you could soften up with flattery or bullshit. It would just make him suspicious. He'd remember Yari, but I'd give him a quick reminder anyway. I didn't want to push it too far, but there was a reasonable case to be made that if it wasn't for what Yari did, we'd have lost Iran. It's impossible to say how that would have changed things, but it sure as hell would've put a crink in Toby's march to the top. I'd composed a snappy punch line to end it with: *He saved our asses, Toby, now we have a chance to save his.* Whether all that would wash—well, like I said, it was a long shot.

I parked twenty yards up the lane, nestling the car under a tall hedge where it would be less conspicuous. As I stepped onto the road, I became aware of a very strange symphony of sounds. It was like some mad orchestra made up of those suspended steel balls that people put on their desktop for no other reason than to watch them click back and forth as they hit up against each other. At first, I thought it might be crickets, but the occasional *croak* in the mix identified the source as some variety of musical frog. They certainly had a lot to say to one another.

The electric gate would've been easy enough to climb, but there were at least two floodlights aimed at it, and there was bound to be a movement sensor that would alert the house to an uninvited visitor. I considered ringing the bell and announcing myself from there, but I didn't want some disembodied voice telling me Toby wasn't available. Besides, I had this image of his face when he opened the door to find me standing there, and I didn't want to miss it.

Feeling my way along the brick wall that surrounded the property, I was disappointed to find that every tree within jumping distance had been shorn of its low-hanging branches. There was a time when a ten-foot barrier wouldn't have presented much of an obstacle, but stepping back to consider my options, I concluded that those days were behind me. Heading back to the car, I keyed the engine, reversed up the lane, and pulled in as close as I could, sacrificing the passenger-side wing mirror in the process. Once I'd clambered onto the Ford's roof, it was relatively easy to hoist myself up onto the wall, and from there it was a short drop to the ground. Unfortunately, it was too dark to see my landing zone, and I was disentangling myself from the rosebushes when I looked up to see my worst nightmare coming at me.

The huge, bloodthirsty, spit-spewing Alsatian bastard came snarling out of the darkness, buried its fangs in my arm, and pulled me to the ground. Before I could react, I was being dragged across wet grass, a helpless rag doll in the lockjaw grip of the wild-eyed beast. I thought about playing dead, but this animal was going for the real thing.

"AUS!"

The dog took three steps back and stood there watching me, a hungry look in its eye. A powerful light hit me in the face, blinding me.

"Just what in the hell do you think you're doing?" I could make out the hulking frame of a big man dressed in a red plaid bathrobe. He had a flashlight in one hand, and a double-barreled shotgun in the other. The rich, Tennessee drawl was unmistakable.

"Visiting an old friend," I said, propping myself up on one elbow.

"Jesus fucking Christ! Jack Teller, is that you?"

"The one and only."

"You crazy son of a bitch!"

"So you haven't forgotten me."

"No such luck. And I was about two seconds away from turning you into a permanent memory." He shook his head. "What the hell's the matter with you?"

"Did I catch you at a bad time?"

"Jesus Christ. Well, I guess you'd better come inside."

Toby was duplicitous, devious, and ruthlessly ambitious, but he'd always had impeccable southern manners. He called off his dog and welcomed me into his home with a wave of his shotgun. I realized, once I got a look at him in the light, just how much he'd changed. He'd lost the athletic posture, along with the wavy black hair, which had been reduced to a couple of patches of unruly gray. The pouches under his eyes told me that he didn't sleep well, or at least not enough, and his once energetic, in-your-face attitude had been replaced with a world-weary resignation. He gave me the once-over, too, probably picking up all sorts of information I didn't know I was giving off. Whatever shortcomings Toby had, people reading wasn't one of them.

"We can talk in here," he said, ushering me through a set of double doors that led to a smallish study. Cozy, with books on the wall, rugs on the floor, and a crackling fire in the hearth. It smelled of stale cigars.

"Drink?"

"Whatever you're having."

"I guess this calls for the good stuff." Toby chose a bottle of Rémy XO from the shelf and poured the honey-colored liquid into two large crystal snifters. I noticed an open copy of John le Carré's latest thriller, *Smiley's People,* on a table beside an armchair. Spies never get tired of reading spy stories. They can feed their egos and their imaginations at the same time.

"Gimme a minute," he said, handing over one of the tumblers, leaving the other on his desk. "My wife'll be wondering who in hell's calling at this hour."

"Sure," I said, and he slipped out of the room.

The brandy was as smooth as it looked, and went a long way toward soothing the aching teeth marks in my arm as it dissolved into the back of my throat and found its way to my brain. I glanced around the room and was drawn to a gallery of photographs that hung along the wall opposite the fireplace. At the center of the display was a group of frames that featured Toby posing with the six presidents he'd served under—Eisenhower, Kennedy, Johnson, Nixon, Ford, and

Carter. The shot with Ike was the only group picture, the rest were one-on-one, and signed with a personal message. The one that made me smile read:

To Toby,
One hell of a son of a bitch,
Lyndon

High praise, indeed.

"So what's your secret?" Toby reentered the room, gently pushing the door closed behind him.

"Secret?"

"Have you got some sort of magic elixir you can sell me? To what do you attribute your goddamned annoying youthful looks?"

I smiled. "Good living and lots of sex."

"Well, I can still manage half of that—but just barely." He scooped up his brandy and plopped himself down behind the antique mahogany desk. I took the seat opposite.

"Christ. Jack Teller." He shook his head again. "Seeing you sure brings back memories. I've got an office, you know. And a telephone."

"I guess you didn't get any of my messages, then."

He smiled cagily. "I won't bother asking how you found this place."

"Let's just say not everyone in Langley hates me."

He chuckled. "I gave you up for dead a long time ago. Where in hell have you been?"

"Here and there. I move around a lot."

Toby leaned back in his leather chair, folded his hands into each other, and gave me a thoughtful look. "I should be pissed off at you, sneaking around my property like that. In fact, I probably should've shot you."

"If I knew you were gonna be so damned important, I would've been nicer to you back then."

"Know what I do all day long? I read memos. A never-ending stream of bullshit memos that all say the same goddamned thing—here's a hundred and one reasons why we can't do our job anymore. Everybody's got an excuse now. Ever since that Church bullshit, you've got everyone pissing their pants because they're afraid to ask some junior congressman if they can go to the bathroom. It's a sorry state of affairs, Jack, and you're damn lucky to be out of it."

The "Church bullshit" Toby was referring to was a congressional committee chaired by a senator from Idaho named Frank Church, which had, a couple of years earlier, conducted a pretty thorough investigation into the United States intelligence community. The resulting report detailed a parade of questionable activities that included political assassinations, paramilitary murder on a grand scale, domestic spying, blackmail, drug experiments, harassment, and consorting with organized crime. The CIA, singled out for special mention, was described as "a rogue elephant rampaging out of control." The findings shocked the country and moved Congress to pass a variety of measures whose purpose was to keep an eye on the spies. Needless to say, Senator Church and his reforms were about as popular in Langley as Fidel Castro.

"The good days are over," Toby grumbled.

"Old guys always say that."

"It's true this time. We're relics, Jack, you and me both, from a time long forgotten."

"The pendulum will swing back," I said, resisting the temptation to launch into what I really thought. I'd seen in Vietnam the kind of damage a rampaging elephant can do.

"Maybe so." He sighed. "But I won't be around to see it." He reached across the desk, handed me his glass. "Fill us up again, will ya, Jack?"

"Sure."

I stood up, poured us both a refill. The tone of Toby's lamentations had taken me by surprise. I don't know what

I'd expected from him, but it wasn't wistfulness. The reason for it became clear when I sat back down.

"Cancer," he said with a smile, accepting his refill.

"Jesus, Toby, I—"

"You don't have to say anything. I'm not sure why I told you. I haven't even told my wife yet. I only found out a couple of days ago, and this is the first time I've said it out loud. I guess you were my practice run."

"I . . . I'm sorry, Toby. I really am," I stumbled. "They have all sorts of good treatments these days—"

"It seems that I'm more in the market for a miracle. But what the hell, the good die young, right?" He forced a smile and raised his glass. "So here's to the dinosaurs. We had a damn good run."

"To the dinosaurs," I echoed, and we drank, using the booze to cover the awkwardness of the moment.

I wasn't sure where Toby's sudden revelation left me, whether I should go ahead with the reason for my visit, or if that would seem a bit cold. I took the lead from him when he leaned across the desk and, grinning broadly, said, "So what in God's good name are you doing here, Jack?"

"Does the name Yari Fatemi ring any bells?"

Toby furrowed his brow and searched his memory. "Sure, sure. Tehran, '53. He was Mossadegh's guy." He pointed his index finger at me. "At least, until he became your guy. That the one?"

"That's him."

"What about it?"

"He's in Qasr prison, awaiting trial."

"Along with a few thousand other poor bastards."

"He's the only poor bastard who used to be a friend of mine," I said.

"A friend, Jack? Or an asset?"

"He was both."

"I see."

Toby paused thoughtfully, absentmindedly pulled on his

earlobe as he stared down into his glass. After a moment he sighed and looked up at me. "Did you come here to assuage some kind of guilt you feel about this guy, or do you really expect me to do something about it?"

It was a good question. I guess I'd known that Toby wasn't going to jump out of his seat and say, "Well, if he's a friend of yours, Jack, let's get him the hell out of there!" but was I really just giving myself a free pass, an opportunity to quiet my conscience by saying, "Hey, I tried"?

"I had a whole pitch worked out for you." I smiled.

"Let's hear it."

I shook my head. "It's bullshit."

"I'm used to it."

"The truth is, Toby, I don't know why I'm here. Maybe I do owe this guy something. Maybe we both do. You remember how it went down, don't you?"

"He tried to fuck you over, that's what I remember."

"Yeah, I guess that's true, too. Depends on how you look at it. But we won in the end, didn't we? And he's sitting in Qasr prison."

Toby gave me a long look. "So you do want me to do something about it?"

"Yeah," I said. "I guess I do."

"Well . . ." He drew it out with southern languor. "Not to put too fine a point on it, Jack, but you're living in cloud-cuckoo-land. Even if I was so inclined, there's not a god-damn thing I can do to help your friend."

"Maybe you need to get permission from one of those junior congressmen," I said, not appreciating his condescending candor. Toby managed a chuckle, but I'm not sure he was overly amused, either.

"What the hell did you think I was gonna say?"

I asked about the State Department, thinking they might have some prisoner negotiations in the works. After all, Iran under the Shah had been one of America's closest allies. I wouldn't be the only one with friends in Qasr.

"It's a waste of time talking to these people, Jack. They're fanatics."

"That seems like a pretty good reason to open up a line of communication," I replied, but Toby dismissed it with a wave of his hand.

"If that phone rang right now, and the president of the United States was on the line, asking me what I could do, I'd have to tell him exactly what I'm telling you. I've got fuck all to work with. Aside from a couple of officers in the embassy, we've got no assets left in Iran. Nothing. The ones who didn't get out six months ago are sitting in Qasr with your friend. It's not just you, Jack. I've got a couple of people I'd love to get out of there, myself."

"Send me," I heard myself saying. I hadn't planned it, hadn't even anticipated it. It just came out. Toby gave me a strange look, like he wasn't sure if he'd heard right, then he burst out laughing.

"I'm serious, Toby," I said. When he saw that I was, he stopped laughing, frowned, and threw back the last of his cognac.

"No, Jack, you're not serious. You're fucking crazy."

"Hear me out," I said, my mind racing to catch up with the idea. "You say you don't have any assets left in the country. Well, I know the people, the country . . . I'll be your man in Tehran. Set me up with an identity—a Canadian businessman, looking for oil contracts—get me some cash, say twenty grand, and I'll nose around a bit, see if we can buy our people out. They may be fanatics, but if we learned anything over there, we learned that even fanatics have a price."

Toby gave me a deeply skeptical look, but I could see that he was intrigued.

"It'll be between you and me," I said. "No one else needs to know anything. Like the old days. Come on, Toby. Fuck 'em!"

He sat there for another few beats, then he leaned forward

and lowered his voice. "Did you ever see that program on TV called *Mission: Impossible*?"

"Sure."

"You know how, at the beginning of each show, the guy turns on a tape recorder and a voice tells him what his mission is gonna be for the week?"

"Right . . ."

"Then, once he's heard it, the tape self-destructs, but not before the voice says, 'The secretary will disavow any knowledge of your actions.' Remember that? Well, that's you, Jack. If anything goes wrong over there, if you fuck up in any way, or if you just get unlucky, your ass will be completely and utterly disavowed. You'll be by yourself, on your own, and all alone, whatever the situation, whatever the consequences."

"Sounds perfect," I said. And, strangely enough, I meant it.

"Goddammit, Jack!" Toby leaned back in his chair and allowed a massive smile to overtake his woes. "I wish to hell I could go with you!"

FIVE

April 1953
Tehran

I got my first view of Tehran through the window of a Lockheed L-749, operated by Air France. As the aircraft pivoted on its left wing, coming around to make its approach from the east, the city lay below me, a collection of low-lying, flat-topped buildings spilling down from the snowcapped Alborz Mountains toward the vast Dasht-e-Kavīr, or Great Salt Desert, to the south.

A feeling of edgy anticipation had been steadily building since I'd left New York, two and a half days earlier. It had been a fairly impulsive decision to accept a job offer that would take me halfway around the world, especially since I had no real idea about what I was signing up for.

"We're consultants," Sam had explained when he phoned me in the middle of the night to make the proposal. "In this case, it's about oil, but we dabble in any number of areas."

"I don't know the first thing about oil," I'd mumbled, still half asleep.

"You won't need to."

"What's the pay like?"

"It's shit, but the money's not the point. You'll see the world, and I guarantee you it won't be boring."

"What exactly will I be doing?"

"We'll discuss the details when we meet up in Tehran," he'd said. "And don't worry, it's the right decision, I promise you. You're getting in on the ground floor of something big. Something very fucking big." Then he hung up. I fell back to sleep telling myself it was just a bad April Fools' joke, but the next morning a special-delivery guy showed up at my door with a ticket for the Friday-afternoon flight to Paris, then on to Beirut, and Tehran.

Sam Clay was one of a kind. Short, stocky, and smart, he sized up the world with a look of constant bemusement in his blue-gray eyes, as if he was waiting for everyone else to get the answer to the riddle that he'd already worked out. I'd met him only once before the phone call, three nights earlier, at the Three Deuces on Forty-seventh Street, where I'd taken a job pouring drinks until something better came along. After a rather public scene with his sexy date, who left in a huff, Sam wandered up to the bar and we'd started talking. Before I knew it, the place was empty and we were most of the way through a thirty-year-old bottle of malt whiskey. He somehow got me to unload my life story, which was very unusual for me, but Sam was like that. Anyway, three nights later, I got the late-night call, and now here I was buckling my seat belt, wondering what the hell I'd got myself into.

"Jack Teller?"

"That's me."

"Toby Walters." He folded an English-language newspaper under his arm and offered a hefty handshake. "Welcome to Iran."

"Thanks."

"Where are your bags?"

"This is it," I said, nodding toward the beat-up old leather case I had slung over my shoulder.

"Okay, then, follow me. The car's out front."

Toby was a big, linebacker type, with deep-set eyes, a high, broad forehead, and a head of wavy, black hair. Dressed in a loose-fitting short-sleeved shirt and khaki pants, he had a relaxed manner, and spoke in an easy baritone drawl.

"You must be tired," he said, leading the way across the pristine green marble floor toward the exit. "I'll drop you at your digs, and you can use today to get settled in. A car'll pick you up tomorrow morning and we'll get you set up in the office."

"Sounds good," I said, avoiding questions that might reveal my ignorance.

Mehrabad's terminal building—spacious, bright, and exceptionally clean—felt more like the lobby at the Ritz than an airport waiting lounge. The locals, dressed to be seen, gathered in small groups, stylish women chatting quietly among themselves while the men smoked cigarettes and conducted business from the spotless white sofas that were set out around the place. A pair of uniformed soldiers, rifles strapped to their backs, kept an eye on things from a discreet distance.

"Ever been to the Middle East?" Toby asked as we stepped into the fresh early-April sunshine.

"First time."

"Well . . ." He gave me a knowing look, then slipped behind a pair of dark glasses. "It takes some getting used to."

The subdued elegance of the airport stood in stark contrast to the scenes we passed on the brief ride into central Tehran. Construction of a broad avenue that cut through the city's old neighborhoods had been abandoned, requiring the driver to slow to a crawl whenever we came across one of the intermittent patches of unfinished roadway. Women, wrapped in the traditional black chador robes, bent over deep puddles of water that had collected along the side of the thoroughfare, doing their daily washing as cars, taxis, and exhaust-spewing trucks whizzed by. Men with push-carts, full of everything from bricks to dried dates, braved the traffic, and we even passed a camel train, fully laden with carpets on their way to the bazaar. There was little green along the route, just the occasional scruffy tree or an untended palm to relieve a relentless parade of dull, concrete buildings.

Things got more crowded as we pushed into the city's center. Double-decker buses and an army of motor scooters joined the fray, while quick-footed pedestrians made well-timed sprints across the wide boulevards, facing down oncoming vehicles with a scornful look or a contemptuous gesture. There seemed to be quite a bit of construction in progress, but again, it all seemed to have come to a sudden, grinding halt.

"So here it is . . ." Toby, who'd been quiet for most of the journey, swung around to face me from his spot in the front seat, beside the driver. "Tehran. About the size of Baltimore, but three times as crazy, and not half as beautiful."

"I suppose it must have some good points," I said.

"Sure." He grinned. "It's got a shitload of oil."

"You are welcomed in Iran, and to the Iranshahr Hotel."

The young man at the reception desk offered a shallow bow and a genial smile as I stepped up to the counter. He placed a small white card and a ballpoint pen in front of me.

"Please, to write your name here, and I may take your passport."

Toby had left me to fend for myself, claiming he had an important meeting back at the office. It was clear that I'd been an unwelcome diversion in his day, but I didn't mind. I was eager to look around and didn't need a guide who used Baltimore as a yardstick.

"What's your name?" I asked the young man as he carefully copied my passport number onto the card.

"My name?"

"Right."

"I am Shamil."

"Good to meet you, Shamil."

"Yes, thank you . . ." He seemed a bit confused by my friendliness, even more so when I placed a twenty-dollar bill on the counter. "Er . . . The room, it has been already paid, sir."

"That's for you," I said.

"Oh. It's very kind. I . . ." He waited for the quid pro quo, and I explained that I was going to rest up for a couple of hours, get myself cleaned up, then I wanted to be picked up by a taxi and taken to a restaurant where I could have a good meal. "Not a tourist place," I said. "I want to see only Iranians."

"Yes, I am understood," Shamil said, grinning from ear to ear as he pocketed the bill. "And I know a very good place. The best place. You will like."

He was more than happy to have the twenty bucks, of course, but I didn't think it was just the money that made him smile.

Café Pars took up an entire city block, with tables set out on the sidewalks and people spilling out onto the street. Located at the edge of Tehran's business district, the lively nightspot was housed in a two-story brick building whose main feature was a circular roof terrace where people could sit under a domed cupola and look out across the city lights. As my taxi pulled away, the soft strains of a small orchestra drifted out the door and across the moonlit evening, adding to the allure of the place.

"Welcome, sir, so nice to see you." I was greeted like a

long-lost friend by the gray-haired maître d' who was waiting by the door. Wearing a finely tailored blue suit and a tasteful silk tie, he wouldn't have looked out of place in the finest restaurant in Paris. "I have saved for you my best table, and tonight we have a very good show. I am certain it will please you."

A white-jacketed waiter led me through a set of pointed arch doors into a large dining room where, at the far end, a ten-piece orchestra was playing a fox-trot in front of a good-size dance floor. A handful of couples were on their feet, but most of the action was at the tables, where dinner service was in full swing. I was given a single, up front and to the side, where I could watch the show without being part of it.

No menu was necessary. As soon as I sat down, food began to appear, starting with a plate of fresh herbs, including coriander, tarragon, cilantro, and watercress. Then came a basket of flat bread, accompanied by a number of fetalike cheeses, and a tray of sliced tomatoes, cucumbers, and onions. There was a delicious relish, too, based on eggplant, but containing cauliflower, peppers, and carrots, among other things. I was poured a glass of a carbonated yogurt drink, but when the waiter saw my reaction, he followed it up with a bottle of local beer, which I gratefully accepted.

At this point, the lights went down, and a spotlight hit the gentleman who'd greeted me at the door (who turned out to be the club's owner, and Shamil's uncle). After a heartfelt introduction, a dark, full-figured beauty undulated onto the stage, dressed to the nines in a black sequined gown, thick mascara, bright red lipstick, and a long string of pearls. She paused, cast her eye across the room, waited for total silence, then smiled seductively. The band picked up the cue and she slid into an interesting version of "Some Enchanted Evening." I wasn't sure until the second verse rolled around that she was singing in English, but what she lacked in vocal talent, she made up for in stage presence. She certainly kept the attention of the male half of the audience, anyway, me included.

The main course was a delicious lamb-and-chickpea stew served over rice. I tried to wave off dessert but got a piece of nut-filled, honey-soaked pastry anyway. I was thankful for the glass of hot lemon tea that signaled the end of the feast, which had been as superb as it was plentiful.

"Are you American or English?"

I'd noticed the young beauty earlier, during the show, when she and her friends had been stealing glances and whispering about me from their table across the room. She was part of a large group, maybe a dozen people of various ages.

"I said that you are American," she continued. "But my friends think you are English."

"You win," I said. "What gave me away?"

"An Englishman would not sit alone in a nightclub. He would be too embarrassed."

"Well . . ." I smiled. "I guess I have no shame."

"Why should you?"

A man appeared behind the girl and placed a hand on her shoulder. He was tall and slender, naturally elegant without being feminine, serious without looking dour. He sported a neatly trimmed mustache, and his dark hair was combed straight back, with a neat part in the middle. "You must excuse my sister," he said. "She thinks she is being modern when she is, in fact, being rude."

"I was just speaking to the gentleman, Yari," the girl protested.

"Jack Teller." I stood up and reached across the table.

"Yari Fatemi," he responded, taking my hand. "And this impertinent girl is my sister Zahra."

"Good to meet you—both." I offered my hand to Zahra, too. She smiled cagily when she took it, and didn't let go.

"Do you know how to tango, Mr. Teller?"

"Ah . . . Well . . . It's been a while."

"I'm sure you can remember."

I glanced over to big brother, who shrugged with resignation. "Please join us at our table afterward."

I thanked him and Zahra wasted no time, flashing her friends a triumphant look as she pulled me onto the dance floor. She was a true beauty. Slender and graceful, like her brother, though she certainly didn't share his sense of propriety. She reveled in her own audacity, the reckless glint in her eye revealing the pleasure she took in the effect it had on people. Her move on me would ensure that she would be the talk of the town for at least a week.

"You see," she said as the tango ended and I was pulled straight into a waltz. "I told you that you would remember."

"Like riding a bicycle."

"A bicycle?"

"Just an expression."

Zahra gave me a funny look, like I was off script, then returned the conversation back to where she wanted it to be. "Yari still treats me like a little girl. He hasn't yet realized that I've grown up."

"It must be nice to have a big brother to look after you." Again, her look told me that it hadn't been the right response.

"How old do you think I am?" she asked, giving me another chance.

"Seventeen?" In fact, I put her at eighteen or nineteen, but I didn't want to encourage her. She frowned.

"I'll be twenty this year. Does that surprise you?"

"Not at all," I said. "But you put me on the spot. It's bad form to tell a lady that she looks her age." Zahra looked skeptical, but we made a couple of spins around the dance floor, and by the time the music stopped, she was smiling again.

"Come," she said, taking my hand. "My friends will be jealous. They all want to meet you."

Waiting at the head of the long table, Yari gestured me

into an empty chair on his right, directing Zahra to the opposite end of the gathering, where her two girlfriends were losing the battle to control their giggles. I was introduced around the table, to Yari's lovely, if somewhat quiet, wife, a couple of brothers and sisters, several cousins, friends, and I think there was a nephew and a niece in the mix, too. Among all the smiling faces, there was one that wasn't. In his midtwenties, and darker than the others—in both skin tone and presence—he was a small, angular man, with a pencil mustache, who wore the uniform of an army officer. He managed a nod in my direction when Yari introduced him as Lieutenant Ali Ashraf Azari, but he made no effort to hide his contempt. I didn't understand it until later in the evening, when it became clear that he felt Zahra's tango should have been reserved for him.

"What brings you to Iran, Mr. Teller?" Yari asked as we settled into our seats.

"Business," I said breezily. "But please call me Jack."

"All right then, Jack . . ." He poured a shot of clear vodka-like liquid into a tall glass, pushed it over to me, then poured one for himself. "Let's drink to the success of your business."

I picked up the glass, studied its contents.

"It's called *Aragh-e Sagi,*" Yari explained. "The English translation would be 'sweat of a dog.'"

"Sounds terrific." I smiled, quickly tossing it back. I'd never tasted dog sweat before, but it couldn't have been any worse than this. I stifled a gag and managed a pitiful "Nice," before realizing that Yari had a very amused—and slightly incredulous—grin fixed to his face.

"You're meant to add water," he said, illustrating with his own glass, waiting until the liquid had turned a cloudy gray before lifting it to his lips and taking a small sip. "And drink it slowly. Like this."

I laughed out loud, helped along by the sudden rush of almost pure alcohol to my brain. "In that case, I'd better try another," I said, pushing my glass back across the table.

Everyone enjoyed the moment, and a warm, relaxed atmosphere took over. The top half of the table listened in as Yari quizzed me about America, and what Americans thought of Iran. I improvised the best I could, not wanting to say that most of my countrymen wouldn't have the slightest idea that a place called Iran even existed, and of those who did, few would have an opinion about it. I got the sense that, aside from Zahra, who was otherwise occupied, Yari was the only one able to follow my English. The rest were just nodding their heads, either out of politeness, or an unwillingness to admit that they had no idea what I was saying. Probably both.

As the evening came to an end, I asked for my bill and was told that it had been taken care of. I tried to protest, but to no avail, so I just thanked Yari for making my first night in Tehran so memorable. On the way out, he gently pressed me about the nature of my business, but he was too polite to push it when I dodged the query. Handing me his card as we parted, he told me that Iran could be a difficult place to get things done if you didn't know the right people, and to get in touch if I needed help cutting through the bureaucracy. As he joined his clan in one of the three waiting cars, I was surprised by Lieutenant Azari, who came up to shake my hand and say a genial good night. He was looking a lot happier, and I soon discovered that it was because he'd managed to secure a place in the backseat, next to Zahra, for the ride home.

After a breakfast of tea, bread, and goat's cheese, I found my driver—the same one who'd picked me up at the airport—waiting in the hotel lobby. I learned that his name was Hadi, but not much else. He pretended not to understand English, and provided no more than fumbling evasions when I tried to extract information about my new employer out of him. He'd managed to understand Toby pretty well the previous day, but I guess he figured that he couldn't get into trouble for what he didn't say.

The company offices were located just off Ferdosi Square (actually an oval), in a nondescript three-story concrete building about halfway between the British and American embassies. The elevator was out of service, so I climbed the stairs to the second floor, where I found one flimsy-looking wooden door, locked. There was no sign, or any other indication of what might be inside, but there was a bell, so I rang it. A few moments passed before the voice of a young female came through the door.

"Ki e?"

"I, ah . . . Do you speak English?"

"Yes . . ."

"Are these the offices of the Americo Oil Company?"

"Yes, but no one is here."

"You're here."

There was a longish pause. "It's better if you come back."

"When?"

"When someone is here."

"When will that be?"

Another pause. "One hour."

It sounded like a guess, so I pressed on. "My name is Jack Teller . . . I'm supposed to start work here today."

Silence. I considered going for an hour's walk, but elected instead to ring the bell again. To my surprise, it worked. The lock clicked over, the door opened, and I was met with a wary set of dark eyes.

"Come in," she said grudgingly.

I didn't want to start my new life with an enemy—especially one as attractive as this—so I put on my best smile. "I guess no one told you about me."

"I didn't expect you until later in the day," she responded, unimpressed.

I tried another tack. "What's your name?"

"Leyla."

"Pretty. What does it mean?"

"It's just a name."

"Right. Well . . . Do I have a desk or something?"

"An office. I can show you."

"Thanks."

What Leyla lacked in charm, she made up in raw sex appeal. In her late twenties, with long, dark hair that had been tinted a rich auburn color, she had full red lipstick-covered lips and a body with curves in all the right places. She wore a tight black skirt with a slit up the back, a white blouse that was a size too small, and heels that made everything jiggle in just the right way. I paid careful attention as she led the way along a short corridor, then through a second door into the back, where three small offices were positioned around a reception area.

"I sit here," she said, pointing to a desk that held a typewriter, a phone, and several cardboard boxes in the process of being unpacked. She explained that the three offices belonged to "Mr. Walters, Mr. Keating, and Mr. Cotton."

"Where am I?" I asked.

"This way."

I followed down a dark, narrow hallway that ended in an empty storeroom. There was no door on it, and certainly no window. Just a space, maybe eight feet by six feet, with a single lightbulb dangling from the ceiling and a desk that had been maneuvered into a cockeyed angle that would allow it to fit between the walls.

"This is my office?"

Leyla crossed her arms and gave me a look that said, "Nothing to do with me."

"Did Sam say this was my office?"

"Mr. Clay?"

"Right. Sam Clay."

"Mr. Clay hasn't yet arrived in Tehran."

"He hasn't?"

"No."

"Then who decided this should be my office?"

She frowned, unhappy about being cross-examined. She got lucky, though, because the answer to my question was striding down the hall, heading toward us with a schoolboy grin on his face.

"Hiya, Jack!" Toby bellowed out. "I see that Leyla's getting you settled in." He also saw that I wasn't smiling. "Listen, buddy, it's just a place to hang your hat. Nobody expects you to actually sit in there. Anyway, it's only temporary, until we get hold of some bigger quarters."

"When will that be?"

"When Sam gets here, I guess."

"When will that be?" Leyla saw this as an opportune moment to slip away.

"He's been delayed in Cyprus," Toby replied, somewhat reluctantly. "He'll come straight here once he's finished up there. A couple of days, maybe. In the meantime, take it easy. Get the lay of the land. There's no rush."

I gave him a look. There didn't seem to be much choice but to pose the question. "No rush to do what?"

"Sorry, buddy, I don't follow you."

"I'm not too sure what I'm supposed to be doing here."

Toby squinted his eyes and thought about it. "What did Sam tell you?"

"Not much," I said. "In fact, nothing at all."

"Well, then . . ." He patted me on the back. "That's exactly what you should be doing."

SIX

I hung around the office for the next couple of days, hoping to get a clue about this so-called company I'd signed up to, which, it turned out, didn't even have a name. They just called it "The Company." Nobody wanted to say much about it, but it didn't take long to figure out that I hadn't thrown in with a bunch of oil consultants.

The longest-serving employee in the group was Al Keating, a quiet thirty-year-old from California who'd been on board for a couple of years, based in Washington. Like everything else about the place, he was elusive, but a couple of things he said made me think he came from an academic background, and the suspicion was backed up by the fact that he spent all day with his feet up on his desk, reading one book after another. He spent a lot of time on *The Seven Pillars of Wisdom* by T. E. Lawrence and the Koran, along with several books on the local lingo, Farsi.

Toby, on the other hand, spent the day hunched over his typewriter, banging out long memos that he'd lock away in a filing cabinet, even if he was only going down the hall for one of his half-hour shits. He pretended to be friendly, but he was wary, and didn't like having me around.

Bob Cotton was the most talkative of the three. A congenial midwesterner with a mischievous twinkle in his eye, he appeared in the doorway of my closet on the first morning and, pretending to shoot the breeze, attempted to pump me for information. I had a feeling that Toby had put him up to it, but it was just a guess. Anyway, I had nothing to hide, but if they were gonna play games, I decided I would, too. I talked him around in circles for the better part of an hour, until he finally gave up and withdrew to his office, with a slightly dazed look on his face. I did manage to get out of him that he'd grown up in Des Moines, Iowa, had served in Italy during the war, and had been a reporter for the *Chicago Tribune* before joining the Company a few months earlier.

I'd arrived in Tehran on Monday. On Thursday morning I woke up cursing Sam, and went straight to a travel agent to check out the price of a one-way ticket back to New York. The answer was eight hundred bucks, which pretty much settled the question. I'd brought just under four with me and Leyla had given me an envelope containing another hundred for expenses, so I was three hundred short, and stuck, at least until Sam arrived.

I decided to make the most of it and spent the next few days floating around Tehran, seeing the sights and breathing in the atmosphere. I'd pass the morning in a museum, or people watching in Pârk-e Laleh, the afternoon wandering through the bazaar, a never-ending labyrinth of streets and alleys where you could bargain for anything from a bag of figs to a chunk of gold the size of your fist. I found a newsstand that carried the *Daily Mail* and the London *Times,* and a friendly place called Café Naderi, where I could sit all evening and read them. I even managed to finish a couple of the crazy crossword puzzles in the *Times.* On the third night, I was invited by a group of old men, who seemed to live in the place, to join them in a game of backgammon, or *takhte-nard,* as they called it. They not only taught me the game, but how to drink hot tea through a sugar cube that's held between your teeth, and the right way to use a *qalyan,* which is a great way to smoke if you've got a lot of time on your hands, which I did.

People were invariably friendly, particularly once they found out I wasn't English. After several decades in Iran, the Brits weren't exactly at the peak of their popularity. In fact, six months earlier, their embassy had been closed and their diplomats unceremoniously tossed out of the country. Saleh, my eighty-seven-year-old *takhte-nard* partner, who was the accepted Champion of Tehran, summed it up between rolls of the dice:

"The British, they are cheater and thief!" He gesticulated wildly as he spoke. "They don't make a good business, they take what is not belong them. It is something like a thief. What else it is when they come in our home and take what is belong us? Where is the oil? It is in Iran! It is Iran oil! We have try to make business with them, but they don't take serious. They don't talk. They make Iranian people like fools . . . Believe me, I have been in Abadan, I have seen what it is. The British have a big house with a green grass for tennis, and the water pool for swimming in the middle of desert, while the Iranian people, they live like an animal. I tell you, it is like this. I saw it myself. There is the sign on the drinking place where it is written 'Not for Iranian.' So now it is written 'Not for British'!"

He paused to smile, proud of his clever turn of the tables. "I tell you, by God, Mossadegh has done the right thing when he throws these British away. Praise God, I believe he is right!"

Mohammad Mossadegh was the Iranian prime minister who, in 1951, had triggered the crisis with Britain by nationalizing Iran's oil and its oil facilities. A Swiss-educated member of the country's elite, he was a quirky, intelligent man, known for quoting poetry, crying at the drop of a hat, and doing business in his pajamas. After making an impassioned case for his actions before the United Nations, cataloging a long list of abuses by the Anglo-Iranian oil company, Mossadegh was named *Time* magazine's "Man of the Year," and became an overnight hero to the people of the world who were struggling to escape their imperialist past.

Winston Churchill wasn't his greatest admirer. The British prime minister, who was doing everything he could to hold on to a rapidly shrinking empire, was determined to save Britain's lucrative oil monopoly, by whatever means he deemed necessary. When he ordered an economic embargo of Iran, and backed it up with a naval blockade, it just hardened Mossadegh's resolve, leading him to declare that he would "rather be fried in Persian oil than make the slightest concession to the British." Upon discovering that Churchill was plotting something very much along those lines, Mossadegh ordered their embassy closed, and rescinded all British diplomatic visas. And that was pretty much the state of affairs when I turned up.

I was surprised to find Leyla sitting in the lobby of the Iranshahr. She stood up as I entered, put her hands on her hips, and gave me an exasperated look. "I have been looking all the day for you."

"I guess you found me," I said. "What's up?"

"Mr. Clay has arrived."

Sam glanced up from the desk, where he was chomping on a cold cigar as he perused one of Toby's epic memos. He looked like he'd been drinking sour milk.

"Where in hell you been?" he said.

"I was about to ask you the same question," I said, stepping into the large office on the top floor.

"Close the door," he said, setting the memo aside. "Take

a seat." I pulled up a chair, sat down, and waited. Sam sized me up for a moment, then broke into a cagey smile. "I'll bet you were starting to wonder about me."

"You could say that."

"Good. Rule number one. Never trust anybody unless you have to, and that includes me. How do you like Tehran?"

"It's different."

He chuckled. "You can say that again. It sure as hell is different. I suppose you're wondering what in Christ's name you're doing here."

"Something like that."

He gave me another long look. "And you probably figured out that we aren't exactly in the oil business."

"Yeah, I figured that out."

He pushed his chair back, swung his feet up onto the desk, and took a couple of puffs on the Havana. "So what do you suppose we are up to, Jack?"

"I was hoping you were gonna tell me."

He nodded. "What do you know about the Central Intelligence Agency?"

"Not a lot," I said, which was true. It might sound implausible now, but in 1953, very few people had even heard of the agency. I recited to Sam what I remembered reading—that Truman had created it in 1947, along with the National Security Council, in order to coordinate the intelligence activities of the military and the State Department. The idea was to cut through the bureaucracy, and provide the president with faster, more accurate information.

"Not bad," Sam said, raising an eyebrow. "It's more than most of the high-octane dimwits in Washington know, anyway. But it's not really their fault, because, up until now, we've been pretty fucking useless. Like you just outlined, our job has been to collect stacks of paper from various corners of government, and turn 'em into bite-size morsels that the White House can easily digest."

"Up until now?"

He punched the air with his cigar. "We just got real."

"Does that mean you get to generate your own stacks of paper now?" I nodded toward Toby's memo. Sam picked it up with one hand, grabbed his Zippo with the other, and, with his eyes locked on me, set the papers alight. He held the document for as long as he could, then threw it into an empty wastebasket, where it disappeared in a cloud of smoke.

"I'm not big on writing stuff down," he said. "It tends to come back and bite you in the ass."

"Is that rule number two?"

Sam laughed again. "You don't sit still for any bullshit, do you? Well, that's good. Neither do I. I guess that's why I chose you."

"Chose me for what?"

"To be a spy, Jack. To be a spy. Or, more precisely, to be *my* spy. I chose you to be my man in Tehran."

I said the first thing that popped into my head: "Why?"

"You mean why would I choose you, of all people?"

"Right. Why me?"

"Well, first of all, I've got a good feeling about you, and I've got impeccable instincts. I know a good operative when I see one. And second, because I checked you out, from top to bottom, and I liked what I saw. You've got a fairly interesting past, Jack, if you don't mind me saying so."

"Checked me out?"

"I know stuff about you that you don't even know."

"Checked me out with who?"

"Oh, you'd be surprised how many federal agencies have a file on you. Or maybe I should say *used* to have a file on you. I'm happy to report that Jack Teller no longer exists, at least as far as the government of the United States of America is concerned. You are what we call a blank slate, my son."

"*Your* blank slate . . ."

"That's right. My blank slate." He paused. "Of course I

can't make you do anything that you don't want to do. If pouring drinks for overpaid executives is more your cup of tea, that's fine, I'll get you a seat on tomorrow morning's flight to Paris, and you can be back in New York for church on Sunday. But I don't think the quiet life is for you, Jack. And I think you have the makings of one hell of a spook."

He paused to take a couple of puffs on his cigar while he sized up my reaction so far.

"You should know two things before you make your decision," he continued after a moment. "One, I don't invite just anybody onto my team. I've got plenty of college-educated geniuses, and I've got savvy operators up the ying-yang, but you've got talents that are a bit tougher to find. You know how to read people, you know how to handle yourself, and, most important of all, you're not out to impress anyone. People don't impress me. Results do."

"What's the second thing?" I said.

"The second thing?"

"You said there were two things I should know before I make my decision. You only told me one."

"The second thing is that once you get involved, you don't get uninvolved. Ever." He paused to see if I had any other questions. I didn't. "So what's it gonna be, Jack? In or out?"

"In," I said simply.

"Good." He picked up another memo from a stack on his desk. "There's a briefing in this office tomorrow morning at ten o'clock. Don't be late."

And that was it. I'd walked into the room as a stranded bartender, and left as an operative for the CIA. I had little idea of what my new duties would entail, but I was excited and intrigued.

SEVEN

Operation Ajax . . .

Sam scrawled the words across a portable blackboard that had been brought into the room for the occasion, along with a group of chairs that were being filled by Toby, Bob Cotton, Al Keating, myself, and a man in a beat-up panama hat whom I didn't know. He'd come in with Sam and sat down without saying a word.

"For those of you who are unschooled in such matters," Sam said as he turned to face his audience, "Ajax was a Greek hero, a great warrior who distinguished himself in the epic battles of the Trojan War. Described by Homer as a man of great stature and a colossal frame, he was the tallest and strongest of all the Achaeans. In other words, he was the meanest, toughest goddamn son of a bitch on the block." Sam paused, waited for the obligatory laugh, then continued.

"Of course he had to be tough, because of all the warriors who appear in *The Iliad,* Ajax is the only poor bastard who never benefited from divine intervention on the battlefield. Instead, he won his contests with hard work, determination, and unflinching perseverance. It is for those qualities that we've named our little operation in his honor. For there will be no divine intervention here. God, apple pie, or your mama's heartfelt prayers ain't gonna do it for us. As with Ajax, it's gonna take hard work, determination, and unflinching perseverance. Along with one other thing. Intelligence. And I mean that in both senses of the word. We're gonna need good information, gathered from reliable sources, but we're also gonna need the other kind of intelligence. The kind that comes from up here."

Sam tapped his forehead, then paused to squint into the souls of his audience, sizing us up like a head coach who's about to send his team of rookies onto the field for the opening game of the season. When he spoke again, it was in a low, measured tone, intended to add weight to his words, and make us inch forward in our seats.

"If you men get this right, you'll have done something important," he said. "Precious few will ever know what you did, and I guarantee that you won't make it into the books, but you'll be making history all the same. Because you lucky sons of bitches are the guys who are going to carry out the first-ever agency-sponsored overthrow of a sitting government. Gentlemen, we are going to effect a coup d'état in this country."

He stood there for a moment, perfectly still, allowing time for the words to sink in. None of us could have appreciated the significance, or the ramifications, of his statement at that time, including Sam himself. After all, history isn't some docile animal you can just saddle up and calmly ride out into the future, choosing your path and tugging at the reins whenever you feel like you're drifting off course. She's a wild, uncontrollable beast, with a mind of her own, and she delights in throwing anyone who's arrogant enough to think they can tame her. History's path is littered with leaders who thought they had her bested, only to find themselves lying on the side of the road, battered and bruised. Of course that wasn't what I was thinking as I sat there, in the company of my new colleagues, listening to my first CIA briefing. I was wondering how in hell five guys, who didn't even speak the language, were gonna overthrow an entire government.

"Since this is the first time we've attempted anything along these lines," Sam continued, "there is no template, no model we can follow. Oh, there's a perfectly good plan, all right, and I'll get to that in a minute, but we all know that when it comes to the crunch, even the best-laid plans have a tendency to turn to shit. So, in large part, we're gonna be making this up as we go along. But here's what we have to start with . . ."

He picked up the chalk and scribbled three points across the board:

1. *Undermine Mossadegh popularity*
   - *media*
   - *mosques*
   - *man in the street*

2. *Demonstrations/riots*
   - *people demand PM resignation*

3. *Shah decree dismisses Mossadegh*
   - *royalist officers arrest him*
   - *new PM appointed*

"One, two, three. Simple, right?" Sam smiled, got back a ripple of soft laughter as he brushed the chalk off his hands and cleared his voice to continue, taking on a more military tone as he got into operational details.

"At the moment Mossadegh is seen as the patriot who stood up to British imperialism and won. Our job in phase one will be to turn him into the traitor who bankrupted the Iranian economy and sold out to the Commies. Using this three-pronged attack—media, mosques, and man on the street—we'll take him from national hero to national goat.

"In the media campaign, we'll be planting editorials and news stories, mainly in the newspapers, but on radio, too, whenever we can. Bob, this'll be your primary area of focus. You'll have support from Washington, of course. We've got two or three Farsi speakers lined up to do translation for you, and you'll have the art department at your disposal. Start out with stories on the economy, and the disastrous effect that nationalizing the oil has had on people. How lives have been ruined. Kids dying in the hospitals because there's not enough medicine, that sort of thing. Then we should get into how Mossadegh's cozying up to the Commies, giving the Tudeh Party more and more influence in the cabinet. You and I can do some brainstorming over the next few days. At the same time we'll be lining up as many imams as we can to whip up resentment in the mosques. The clerics have been playing ball with Mossadegh up to now, but they're not exactly fond of him. His ideas about a Western-style democracy don't sit too well in their fifteenth-century minds, and we can use the Communist card with them, too. These guys can swing a lot of resentment our way, so let's put on our thinking caps and figure out how to get them real pissed off at Mossadegh. Al and Toby, you two get together on this, see what you can come up with."

"As far as the man in the street," Sam continued, "we'll use pamphlets, cartoons, graffiti, and whatever else you can come up with. Bob, you're in charge of production, and Toby will handle distribution. Somebody suggested we start with a rumor that Mossadegh has a Jewish grandmother."

"That's good," Bob jumped in. "We can do a cartoon featuring the big nose, maybe have a rabbi whispering in his ear."

Sam nodded. "Good. And put a hammer and sickle on the

rabbi." Bob made a note of it, and Sam continued. "The next phase will kick in a couple of months down the line, once we've knocked Mossadegh down a peg. Toby, I want you to take the lead in this area, too. Start organizing now. We'll begin with small protests, unemployed workers demanding jobs, better conditions, that sort of thing. Then we'll bring in the students to ratchet things up, and finally, we'll get the riffraff into it, create some real chaos. And the more violent it gets, the more red flags I want to see. Workers unite behind Mossadegh and down with the Shah."

"What kind of budget do I have?" Toby inquired.

"We'll get into that later. But don't worry, we'll get everything we need. We're the number one priority right now, all the way to the top." Toby nodded with satisfaction, and Sam went on to the next point on the board.

"Once things look like they're starting to spiral out of control, in late July or early August, we'll be ready for phase three, which is the critical stage. The Shah hasn't been brought into this yet, but we've got people he trusts coming in over the next couple of weeks to talk to him. He'd dearly love to see the last of Mossadegh, but from what I hear, his backbone ain't exactly made of steel, so he'll have to be handled with kid gloves. That's not your concern, though. Your job is to be ready once we get him to sign that decree dismissing the government. The army could go either way at that point. Mossadegh's got units that'll stay with him to the bitter end, so we need to identify officers sympathetic to the Shah and ensure that, when push comes to shove, we have them in the right place at the right time. We want it to be Mossadegh who ends up in jail and not the Shah."

"That'll mean bringing in a lot of people over an extended period of time," Bob Cotton interjected. "All it takes is one to turn on us and we're screwed."

"That's right," Sam agreed. "But there's no way around it. We need the army. The rest is just window dressing. I can't stress it enough. When Mossadegh gets handed that decree from the Shah, dismissing his government and putting him under arrest, there'd better be a line of tanks staring him in the face to drive the point home." Sam leaned back against his desk, removed a Havana from his jacket pocket, and clipped the end. "So that's it, in a nutshell," he said as he fired it up. "Questions?"

There were none.

"Hang back a minute, Jack," Sam called out as I headed for the door. I stepped back into the room, noted that the man in the panama was watching me out of the corner of his eye while he pretended to gaze out the window onto the busy street below.

"Got any lunch plans?"

I said I didn't.

"Good. We're gonna catch a bite down the street. Why don't you join us?"

Nothing much was said as we made our way through a web of back alleys to a small family-run restaurant, where we were led into a private room in back. The proprietor, a short, wide-bodied man with a welcoming smile, seemed to be on good terms with our unnamed companion, who, as far as I could tell, spoke fluent Farsi, albeit with an Oxford accent.

"Timothy Spry, Jack Teller. Jack Teller, Timothy Spry." Sam made the formal introduction once we'd sat down.

"Pleasure," Spry said in a crusty voice. I nodded in his direction and he offered a pack of Oshnu across the table. "Cigarette?"

"No, thanks," I said, retrieving my own pack. I'd tried the local weed a few days earlier when I'd run out of Luckys. After struggling through half a pack, I'd dedicated the rest of the day to finding a shop that sold American brands, and I now had a two-month supply sitting in my hotel room.

True to form, Sam got straight to the point. "I asked you to join us, Jack, because the Professor here doesn't think you're up to the job I have in mind for you. He can't do anything about it, you understand, but I said I'd let him look you over so he can report back to his people that we're not the Neanderthals they think we are."

In fact, Spry did look a lot like a university professor. Quiet, watchful, and somewhat disheveled, he was in his midfifties, maybe a little older, and wore an enigmatic expression on a narrow, freckled face topped by a mop of reddish-brown hair. His thick, heavily lined skin, hardened by years in a harsh sun that he wasn't built for, was the only clue that he had a life outside the classroom. He tried to put on a smile, met with limited success.

"Sam is being his usual hyperbolic self," he said. "He intends quite an important role for you and I just wanted to meet you before any final decisions were made."

"The decision's made," Sam mumbled.

"I understand you were mixing drinks when he found you."

"That's right."

"Interesting." He shot Sam a look. "Tell me, Jack, what's your assessment of Operation Ajax? I'd like to hear your thoughts on it."

"My thoughts?" I blew a couple of smoke rings in his direction.

"If you have any."

"Well . . . It's certainly an ambitious plan."

"Too ambitious?"

I shrugged. "I thought so at first, then I changed my mind."

"Oh? What made you do that?"

"You."

"Me?"

"Right."

"How did I do that?"

"You spoke."

"I spoke?"

"That's right."

"I . . . I'm afraid I'm not following you."

"Yeah, I can see that. Shall I explain it to you?"

"Please do."

"Well . . ." I noted that Sam was sitting back, watching the Professor as I spoke. "While I was listening to the briefing, I was thinking about all the various elements we'd have to have in place in order to have any chance of pulling something like this off. We'd need friendly locals in pretty much every segment of Iranian society. Journalists, religious leaders, politicians, the military . . . It's not the sort of thing you can put together in a couple of months, especially if you don't know the place, which none of us do. So I was skeptical. Then, when we came into the restaurant, I heard you say something for the first time. You spoke with the owner in what sounded like pretty good Farsi, but I could hear your English accent, too. I couldn't place it then, but now that I've heard a bit more, I'd say you're from the north—Liverpool or Manchester—but you've made an effort to take on a more polished way of speaking. It's not bad, but there are still traces of your working-class background in there."

I paused to let the Professor react. He didn't, so I continued.

"Anyway, all that's beside the point. The point is that when I realized you're English, I assumed that you represent British intelligence, which means that this is being run as a joint operation, or at least with the support of MI6. And since you guys have been in Iran for something like four decades, and pretty much ran the place until Mossadegh kicked you out, you must have a pretty extensive local network that we can draw on. So that's when I changed my mind and thought, with British assets and American resources, there's no reason why Operation Ajax can't succeed. Does that make it more clear for you?"

Spry sat there, staring at me with a look that split the difference between bemused and annoyed. "Yes," he said. "Yes, it does. Thank you."

"Any more questions?" Sam gloated.

"No." Spry shook his head. "I think that clarifies the situation."

"Good." Sam smiled. "Then I have a question for you."

"Go ahead . . ."

"Where were you born?"

The Professor gave him a look, and then, with a resigned shrug of his shoulders, said, "Liverpool."

Lunch arrived, consisting of saffron rice and kebabs, which we washed down with bottles of strong beer. The atmosphere lightened up, and soon Sam and the Professor were digging into the past, vying to top each other with stories of wartime adventure and intrigue. They clearly had a history together, and didn't dislike each other as much as they pretended to. Sam, I discovered, went back to the early days of the OSS, when he worked with the father of American intelligence, "Wild Bill" Donovan. The Professor had been pretty much everywhere, it seemed, but was continually drawn back to the Near East.

"I suppose it's the idea that it could fall apart at any given moment, and it's been that way for thirty centuries, that appeals to me," he mused.

"How did you manage to stick around when the rest of your countrymen were shown the door?" I asked, causing a roguish smile to creep across his face.

"As a matter of fact," he confided, "they personally escorted me onto the plane. The truth is, I'm not actually here. I'm in Egypt, supervising a very important archaeological dig that is being sponsored by the British Museum."

We talked a bit about the operation, and the extent of the organization that the British had left behind, which was substantial. Until Mossadegh showed up, they'd run Iran like the Wizard ran Oz, pulling the levers of power from behind a little curtain in a corner that everyone knew existed, but no one acknowledged. I learned that Operation Ajax had been conceived by the British (they'd called it "Operation

Boot"), and they'd intended to carry it out on their own until Mossadegh got wind of it and tossed them out. At that point, they'd taken it to Washington and, after being rejected by the Truman administration, found a friendlier reception when Eisenhower moved into the White House.

"I guess you must be wondering about that job," Sam said as tea and sweet cakes were served. Before I could answer, he threw a business card onto the table. Printed on thick, textured paper, were the words:

JACK TELLER
EXECUTIVE VICE PRESIDENT

AMERICO OIL
227 PARK AVENUE, SUITE 475
NEW YORK, N.Y.

"Congratulations," he said. "You just made captain of industry."

I picked up the card, ran my finger over the engraved lettering. "Does it come with a raise?"

Sam chuckled. "I'll buy you a new suit."

"Is anybody gonna believe this?"

"People will believe anything when it's in their interest to believe it," Sam said, breaking off a piece of cake and popping it into his mouth. "And it's in the Iranians' interest to believe that you are who you say you are."

"Why?"

"Because they want what you're selling."

"Oil?"

Sam shook his head. "Know-how."

"You see . . ." The Professor stepped in, allowing Sam a chance to chew the sticky sweet without spewing it across the table. "The Iranians have a problem. When they nationalized the oil, and sent the employees of Anglo-Iranian packing, they lost everyone with any sort of technical expertise. They were left with a sea of oil in the ground, but no way to get it out."

"And without the oil revenue, their economy's fucked." Sam took over again. "Mossadegh's been trying to hire engineers out of France and Germany, but so far the Brits have been able to keep the embargo in place. They're getting desperate."

"Americo Oil to the rescue?"

"Bingo." Sam brushed the crumbs off his lap. "As far as Mossadegh knows, he's got an excellent relationship with the government of the United States. He'll be pleased and grateful that we've decided to come to his country's rescue in its hour of need." He handed me a sealed envelope.

"What's this?"

"A letter from the Department of Commerce signed by the secretary himself. It grants Americo Oil exclusive rights to provide technical advice and assistance to the Iranian government in order to rebuild their oil production capability. Mossadegh's been asking for this kind of assistance for six months."

"What am I supposed to do with it?"

"Get it to Mossadegh," Sam said, deadly serious.

"To Mossadegh?"

"You're our man on the inside, Jack. You're gonna worm yourself into these people's good graces, get close to them, make 'em dependent on you, and . . ."

The Professor took over. "Once you've gained their confidence and signed a contract, you'll have reason to be dealing with all the various elements of the government—ministers, bureaucrats, the military . . ."

"Especially the military." Sam jumped back in. "You'll need to meet with all the top brass in order to coordinate security in the oil fields. Whenever possible, get a one-on-one with them. Get to know them, feel them out, see who's really with Mossadegh and who might be willing to turn on him."

"What happens when I have to start delivering on the contract?"

"You stall for three months," Sam said. "By then, it'll all be over."

There were probably a thousand other questions I should've been asking, but at that moment, I couldn't think of one. Sam must've interpreted my silence as a hesitation, and his eyes bore down on me so hard I thought he was trying to make me levitate out of my seat.

"Are you up to this, Jack?" he said.

"Sure."

He leaned forward. "Good. Because I looked at a whole shitload of guys before I decided on you. They came from all walks of life, with all kinds of smarts, and there were all sorts of reasons I should've gone with them. But I didn't. I chose you, in spite of what guys like the Professor here said. So I sure hope to hell that you're not gonna prove me wrong."

I looked him in the eye, smiled, and said, "How do I get started?"

Sam nodded and sat back in his seat, allowing Spry to answer the question. "We'll arrange a meeting with his chief aide," he said. "Mossadegh's more of a dreamer than a politician. This guy handles the day-to-day business. If you convince him, you'll have Mossadegh."

I nodded. "What's his name?"

"Fatemi," the Professor said. "Yari Fatemi."

It took me a moment to place the name, and then I laughed out loud.

"Something funny?" Sam asked.

"I know him."

"Know him? How in hell do you—"

"I did the tango with his sister."

EIGHT

"Hey, Jack!"

Toby called out from inside his office just as I was about to make my escape. He'd spent the afternoon trying every angle he could think of to find out what Sam had said over lunch, and up until now, I'd been having fun keeping him guessing. But it was late, the offices were dark, and I'd had enough of that game.

"Didn't know you were still here," he lied, stepping into the reception area.

"Yeah, I was up with Sam."

"Working things out, huh?"

"Right."

"Good. Well, let me know if you need any help. Sam can be a pretty tough customer." He chuckled. "You're probably finding that out."

"So far so good," I said.

There was no reason that Toby couldn't know about my assignment, and if he'd just asked me straight out, I probably would've told him. But the direct approach never occurred to Toby.

"Well . . ." I took a backward step toward the door.

"Christ!" He made a show of checking his watch. "I didn't realize it was so late. How about I wrap things up and we get a drink? I know a place that's got a belly dancer who, I swear to God, Jack, defies the laws of nature. You gotta see it to believe it!"

"Sounds wild," I said. "But I've got an early start tomorrow." The last thing I wanted was to spend the evening being plied with alcohol while Toby tried to get his hand up my skirt. I took another step toward the door.

"Sure, no problem. Some other night." He followed me across the room. "And listen, I meant what I said about Sam. Give me a shout if you need any—"

"I'll let you know," I said, backing into the hallway.

The evening air was a welcome relief, so I took the long way back to the hotel, strolling through Ferdosi Square then over to Shareza Avenue, where the sidewalk cafés were filled with lively crowds of students from nearby Tehran University. The atmosphere was casual and upbeat, young men and women smoking cigarettes and, for the most part, drinking tea and coffee as they discussed the politics of the day and the latest fashion from Europe. You could sense the youthful optimism in the air.

Odd, I thought. If Shamil wasn't sitting behind the reception desk, he'd invariably be in back, napping or listening to the radio, and would come scampering out after a ring or two of the service bell. I gave it one more try—*Ding! Ding! Ding!*—then gave up and reached across the counter to slip my room key off its hook.

Starting up the four flights of stairs, I wondered if there would be any hot water left. It usually disappeared around eight, but with a little luck I'd be able to squeeze a shallow, tepid bath out of the faucet. Between that and the mostly full bottle of scotch I'd left on the bedside table, I had hopes of getting to sleep at a reasonable hour. As exciting as life as a spy sounded, so far it had consisted of a long afternoon being schooled in the extensive details of my new life as an oilman, and Sam wanted to pick up where we left off at 7 A.M.

I slipped the key into the lock, opened the door, and stopped in my tracks. Someone was in the room. I could smell the perfume.

"Hello," said a honey-flavored female voice.

I turned toward the bed, and there, lying under the cool white cotton sheet, I could make out the soft curves of my interloper's form. A step closer and Leyla's face came into focus, her dark eyes glinting in the moonlight as they sized me up, her lips formed into a mischievous smile.

"And here I thought you didn't like me," I said.

"What do you think now?"

I smiled, but it was just a reflex. Leyla was sexy beyond words, but what the hell was she doing in my bed?

"How did you get in?" I asked.

"I give the boy at the desk twenty rial. Are you happy?"

"I'm surprised."

Leyla frowned. "If you don't want, I can go."

I took a step toward her.

"You like whiskey?" I reached across her to grab the bedside bottle.

"I never tried it."

"Want to?"

She shrugged. "Why not?"

I found a second glass in the bathroom, sat on the bed, and poured a couple of shots. Leyla smiled seductively and pretended to like it, but she put the glass aside after a couple of sips and lay back on the pillow, strategically positioning one arm behind her head, hand gripping the metal bed frame. It was an interesting turn of events, all right. I would've loved to believe that Leyla had finally succumbed to my irresistible charm, but even my ego didn't extend that far. No, she was after more than a night of uninhibited sex. But hell. There's a time and a place for everything.

"What are you gonna tell Toby?"

If Leyla was startled, she didn't show it. She'd slipped out of bed as the first predawn light filtered through the open window and, thinking I was asleep, deftly pulled her underclothes on. She was wriggling into a low-cut black dress when I decided to speak up.

"What do you mean?" she said matter-of-factly.

"When he asks you how it went. What will you say?"

"Are you talking about Mr. Walters?"

"Right. He told you to come here, didn't he?"

She tried a laugh. "I don't know what are you talking about."

"Did he give you any money?"

She gave me a look. "What do you think I am?"

"I guess different people would have different words for it, but that's not important. What's important is that you tell me the truth."

"There is no truth."

"What did he tell you to do? Aside from the obvious, of course."

She found her shoes, sat on the wooden chair opposite the bed to pull them on while she thought about how to respond. "Nobody has told me to come," she said. "I did it because I like the way you look at me."

"Okay." I sat up, turned on the bedside light, and reached for a cigarette. "I guess I can ask Toby. Of course if I do that you'll not only lose out on whatever he's giving you, you'll lose your job, too." I let that sink in for a moment before continuing. "But it doesn't have to be that way. You and I can work something out." I struck a match. "If you tell me the truth, that is."

She fixed me with a long, silent stare and weighed her options. "How did you know?" she finally said.

"It was an educated guess until just now. You should've stuck to your story. Toby would've backed you up."

I passed my smoke over to her, and lit another one for me. She took a long drag, then leaned forward and rested her chin in her hands. It was the first honest move she'd made all night.

"What does Toby want?" I asked her.

She shrugged. "He wants me to . . . to become close to you. To win your trust. So you will tell me things."

"What things?"

"He didn't say. Maybe later he would."

"How much did he give you?"

"One hundred dollars. He said I can have it for every month that I . . ."

"Have my trust?"

She crushed her cigarette in a glass ashtray. "What shall I do?"

I could've confronted Toby, of course, or even told Sam what he was up to, but that seemed kind of ridiculous, and besides, there was nothing to gain from declaring open warfare. Leyla would've been cut loose, which seemed unnecessarily harsh, and I would have made a formidable enemy. I had no desire to spend the next few weeks watching my back.

"Tell him it all went perfectly," I said. "And that I don't suspect a thing."

Leyla smiled. She'd worked for the Brits before we arrived and understood right away what I was driving at. Turning her into a double agent would let me keep track of Toby's intrigues while he paid the tab, and I could have some fun feeding him all sorts of false information. Leyla sauntered over to the bed, leaned in, and gave me a long good-bye kiss.

"It's smart," she whispered when we came up for air. "This way, I can come again. Would you like that?"

"I'd love it," I said honestly. "But I never mix business with pleasure."

She didn't seem too surprised, but I was happy to see that she looked genuinely disappointed. "It's a pity," she said. "We did well together."

"Yes," I agreed. "We certainly did."

Once she was gone, I lit another cigarette and ran a bath. A quick dip in a cold tub was exactly what I needed.

NINE

Hadi had become a lot more talkative in the month since he'd been assigned as my permanent driver, and I quickly discovered that he was a reliable source for all sorts of useless information and incomprehensible homilies. Things like "It is impossible to ride a camel underground," and "The witness of the cat is in its tail," kept popping out of his mouth. I'd wasted a lot of time trying to squeeze some meaning out of these gems, and even more time listening to long-winded explanations that made even less sense, then I came up with a strategy.

"Marriage it is like the uncut watermelon," he said, catching my eye in the rearview mirror.

"Birds of a feather flock together," I shot back.

Hadi solemnly nodded his head, as though I'd made some sort of profoundly important statement, and I smiled to myself because I knew that he was just as confused as I was. I guess we were talking across some sort of culture gap. Marriage was the subject of the day because I was on my way to a wedding. The invitation had come late one afternoon in Yari's office as we wrapped up our latest unproductive meeting to discuss a potential agreement between Americo Oil and the Iranian government.

"My sister will be married on Saturday," he'd said as he walked me to the door.

"The one I danced with?" I'd wondered if the love-struck lieutenant had met with success.

"No, no, not Zahra. I have three sisters. It is the middle one, Roxana, who will be married. Now that she will be settled, we can begin to think of Zahra's future."

"Wonderful," I said, not sure what, if anything else, was expected of me. Yari dipped his head slightly, by way of a thank you, then handed me a large white envelope with a curly white ribbon attached to it.

"The ceremony will be in our home, with celebrations to follow. It would greatly honor us if you would share the occasion. I believe you would enjoy it." He punctuated the formalities with an engaging smile.

The significance of the gesture wasn't lost on me, and the prospect of seeing an Iranian wedding from the inside was certainly appealing. But there was another, more practical reason to be pleased. I'd been trying for weeks to break through the unrelenting politeness that had thus far defined my dealings with Yari. He was an educated, forward-thinking, twentieth-century man, and while his openhearted friendliness was genuine enough, he maintained a wary distance that was frustrating my attempts to gain his trust. I needed him to open up, and the wedding invitation was the first sign of a crack.

"Thank you, Yari," I'd replied. "I'm both honored and touched."

"A car," Sam had said when I told him.

"What?"

"The wedding present. You should give her a nice, new shiny car."

"Isn't that a bit flashy?"

"You're American. You're expected to be flashy. And it shows that you don't mind spreading a few dollars around. Maybe that's what he's waiting for."

I shook my head. "I don't think money is what motivates this guy." Sam gave me a long, gloomy look, then leaned back in his chair.

"You've been over there, what, three times?"

"Four."

"Four times at bat and you haven't got to first base yet. If he's not looking for a backhander, what's he waiting for?" Sam had been spending a lot of time coaching me on the negotiations, but Yari had so far resisted getting into details. It had thrown Sam. He'd assumed that the Iranians would be so desperate they'd lunge for the lifeline he was tossing out.

"He's being cautious," I said.

Sam nodded. "I know. The Iranian ambassador's been asking about you around Washington."

"And getting all the right answers, I assume?"

Sam didn't feel the need to respond with more than an annoyed look. "You gonna be able to win this guy over? Because I'm making moves out there and I need to know if any of it is getting back to Mossadegh."

"The invitation's a good sign," I said. "He'll be relaxed, maybe more receptive. I'll work on him."

Sam nodded, but he had his unhappy face on. I got up to leave, but he stopped me before I could get to the door. "And, Jack . . ."

"Yeah, Sam?"

"There's a baby-blue Olds in a window down the street. Make sure you get the whitewalls, and the radio, too."

It was a beautiful set of wheels, all right, and looked particularly smart parked up on the grassy slope in front of the house, for all the wedding guests to marvel at as they made their way up the path toward the main entrance. Hadi, who'd delivered the gift the previous day, dropped me at the bottom of the path, then joined the other drivers on a rug that had been laid with food and refreshments in the shade of a tall date tree.

A white-jacketed attendant greeted me as I stepped through the front door, and directed me along a floral-lined corridor, at the end of which was an open archway leading into a large reception room. There were about fifty people milling around, buzzing with excitement, greeting friends and family and exchanging the latest gossip.

A handsome gray-haired woman in a blue silk dress was stationed at the top of the room, greeting every guest with a warm, gold-toothed grin, a hug, and a kiss on each cheek. I stepped forward, expecting a less familial welcome, but got the full treatment. I smiled and thanked her in Farsi (*tashakor* was one of the handful of phrases I'd picked up), then she stepped back to admire me with motherly pride. Taking my hand, she pulled me across the room and placed me in front of a broad-shouldered man of medium build, who I assumed was her husband. The patriarch stood there, projecting a timeless poise that had, no doubt, been handed down through many generations. He listened carefully to the long introduction offered by his wife, then he stepped forward, took my hand, and held it firmly in his.

"You bring the honor onto our . . ." He paused to formulate the next phrase, but decided it would be best to continue in Farsi. I guess he felt it was more important to say it correctly than for me to understand it.

"It's an honor to be here," I responded when he'd finished. "*Tashakor.*" I thought that might conclude the formalities, but instead of letting me go, my host held on to my hand and pulled me closer. He gave me a studied look, turning his head from side to side as he searched my eyes, as if that would give him a better angle on my soul. After a moment he nodded his head and added his left hand to our grip, squeezing it in a gesture of newfound intimacy.

"We will to be good friends," he said. "It is a certainty."

Among the sea of unfamiliar faces, I recognized one.

"Lieutenant Azari," I said, surprising myself by recalling his name.

"Ah, hello . . ."

"Jack Teller," I reminded him. "We met about a month ago, at the Café Pars. It was my first night in Tehran."

"Yes, yes, of course . . . Mr. Teller . . ."

He seemed a bit flustered, unsure how to proceed. I had interrupted an intense conversation he was having with a tall European-looking gentleman who stood out in this crowd as much as I did. In his late fifties, with a receding head of dark wavy hair, he had a narrow, weathered face that was defined by the heavy black frames of his eyeglasses. He'd taken a step back when I approached, and was now watching me with studied concentration. I turned to him and thrust my hand forward, taking him by surprise.

"Jack Teller," I said again. He paused, then smiled stiffly, gripped my hand, and shook it firmly.

"Viktor Kerensky," he said in a deep, rich voice.

"Good to meet you," I said amicably, trying to mask the fact that my heart had just jumped into my throat. I had, it seemed, just stumbled upon the enemy.

A sudden, rolling burst from a small, goblet-shaped drum announced the beginning of the ceremony. Dressed in white from head to toe, a wreath of multicolored flowers slung around his neck, the groom stepped into the room, trying hard to look serious, but unable to control the boyish grin that kept creeping onto his face. Once the crowd had organized itself, creating an aisle down the center of the room, the drummer, joined by a man on a lutelike instrument and another playing a reed flute, led the nervous groom to the front, where he took up his place on one of two small stools, his back to the assembly.

Spread out on the floor in front of him was what looked like an extravagant picnic lunch. Laid onto an intricately designed silk, the meticulous arrangement included groupings of painted eggs, flat naan bread and cheese, spices, apples and pomegranates, nuts, and a tray of sweet pastries. At the center of the display was a book that I assumed was the Koran, and next to that, a bowl filled with gold coins. A full-length mirror had been placed at the front of the spread, flanked by two floral arrangements and a pair of silver candelabras, candles burning.

Attention shifted back to the top of the room, the group holding its collective breath in anticipation of the bride's appearance. The music surged forward, each drumbeat hastening hearts and galvanizing the excitement until it spilled over into spontaneous clapping. A young girl, probably ten or eleven years old, stepped through the archway and stood there, her feet planted firmly on the floor, her eyes fixed resolutely straight ahead. Gripped tightly in her hands was a silver tray that held a small metal brazier, which sent a sweet, smoky fragrance wafting into the air.

When the veiled bride finally walked through the doorway, satin and lace in full flow, the crowd emitted a doting sigh, the men nodding their heads, the women whispering breathless words of approval to one another. The groom's eyes were the only ones not turned toward his betrothed as she made her way down the aisle. He was focused on the mirror, a proud smile fixed to his lips as he watched her reflection grow in the silver-plated glass. Two women stepped forward to help settle her onto the empty footstool to her fiancé's left, then they lifted a length of white cloth and held it like a hammock over the couple's heads.

A religious figure—clearly an imam of some distinction—appeared out of nowhere and positioned himself in front of the couple. An old, cadaverous man with a frazzled, gray beard and big round glasses, he wore an ocher robe over a dark suit and starched white shirt, buttoned to the top. An equally spotless turban covered his mostly bald pate. Looking poker-faced back and forth between the bride and groom, he waited for the congregation to settle, then began to speak.

Standing toward the back, I stole a look across the room at Kerensky, who'd quickly excused himself after our handshake, claiming he needed to find his wife, who'd disappeared into the crowd. I had managed to get out of him that he was attached to the Soviet embassy, but he'd been evasive about the details, and I didn't want to seem overly inquisitive. He didn't seem the least bit curious about me, which made me think he already knew more than I would tell him, and that, in turn, led me to suspect that he was KGB, an assumption that Sam later confirmed. I wondered how he'd come to be invited to the wedding.

"You look like a man who wouldn't say no to a glass of scotch whiskey."

I'd seen Yari only briefly during the dinner reception, when he and his wife had brought the bride and groom over to thank me for my generous gift. The newlyweds had gushed for a few minutes while I'd acted suitably embarrassed, then Yari had ushered them on to the next table. There was a lot of ground to cover, with upward of three hundred people being fed and watered in the spacious courtyard behind the family house.

"I never do," I said.

"Come . . ." He beckoned with a flick of his head. "I think I know where to find one."

The sun had slipped down below the trees, leaving behind a pink-and-golden sky with a full, silvery moon in ascendance. Yari led us into a broad, neatly tended garden at the bottom of the courtyard, where gas lanterns lit our way along a winding, gravel path. It was a clear, balmy evening, with the scent of night-blooming jasmine in the air, and I felt as though I'd been transported into one of Scheherazade's *Thousand and One Nights*.

We made our way down a gentle slope toward the sound of running water. Yari, in an expansive mood, talked animatedly about the symbolism of the wedding ceremony, which apparently had its roots in the two-and-a-half-thousand-year-old Zoroastrian tradition. He was in as relaxed a state as I'd seen him, and I wanted to take advantage of the moment.

"It's been a wonderful day," I said.

"You've enjoyed it?"

"I've met some very interesting people."

He chuckled. "My father tells me that he looked into your heart, and saw that it was pure."

"He must've got my heart mixed up with somebody else's."

"Yes." Yari laughed. "That's what I told him, too."

"I met Viktor Kerensky," I said, as nonchalantly as I could manage.

"Oh, yes . . ." Yari seemed to think nothing of it.

"He was interested to know more about our discussions," I lied. "I put him off, in the nicest way I could, of course."

"Yes. Of course."

"But I did wonder how he knew that we were having any discussions at all . . ."

Yari stopped walking, gave me a sharp look. "You're not suggesting that I told him?"

"No, of course not. No, I wouldn't suggest that. I just wondered if, perhaps, someone in your office . . ."

"I can promise you, Jack, that no one in my office would have told anyone about our discussions, and particularly not Kerensky. I hardly know that man. He was invited today as a courtesy, a favor to someone . . ."

"I'm sorry. I didn't mean to suggest—"

"You needn't apologize." He put his hand on my shoulder

in a gesture of friendship. "I understand your feelings, Jack. But if we are to go forward, it must be on the basis of mutual trust. Agreed?"

"Yes," I said. "And you shouldn't misinterpret what I said. Because I do trust you."

"Good." He smiled genially, and we continued along the path.

A narrow river—maybe it was more of a stream—ran along the end of the garden, overhung on the opposite bank by a string of soft willow trees. The sound of laughter caught my attention, and I could see candles flickering all along the water's edge, where groups of mostly young people had gathered on rugs to play music, tell stories, and flirt with one another.

"Do you mind sitting on the ground?" Yari asked.

"It wouldn't be the first time," I replied. A young servant called out, waving us over to the spot where he'd unfurled a rug in the light of an oil torch, its orange flame dancing languorously atop a bamboo pole that had been planted in the ground. Yari and I sat down, a bottle of thirty-year-old Glenfiddich, two crystal glasses, and a tray of sweets between us. The boy filled our glasses then withdrew to a discreet position a few yards away.

Yari inhaled a lungful of night air and stared out across the darkness, tilting his head slightly, as if listening to the sound of the stream coursing over a shallow bed of time-worn pebbles before it slipped into the deeper, more turbulent waters ahead. Behind us, in the distance, you could hear the orchestra strike up a tune, and I imagined that the tables had been set aside to make way for a dance floor. A firefly flitted by, briefly revealing itself against the night sky, only to disappear once again into the void.

"This is Iran," Yari said softly, letting it hang in the air for a moment before turning his eyes toward me. "Do you understand what I mean, Jack?"

I nodded, and I think I did understand. For me, it would've

been Yankee Stadium on a warm night in late July, the lights flooding the outfield, the *crack* of the bat against the distant hum of the city, the guy in the next row keeping a careful scorecard with his ten-year-old son. It's those accidental moments that connect us to a place more than any flag, anthem, or loud marching band ever could. With no particular event attached to them, and nothing to separate them from the millions of other moments just like them, they could easily pass unnoticed, but they don't. Something makes us step back and observe that, in some inexplicable way, this moment sums up everything I love about this place. I guess that's what Yari was feeling at that moment.

I had other things on my mind.

"Have you discussed the company's proposal with the prime minister yet?" I asked.

He took his time then responded with a question. "Was the car meant as a bribe?"

"No . . ." I said, caught off guard. "It was a gift . . ." Yari made a face and I shrugged. "Call it a token of my company's esteem for you and the people of Iran."

"Most of the people in Iran are lucky to have a donkey."

"I hope we can help you change that," I said, eliciting another unhappy look.

"I considered sending it back." He tasted the scotch for the first time, didn't seem to like it much. "But I decided that would be impolite. And it would have made my sister unhappy on the day before her wedding, which would not have been very good of me."

"It was only a gesture, Yari—"

"It was a bribe," he said sharply. "An attempted one, anyway. And I don't approve of it."

I was taken aback by the vehemence of his sentiment. "All right, then," I said. "It won't happen again."

He sighed. "I'm sorry, Jack. It's not your fault. This is the way things have been done for a long, long time. It is one of the things we hope to change."

"I understand," I said, waiting for more.

"The world is changing," he mused. "The days of empire are gone, thank God, a part of history, never to come back. The British can't accept this. Not yet, anyway."

"They can make things difficult," I said, and Yari released a caustic laugh.

"Difficult? Go to Abadan if you want to see how they make things difficult! See for yourself how they treated the men who worked for them. Worse than dogs." He shook his head. "These men worked fourteen, fifteen, sixteen hours a day, and went home to a house made from a discarded oil drum. When they became sick, they received no pay. When they were injured in their jobs, they were let go, with no compensation. In the winter, the rain turned the streets to a lake of mud, and in the summer their children suffered and died from the impossible heat, or the diseases that were spread by the insects, which were everywhere. There was no running water, no electricity, no shop, no place to bathe, not even a tree to give them shade . . ." Yari stopped, but only long enough to catch his breath. "And do you know how much profit the British made each year from the work of these people?"

"No," I replied quietly. "I don't."

"Neither do I!" Yari laughed. "No Iranian knows. Because we did not have a legal right to look at the accounts. Can you imagine something like that? Our only natural resource, and all we could do was hope that the British would be honest enough to give us the sixteen percent share of profits that we were entitled to. And the worst part of it, Jack, was that they truly believed that it was their God-given right."

"That's not the kind of arrangement my company is suggesting," I said.

"Yes, yes, I know that," he replied, in a softer tone. "I'm sorry that I've gone on about it, but—" He paused to reflect. "Of course it's easy to blame the British. But it's what you would expect from them. It was our leaders—the Shah, and his father—who allowed them to do what they did. The British were welcomed with open arms, and with open palms." He gave me a look. "So perhaps you understand why I considered returning your beautiful car."

"We're not the British, Yari," I said. "And we're not looking for a colony. We're looking for a business partner."

He nodded slowly, then, through the darkness, turned to look me in the eye. "That is a very important statement, Jack. Very important. And I hope it is true. It *should* be true. After all, you were a colony of Britain yourself at one time. Of all the people in the world, the American people must understand what it means to make a declaration of independence."

TEN

I was caught in some sort of spell. The ceiling fan was supposed to be off, but it kept moving around, marking each slow rotation with a soft *click* as one of the blades caught a loose screw in the motor's housing. I'd asked Shamil to have it repaired every morning for a week before I finally gave up and disconnected the wiring myself. Apparently, they'd finally got around to fixing it, meaning they had reconnected the wires that I'd detached, putting the thing back into perpetual motion. I was too tired to do anything about it, so I just lay there, watching it, transfixed.

It had been a productive day. Yari seemed ready to stop procrastinating about a deal, and I'd finally been able to provide Sam with some useful intelligence. I'd telephoned him with the news about meeting Kerensky as soon as I got back to the hotel.

"No shit? Kerensky," he'd said. "That's news all right."

"KGB?"

"We're pretty sure he's Tehran station chief."

"You think they're planning something along the lines of what we're planning?"

"Washington figures they'll be in a holding pattern until the white smoke goes up at the Kremlin . . ." Sam was referring to the ongoing power struggle in Moscow following Papa Joe Stalin's death a couple of months earlier. "But I'm not so sure. It means they have some kind of foot in the door, anyway. Who'd he spend his time with?"

"Aside from his wife, the only one I saw him talking to was an army officer."

"What's the name?"

"Azari," I said, getting the sense that Sam was writing it down. "Lieutenant Ali something Azari. I can't remember the middle name."

"That's fine. Good work, Jack," he said as we hung up. "Very good."

So I should have been feeling good, but I was on edge. I'd spent the better part of an hour trying to figure out what was bugging me, but I'd been going round and round, like the goddamned fan.

I liked Yari. He was a classy, sincere man, with a sharp mind, a good sense of humor, and he certainly had the best of intentions. I was even sympathetic to what he was trying to achieve for his country. The problem I had—the thing that seemed to be keeping me awake—was that he was naive to the point of foolishness. What was it he'd said?

Of all the people in the world, the American people must understand what it means to make a declaration of independence.

For Christ's sake, did he think Thomas Jefferson was running American foreign policy? Could he really believe that the American people would rise up in support of their Iranian brothers and sisters, demanding that they receive their inalienable Right to Life, Liberty, and the Pursuit of Happiness? Was he going to bet his country's future on America's sense of fair play?

Yari seemed to believe that standing on the moral high ground was as good as holding a strategic position. He hadn't even understood the implication of Kerensky's presence at the wedding. At least, he didn't seem to. Was I underestimating him? Was Kerensky's presence supposed to send me a message? Was my presence supposed to send Kerensky a message? It would've been a good play, but I didn't believe it. Yari was an open book, and so certain in the justice of his cause, and in America's inherent sympathy for it, that he failed to see his country's place in the scheme of things. It was a stunning display of schoolboy idealism, coming from a man who should have been making a cold, calculated reading of the world's intentions.

Washington, of course, had no trouble with cold and calculating, and the reading on Mossadegh was that he was a weak, guileless dreamer, ripe for manipulation by the Communist Tudeh Party. Enter Viktor Kerensky. The Red Scare was all the rage back home, with a Commie hiding under every bed, and no shortage of red-white-and-blue patriots who were ready to pull back the covers. Things had gone too far, of course, as they always do when fear is involved. A few cynical men had dressed up the danger to use as a political sledgehammer, but that didn't make Kerensky's crowd any less of a threat.

The Soviet Union was second to none when it came to brutal tyranny, and having sentenced millions of their own innocents to death, there was no reason to believe they'd hesitate to use their newly acquired A-bomb if they thought they could get away with it. The old men in the Central Committee had no trouble with cold and calculating, either, and only a fool would believe that, given half a chance, they wouldn't make a play for Iran. Yet Yari seemed blissfully unconcerned. I'd tried to approach the subject from another, more oblique angle, later in our conversation.

"I think one of the reasons Washington gave us permission to talk to you," I'd said, ". . . is that they think if we don't give you help, somebody else will."

"Don't think we haven't tried." He'd shrugged. "But the British are very effective. They've bribed or frightened everyone into honoring their embargo. Even the French refuse to make a deal."

He'd missed the implication completely, and gone back, as usual, to the terrible injustice of the British. There was no doubt that Iran had been treated unfairly, but they weren't alone in the world, and while that kind of play for sympathy might go over well at the General Assembly, it wasn't going to get Yari and his dream very far in a world full of Sam Clays and Viktor Kerenskys.

I got up off the bed to retrieve my smokes, which were in my jacket pocket. Sleep wasn't going to come and there was nowhere to go, so I stood at the window and stared out at the empty street below. The only sign of life was a stray cat that was stretched out on the hood of a parked car, absorbing the last bit of heat from the cooling engine.

Why should Yari's naïveté bother me? If anything, it would make my job easier, and it was evidence that we were doing the right thing. We'd learned the hard way about the perils of ignoring a hungry autocracy, and Yari's wide-eyed approach to the world only confirmed Washington's assessment that the Mossadegh government was dangerously out of touch and vulnerable. It was clear that Iran needed a new, stronger leader, one who understood and could deal with the Soviet threat.

I took in a lungful of smoke and let it out slowly. The bottom line was that if Yari was naive enough to trust me, it was proof that betraying him was the right thing to do. Christ. No wonder I couldn't sleep.

"So this is where you've been hiding!" Zahra had come up behind us and plopped herself down on the rug. "Everyone has been looking for you, Yari. Especially Mama."

He'd given her a look, got one back, then turned to me. "Please excuse me. It seems that my presence is required."

"I'll go with you," I said, standing up with him. "I'd like to thank your parents before I go."

"Oh, no." Zahra sulked. "I wanted you to stay and talk with me," I looked to Yari for help, but it wasn't forthcoming. In fact, he seemed amused by my plight.

"There's no need for you to go." He smiled. "Please . . . Stay and entertain my sister."

"Yes, entertain me!" Zahra grabbed my hand and pulled me back onto the rug. Yari brushed the grass off his suit as he confirmed our arrangement for the morning.

"I'll pick you up at nine o'clock outside your hotel."

"Are you and Yari going somewhere?" Zahra asked once he'd gone.

"He wants to take me for a day in the country. He thinks I need to see what Iran is like outside Tehran."

"Wonderful! I'll come with you!"

"I'm not sure that your brother—"

"He'll try to say no, but he won't be able to. All I have to do is put on a face like this . . ." She'd demonstrated a coquettish pout, then broke into a smile again. "Where is he taking you?"

"He didn't say, but . . . I think the idea is to talk business."

"All the more reason for me to come. I'll keep you from boring each other to death. Can you give me a cigarette, please, Jack? I've been dying for one, but Mama and Papa have been hovering over me all day. They don't approve of women who smoke. I'm afraid they're not very modern. Like most of Iran."

I gave her one and lit it up. Zahra took a shallow drag, then fell back onto her elbows, turned her head toward me, and smiled, knowing full well the effect of the moonlight on her face. It was time to come to an understanding.

"If you want to be friends, Zahra, you're gonna have to knock that off," I said.

A quizzical expression came over her face. "Knock it off? What does it mean?"

"Stop it."

"Stop what?"

"The flirting. You're gonna have to cut it out."

"Did you think I was flirting with you, Jack?" She batted her eyes, and I gave her a scolding look. She got it, and shrugged. "All right, then. Let's be friends." She offered her hand and I took it.

"Friends."

She tucked her legs up under her chin and stared out at the darkness, as her brother had done. When she spoke again, it was uncanny how her demeanor had changed. Relieved of the need to play the femme fatale, Zahra was suddenly a pretty young girl with an unaffected smile. She even tossed the cigarette aside.

"Why aren't you married?" she asked out of the blue.

"How do you know that I'm not?"

"You don't wear a ring. *Are* you married?"

"No."

"Have you ever been?"

"No."

"Why not? You're a good-looking man in a successful position. Don't you want a family?"

"It's not always as straightforward as that."

"Are you waiting for love?"

I smiled. "I guess that's it."

She nodded sagely. "You're right to wait, of course. It's not how it's done in Iran, though. It's all very practical. My sister and Hooshy, for example. She likes him well enough, I think, but she's not in love with him. It was all arranged between my parents and his parents. And Yari, of course. The two families sat down and decided that it would be a good marriage, and that was it. Roxana had nothing to say about it. It's very wrong, don't you think?"

"I'm sure they have her best interests in mind."

"They try to make her comfortable, but they don't think about what will make her happy."

"She looked happy today."

"I don't want to be comfortable. Comfortable is boring."

"You're right about that," I said, more to myself than to her. She smiled, proud to have struck a chord in me.

"They can't force me to marry," she declared.

I paused, wary of getting into the middle of family issues. The last thing I needed was for Zahra to be quoting me on the subject. "Maybe you can agree on someone," I said diplomatically.

"They have already chosen for me."

"Don't you like him?"

"I don't know him."

"Why don't you give him a chance?"

She shook her head. "No. It's impossible."

"Impossible? Why?"

"He's a . . . What do you call the man who takes care of the dead people?"

"An undertaker?"

"Yes," she said gloomily. "An undertaker. I could never love an undertaker."

I tried not to smile, but how could I resist?

"It's not funny," she said testily. "It's my life."

She was right, of course, it wasn't funny, but to my Western mind, it was just a matter of making her feelings known to her parents and Yari, and they would have no choice but to accept her decision. I said something along those lines, which made Zahra smile wistfully and shake her head.

"I wish it was so simple as this," she said. "But they will say that I'm just a girl and that I don't know what's best. I need someone to speak on my behalf. Someone that Yari respects, someone that he'll listen to . . ."

I saw it coming, but too late to head it off. Zahra sat forward eagerly.

"Will you talk to him, Jack?"

"Me?"

"I know it's a great deal to ask, but . . . You are an American. A modern man. You can explain to them how wrong it is what they ask."

"Zahra, I—"

"Just a little word from you can change my whole life!"

"I know, but—"

"It's true that we've not known each other for a long time, but you said that we will be friends. Did you mean it?"

"Yes, of course, but—"

"There is no one else I can turn to."

She fixed her big, brown, childlike eyes on me and I heard myself saying, "All right. I can't promise anything, but—"

"Thank you," she purred happily as she nestled into me and gently laid her head on my chest. "You are truly a good friend."

I wasn't expecting to see the baby blue Olds, but it was hard to miss as it rounded the corner and cruised up the block toward the entrance to the Iranshahr Hotel, where I'd been waiting for about ten minutes. I wasn't really expecting to see Zahra, either, but there she was, all smiles, sitting in the passenger seat, next to Yari, who was behind the wheel. I should have known that she'd get her way.

"Flashy car," I said, sliding into the front seat, which Zahra had relinquished to me for a place in the back.

Yari smiled back at me. "Made in America."

He found first gear, and as we pulled away from the curb, Zahra leaned forward and spoke into my ear. "Are you surprised to see me?"

I twisted around to see the coy look I knew she had on her face. "I never underestimate the persuasive powers of a woman," I said. She seemed happy with that, and sat back with a contented smirk to keep her company.

There was a smattering of small talk—what a wonderful wedding it had been, how beautiful the bride had looked, funny stories about various relatives—then we fell silent as

Yari negotiated our way through the slums of south Tehran. It was a bright, beautiful day in mid-May, but the sunlight did nothing to alleviate the unrelenting dinge of those neglected streets. If anything, it just made the grayness more gray, and it was impossible not to feel like a heel driving through there in that car.

The mood lightened again as we broke free of the city, the vast, empty salt plains of the Dasht-e-Kavīr stretching out before us. We opened the windows and sat back, letting the warm, dry air blow across our faces as we watched the strange, bleached landscape rush by. Yari pointed out a group of lakes, lying to the east, that were so white with salt that they seemed to be made of milk. Zahra sang a quiet song to herself in the back, and though the words were lost on me, the mournful melody seemed to go with the moment.

After an hour or so, the desert gave way to a cluster of low-rising, scrubby hills, where young men with heavy coats flung over their shoulders and long staffs cradled in their arms, watched over flocks of grazing sheep and herds of goats. We passed a caravan of heavily laden camels that were being driven along the side of the dusty highway, then a series of small villages appeared, flat-topped concrete bunkers tucked into the side of the hills. There were people on the road now, in small and large groups—men, women, and children, some on donkeys, but most walking, all moving forward with a sense of great purpose.

Within a few moments, an ancient city emerged from the desert sand. With muted colors, its shapes distorted by the rising waves of heat, it seemed unreal, some sort of illusion that was being magically projected onto the long horizon. There was a strange sense about it, too, a feeling that whatever this place held inside it, no one who entered would come out unscathed.

ELEVEN

The shrine of Hazrat-e-Masumeh rose above the rooftops of the holy city of Qom, its gleaming gold dome a beacon to the steady stream of pilgrims who came to pray, beg a favor, or cleanse a spirit soiled by human frailty. We left the car beside the city's crumbling medieval wall and joined the true believers as they advanced on sacred ground along the bank of the river, its bed as dry and dusty as the street above it.

"Allah hu Akbar . . . ! Allah hu Akbar . . . !"

The plaintive call to midday prayers floated out across the sky, quickening the pace of the travelers, who hurried to reach the mosque before the muezzin completed his cry. The words were a mystery to me, of course, but the silky richness of the disembodied voice was enough to send a shiver up my spine.

"What's he saying?" I asked.

"He says that God is great. God is great . . ." Yari waited for the next phrase, which was repeated three times.

"Ishhad lá allah illá 'llah!"

"Confess that there is no God but God . . ."

"Ishhad Muhammad rasúluhu!"

"Confess that Muhammad is the prophet of God . . ."

"Hayá 'alá 's-salát, Hayá 'alá 's-salát . . ."

"Come to prayer, Come to prayer . . ."

"Inna 's-salát khair min an-naum!"

"For prayer is better than sleep."

The midday sun was merciless, so I was glad to be sheltered under the faded green awning. Yari had led us straight to the little restaurant behind the shrine, suggesting a leisurely lunch followed by a walking tour of the city's monuments. Zahra, it turned out, had been to Qom only once herself, and that had been when she was just five or six years old.

"My sister and her friends prefer the mountains, where they can ski in the winter and swim in the lakes in the summertime," Yari explained.

"I didn't see you go into the mosque for prayers," Zahra fired back.

"I pray in my heart," Yari said, adding with a smile, "I pray that my sister will learn politeness to her elders."

Zahra shot me a "see what I mean" look, then changed the subject. "I want to buy a silk rug," she announced. "As a present to Roxana. I haven't given her a gift yet, and Qom is known for its silk rugs."

"A rug?" Yari frowned.

"A small one, with a lovely design, that she can put in the entrance of her apartment. I know that she'll like it."

"Yes, all right," Yari agreed. "We can look in the market after our walk. Do you have enough money?"

Zahra laughed, then leaned over to hold Yari's face in her hands while she kissed him on the cheek. "Why would I need money when I have such a generous brother?"

Yari smiled, then folded Zahra under his arm. She laid her head on his chest and they stayed that way until a waiter appeared to take our order. I'd been thinking about a beer since we left the car, but when I asked for one all I got was a scolding look.

"It's Qom," Yari apologized.

The food was light, and so was the atmosphere. I enjoyed watching brother and sister spar over every subject that came along, neither one willing to give an inch, no matter how insignificant the issue. If Zahra said the heat was stifling, Yari would say, nonsense, there's a lovely, fresh breeze; if he said I should try the lamb stew, she would say, no, no, no, the saffron chicken would be a much better choice on such a hot day. And so on. Although it was played with dogged determination, it was clearly a game, and I took it as just another sign of the genuine affection that existed between the two siblings.

Once the plates had been cleared away, we sat back over hot tea, served with the local specialty of pistachio and caramel brittle, and watched the city come back to life while we smoked our cigarettes. Yari didn't object when I provided one for Zahra, though I could see that he didn't approve.

"Did you know, Jack," he said after a moment of easy silence, "that a community has existed on this site for over two and a half thousand years? Since the time of Cyrus the Great."

"Be careful," Zahra groaned. "It's Yari's favorite subject. He'll lecture you for hours if you let him." She pushed her chair back and got to her feet. "And since I've heard the stories too many times to count, I will now go shopping for a rug!"

Yari made a face. "Let's go together, Zahra."

"You'd only tell me to hurry."

He sighed. "You don't even know where—"

"We passed the market on the way here. It's two blocks that way." Yari shrugged his shoulders, defeated.

"How long will you be?"

"An hour should be enough."

He frowned, but reached into his pocket and handed her a stack of bills. "Don't pay more than half the first price you're told. They'll try to take advantage of a woman."

"They'll be disappointed," she said as she stuffed the bills into her bag.

Once we'd agreed to meet an hour later, in the square in front of the shrine, Zahra leaned over and kissed her brother good-bye. She started to leave, but hesitated, turned back toward me.

"Perhaps you will have an opportunity to talk about other subjects, as well," she said, affecting an overtly conspiratorial look. I hoped that Yari wouldn't notice, but she drove it home by waiting for an answer.

"We'll try," I said. She nodded, smiled sweetly, then, with a nervous glance in her brother's direction, turned, and walked away.

"What did she mean by that?" Yari asked, watching his sister cross the square.

"Nothing," I said. "Nothing important."

"They say that if you could see into a man's past, you would have a window onto his soul. I think this can be equally true for a nation. Don't you agree?"

We'd left the restaurant and had been meandering through a maze of narrow streets long enough for me to lose any sense of direction, and the conversation had followed pretty much the same path. Every time I tried to take the lead, Yari would circle around and we'd end up back in some poetic dead end. I thought I'd try one last stab at getting us on course.

"Maybe it's best to leave the past to historians," I said. "You and I have enough to deal with in the present."

"Perhaps you're right," he said, unconvincingly. I decided to press the issue anyway.

"You never answered me last night when I asked if you'd discussed the company's proposal with the prime minister."

Yari gave me a sideways glance, but ignored the question again. His attention was drawn to a figure sitting, cross-legged, on the cobbled pavement, a worn cotton blanket draped over his head. He seemed to be asleep, but as we approached he lifted his eyes to reveal the drawn, weary face of an old man, absent one eye and most of his teeth. He whispered something inaudible as we approached (perhaps it was *"as-salam alaykum"*—peace be upon you), then a skeletal arm emerged from under the wrap, long, knurly fingers reaching out in an appeal for alms. Yari slowed his pace, responded *"as-alaykum-salam,"* then dug into his pocket and placed a coin in the man's palm. I followed suit, and we continued on without comment. We didn't speak for some time, the only intrusion on the silence the sound of our footsteps echoing off the ancient stones. Then Yari turned to me.

"Have you ever been in the presence of greatness, Jack?"

"Greatness?"

"Yes. A man who has done something so important—given something so important—that he will be remembered for as long as there are people to remember. Have you ever met a man such as this?"

"Joe DiMaggio."

Yari gave me a strange look.

"A baseball player," I explained. "I never actually met him, but I've been in his presence more than a few times. He had a fifty-six-game hitting streak in 1941, and it doesn't get much greater than that."

Yari frowned. It wasn't exactly what he had in mind. "I was thinking of men who, with their deeds and their ideas, changed the world for the better. Men like George Washington, Thomas Jefferson, and Abraham Lincoln."

"No, never met any of them," I said, earning another admonishing look.

"Men like those don't appear very often," he continued. "But when they do, there is a sense of destiny about them. One could even say a divine will." He looked over to see if I had anything else to contribute. When I didn't, he proceeded with his thought. "I believe there is much in common between those men you call the 'Founding Fathers,' and Cyrus the Second, who was the founder of Iran."

"In what way?" I asked, bowing to the inevitable. Yari smiled, pleased that I'd finally decided to go along.

"Well, you see, like Washington, Cyrus was a great general—a natural leader and a brilliant battlefield tactician. By the time of his fortieth birthday, he had created the greatest empire the world had ever seen, stretching from the Indus River in the east to Gaza in the west. Babylon, Phoenicia, Damascus, Jerusalem—they were all in his domain."

I nodded, signaling that he should go on.

"But, of course, there have been many conquerors in history. Cyrus was more than that. Like Jefferson, he was a great philosopher, and believed passionately in the idea of a government founded on social justice. Did you know that your Bill of Rights was fashioned from the principles put forth in what is called the 'Edict of Cyrus'?"

No, I said, I hadn't heard of it.

"You should have!" Yari scolded. "It is a document of great historical importance. Cyrus understood its importance, too, so he had the words inscribed on a clay cylinder that would survive through the ages. It is on display, today, in the British Museum. I've seen it myself. It's really quite something. Mankind's first declaration of human rights.

"In it, Cyrus set forth the principles he would use to govern his empire, and they are the very same tenets on which America was built. Freedom of thought and expression, the right to practice a religion of your choice, the right of every individual, no matter what his place in life, to receive fair and equal justice. Equal justice! Can you imagine what a radical idea it must have been! And to show that these were more than empty words, his first act as governor of Babylon was to free the thousands of Jews who had been taken into slavery by Nebuchadnezzar a half century earlier."

"Lincoln . . ." I said, before Yari could get there. He grinned sheepishly and shrugged.

"Perhaps some Americans would be surprised to learn that the emperor of Persia freed the slaves two and a half millennia before the Emancipation Proclamation."

"I guess I'm one of them," I admitted.

"Then you must not have read your Bible. The story is told in the Old Testament."

"I was never much of a churchgoer," I said, and Yari nodded sympathetically.

"One can be a believer without being a follower. I'm the same. In fact, I think you and I are more alike than it may appear on the surface. We are the silent ones, men who will be forgotten by history. But we will play a part in it. Perhaps we can even have an effect on it. One need not aspire to greatness in order to achieve great things, if there is the will to do so."

The old walls of our dark alley came to an abrupt end, leaving us on the verge of the large, rectangular square that was the geographical and spiritual heart of Qom. At the far end, bathed in bright sunlight, was the shrine of Hazrat-e-Masumeh, which to my Western eye looked like a disorganized mess of low-lying buildings, high towers, and sparkling domes, all decorated with mind-numbingly elaborate mosaic designs. Standing in the shadow of the mosque were hundreds of pilgrims—mostly men, but women and children, too—all dutifully awaiting their turn to enter the holy site.

We hung back, at the periphery, where we could watch

the scene without being part of it. When Yari turned to face me, his brow was set. When he spoke, his voice quivered with emotion.

"We are alike, Jack," he said in a near whisper. "Iran is like America was at the beginning, when you removed the shackles of colonialism and declared your independence. And, like you, we wish to make something good for our people, to create a just society for Iran. We wish to restore our country to greatness, to build it on a foundation of those principles established by Cyrus, which were picked up by Washington, Jefferson, and Lincoln. We had it once, long ago, but it was lost, taken away from us by one foreign power after another."

Yari paused to control his feelings. His eye drifted upward, scanning the sky until it fixed on a high-flying bird floating across the empty stratosphere. He followed its flight until it disappeared into the blinding halo of the afternoon sun.

"I asked you if you had ever been in the presence of greatness," he said, returning his gaze back to earth. "I'm certain that I have, for I believe that Mohammad Mossadegh can be one of those men who will be remembered for as long as there are people to remember. He can give Iran democracy, Jack, and if he is successful, the idea will spread across this region, as the Persian Empire spread, and it will mark a new era for the Middle East. An era that can give us peace, and justice, and, finally, a government that runs not on greed and self-interest, but on justice and respect for human rights."

I was taken aback by the almost religious fervor of Yari's sentiments, and I wasn't sure how to react. "It's a noble goal, Yari," was all I could muster. He held my look for a moment, then let out a long sigh, and smiled, perhaps thinking that he'd gone too far, and feeling embarrassed about it.

"You asked me earlier if I had spoken with the prime

minister about your proposal," he said, his voice flatter, more controlled now. "The answer is, yes, we have spoken." I waited for more, but nothing came.

"If there's a problem, Yari, tell me what it is. I'm sure we can fix it."

"There is no problem," he said. "Haven't you been listening to what I've said?" He offered me his hand. "Let us today, at this moment, begin a strong and lasting partnership between our two great countries. Two nations that share in the ideals of freedom and democracy."

TWELVE

Zahra smiled and waved as she crossed the square, coming toward us. Following a few feet behind were a couple of young boys, twelve or thirteen years old, trying to keep pace as they struggled with the long roll of heavy rug that was slung between their shoulders. I had realized as soon as they came into view that I'd forgotten all about the conversation I was supposed to be having with Yari on her behalf. I knew that my interference in a family matter was likely to be received coldly, and I had no illusions about having the effect that Zahra hoped for, but I had decided to bring it up anyway, just so I could say that I'd tried. The subject had simply slipped my mind.

"You said a *small* rug!" Yari exclaimed as the retinue reached our position in the shade of a lonely palm tree.

"Wait until you see it, it's beautiful! Roxana will be so happy, I know she will!"

"How much did you pay?"

"It's one of a kind . . . A very unique design."

Yari shook his head and looked to me. "She's been cheated."

"My brother has no faith in me." Zahra frowned, managing to shoot me an inquiring look at the same time. I smiled and pretended that I didn't know what it meant.

Yari pressed the issue. "How much is left from what I gave you?"

"Why are you being mean?" She pouted.

"All right." Yari relented, wrapping his arm around her. "It doesn't matter. I'm sure it will make a beautiful gift."

Zahra reverted to her smile, and we all agreed it was time to head back to Tehran. She was eager to present Roxana with the rug, and I was eager to report back to Sam that we were in business.

As we exited the city through the eastern gate, my attention was drawn to a vacant lot across the road from where we'd parked the car. A large crowd had gathered at the center of the tract, and was being addressed by a man whom I couldn't see. He was using a loudspeaker of some sort, perhaps a bullhorn. Every so often the distorted voice would pause, allowing a great cheer to go up, then it would pick up again, inciting the group to an even greater roar the next time around.

"What's that all about?" I asked Yari.

"Nothing," he replied dismissively. "Just a game. Some sort of silly game."

"Let's take a look," I said, curious.

"No." He glanced nervously across the street and picked up his pace, in a hurry to get to the car. "It's not of interest. Let us go."

"I want to see, as well." Zahra was halfway across the road by the time we turned. "Come, Jack, I'll go with you!" she cried out.

"Zahra!" Yari shouted after her. "*Zahra! WAIT!*" But she was gone.

Yari took off after her and I followed, but by the time we reached the edge of the field, she'd disappeared into the sea of people. Yari pushed through, in desperate pursuit, while I moved around to the other side of the crowd. I could see now that the gathering—all men—was organized in a wide circle, four or five people deep, with about ten yards of open ground between them. As I pushed forward, elbowing my way to the front, the group began a frantic, almost delirious chant, egged on by the man on the bullhorn.

"ALLAH HU AKBAR! ALLAH HU AKBAR! ALLAH HU AKBAR!"

It took me a moment to pull together everything I was seeing and realize, with growing horror, what was about to happen. At the center of the circle, protruding from the sandy earth, was an object that I, at first, didn't recognize. Two men with shovels were patting the earth down around the object, which was wrapped in a clean white sheet tied in a double knot at the top. A third man held the object in place. It wasn't until they moved away, and the object started to shake violently with fear, that I understood—a living human being had been wrapped in the sheet, and buried in the sand from the waist down.

My heart froze as a sudden, piercing, terrified shriek erupted from within the shrouded victim, only to be absorbed by the increasingly furious chant of the crowd. It was the cry of the victim—a young girl, calling out for help, or mercy, or perhaps simply in sheer terror at the thought of what was about to happen to her. She began to violently twist and turn the upper part of her body in a desperate and hopeless attempt to escape the horrendous fate that she knew would meet her at any moment.

I looked up, quickly scanning the crowd, hoping to spot Yari, who I was sure would be able to put a stop to this insanity. But my frantic search was met with another set of eyes—eyes so filled with cold, hard, twisted hatred that their image would be burned into my mind from that moment on. In his midtwenties, in the long black robe and white turban of a mullah, a short, dark, scruffy beard growing around his bloated face, was the man with the bullhorn, the one who had whipped the crowd into this murderous frenzy.

I held his poisonous stare for a moment, unable to pull away until the sudden movement of the crowd broke the spell. All at once, in unison, the men began to hurl, with all the force they could muster, palm-size stones at the head of their trapped young victim. The first few projectiles went wide of the target, but the sickening sound of stone hitting flesh and bone quickly filled the air.

My first—my *only* impulse—was to grab hold of the nearest killer and shove him off his feet, but it made no difference, of course. The assault went on. The poor girl, under attack from all sides, cried out in agony, recoiling in fear, writhing, struggling to find some hope, some way to hold on, to stay alive.

The rest was a blur. I was frantic, incensed—gone suddenly and violently mad, I think. I probably cried out, cursing the bastards. I probably hit a few, but they were too worked up to even care. I would have killed them all if I could have, mowed them down and sent them to hell, but I was helpless and the hail of stones continued. I'm not sure how I got there, but the next thing I knew I was on my knees, beside the girl, my arms around her, trying to protect her with my body as I whispered encouragement in her ear. She didn't hear me. The pristine sheet was now crimson with blood, the cloth torn to shreds, revealing the battered and beaten head of what had been, only a moment ago, a girl—a child—of no more than sixteen.

I remember turning to face the mob and coming up against a sea of angry faces, and I can recall that in all that fury, amid all that angry wrath, there was one face that stood out. It was the face of the young mullah, looking at me from across the distance, a much-amused grin plastered across his face. I remember thinking that it was the look of a madman.

Then the world went dark.

I was on my feet when I came to, walking—or, more accurately, stumbling across the road toward the car, being pulled along by Yari. On his other side, under his arm, was Zahra, who I could see was in real distress, her face distorted with desperate sobs, her eyes bloodred with tears. Behind us, a handful of men stood at the edge of the field, seeing us off with a few last ugly taunts.

Yari pushed me up against the front of the Olds, looked into my eyes, and asked me if I was all right. I wasn't sure yet, but I said, yes, I was, so he went back to Zahra and gently led her into the front seat of the car.

The pain hit suddenly, and I realized that my hand was pressing against an open wound on my right temple. As my senses returned, I could feel the warm stickiness falling across my face and I looked down to see that my white shirt was soaked in blood. The horror of what I'd seen shot back into my awareness—that horrible image of the poor girl's battered head, wrapped in the crimson white sheet. I felt sick, physically ill, and I thought I was about to pass out. Leaning forward, I placed my hands on my knees, lowered my head, and tried to breathe. The world seemed to fade away for a moment as I watched the steady *drip, drip, drip* of my blood as it fell to the earth beside my feet, staining the ground only briefly before it disappeared, absorbed into the ageless sand.

We made the journey back to Tehran in silence. Sitting in the back, resting my head against the roll of carpet, which the two boys had managed to fold into the car as we left, I stared out the window at the seemingly endless desert and tried not to think about what we'd just witnessed. What had she done? I wondered. What heinous crime did a sixteen-year-old girl have to commit to merit such a brutal punishment? I recoiled at the thought. It didn't matter. Of course it didn't matter. The poor girl's only offense had been to be born in the wrong place. In Qom.

I thought about Yari's vision of a democratic Iran, a just society based on the venerable principles of Cyrus the Great. How did the people of Qom fit into that dream? What would the mad mullah think of the idea of a nation built on freedom of speech and thought and the respect for individual rights?

Zahra was softly crying in the front seat. Yari reached out to her, and said a few gentle words, but neither had any effect. She continued to weep.

"There's blood on your carpet," I heard myself saying in an oddly distant voice, unaware that the stain was my own.

"It's all right," Yari replied quietly, in a voice both empty and flat. "It can be cleansed."

THIRTEEN

November 1979

They were burning an effigy of Jimmy Carter outside the U.S. embassy, but their hearts didn't seem to be in it. Maybe it was starting to get a bit old hat, or maybe it was just too early in the day for that sort of thing. It's not easy to work yourself up into a vitriolic frenzy before breakfast, especially when the evening news has stopped coming to the party. Anyway, for whatever reason, the small group of students who'd gathered on this clear, bright Sunday morning in early November were just going through the motions as they set a match to the president and began their familiar "Death to America!" chant.

I'd arrived the previous evening, on a Turkish Airways flight from Istanbul. My arrival had gone smoothly, due in part to the impeccably forged Canadian passport Toby had provided, helped along by the ten-thousand-rial note that I'd folded into its pages. I didn't know if that was still standard operating procedure in postrevolution Iran, but I didn't think it would hurt, and it didn't.

It had been necessary for me to spend a couple of days in Washington while the papers were processed and travel arrangements made, but I didn't mind because I'd managed to convince Toby to book me into the Four Seasons, the recently opened five-star in Georgetown. I'd tried calling Lenni to see if she could come down and luxuriate with me, but all I got was her answering machine, and since I didn't like talking to a tape, I went it alone. In truth, I was just as happy to spend the time brushing up on my Farsi and trying to figure out what the hell I was gonna do once I got to Tehran. I did drop her a postcard saying that I might be gone a bit longer than the couple of days I'd originally anticipated, but I didn't say why.

A blue-eyed marine appeared from inside a sentry box. "Good morning, sir," he said crisply. "May I see your passport?"

He took a careful look, glancing up to compare my face with the photo, then checking to see what visas had been stamped onto the inside pages. Once satisfied, he handed it back with a sharp nod of the head.

"Is anyone expecting you this morning, Mr. Phelps?"

"Bill Donnelly," I said. "I have a nine o'clock appointment."

"I'll let him know that you're here."

The sergeant stepped back into his box, had a brief phone conversation, and a couple of minutes later, I was following a pleasant young lady with shoulder-length brown hair and a clipboard under her arm across the compound to the chancery building, where most of the embassy offices were located. The two-story brick structure, located at the center of the twenty-seven-acre site, looked more like a state penitentiary than a diplomatic mission, a result of the heavy steel bars that had been welded over all the windows. Local security, in the form of a few tattered revolutionaries who wandered the grounds with automatic weapons slung over their shoulders, seemed to me to be a good example of putting the foxes in charge of the henhouse.

We passed through the building's mausoleum-like main entrance, climbed a wide circular staircase, and passed through a heavy, wood-laminated steel door onto the top floor. Turning left, we proceeded along a wide, high-ceilinged corridor, to the western end of the building, where Donnelly's office was located.

Toby had warned me not to expect too much. The newly assigned junior operations officer was fresh off the sixteen-week FTC (Field Tradecraft Course) at the agency's Chesapeake Bay training center. That would've been preceded by an eight-week "Initial Operations Course," and six months of "Interims," which consisted of a series of eight-week rotations at the various desks within the Directorate of Intelligence at Langley. Initiation into the Company had come a long way since my baptism, when Sam unceremoniously tossed me in at the deep end. All that training no doubt produced highly competent, well-informed agents, but there was something to be said for the old school, too. Nobody ever learned how to swim without getting wet.

"Mr. Phelps. Please come in. I'm Bill Donnelly . . ."

A lanky, down-home, high-school-quarterback kind of a guy stood up and extended a big, welcoming hand across his desk. In his late twenties, with a long, friendly face, soft bloodhound eyes, and short-cropped curly hair, he wore khaki trousers with a sharp military crease down the front and a well-pressed white shirt with the sleeves neatly rolled up to just below the elbows.

"You know that Phelps isn't my real name, don't you?" I said as I took his hand. "It's just my cover."

"Well, yes. I did know that, but . . ." He forced an uneasy smile. "It's best not to deviate in the use of a cover name. It can confuse things."

"Is that what they teach at spy school?" I said before I could stop myself. His grin faded to nothing.

"What would you like me to call you?"

"Jack," I said, a bit sheepishly. "Call me Jack." It hadn't been my intention to alienate the guy before we'd finished shaking hands. It just came out that way.

"Okay, Jack," he said. "Take a seat."

I sat and he slipped back down behind his desk.

"The name was Toby's idea of a joke," I said, trying to make amends.

"Sorry, I . . . I don't follow you."

"James Phelps . . . ?"

"I still don't—"

"The gray-haired spook on *Mission: Impossible.* His name was James Phelps. I guess Toby thought it'd be funny."

"Oh, right. I see." I wasn't sure he did. "Would you like a cup of coffee or something?"

I ordered it black, with two sugars. Donnelly went to the door to place the order with the clipboard lady, giving me a chance to have a look around the office. It was a good-size room, with a view onto a parking area and, beyond that, an open athletic field, and some low-lying buildings in the distance. The walls were painted the usual institutional cream and decorated with standard-issue prints of various scenes of Americana—the Capitol building at night, the Grand Canyon, the Golden Gate Bridge, and, of course, the obligatory portraits of the commander in chief and the secretary of state. The only personal touch was a group of a half-dozen photos neatly displayed on a bookshelf behind the desk. Divided equally between family and career, and arranged accordingly, they summed up Donnelly's life in six simple frames. On the right side were the personal shots—a studio photograph of a heavily airbrushed mom and dad; a wedding-day shot of Donnelly and his bride standing on a wooden footbridge; and, finally, an out-of-focus snapshot of his beamingly happy wife arriving at a suburban home with a newborn baby in her arms—a daughter, judging by the amount of pink she was loaded down with. The career group featured a shot of Donnelly as navy pilot, helmet tucked under his arm as he posed in front of an F-4 Phantom; a graduation photo taken at Annapolis; and a more recent shot of Donnelly standing with a group of men outside the State Department building in Washington. The last one was almost certainly an agency product.

"Thanks for seeing me," I said when he'd returned to his seat.

"No problem." He reached into a drawer, withdrew a sealed envelope, and passed it across the desk. "There's twenty thousand in there."

"Thanks," I said, slipping the envelope into my jacket pocket.

"Don't you wanna count it?"

"Am I supposed to sign for it?"

"No."

"Then I don't see much point."

"I guess not," he admitted.

Instant coffee arrived and I took my time adding in a couple of packets of sugar then slowly stirring it up. I thought if I let Donnelly do the talking, I might get some idea about what he'd been told about me, and what I was up to, but he didn't bite. He just sat there, stone silent, smiling across the desk, waiting for me to say something. We stayed like that for quite a while, each of us waiting for the other to give in. I lost.

"Must be fun, flying those F-4s," I said, nodding toward the photo.

"Nothing like it."

"Why would you want to trade that in for a life sentence behind a desk?"

He considered it for a moment, decided to give me a straight answer. "I guess I thought I could contribute something. I hope to, anyway."

I smiled and allowed a little chuckle to escape. He looked a bit put out.

"Something funny about that?"

"Come on, be honest. The truth is that when the guys from Langley turned up at your door, the first thing you thought of was James Bond."

He tried not to, but he couldn't help cracking a smile.

"Maybe you didn't really expect fast cars, beautiful women, and evil villains, but I'll bet you were hoping for more than a desk, a secretary, and a long list of reports to write."

Donnelly shrugged. "Gotta feed the beast."

"Yeah, well, that's why I asked you about the F-4s. You don't strike me as the kind of guy who likes to sit around doing nothing."

Donnelly tilted his head back and studied me for a moment. I waited for a response, but he was pretty good at the silent game, and I was the one who was after something.

"In fact," I continued, "I'll bet that in the two months you've been here you've already started to put together the beginnings of a network—government officials, informers, maybe even a couple of military guys."

"You've obviously got a point, Jack, so why don't you just spit it out."

It was the best I was gonna get out of him, so I inched my chair closer to the desk and leaned forward. It was just for effect, but it seemed to work. He leaned forward, too.

"How much do you know about what I'm doing in Tehran?" I said.

"Not much," he admitted. "Nothing at all, in fact."

"You know I was sent by the deputy director?"

"Yes, I am aware of that."

"Toby and I go back a long way. Did you know that?"

"No. No, I didn't."

"Well, we do. And from time to time, he . . . well, he contacts me, and asks me to do a little job for him. The jobs vary, but they all have one thing in common. They're extremely sensitive. Too sensitive to be put through normal channels."

"Go on," Donnelly said, looking sufficiently intrigued, if not yet sold.

"I'm not telling you this to impress you. I'm telling you because I need your help."

"To do what?"

"I need to get someone out of Qasr prison."

He tried to hide his reaction, but I could see him flinch. "Qasr? That's . . . Christ. Just how in hell do you hope to do that?"

"I thought I'd start with twenty thousand bucks."

Donnelly picked up a pen and absentmindedly twirled it around on his fingers. "You start flashing money around to the wrong people and you might end up in Qasr yourself."

"That's why I need your help. I need introductions, to people you trust."

He laughed. "I don't trust anyone in this country."

"Just get me started."

He shook his head. "Look, I wasn't lying when I said they didn't tell me what you're up to, but that doesn't mean they didn't give me any guidance at all."

"No?"

"No."

"What'd they tell you?"

"To give you the money, then wash my hands of you. They said not to get involved with you in any way. They said you're trouble waiting to happen, and that under no circumstances should I believe a word you say."

"They said all that?"

"Yep."

I smiled. "Who you gonna believe, them or me?"

"Sorry, Jack, but I'm afraid you're on your own. Even if I could help you, I don't think a bribe's gonna cut it, not as far as Qasr is concerned. You're right, I have made some inroads, and I know government officials, guys who are pretty high up, who can't even get into that place. It's run by this mullah, a real nutcase, even by their standards. He operates this one-man kangaroo court over there. They call him 'The Forty-Five-Caliber Judge' because he declares the defendant guilty, has him taken out into the courtyard, counts down from ten, then personally shoots him in the head. Always uses a Colt M1911. And it's not just the Shah's crowd, of course. Actors, writers, teachers, journalists. He's an equal-opportunity killer, and he's responsible for hundreds of deaths."

"That's why I need to get my guy out," I said.

Donnelly placed the pen down and took a moment to study it before looking up at me. "I'm sorry," he said. "I wish I could. I really do."

I nodded, but before I could say anything, the phone rang.

"Yes?" Donnelly picked up quickly.

I became aware of a commotion coming from outside. Going to the window, I tried to get a view of the main gate, where the cheers, or screams—I wasn't sure which—seemed to be coming from. There was nothing to see, so I assumed that it was just the protest coming to life. Maybe the cameras had turned up, after all. I was about to turn away when something caught my eye.

"Look at that," I said as Donnelly hung up the phone, but I could see by the look on his face that he already knew.

"We've got a problem," he said.

FOURTEEN

People were emerging from their offices with a variety of bewildered looks on their faces. "What's going on?" . . . "I dunno." . . . "What did you see?" . . . "How in hell—"

"Listen up, everybody!" Donnelly called out along the corridor. "We've had a breach of security! It's nothing to worry about, but we're going to put into effect the drill that we've all practiced!"

"What's happened, Bill?" a man with thick glasses asked.

"We think it's just a few overzealous protesters who've come over the fence."

"More than a few," a nervous secretary added. "They're all over the grounds."

"Okay, it doesn't matter who they are, or how many, the procedure is the same. I was just on the phone with security, and they've already locked the main entrance to the building and are in the process of escorting everybody on the first two floors—that's both U.S. personnel and local employees—up to this level, so it's gonna be very crowded up here in a couple of minutes. Once we're sure the lower floors are clear, we'll be locking the door that leads to this floor, and I assure you that nobody is going to get through that. We'll be safe here until the local authorities arrive to remove the intruders."

It all sounded very reasonable—up until the last sentence. I had serious doubts about the Iranian cavalry riding to the rescue. And from what I'd seen out the window, this wasn't a spontaneous act by some overzealous protesters, either. This crowd was well organized, and they were dressed for the occasion, too, with red armbands for identification and laminated photographs of the Ayatollah Khomeini pinned to their shirts. A play for attention probably. A ploy to get the cameras back. Odds were that once they had their pictures taken, they'd leave. Then again, maybe not.

Donnelly chose two young men to station on the door leading up from the center stairwell. He gave them a key and instructions to use it once everyone from the lower levels had been accounted for. Then he turned to me.

"Okay, Jack. You're gonna help me do the burn."

Every CIA station in the world has contingency plans for a paper burn, in anticipation of just such an occasion. In sensitive locations, where an incident is considered more likely to occur, there would be a "read-and-burn" policy in effect, but, believe it or not, on November 4, 1979—eight months into the Islamic revolution, with daily rantings and ravings taking place outside the embassy gate—the risk to the U.S. embassy in Tehran was judged to be moderate. So the station was functioning under the "half-hour rule," which meant that critical documents could be kept on file, but only so many as could be destroyed within a thirty-minute time frame. Unfortunately, whoever was in charge of deciding what volume of documents that constituted must've had a wildly optimistic idea about how fast paper can be shredded and burned. When we entered the twelve-by-twelve-foot vault where agency documents were kept, there were already several mountains of files stacked up on the floor, and the clipboard lady was still emptying armloads of paper from four very large safes.

Donnelly moved to the back of the room, where a big barrel-shaped contraption sat looking like an overgrown beer keg that had been converted into a furnace.

"Okay. Let's get this thing fired up."

He flicked a switch and the machine shuddered to life, sounding pretty much like it looked. The idea was to feed paper through a rectangular slot in the front, where it would be shredded into quarter-inch-wide strips before falling into the belly of the beast, to be incinerated. We organized ourselves into a sort of human chain, with the clipboard lady handing me a stack of top-secret files, which I fed in stacks of about thirty pages to Donnelly. Naturally, I read as much as I could in the process, for no other reason than idle curiosity. I managed to gather that Donnelly and others at the embassy had been trying, with increasing vehemence, to warn the rest of the government about the pressures that were building in Iran.

One page read like this:

TOP SECRET

TO: W.DONNELLY, TEHRAN STATION
FROM: DC/NE
DATE: OCTOBER 14, 1979

RE: SHAH/VISA

You'll be glad to hear that your points re: entry visa for the Shah have been noted and were included in today's PDB. You're not alone in your concerns. Unlikely to become a problem.

It was a shame to burn it, I thought, although given the present circumstances, the deputy chief/Near East division, who was its author, probably wouldn't have minded having it consigned to oblivion. On the other hand, it was pretty clear evidence that this particular screwup had been accomplished with no help from the CIA. In fact, it looked like the agency was ahead of the game this time, warning in the PDB (President's Daily Briefing) about the danger of allowing the deposed Shah into the United States.

A few days after the memo was written, in a truly inexplicable move, the White House had decided to ignore an avalanche of advice from people who knew what they were talking about, and issue the former monarch an entry visa. It seemed that the Shah, who was seeking medical treatment for his cancer at a New York hospital, had some pretty impressive advocates himself. People like David Rockefeller, who held a large chunk of the Shah's $16 billion fortune in his Chase Manhattan bank, and former secretary of state Henry Kissinger, who was a Rockefeller employee at the time. In the end, the president went with Rockefeller and Kissinger over Bill Donnelly, and granted the visa, citing "humanitarian grounds." I don't think even Jimmy Carter, who was as close to a preacher as you'd want in the Oval Office, thought anyone would buy that it was just a kind-hearted gesture to a sick man, but I suppose they thought the world would see it as a sign that we were no fair-weather friend. The United States of America would stick by its brutal dictators to the bitter end. Personally, I thought the $16 billion probably had a little something to do with it, but that's just me.

At any rate, the move played right into the hands of the Grand Ayatollah Seyyed Ruhollah Khomeini. Since his return from exile, the imam had been doing everything in his power to undermine the moderate forces in the new government, with an eye toward establishing a fundamentalist Islamic state in Iran. But as much as he was revered as the country's spiritual leader, popular support for his cause was limited. By late October, revolutionary fever had cooled and the government was slowly moving toward some sort of accommodation with the Great Satan, even meeting with top administration officials in Algiers to map out a way forward. Khomeini needed something to hang his hat on, and the Shah's visa was just the thing. The Iranian people were well aware of America's past meddling in their affairs, and they were all too ready to believe Khomeini's assertion that the Shah's welcome into the United States was a sign that the great and powerful CIA was once again plotting to reinstall their puppet king to the peacock throne.

Rockefeller and Kissinger, it turned out, gave the Ayatollah's crowd a wonderful gift. One of those gifts that keeps on giving.

Ker-chunk—ker-chunk—ker-splack!!!

The paper-burning gismo spluttered to a sudden, wrenching stop. We all froze, did a group double take, then Donnelly started madly flipping the switch back and forth. He did that five or six times, until he realized it wasn't going to have any effect, then he took a step back, put his hands on his hips, and looked the machine up and down.

"Damn," he said quietly.

"Have you got a backup?" I asked. Donnelly turned to the clipboard lady.

"Do we?"

Her look said that they didn't. "I'll see what I can locate," she said, and hurried off, leaving Donnelly and me standing in the middle of the room, looking at each other. Helpless and hapless.

A baby-faced marine appeared in the doorway. "Sir . . ."

Donnelly spun around. "Yeah?"

"They want you down the hall, sir. There's something you need to see."

"What?"

"You'd better have a look for yourself, sir. They're in Colonel Stark's office."

Donnelly nodded, started out the door, but had second thoughts when he remembered the stacks of top-secret documents strewn across the floor. He turned back to the sergeant.

"You know my assistant, Carol?"

"Yes, sir."

"Good. You stay here. She's the only one who gets past you."

"No problem, sir."

Donnelly shot me a look. "You come with me."

The hallway was packed with people, most of them nervous-looking Iranians who were smoking so many cigarettes that I thought at first the place was on fire. The faint scent of tear gas, which must've been released on the lower floors, made me wonder how far the marines were authorized to go in order to protect the embassy. Things could easily get out of hand.

The center door was closed now, and barricaded with various pieces of office furniture. We pushed through the crowd to the other end of the building, where we entered a large, corner office. You could sense the nervous energy in the room—that underlying tension that comes with a quickly escalating crisis.

Colonel Stark, dressed in a light gray civilian suit, was standing beside his desk, speaking in hushed tones into a telephone. A tightly packed man in his midforties, with a receding hairline, a small nose, thin lips, and big aviator-style eyeglasses, he acknowledged Donnelly with a nod, then gestured toward the window, where a tall, willowy man was peering out onto the compound through a pair of binoculars. I was pretty sure he was agency, too. He had that air about him.

"What's happening?" Donnelly asked him.

The man handed him the binoculars without comment and pointed him in the direction of the rear parking area, about forty yards away. I didn't need any magnification to see that five men had gathered there, four of them young, bearded Iranians, the fifth an American. You could tell he was American, even from this distance, by the way he was blindfolded with his hands tied behind his back. His captors—two of them armed with AK-47s—were involved in an animated discussion, presumably about what to do with their catch.

"Christ," Donnelly whispered as he lowered the binoculars. "Is that Zakowski?"

"That's him," the spindly spook replied.

"What the hell's he doing out there? He was supposed to be securing the lower floors."

"He was. Then he decided to go out and negotiate."

"He's got an interesting style," I said, earning a dark look from the guy whose name I didn't know.

"Who's this?" he sneered.

"Jim Phelps," I said quickly, before Donnelly could answer.

"He's here under the auspices of the deputy director," Donnelly explained.

The unnamed spy shot a glance my way, tried not to look too impressed, then took up his binoculars and returned to what was happening outside. After a moment's observation, he called out to Stark.

"They're on the move. Looks like they're bringing him inside."

"They're bringing him into the building," the colonel repeated into the telephone. Donnelly asked who was on the line and was told that it was Bruce Laingen, the acting ambassador, who'd been attending an early morning meeting at the Foreign Ministry.

"He wants to know if anybody has communicated with the protesters," the colonel reported.

"No," the guy with the binoculars replied. "As far as we know, nobody's communicated with them."

"Aside from Zakowski," I muttered, which earned me another dirty look. I knew I was getting on the guy's nerves, but that was okay. He was already on mine.

"We've got a serious situation here, Mr. Phelps," he said. "Perhaps you wouldn't mind stepping out into the hall."

"They'll try to use him to get in," I said.

I got silence and a cold stare. "That's not your concern."

"It's very much my concern," I said. "I didn't come halfway around the world so I could be taken hostage."

"Nobody's going to be a hostage."

"Tell that to Zakowski."

Colonel Stark interrupted. "They want to know if there have been any injuries."

"No," the arrogant one said, his eyes still locked on me. "There have been no injuries. Not yet."

"No injuries," the colonel reported into the phone. He was about to relay another question when a breathless bald man came stumbling into the room.

"They . . . They . . . They've got . . ."

"Slow down, Mike." Donnelly led the man over to a sofa and sat him down. "Take a couple of deep breaths and start over."

He did exactly that and tried again. "They have Jim . . . Jim Zakowski . . . He's . . . he's a hostage . . ."

"Yes, we know."

"They've got him . . . on the other side of the door . . . with a gun to his head." The poor guy was doing the best he could not to panic. "They . . . they say if we don't open up . . . they . . . they say they're gonna shoot him!"

Donnelly glanced over at me, then at the lanky spy. Everyone waited for the colonel to explain the situation to the ambassador, which seemed to take a lot longer than it should have. Meanwhile, another marine appeared at the door.

"The situation's getting kind of intense out here, sirs," he said. "They say if we don't open the door in two minutes, they're gonna kill Mr. Zakowski."

"Did Zakowski say anything?" Colonel Stark asked.

"Yes, sir. He said that we should open the goddamned door right now. He sounded pretty stressed, sir. I . . . I think they might actually do it. What should we do?"

"We're working on it," the nameless spy said as the colonel relayed the latest information down the line.

"Okay, the ambassador's up to speed," he said after a moment. "He wants a recommendation."

Nobody was in a rush to speak up, so I did.

"Call their bluff."

I was met with a stunned silence.

"What the hell's that supposed to mean?" the colonel finally growled.

"They're bluffing," I said. "You should call them on it."

"That's kinda cold, isn't it?" Donnelly said. "You're talking about a man's life here. What if you're wrong?"

"If they're really willing to kill him, then they'd be willing to kill everyone in here. Every American, anyway. If that's the case, it'd be nuts to let them in. And if they're not willing to kill him . . . well, then it's a bluff and you should call it."

Donnelly looked to his agency colleague. "What do you think?"

He shook his head, signifying that I might have something, but it was a tough call. He asked the colonel what he thought. The colonel thought what I said made some sense, but on the other hand, they just might do it, and then the whole thing could spin out of control. When he completed the circle by asking Donnelly what he thought, I'd had enough.

"How about we form a committee?" I said. "We could report back to ourselves in a couple of months."

"That's really not very helpful, Jack," Donnelly said. "This is a man's life we're talking about." He turned to the marine. "Do they speak English?"

"Yes, sir, one of them does. Sort of."

"Okay. Go back and tell them we need more time. Fifteen minutes. Say we need to discuss it with the ambassador." The sergeant nodded and headed back up the hall.

"Well?" The colonel was holding his hand over the phone's mouthpiece. "What are we gonna say?"

They managed to come to a consensus without anyone having to make a decision. It was a mistake, but I understood it, even respected it. I'd given them a perfectly good argument for staying safe behind the big steel door, but they chose to risk their own lives rather than risk their colleague's. Zakowski was just a name to me, but to them, he was a living, breathing human being. They'd worked with him, shot the breeze with him, maybe even shared a few drinks and had a few laughs with him. He'd shown them pictures of his family from in his wallet, and shared stories of his hometown. He was one of them, one of the team, and it just wasn't in the makeup of these military-minded men to abandon one of the team in order to save their own skins.

Of course the problem with doing the honorable thing was that by opening the door they'd be putting the better part of a hundred people in jeopardy. And these weren't Company men or air-force colonels, or even "political officers," as they call them in the State Department. These were ordinary men and women doing ordinary jobs. Maybe they'd been attracted by the few extra dollars they'd get in "danger pay" at a posting in Tehran, and they would've arrived with little or no idea about the power struggle that was being played out in Iranian politics, or what it had to do with them. Those who'd thought about it at all would've seen themselves as innocent bystanders in that game. And they would have been partly right. They were innocent. Maybe too innocent. But if they'd ever really been bystanders, that was about to come to an extremely uncomfortable end.

FIFTEEN

"No eh-speak!"

Our young Iranian guard seemed to be getting jumpier by the minute. He kept playing with his pistol, spinning the cylinder, then nervously cocking and uncocking the hammer as he paced back and forth across the front of the room. It had been unsettling at first, but now it was just pissing me off.

I wasn't sure how many of us were in the room, but I estimated that half a dozen of my fellow hostages were seated on the floor around me. It had been a little over an hour since we'd been blindfolded, our hands tied behind our backs, then taken in small groups to various offices, presumably to wait for our captors to figure out what to do with us. The taking of the embassy had been swift and easy, but none of the intruders seemed to have had the slightest idea about a plan once they got in. I suppose they hadn't counted on such a spectacular success.

Once the security door was opened, a flood of scruffy-looking students had burst through, waving guns and spitting insults as they surged forward along the corridor, shoving people aside and throwing random punches. A few Americans were knocked to the floor, where they could do nothing but roll up into a fetal position while they were kicked and beaten with rolled-up newspaper, sticks, or whatever else was at hand. It was as if some huge, pent-up well of hatred had been suddenly released, engulfing and overwhelming everything in its path.

I'd pushed my way up the corridor, trying to get a sense about who, if anyone, was in charge. Searching for the red armbands worn by the organizers, I finally spotted two men standing off to the side, involved in a heated discussion. It was tough to follow them, but I understood enough to get the gist of the debate, which boiled down to *"What the hell do we do now?"*

"You need to control your people!" I yelled above the din. "Before something bad happens!"

Either they didn't speak English, or they were too surprised to respond, because all I got back was a couple of blank expressions. I switched to Farsi.

"You must stop this! Before people get hurt!"

They both nodded their heads in agreement then shrugged. What were they supposed to do?

"Talk to them!" I said.

That fired up the argument again. After going back and forth for a couple more minutes, they finally reached some kind of understanding, and the smaller of the two men, an impish-looking guy with a mop of straight black hair and a thin, scraggly beard, climbed onto a table, one of the pieces of furniture that had been barricading the door. He made a few attempts to speak, but was drowned out by the chaos. He looked to his friend, who joined him on the table, raised his arms up over his head, and let loose a great, long, whooping cry that really shouldn't have been humanly possible. It got everybody's attention.

"We must do it correctly!" the little guy called out across

the sea of faces. *"The world must know that we have acted in the right way!"*

It worked, calming things down considerably, but I couldn't help wondering if these people actually believed that the world was gonna be impressed with their actions. Could they really be that out of touch? It didn't bode well for a quick resolution to the problem.

Things progressed in a slightly more orderly fashion after that. Those who were still in their offices were brought out to join a line of non-Iranian employees that was formed along the wall of the corridor. Locals were led away, to be released, I assumed, and the invaders, giddy with success, set about blindfolding and binding their prisoners. As I stood in line, waiting my turn, I caught sight of the baby-faced marine, the one Donnelly had charged with protecting the vault. His hands were already bound behind his back, and he was being taunted and laughed at as the strip of white cloth was tied over his eyes. It was tough to watch. This was a good kid, not long out of high school, no doubt, proud to have made it into the elite brotherhood of the United States Marine Corps. He'd been prepared to fight, even to die for his country, but no one had prepared him for this. He'd been told that the word *surrender* doesn't exist for a marine, yet there he was, being tied and bound by a ragtag mob of clapped-out, grungy students, without having had the opportunity to raise his weapon, let alone fire it. He probably felt he'd let us down, let the uniform down, but of course he hadn't. The truth was that somebody had let him down. I'll never forget his expression as that blindfold went over his eyes. He looked embarrassed. No, it was worse than that. He looked humiliated.

"No eh-speak!"

There hadn't been a peep out of anyone, but the kid with the pistol continued to feel the need to assert his authority every few minutes. I thought there was a growing anxiety in his voice, and the addition of fear to the already lethal combination of inexperience and a loaded weapon did nothing to calm my nerves.

"Nobody said anything," I said in as calm a voice as I could muster. "And nobody's going to say anything, or do anything except sit here quietly until we're told to do something else. So why don't you just take it easy? Everything's under control."

I heard footsteps coming at me, then I felt the hard steel of the gun barrel pressing against my left ear.

"NO EH-SPEAK!" he screamed. It probably would've been best to leave it at that, but I couldn't help going for the last word.

"Okay," I said. "No eh-speak."

I suppose I was lucky not to get the bullet. As it was, I didn't feel a thing. Not until I woke up, anyway. Then it hurt like almighty hell.

The only thing that existed in the entire universe—the only thing that let me know I was still alive—was the relentless pain at the back of my head. Christ, it hurt! Like my skull was in the grip of a vise, ready to crack wide open at any moment.

Slowly, other messages started to get through. I was on my feet. Walking down a set of stairs. No, not walking, being dragged down. There were two men, one on each arm. Where the hell was I? What was happening? The men were talking to each other but I couldn't make sense of what they were saying. Oh, yes . . . Farsi. They were speaking Farsi. Iran. The embassy. It all started to fall into place as we reached the bottom step.

"You can stand?" one of my escorts asked in a friendly voice. I nodded and stiffened my legs, allowing them to take my full weight. The men eased their grip on my arms, without letting go, and pulled me forward.

We stepped outside, into a light afternoon drizzle. The

fresh air was a relief, and helped bring me around. Where are they taking me? I wondered. Am I alone or are the others with us?

"Don't to be afraid," the friendly escort whispered in my ear. "It's not will hurt you."

What the hell does that mean? I thought. Did he want to say that I'm not going to be harmed, or did he mean that the end would be quick and painless? It wouldn't make sense for them to kill us. We're only valuable as long as we're alive. I hoped to hell they knew that.

As we stepped forward, we were greeted by the wildest, most earsplitting, ground-rattling roar you could imagine. The sheer force of what felt like ten thousand screaming voices nearly knocked me off my feet. Buildings shook and windows rattled, and a massive dose of adrenaline jump-started my heart.

"You don't to worry!" my escort shouted above the din. "Is just the people! They are happy!"

Happy? No. That's not happy, I thought. Happy would be if they'd gathered to celebrate the local team's unexpected victory over that long-standing rival, the Great Satan, or if they'd brought their children down to witness and cheer a great moment in Iranian history. But that wasn't why this crowd was here. They had something very different in mind, and it was what they were screaming for now. They'd come to see blood.

"Who are you?"

"James Phelps."

"Yes, I can see this name in your passport. I wanted to know what you do in the embassy of the United States government."

"I don't do anything. I'm a Canadian citizen."

My interrogator sat back in his chair and stroked his thick black beard. A tall, spare man, in his late twenties, he spoke in a soft voice and had a serious, thoughtful air about him.

He'd taken his time starting the interview, and he was in no hurry to move on. Maybe he thought the long silences would unnerve me, but I was happy to go slow. It gave me a chance to size him up.

After I'd been paraded past the bloodthirsty crowd outside the main gate, my two escorts had hauled me aimlessly around the grounds for a while, stopping once for a quick photo call, with dozens of cameras madly clicking away. I was then taken to the small, stuffy, windowless room where I now sat. After I was placed in a hard chair, my blindfold was removed, but not the tightly bound nylon cord that was cutting into my wrists. I was given a glass of water, and a couple of minutes later, my interrogator came through the door. He pulled up the only other chair in the room and straddled it like a horse.

"Why do you carry twenty thousand United States dollars in your pocket?" he said. "What was the purpose of this?"

"Expense money."

"Expense money?"

"Right."

I'd determined to give the shortest answers possible, offering no explanation or amplification until I was explicitly asked for it, at least until I had a better sense of what they knew about me. There was no reason to believe that they knew anything other than what they could glean from my documents, which I was certain they would accept as genuine, but it would be easy to let something slip if I was too talkative. The less said, the better.

"It is a very big amount of money."

"Yes, it is."

"Too big."

"I don't know about that."

"Who gave it to you?"

"My company."

"What is the name of the company?"

"Hudson Oil."

"I see. So you have not received this money here, in Iran."

"No."

"You have brought it with you, from United States."

"Canada," I corrected him. It was a pathetic attempt at a trap, which he seemed to acknowledge with a shrug.

"Then you have declared it in the airport, when you have entered Iran."

"No."

"Why not?"

"No reason."

"But you are required to do so."

"Well, I didn't."

"This is a crime. You can go to jail for it."

"Fine," I said. "Call the police and I'll be happy to confess."

He paused, dug a pack of cigarettes out of his pocket, and took his time lighting up, fixing me with a long look as he did. My head was still pounding and all I wanted to do was lie down.

"I find this too much to believe." He picked a stray piece of tobacco off his lower lip.

"Well, it's the truth."

"No, I don't accept. This amount of money cannot be used for expense alone." He leaned forward and lowered his voice. "It will be much better for you to tell the truth. Believe me."

"Make all the threats you want," I said, looking him straight in the eye. "It won't change anything."

He gave me a sad look, then shrugged his shoulders and twisted around in his seat, looking toward the two guards who were standing by at the door. Understanding the silent message, the bigger of the two men stood his rifle against the wall, then circled around behind me, got to his knees, and wrapped his arms around my torso, pinning me to the chair.

My inquisitor leaned forward, so close that I could taste his warm, sour breath as it wafted up my nostrils. Narrowing his eyes, he lifted his cigarette to within a couple of inches from my cheek, and held it there, not saying a word. I could feel the heat of the burning cinder against my flesh and the smoke was drifting into my eyes, making them water.

"Shall I continue?" he said.

"No," I said, shaking my head. "I'll tell you."

"Good. Very good." He sat back, the trace of a grin having crept onto his face, and signaled the guard to release me. "I have no wish to hurt you. But, as I have said, it is best for you to tell the truth. Now please, what was the purpose of this money?"

"It was meant for, well . . . It was to be given as gifts."

"Gifts?"

"Yes."

"What kind of gifts?"

"For officials . . . Officials in your government."

"Do you mean to say bribes?"

I shrugged. "Call it what you like. The facts are that my company is bidding for a contract to provide equipment for your country's oil industry, and these monetary gifts—or bribes, as you call them—were to be given to the people who'll be making the decision about whether or not we get the job. You might not like it, but that's the way business is done in your country. Even after your revolution."

He dropped his cigarette to the floor, crushed it with his heel, then looked up and smiled broadly, revealing a chink of glistening gold where his front left tooth should have been.

"So you see?" he said. "Everything can be just fine when you tell the truth. Now let us take a cup of tea."

I'd anticipated all sorts of responses to my tale, but that wasn't one of them. "Sure," I replied. "A cup of tea would be great."

The smaller guard was dispatched to fetch the refreshments, and silence descended on the room. In all the excitement of the takeover, I'd simply forgotten to dump the money, but quickly realized it would be my most vulnerable point. The story I'd worked out was a perfectly plausible one, but I knew they'd be more likely to buy it if they thought they'd forced it out of me. I'd even planned to take a bit of physical abuse before caving, but in the end, I didn't think it would be necessary. This guy was a rank amateur.

"Do you have a name?" I asked him.

"Me? I am Hesam."

"I meant your group. Does your group have a name?"

"Oh. Yes. We are Muslim Students Who Follow the Line of Imam."

"Catchy," I said. He fixed me with a look, not sure if I'd just insulted him. I let him wonder. "What are you after?"

"After?"

"What do you want? I assume you took us hostage for a reason. What do you hope to get out of this?"

The question seemed to take him by surprise, but after some initial thought, he warmed to it. "We will teach a lesson."

"Yeah? What kind of lesson?"

"We will show to the world that America is a great oppressor. Our action can make an example, to bring hope in the hearts of all the good and spiritual people who are enslaved by the imperialist superpower. They will learn how it is possible to rise up, and then together we will destroy the political, economic, and strategic hegemony of United States."

I couldn't help smiling. "How long did it take you to memorize that?"

"This is not joke," he spat back.

"No, you're right. It isn't. But it is a pretty ambitious agenda."

"It must be done."

"I thought you were gonna say that you wanted the Shah returned to Iran."

"Yes, this, too, of course. He must stand on trial for his crimes."

"What if that doesn't happen? What if the Shah isn't shipped over, and there's no uprising to overthrow the evil oppressor? What then?"

He gave me a long, hard look. "There is much time, and we have much patience."

A tray of tea arrived, accompanied by egg-salad sandwiches which had been cut into quarters. The big guard cut my hands free, and I was even allowed a bathroom break and a cigarette before we went back to work. I hadn't had a smoke in two years, and all it did was make me feel dizzy.

"How have you come to speak Farsi?" I was asked when we were all in position again.

"What makes you think that I do?"

"You spoke it to someone as we entered the building." I had hoped that that would've been lost in the confusion, but I had an answer ready, in case it wasn't.

"I do a lot of business in this country," I explained. "At least, I used to, before the revolution. So I took a course in Farsi a few years ago. I don't speak it very well."

"Yes, I have been told this, too."

"What about you?" I said, seizing the opportunity to change the subject. "Where did you learn to speak English so well?"

"Berkeley," he said, allowing a hint of pride to show through. "I have made a degree there, in the study of political science."

"Berkeley?" I had to laugh. Who says God doesn't have a sense of humor?

We spent the rest of the night alternating between Hesam's clumsy attempts at interrogation and regular tea breaks, where we'd engage in more or less friendly chatter. I found that, even during the cross-examination, I could steer the discussion away from uncomfortable areas—like why I'd been at the embassy in the first place, and who I was there to see—by bringing up politics. All I had to do was toss out a remark like "Maybe the Shah wasn't perfect, but you have to admit, he did a lot of good things for Iran," and I could count on a twenty-minute diatribe, detailing how the former monarch had destroyed an otherwise perfect country. Of course, like all the evil in the world, the true source of Iran's woes was America. It always came down to America.

"United States has been enemy of Iran for six hundred years!" the little guard exclaimed during one of our breaks. When I pointed out that the United States had only been a country for two hundred years, he would have none of it. The imam had said six hundred years, and an imam cannot be wrong.

"Why not?" I asked.

"Because he is imam."

"What qualifies him to be imam?"

"Because he is never wrong."

Tough to argue with that kind of logic.

As dawn rolled around, Hesam had long since run out of questions. I was exhausted and feeling sick to my stomach after bumming cigarettes all night, but I kept talking, holding forth on anything that came to mind, just to fill the space. I was controlling the room now, and the longer I went on about nothing, the less likely it was that they would stumble onto something.

Hesam never did ask me what business I'd been conducting at the embassy, or who I'd been to see. Believing that he'd broken me with the cigarette-in-the-face stunt, he didn't have a clue about what to do with it. He'd probably been on the receiving end of that kind of treatment himself, so he knew its effectiveness, but he just didn't have it in him to take it all the way. It takes a special kind of person to pull that off, and I didn't see it in Hesam. So, in the end, rather than breaking me, I'd broken him.

My throat was sore, I had a headache, and I was fighting to keep my eyes open, but I kept talking. I'd done over an hour on my childhood in Hamilton, Ontario—a place I'd never been—and was shifting into my passion for ice hockey—a game I'd never seen—when the door burst open and a man stepped into the room. He was older than the others, probably late thirties, and better dressed, though not by much. One of the rules of the revolution seemed to be that everyone had to buy their clothes at the secondhand store.

Anyway, this guy was clearly somebody. He was followed into the room by a young girl in a chador—she couldn't have been more than seventeen—and a young man with a notebook under his arm. Hesam jumped to his feet, offered a fawning greeting to the VIP, then ushered him into a corner, explaining that I spoke enough Farsi to understand what was being said. The group huddled for a few minutes, Hesam answering the older man's questions with long, whispered soliloquies, which the young stenographer did his best to keep up with. There was a bit of back-and-forth, then, when things were resolved, they turned their attention back to me. Stepping forward, the VIP mumbled a few offhand words to the girl, which I didn't catch.

"It's been decided that since you're a Canadian citizen, you'll be released," she said in an American accent.

"Am I supposed to say thank you?"

"You'll be taken to the Canadian embassy now," she continued. "But first, we want you to sign a statement saying that you weren't mistreated in any way."

The boy with the pad produced a typewritten document, handed it to the girl, who, in turn, offered it to me. I left her hanging.

"You know, I'd love to sign it, but I've got this problem." I displayed a limp right hand. "It's completely dead. Can't feel a thing. Probably due to the lack of blood supply when my hands were tied behind my back with a nylon cord."

The VIP asked the girl for a translation and she explained it pretty much word for word. He looked me over, frowned, then shrugged it off. He had more important things to do than deal with a wiseass Canadian. He dismissed the whole thing with a wave of his hand, then spun on his heel and led his entourage out.

I had mixed feelings about my good fortune. Though I hadn't said a word to any of my fellow hostages since we'd been taken, I felt a natural affinity with them. Anyone would in that situation. It was in no way fair that I was getting a free pass when I was the least "innocent" among them, and I hated to think what awaited Donnelly, or anybody else they were able to connect to the agency. But, of course, I didn't feel bad enough to stay.

I wondered if Toby knew that I'd been taken, and whether he would have alerted the Canadians about me. Unlikely. Sovereign nations—even friendly ones like our neighbor to the north—tend to frown upon having their passports forged by foreign intelligence services. No, I was on my own. Toby had been very clear about that. I hoped that the Canucks would play along and claim me as one of their own. It'd be a shame if, after slipping through the grasp of the Muslim Students Who Follow the Line of Imam, the Canadian government blew my cover.

There was no roar from the crowd this time. Just the low hum of morning traffic from beyond the embassy wall. My sense, as I stepped back into the fresh air, was that we were somewhere near the back gate, but the blindfold made it impossible to be sure. As my escorts guided me along a gravel path, I became aware of a car idling a few feet in front of us. Then a door opened. A sliding one, like you'd find on a delivery van.

"Put him on the floor!" someone said in Farsi as we neared. *"Put the blanket over him!"*

I was bundled into the vehicle and was in the process of being shoved down between the seats when a deep, authoritative voice called out from a distance.

"Wait!"

Everyone froze.

"Take him out!" the voice commanded. *"I want to see."*

I was yanked back out of the van and spun around, to face the disembodied voice. I could sense someone standing there, a malevolent presence, breathing heavily, literally snorting as he looked me over. It didn't feel good.

"It is a Canadian," someone said, attempting an explanation without being asked. *"We have been told to take him now to that embassy."*

"Remove the blindfold."

After some nervous fumbling around, one of the guards managed to untie the strip of cloth that had been covering my eyes. Once I had adapted to the sudden surge of bright sunlight, I found myself looking into the face that had haunted me through many sleepless nights before I was finally able to bury it in some dark, distant corner of my mind. The face had changed very little since our first encounter, on that afternoon in May, in the city of Qom, twenty-six years earlier—more gray in the beard, perhaps, the face a bit more bloated, the eyes a bit more menacing—but there was no mistaking it. It was the face that had grinned with cruel amusement as I tried to protect that poor young girl from the cruel death this mad mullah had meted out to her in the name of some kind of perverted justice.

"I know this man," the cleric whispered, a look of startled recognition on his face. *"Yes, I know him. He is a spy! This man is a CIA!"*

It was true. He did know me. But not from our first encounter in Qom. That had been no more than a passing amusement for him, certainly not something he would recall twenty-six years later. No. The imam remembered me from our second encounter, two months after Qom. It was then I learned that this psychopath had been recruited to the struggle to keep democracy safe.

SIXTEEN

July 1953

Three months had passed since my encounter with Leyla and the little game of spy-counterspy with Toby had faded to nothing, lost in the day-to-day of real covert activities. I spent most of my time holding endless meetings, handing out stacks of cash to various civil servants, military men, and even a cabinet officer or two.

"He phoned," Leyla said as I came through the door that morning. "He wants to see you."

"When?"

"Now. "

"Call him back and say I'm on my way."

I found Hadi parked up the street, sitting behind the wheel with an open newspaper over his face. Rousing him with a bang on the roof, I jumped into the backseat, told him our destination, and lit a Lucky. He mumbled something unintelligible, then keyed the engine, pulled into traffic, and did a U-turn, heading toward Tehran's wealthy northern suburbs.

I was feeling uneasy about meeting the new chief. Sam, who'd headed back to Washington to take up the position of deputy director of plans, had assured me that Operation Ajax would proceed unchanged, but I was doubtful. He'd given me a lot of latitude, allowing me to operate more or less independently, and things were finally starting to pay off. The last thing I needed was some blue blood with something to prove breathing down my neck.

There was reason for concern. It turned out that the new boss, who'd arrived the previous day, in a dusty car he'd bought in Beirut and driven across a thousand miles of Syrian and Iraqi desert, wasn't James Lockridge, as advertised, but someone named Kermit Roosevelt—as in grandson of Teddy. I was half expecting to find a latter-day Rough Rider, ready to charge up San Juan Hill, flags flying and guns blazing.

Hadi swung the car into the drive, sped past the open gate, then climbed a slight incline toward the white stucco-and-stone structure that had served as base of operations for the past two months. The villa, which was leased from the Brits, had become something of a frat house under Company control, with everyone in the group (aside from me) working, sleeping, eating, and playing there. While I missed out on the camaraderie of the frat house, I liked the freedom, and hoped Roosevelt would see the advantage of maintaining the status quo.

I left Hadi stretched out in the shade of an old oak tree at the back of the house and headed across the very green lawn toward the house. The British, who love their grass, had provided a gardener as well as a cook and a maid with the house. It was assumed that their primary responsibility was to spy on us, so the guys went out of their way to insult anything English, including the newly crowned Queen

Elizabeth, whenever one of them was hovering. Like I said, a frat house.

The mid-July sun was relentless, so I took a detour, stopping at the little garden pool to splash some water on my face before I rolled down my sleeves and slipped into my jacket. The trade entrance, which was used for all comings and goings, was open, so I let myself in.

The house was quiet, to the point where it felt deserted. I paused in the vestibule to remove my sunglasses, waited for my eyes to adjust, then proceeded down a narrow, black-and-white-tiled hallway toward the front of the building. Coming in behind the mahogany staircase, I stuck my head into the formal reception room, where you could usually find someone lounging around, reading a newspaper, or listening to LPs on the combination radio/phonograph unit that was the agency's sole contribution to the men's-club decor the Brits had left behind. Finding the room empty, I stepped back into the entryway and called out from the bottom of the steps.

"Anybody home?"

Nothing. I started up the stairs, and was halfway to the second floor when a figure appeared on the landing.

"You must be Teller," he said, showing a slightly crooked, toothy smile as he stole a glance at his watch. "Come on up."

This particular Roosevelt looked more like a history teacher than a Rough Rider. In his late thirties, he had a receding nest of wiry brown hair and a face defined by a pair of thick, horn-rim glasses that made him look a bit cross-eyed. Lanky and unimposing, with a stoop that seemed to be the result of having a head too big for his narrow shoulders, he seemed completely ill at ease with his body.

"I've been looking forward to meeting you." He extended his right hand as I reached the top step.

"Same here," I said, getting a firmer grip than I'd expected.

"Kermit Roosevelt," he introduced himself. "Normally, I'd say call me Kim, but we'd better stick to J.L. I'm going by James Lockridge. You can imagine that it's not easy keeping a low profile with a name like Roosevelt."

"I'll bet. Call me Jack."

"Fine. Shall we sit outside?"

"Sure."

As far as I knew, Sam hadn't so much as opened the French doors that led onto the terrace, but that wasn't the only change I saw as we entered the room at the back that Roosevelt had taken over. There were new books on the shelf, new art on the walls, and a myriad of exotic plants scattered around the place. There was even a cat stretched out on one of the armchairs, an act that would've cost him at least one of his lives under Sam's regime.

"What would you like?" Roosevelt headed for the bar, which I was glad to see had remained intact. "There seems to be some pretty good whiskey on hand."

"Sounds good," I said.

"Neat okay?"

"Perfect."

He poured a couple of doubles into crystal tumblers. "I shouldn't, but what the hell. Best not to take the doctors too literally. They'd have you believe that the sole purpose in life is to avoid death." He handed me a glass.

"You gotta live a little if you wanna die happy."

"If I'd listened to them, I'd be lying in a hospital right now, my most pressing concern when I could stop urinating into a plastic bag. I'd much rather be here."

He threw the whiskey back, came up smiling, and allowed himself another. I followed suit and he refilled me, too. Maybe Mr. Roosevelt was more of a Rough Rider than I'd given him credit for.

There was a soft, cooling breeze blowing across the terrace that hadn't existed at ground level. Roosevelt was one of those people who seem to have a cooling breeze follow them wherever they go.

"Why don't you sit there, in the shade," he said, gesturing toward one of the four wicker armchairs that were arranged around a low-lying, circular glass table. Once I was settled, he slipped into the seat on my right and got straight to the point.

"Sam has, of course, briefed me on what you've been up to. But I'd like to hear it from you. Chapter and verse, if you will. Who, what, when, where, and why."

I started at the beginning, with my accidental meeting with Yari at the Café Pars, then explained how, over the next few weeks, I'd slowly built the relationship to the point that I was invited to the family wedding. I even recounted the story of the baby-blue Olds, which elicited a passing grin. Roosevelt's ears perked up when I mentioned that I'd run into Viktor Kerensky at the occasion.

"Did you relate that to Sam?"

I was sure that I had, but I hedged. "There wasn't much to tell," I said. "We didn't say more than two words to each other."

"It's the sort of thing that should've been in the reports." Roosevelt removed his glasses and wiped his eyes with a handkerchief.

"I guess I didn't see it as significant," I lied. Sam was Roosevelt's boss and didn't need my protection, but my instinct was to cover for him, anyway. Roosevelt dismissed the subject with a wave of his hand.

"Please continue."

I went on to describe the day trip to Qom, leaving out the grim details of the stoning, concentrating instead on Yari's long discourse on Persian history, and his passionate defense of Mossadegh. I recounted how he'd portrayed the prime minister as a man of destiny, someone who could restore to Iran a government based on the lofty principles of human rights, freedom, and democracy, as introduced by Cyrus the Great, two and a half thousand years earlier. Roosevelt was riveted, hanging on every word as I went on to describe Yari's declaration of trust, and his government's desire to go forward as partners, Iran and the United States, two great nations, with common values and a shared vision for the future of the Middle East.

"They see the oil deal as a first step in a larger alliance, perhaps leading to a regional version of NATO," I explained.

Roosevelt nodded thoughtfully and shifted in his seat. "And you feel it's genuine? You feel that you have this man's trust?"

"Yes," I said truthfully. "I do."

"Good. Very good. You've done well, Jack. And your position is going to be absolutely critical over the coming weeks."

I was ready to continue, adding to my account the profiles and judgments I'd formed about the various members of the government and military officers I'd been meeting with since then, but Roosevelt looked away—nowhere in particular, just off into the distance. I got the sense that he had something to say, so I waited. The cat appeared at his feet, and he absentmindedly reached down to scratch its head. She let out a croaky meow, demanding more, but when she tried to jump onto his lap, he shooed her away.

"You know, Jack, listening to you describe the way this man laid out his hopes and dreams, I can't help feeling a certain amount of sympathy for him, and for what he'd like to achieve. How can one not be sympathetic toward that kind of idealism? It's very appealing. I felt exactly the same when I met Mossadegh in Washington a couple of years ago. It's only natural. You must have similar sentiments."

I didn't much like the implication, which wasn't very well disguised, but there was no point in making a big deal out of it. "I'm not much of a romantic," I said.

Roosevelt smiled. "Good. Because this is an age in which

we must be realists. Our very survival depends on it. And whatever Mossadegh might or might not be, he is most assuredly not a realist."

"I've never heard him be accused of that."

Roosevelt placed his empty glass on the table, stood up, and walked to the edge of the terrace. He seemed agitated, maybe even a little annoyed, though it wasn't directed at me.

"That doesn't mean we've abandoned our ideals," he said as he turned to face me. "I'll put my passion for freedom and human rights up against Mossadegh, or anyone else in the world, for that matter. But, we . . ." He paused to tamp down his rising emotions, then continued in a more even tone. "I'm sure that I don't have to tell you, Jack, that we're up against a ruthless adversary. And an extremely dangerous one. If Joe Stalin hadn't died in March, you can bet that we'd have a lot more on our hands down here than we do now. We've got a window of opportunity while the various factions in the Kremlin fight it out. Viktor Kerensky and others like him are playing a slow game now, unsure who's going to come out on top, but you can be sure that as soon as there's a winner in Moscow, one of the first items on the agenda will be Iran. Washington feels that Mossadegh is vulnerable."

"I can't disagree," I said. The answer seemed to frustrate Roosevelt.

"Look, Jack." He sighed. "I can see that Sam was right about you, and I'm not one for these loyalty oaths that are so popular these days, but—"

"Am I now or have I ever been a member of the Communist Party?"

He gave me an unhappy look. "You've been closely involved with this group for more than three months now. I'm sure this man, Yari Fatemi, has the best of intentions. So does Mossadegh. But he's a wild card, and I intend to remove him from office in order to replace him with someone we can depend on. If you're going to be on my team, I need to know that you're willing to go all the way, Jack. It's as simple as that. There can be no half measures."

"I'm ready to go all the way," I said, looking him straight in the eye.

Roosevelt was about to respond when he was distracted by the sound of a car coming up the drive. He checked his watch again as the black sedan pulled in and parked next to my car.

Toby Walters waltzed onto the terrace like he owned it. "Hiya, Jack," he greeted me.

"Hello, Toby." I didn't bother to get up.

"How's the oil business treatin' you?"

"No complaints."

"Well, maybe you should have. You're missing all the fun stuck up there in that office."

A weary-looking Bob Cotton followed him through the door. I shot him a look. "How about it, Bob? You having nonstop fun?"

"Hello, Jack," was all he would commit to.

"Sit down, guys." Roosevelt remained standing, possibly because he wanted to stay above the fray, or maybe it was because the cat had taken over his chair. Bob sat on my left, Toby opposite, and Roosevelt leaned back against the railing, his arms crossed over his chest.

"I've asked Toby and Bob to join us, Jack, in order to look for ways that you can support each other's activities."

Judging by the smug grin plastered across Toby's face, they'd already found a way, and the point of the gathering was to let me in on it. And I had a feeling that this mutual support network would turn out to be a one-way street.

"Great," I said, sitting back to await the pitch.

"Toby," Roosevelt said, ceding the podium. "Why don't you kick off?"

Toby nodded and sat forward, taking a moment to set his brow. "As you know, Jack," he began, "one of the things Bob and I have been working on over the past couple of months is to tie the Tudeh Party in with Mossadegh's National Front. We've had quite a bit of success by using the press, putting out flyers in the Tudeh Party name, and spreading the word through various groups, like the athletic clubs and the merchants' association. We're confident that, in the public's mind, the Communist Party and the government are now seen as inseparable allies. We're helped along by the fact that Mossadegh needs these guys in his coalition, so he can't—or won't—do much to counteract the impression we're putting out there."

"He thinks he's supporting a free press," I said.

"That's certainly working in our favor," Toby agreed. "We feel that it's time to take the next step."

"Which is?"

"To start pushing the negatives up. The more we can portray the Tudeh Party as a bunch of troublemakers—anarchists and agitators—the more dissatisfaction we'll create with Mossadegh. All the bad will we can generate toward the Commies will transfer directly to him."

"Like the bomb at that mosque last week," I noted.

Toby grinned like a proud father. "We'd been making phone threats in the name of the Commies for weeks, saying if the mullahs don't start supporting Mossadegh, something like that was gonna happen. We had to make good on it."

"Nobody was hurt," Bob added.

"No, it wasn't much of a bomb." Toby shrugged, looking a bit embarrassed. "But it made the point, and every cleric in the country spent this week condemning Mossadegh for being in bed with a bunch of terrorists. Anyway, that's the sort of action we're looking for now."

"Where do I come in?"

Roosevelt took that as his cue. "Toby is proposing an action that has the potential to be a defining moment in the campaign to discredit Mossadegh. And you'd play a critical role, Jack."

"And if we pull it off . . ." Toby enthused, "it'll not only turn the entire country against Mossadegh, it'll create an enormous shift in sympathy toward the Shah."

"Pull what off?" I asked.

He smiled. "We plan to kidnap Afsharti."

"General Afsharti?"

"That's right."

I nodded coolly, but my mind was racing. It didn't make sense. In fact, it was ridiculous. Afsharti, whom I'd recruited myself, wasn't just Tehran's chief of police, he was a great supporter of the Shah and one of our strongest allies. He was an extremely valuable asset because, with all the disinformation and double-dealing games Toby was playing, the coup would come down to who owned the streets on the night. I saw what Toby was getting at, but it was a twist too far. Kidnapping such a key ally in order to gain public sympathy just wasn't worth risking the loyalty of a man who was so important to our plans. I tried to say as much, in diplomatic terms, but Toby hadn't come to listen.

"Afsharti will never know we had anything to do with it," he said. "The guys who nab him will be in black hoods, and we'll have them spouting all sorts of Commie slogans. You know, hail to the proletariat and all that crap. We'll hold him for a few days, build it up with a lot of front-page rage, then we'll release a statement from the Tudeh Party, saying they'll kill Afsharti if the Shah doesn't resign immediately."

"The Tudeh Party will deny it," I said.

"They can deny it until they're blue in the face. Maybe they'll get covered in the *Daily Worker,* but we've got all the mainstream press tied up. Bob's done a great job on that front."

Bob took the compliment with a wry smile. "It's amazing

how many editors respond to a reasonable argument, as long as it comes with a bag full of money."

I tried another tack. "Mossadegh won't sit still for it. He'll have to condemn the Tudeh Party in the harshest terms and you could end up undoing all the work you've done."

Toby looked over to Roosevelt, standing off to the side, taking it all in, then back to me. "That's where it gets absolutely diabolical," he said, a huge, shit-eating grin plastered across his face. "Mossadegh will condemn it, sure, he'll have to, but it'll just look desperate and defensive."

"Why?"

"Because he'll be implicated."

"Mossadegh? Implicated in the kidnapping?"

"As good as."

"How?"

"Afsharti is gonna be nabbed at the home of his key political operative."

I hesitated. "Do you mean—"

"That's right. Your friend Yari Fatemi."

SEVENTEEN

I had Leyla cancel my dinner engagement with the deputy minister of oil and replace it with a reservation for one at the hotel. I needed time to think things through, and the Iranshahr's tiny dining room was almost always empty. This night was the exception.

"I'd stay away from the chicken if I were you."

It took me a second to place the smoky voice of the man at the next table. Timothy Spry—the Professor, as Sam called him—had a new look. Instead of the mop of unruly, ginger hair, he now had a shiny head of lacquered black, with a neat little goatee that had been dipped in the same dark dye. The disheveled, absentminded wardrobe was gone, too, replaced by a baggy white linen suit and a pale blue cotton shirt. He gave me a moment to make the connection, then leaned over his table and produced a Cheshire-cat grin.

"Imagine finding me here!" he exclaimed in a mock whisper.

"Yeah." I smiled. "Small world."

I had no misconceptions about this being a chance meeting, of course, and I doubt that Spry thought I did, either, but we played the game, for a while anyway. I invited him to join me, he protested that he didn't want to intrude, I insisted, and he relented. Shamil, the all-purpose hotelier, quickly transferred his place setting over to my table.

"I didn't know you were in Tehran," I said once he was settled.

"Oh, I'm always around, in one way or another."

He offered a pack of Oshnu across the table, but I deferred and went for my Luckys. He lit us up, then sat back and smiled.

"So . . . What's the verdict on the new boss?"

"Too early to say."

"He comes with quite a pedigree."

"Have you met him?"

"Oh, I've known J.L. for years," he said, blowing smoke into the air.

"And what's *your* verdict?"

He flicked his cigarette in the ashtray and shrugged. "Enthusiastic. Very enthusiastic."

"That's good, isn't it?"

"Of course. Why? Did I sound insincere?"

"No more than usual."

The Professor smiled and poured a bit more beer into his glass, though it was still more than half full. "I understand you have reservations about this latest operation."

"Who told you that?"

"J.L. He rang me this afternoon. Asked me what I thought."

"About the operation?"

"About you."

"What did you tell him?"

"That I'd get back to him. *Do* you have reservations?"

"Sure, I have reservations. It's a goddamned stupid idea."

"You think so?"

"Yes, I do."

Spry took a last, long drag off his cigarette, stubbed it out in the ashtray, then shot me a cagey look. "I agree with you."

"You do?"

"It's one thing to be bold, quite another to be reckless. And this is reckless. Damned reckless. Afsharti is far too valuable to put at risk for the sake of a bit of publicity. But I have an even bigger concern than losing him."

"What?"

"Losing Fatemi. If he realizes that you've set him up, the party's over. Because if they connect you to the kidnapping, they'll connect Washington, and Mossadegh will have you all out on your ear, just as he did us."

"Did you say any of that to Lockridge?"

The Professor shrugged. "I can't."

"Can't?"

"I'm not supposed to rock the boat. You see, I take orders, too, and the feeling in London is that we shouldn't dampen enthusiasm."

"You're kidding."

"It's a direct quote. You see, it took us quite some time—over three years, in fact—to sell this project to Washington, and now that they've taken it on board, and with such zeal, the last thing my crowd wants to do is to appear negative. They want me to offer all the encouragement and support I can."

"Encouragement and support? Christ, it sounds like a mother sending her kid off to his first day at school."

The Professor grinned. "Perhaps that's not so far off the mark. At any rate, that's where it stands."

I had to laugh. "So Lockridge sent you here to take my temperature, but what you really want is to encourage me to kill the plan."

"That sums it up nicely." The Professor went into a

coughing fit, which he treated by lighting another Oshnu. I shook my head.

"What makes you think they'd listen to me?"

"Without you they've got no Fatemi."

"I don't know. Lockridge already had doubts about me. He tried to get me to say the Pledge of Allegiance this afternoon."

"Don't take that personally. He doesn't think you're a traitor. He's just concerned that you might've gone a bit native, that's all. I get that sort of thing all the time." Shamil appeared with a tray of food. Spry tore off a piece of pita bread, scooped up some hummus, and tossed it into his mouth. "You haven't, have you?"

"What?"

"Gone native."

It didn't deserve an answer, and Spry didn't press for one. Conversation turned to the historical influences on the various cuisines of the Middle East, with Professor Spry doing all of the talking while I sat there, looking across the table at this dressed-up superspy who was afraid to rock his powerful ally's boat for fear that he might be tossed overboard. I couldn't help feeling that I was seeing the sun set on the British Empire.

"What will you do, Jack?" he asked as we parted.

"I'm not sure," I answered truthfully.

It was early yet, and a cool, pleasant evening, so I decided to take a stroll before calling it a night. There was still lots of activity in the cafés and bars, but I wandered past and soon found myself standing at the main entrance to the bazaar, on Khordad Avenue. I decided to see if my old *takhte-nard* partners were in residence at Café Naderi.

"Jak-eh!" They greeted me like the Prodigal Son. "Where you gone? You have forgotten your friends!"

"Not in a million years!" I said, feeling my spirits rise as I was plunked down at a table to face my old instructor, Saleh, the Champion of Tehran. The eighty-seven-year-old wasted no time bringing me up-to-date on local politics, launching into it before the first roll of the dice.

"Mossadegh is cheater and thief!" he proclaimed. "He makes a business with these Communists. Yes, it is a fact! The British have paid too little for the oil, but Mossadegh will give to these Russians, free of charge! I believe he is himself a Communist! Yes, there can be no doubt of it!"

Toby and Bob had done their work well, I thought. One or two of the old men were skeptical, but they were quickly shouted down by the others. The final blow was dealt when Naderi himself handed out free drinks in order to toast the Shah, who "must be given a stronger hand to deal with these leftist troublemakers." The feeling was pretty much unanimous after that.

As I made my way back to the hotel, in the now quiet streets, I thought about something else Saleh had said. He'd pulled me aside as I was leaving, his expression so weighty that it looked as though he was about to impart the world's wisdom to my ears, and mine alone. He'd put his hand on my shoulder, fixed me with his old eyes, and sighed. "You are a very lucky, in United States," he said. "And it is because you have the leaders who give their respects to the people. Here, in Iran, it is not so."

It would've been easy to laugh off the old man's sentiments. Leaders who have respect for their people? Whoever heard of such a thing? Crazy! But I didn't laugh. Quite the contrary. Because, in the end, it really wasn't all that crazy. In fact, it kind of struck home. America wasn't anything like the utopia that Saleh and his friends imagined, of course, but there was a reason that they, and much of the world, looked to it with such hope and admiration. It wasn't that we had better men to be our leaders. God, no. Nor was it that our leaders had an unwavering respect for the American people. Certainly not. No, it wasn't the men who walked the halls of Congress or filled the offices of the White House that made Saleh admire America. It was the system.

The Constitution of the United States begins with these words:

> *We the People of the United States, in Order to form a more perfect Union, establish Justice, insure domestic Tranquility, provide for the common defence, promote the general Welfare, and secure the Blessings of Liberty to ourselves and our Posterity, do ordain and establish this Constitution for the United States of America.*

Quite a sentence. Did it mean that the country was a beacon of peace and harmony? Or that there actually was equal justice for all? Or that the blessing of liberty was never abused? No. Not by a long shot. You didn't have to go as far as Montgomery, Alabama, to see the injustices that America piled onto its people, and a cursory look through J. Edgar Hoover's private files would be enough for any American to see what their liberty was up against. But when men with power, who wanted more power, played fast and loose with the Constitution, the last say was reserved for the people. The normal, everyday people you see wherever you go. Teachers, salesmen, farmers, nurses, cops. The family upstairs and the nice couple next door. These were people who didn't seek power, and because of that, they were the only ones who could be trusted with it. Sometimes it took them a while to catch on to the greed or arrogance of their leaders, but they always seemed to get it in the end. And when they decided it was time to stand up and fight the good fight, they had the system on their side.

That was what Yari and Mossadegh were fighting to achieve for the people of Iran. It was a noble goal, and, sure, I respected them for pursuing it. How could any freedom-loving person not? If that's all that "going native" meant, then, okay, maybe I had. But what stuck in my craw—*what really pissed me off*—was the insinuation that I would let my sympathy for their cause blind me to what we were doing and why we were doing it.

I wasn't, and never had been, the flag-waving kind of patriot, but when it counted, I didn't hesitate to pick up a gun and fight for my country. I hadn't put my life on the line for anyone named Roosevelt, though, or for any other of those leaders who, according to Saleh, had so much respect for the people. No, like a million other guys, I fought for the idea. For "*We the people.*" It was what allowed me to believe that all those great sacrifices I'd witnessed had been worth something.

Now we were in another war. A very different kind of war, to be sure, but a war just the same. This was a quiet, insidious war, but the enemy was no less malevolent and just as dangerous as it had been a decade earlier. And the consequences of defeat would be even more devastating.

Maybe Roosevelt was wrong when he said that the times called for realists. Maybe we needed a little more romanticism, a little more idealism. Or maybe it was the other way around, and we thought we were being realists when, in fact, we were just a bunch of wild-eyed romantics, carrying the flag of freedom around the world, and not afraid to beat people down with it if they got in our way. I don't know the answer. I know that my sympathy for Yari's cause was real, but I didn't believe they could pull it off. He saw Iran as an ancient land, the birthplace of human rights, a country that could be great again. I saw it as a battleground, part of a bigger struggle, in which his dreams of democracy would have to be sacrificed in the name of democracy.

I guess all that doesn't matter now. Whatever my rationale, on that summer night in Tehran, in July of 1953, I decided to be a good soldier.

EIGHTEEN

General Mohammad Afsharti had a big, rectangular head, with watchful eyes that peered out from below a set of thick black eyebrows. An intelligent man, with a reserved manner, he had an unmistakable family resemblance to the Shah, but unlike his distant cousin, who was known as a weak, vacillating man, Afsharti was like a rock. He knew people, and how to make them do what he wanted them to do. A handy trait in any chief of police, but particularly useful in Tehran, where the position was more complicated than just keeping the peace.

I'd established a good rapport with him, and though he wasn't aware of the full extent of what we were up to, he'd been more than happy to cooperate when he could, such as when I suggested the Tudeh Party might've had a hand in the mosque bombing. He'd smiled cannily and shrugged his shoulders, but the next day a half-dozen members of the party were rounded up and tossed into prison.

Yari didn't like him. Or, more accurately, he didn't trust

him—and for good reason. Afsharti scoffed at Mossadegh and his dreams of democracy. He saw the prime minister as a weak old man, a dangerous poet who was leading the country down the garden path, at the end of which lay total ruin. I'd lent a sympathetic ear to many hours of his well-considered arguments, all of which boiled down to one simple idea. General Afsharti thought his fellow citizens were incapable of participating in the kind of free society Mossadegh envisioned.

"Iran is not like America, or France, or Britain," he'd said to me. "The Iranian people are like children, and must be treated as such. They must be shown a strong hand, and know that it will be used against them when they misbehave."

The general made no secret of his contempt, either, openly ridiculing Mossadegh every chance he had, which made it something of a challenge to convince Yari that he should host a dinner in honor of the chief of police. I made the proposal under the pretense that some of the Americo executives back in New York were expressing reservations about the deal, fearing that Iran's internal politics were too shaky to invest the kind of money we were talking about. The dinner, I'd argued, would help put my colleagues' minds at ease. Besides, I counseled, quoting the old Chinese adage, "A wise man keeps his friends close, but his enemies closer."

Yari had listened carefully, but not said a word. I'd let it go for a couple of days, then, just as I was about to bring up the subject again, he'd surprised me by announcing that the dinner would take place the following week. I wondered if my argument had won him over, or if Mossadegh had overruled him, but it didn't really matter. One way or another, we were on.

There was unusually light traffic in the city, and we arrived in the suburbs almost a half hour early. Not wishing to have too much time alone with Yari before Afsharti arrived, I asked Hadi to take us for a spin around the neighborhood.

"Sure," he said, flashing a smile in the mirror. "I can to show you something."

"What?"

"I show you."

I sat back and breathed in the richly perfumed evening air as we drove north, up a gently winding road that was lined with tall pine trees then west along a dark track that skirted the side of the mountain. After a few twists and turns, we reached a clearing, where Hadi pulled up and engaged the hand brake.

"Come," he said, rushing out into the gathering darkness. "You will see something."

I followed to the edge of a cliff where I saw, laid out below us, the sparkling lights of Tehran, stretching out from the foothills of the Alborz Mountains to the silky stillness of the Dasht-e-Kavīr desert beyond. A full moon rising cast a soft, pale light across the city, imbuing it with a ghostly depth that was out of character for the normally spiritless mass of concrete. It was quite a sight. The kind that takes you out of yourself, allowing you a moment of that sense of timeless wonder that's so difficult to hold on to. We stood there for a moment, side by side, silently taking it in, then Hadi drew in a lungful of clean, mountain air.

"By the light of a thousand candles"—he sighed—"even the camel is a princess."

I smiled and nodded, and then I had to stop and laugh. For Christ's sake, I thought. I'm actually starting to understand this stuff.

"You're late," Zahra gently scolded me as I came through the door.

"How long has he been here?"

"Ten minutes."

"Is everybody happy?"

"Happy is perhaps asking too much."

"I'd better go stand between them before civil war breaks out."

She led me up the hallway, toward the door that opened onto the courtyard. "We haven't seen each other in so long, Jack . . ." She tried to sound lighthearted, but failed miserably. "Promise me that we can speak tonight."

"Sure," I said. "We'll have a long talk later."

She stopped short of the door and turned to face me. "Have you spoken with Yari yet? About me? They . . . they are planning my wedding and I . . ." She started to break down. "I can't marry this man, Jack . . . I . . . I don't love him."

Her emotion was bubbling over, tears welling up in her eyes. I wasn't ready for it, and was at a loss. I pulled her aside.

"I . . . I love another man," she said. "Please, Jack, you are the only one who can understand. You are the only one who can help me. Yari will listen to you . . ."

"I understand," I said, giving her my handkerchief. "We'll . . . we'll work something out. We'll have a long talk about it. Tonight. I promise." She nodded and attempted a smile. I hesitated, but there was nothing else I could do, not then, so I gave her a kiss on the cheek and stepped through the door.

The courtyard was set up for lavish dining under the stars. A long banquet table, laid with sparkling silver and three colossal floral arrangements, was placed in front of an ivy-covered stone wall, with eight smaller tables, seating six each, clustered around it. The invited guests stood in small cliques, drinks in hand, engaging in quiet conversation while a string quartet played soft Western music in the background. A ring of oil-fired torches encircled the setting, which lent a strange, ritualistic quality to the scene.

"Jack . . ." Yari rushed over as soon as I appeared, looking more than a bit relieved. "Why are you late?"

"Traffic," I apologized.

He took me by the arm and pulled me over to his group, whispering along the way that the next time I wanted to give a dinner in honor of an ass, I could do it on my own. Afsharti lived up to the characterization by greeting me with cool arrogance, presumably because I'd upstaged him with my late entrance. I couldn't help thinking, with some satisfaction, that he might not be so puffed up by the end of the evening.

I was introduced around to the collection of politicians and prominent businessmen, some of whom I'd run into at other occasions, then the small talk resumed. I struck a listening pose, nodding and smiling on cue as I stole furtive glances around the area, trying to pick up clues about how Toby had set things up. He'd been reluctant to give me operational details, claiming the fewer specifics I knew, the more authentic my reaction would be when "all hell broke loose," as he put it. There was some truth to that, and it would've been a waste of time to argue the point, anyway, so I'd let it go.

The bodyguards weren't hard to spot. Afsharti often had as many as a dozen thugs following him around, but it looked like Toby's assumption that he wouldn't bring his entire security detail into the home of a government official had been on the mark. There were just four of them, one at each corner of the courtyard, an identical "don't fuck with me" look fixed to his face. So far, so good. Still, I knew that each would have a Browning 9mm Parabellum semiautomatic under his coat, with a spare clip in his pocket. With more than a hundred rounds between them, they could create one hell of a cross fire.

A boy of about twelve came through the crowd ringing a small chime, signaling the start of dinner. As guest of honor, Afsharti was seated at the center of the main table, with Yari on his left and me to his right. After a shaky start, the general and his host seemed to find some common ground and they spent the rest of the meal absorbed in a deep discussion, leaving me to a fat banker's tale of his family's Caspian Sea adventure. It was a very, very long adventure.

Once the plates had been cleared away, the after-dinner speeches began. Various dignitaries, including the mayor of Tehran and a couple of members of the Majlis (the Iranian parliament), rose to offer long-winded tributes to the honoree, each man feeling the need to find prose that soared higher and praise that went further than his predecessor's lofty citations. Afsharti sat there, stone-faced, coolly accepting each eminent, illustrious, resplendent superlative with cool aplomb, as if it was all too obvious to merit acknowledgment. When the last of the silver-tongued sycophants finally sat down, and there seemed to be nothing left to say, Yari got to his feet.

"I, too, would like to say a few words," he declared as an anxious silence descended over the group. No one knew what they were about to hear, but it was certain to be more than just another empty testimonial.

"I hope that General Afsharti will be kind enough to forgive me if I don't simply repeat all the wonderful things that have been said about him tonight. I'm certain that they are all true, but . . . Well, I would like to speak along slightly different lines . . ."

He paused, perhaps to get his thoughts in order, or maybe it was just to set the stage, but whatever the reason, he had the group's rapt attention. The only sound was the soft swish of the trees as they turned in the gentle evening breeze, the only movement the gentle flutter of the yellow flames as they danced atop their wooden stakes.

"Perhaps I should start with a confession." Yari's voice cut through the tension. "It was not my idea to honor General Afsharti with this banquet. In fact, I resisted the idea. Perhaps that is shocking for you to hear, but I think it is not the statement that surprises, but the fact that I would express it so openly. Let me try to explain why I have chosen to do so.

"It will surprise none of you to hear that I disagree with the general on most subjects. In fact, our politics could not be further apart. I deeply disagree with his beliefs about what our country should be, and he disagrees with mine."

I stole a glance at Afsharti, who was as entranced as the rest of the guests. His eyes were locked onto Yari as he waited to see where this was going.

"General Afsharti believes that the people of Iran need a strong hand," Yari continued. "I believe that they need a strong voice. Perhaps that is an oversimplification, but I think it comes close to describing our differences. While I dream of a democracy based on the values of individual rights and equal justice, General Afsharti sees the need for a society based on order and security. These are genuine, strongly held differences about what kind of Iran we want to build in this postimperialist world, and the disagreement must not be underestimated. It is significant.

"The general and I have met on several occasions in the past. In each instance, a few polite words were spoken, then we hurried to escape each other's presence. We left our disagreements to be carried out through proxies, in the newspapers and in the Majlis, where the purpose is never to bring us together, but to push us further apart. Tonight has been different. Tonight, we have not been able to escape from each other."

Yari smiled and a hesitant, nervous laughter arose from the audience. I noticed that even Afsharti couldn't hold back a tiny grin.

"Tonight, at this table . . ." Yari raised his voice a notch. "General Afsharti and I have been able to engage in an honest exchange of views. We have both spoken, but more important, we have both listened. I have found him to be an intelligent, thoughtful, and selfless man. A man who takes his duty very seriously. What I had previously seen as arrogance and intransigence are, I have learned, pride and determination. Qualities that are to be admired. Don't misunderstand me. My views have not changed. I still disagree with the general on many of the serious issues we face, but I have tonight seen that his ideas, like mine, are born of nothing other than a desire to build a better future for the people of Iran. Yes, there are many parties in Iran who strongly disagree with each other, but it is important that we remember—we must remember—that our differences are outweighed by something that we share: a deep and unshakable love for our country.

"Perhaps the most important lesson I have taken from this night is the simplest one. That we must *speak* with each other. And we must *listen*. For what is the alternative? What will we do if we do not talk with each other? There is only one answer. We will fight. And when we fight among ourselves, we become weak, allowing others to prey on us, as they have done for so many years.

"General Afsharti and I agree about one thing. Iran must be strong. And we are stronger when we are together. We need not always agree about everything, but we must work with each other. We need not choose between black and white. Let us talk together, and perhaps we will find a gray area on which to build a future for our children. Let us talk and listen and let us honor each other. So, with that, it is my pleasure tonight to honor General Afsharti. A great patriot for Iran."

A deadly silence greeted Yari as he took his seat. This was too different, too far removed from the norm. Too honest! They had no idea how to respond, and no one dared be the first. Then, just as the weight of the silence was about to become crushing, Afsharti got to his feet. He stood there for a very long moment, perfectly still, a dark and indecipherable expression fixed to his face. I thought he might turn and walk out, or worse, sneer at Yari's childlike naïveté. But he did neither. He nodded his head, almost imperceptibly, then lifted his hands, and started to clap. Alone, at first, then joined by one, and another, and yet another, until, finally, the floodgates opened and we were all on our feet, offering a standing ovation. When Yari stood to accept the accolade, General Afsharti shook his hand, causing an even greater cheer to rise up from the crowd. That's when it started.

Bang! Bang! Bang! Bang!

Four shots, in rapid succession. Everything stopped. Every movement, every breath, every thought, frozen, in a state of suspended animation for one long-drawn-out fraction of a second. Then, as Toby had promised, all hell broke loose. Women shrieked and glass shattered as people threw themselves to the ground in a mad scramble to get under the tables.

Damn it! I thought. *It's gone wrong!*

But it hadn't, of course. It was happening exactly as Toby had planned it. A hooded gunman stood in the middle of the courtyard, his Soviet-made Tokarev SVT semiautomatic rifle pointing into the night sky. He fired off a couple more rounds, either to keep the guests under the tables or as a warning to Yari, the general, and me, who were the only people left standing. A second gunman appeared out of the darkness and trained his weapon on the three of us, then a third man, this one unarmed, stepped forward. I guessed from the way the others looked to him that he was in charge, and he confirmed it when he started barking orders at us.

"Don't move!" he yelled in Farsi. *"Don't speak and don't move!"*

"What are you doing?!" Yari spat back. *"How dare you come into my home and . . . Get out! Get out immediately!"*

"Don't speak I said!" The leader was screaming at the top of his lungs and waving his arms around like a madman. *"DON'T SPEAK AND DON'T MOVE!"*

I quickly scanned the courtyard, spotted one of the general's bodyguards laid out on his back under a tree. I could see that he was breathing, and that the handle of a broken cup was hanging off his index finger, as if he'd keeled over in mid-sip and shattered the cup in the fall. A second was in a similar position in the opposite corner, and I assumed the other two wouldn't be far away. I noted that the catering staff was nowhere to be seen, and assumed they'd made a quick exit after tea was served.

It all happened quickly from there. A fourth and fifth abductor appeared from inside the house. They raced toward the table as the two armed men kept us in their sights from about ten yards away, then split up and swung around opposite ends of the table so they could approach from both sides.

"Where is my family?" Yari demanded, his fist clenched with rage.

"Quiet!"

The two unarmed men came up from behind and yanked Afsharti aside. Working quickly, one pulled a black hood over his head, the other bound his hands behind his back. I wasn't sure if Afsharti was too shocked to resist, or if he was simply managing the moment with exceptional dignity, but he just stood there, stiffly accepting the assault.

Yari, on the other hand, was losing control. Sensing what was about to happen, I reached out, tried to get hold of his arm, but it was too late. He spun away, shot forward, and shoved one of the kidnappers aside, hitting him with such force that he was knocked off his feet. The man fell backward and hit the ground with a loud *thud,* knocking the air out of him. The second intruder, taken by surprise, took a quick step back, leaving the general free, but blind. Yari coolly stepped forward and started to remove the rope from his hands.

"STOP!" the leader cried out. *"STOP WHAT YOU ARE DOING!"* Yari shot him a contemptuous look as he continued to untie the general. *"SHOOT HIM!"* the leader ordered. The two gunmen took aim, and I quickly stepped in front of the rifles. Christ, I thought, I hope to hell these guys know who I am.

"Take it easy," I said as calmly as I could. "No one needs to get hurt here . . ."

It seemed to work; the leader signaled his men to back off. I breathed a sigh of relief, and was turning to Yari, hoping I could calm him down, too, when the man who'd been knocked down came flying out of nowhere and buried his shoulder in Yari's side. The pair went sailing through the air, landed hard on the banquet table, and tumbled to earth on the opposite side.

I leaped across, found the hooded man sitting on Yari's chest, using a silver candelabra to pummel him with blow after merciless blow across the side of his face. Yari was bleeding heavily and losing consciousness and I could see that a couple more blows would finish him off.

Before I knew what I was doing, I had the attacker in a choke hold. I jerked him away, and heard a loud, sickening *crack.* I knew right away that I'd snapped his neck. When I released him, he fell in a lifeless heap onto the courtyard tiles.

The next thing I felt was the cold metal of a rifle barrel pressing against my right ear. The man who was holding it seemed to have gone mad, screaming wild invectives, cursing me and crying about his brother, who I assumed was the guy I'd just killed. I held my breath and had what I was sure would be my last thought—

"No!" The leader raced forward and pushed the gun away from my head. *"Not him!"* he said. *"He cannot be harmed!"*

I could feel Yari watching me as the intruders gathered up their dead partner and escaped with General Afsharti in tow. When I turned to meet his stare, I saw that, though his face was covered in blood and swollen with bruises, the real pain was in his eyes, when he looked at me.

NINETEEN

"It's a shame you had to kill him, but these things happen. No harm done." Toby was still in his bathrobe when he greeted me at the door of the safe house.

"His brother didn't see it that way," I said.

"You had no choice, right?"

"Right."

"Well then."

I followed him into the dining room, where we found Al Keating and Bob Cotton at the table, each with a cup of coffee and a bowl of Kellogg's Corn Flakes (shipped in from Washington) in front of them. Bob said hi while Al kept his nose buried in the morning paper. The only one of us to come close to mastering Farsi, Al served as the group's eyes and ears on the local scene.

"Ah, the reviews are in!" Toby bellowed, showing a bear-size grin. "How'd we do?"

"Everything we asked for and more."

Bob picked up a copy of *Kayhan,* Tehran's most popular

daily, and shoved it in front of Al. "Read it to them," he said. Al waited until we'd settled into our seats, then read the lead story out, providing a halting translation as he went:

Last night, at the home of Yari Fatemi, who is one of Prime Minister Mossadegh's most influential advisors, a group of leftist hoodlums broke into a dinner party being held in honor of General Mohammad Afsharti, and kidnapped at gunpoint the popular chief of the Tehran police force. General Afsharti, who is a strong supporter of the Shah, has made great strides in battling the criminals and Communists who have been trying to disrupt life in our capital. The general has been the target of strong attacks from the Tudeh Party since five of its members were arrested, two weeks ago, for carrying out the bomb attack at the Soltani mosque. Informed sources believe that the abduction is a response to those arrests . . .

"Bob wrote most of it," Toby interjected as he poured himself a bowl of flakes. "But I put that part in. Informed sources. Funny, huh?"

"The editorial is even better," Al said.

"Let's hear it."

He found the page and folded the paper back. "I'll skip to the important part," he said, skimming down to the article's second paragraph.

Can it be a coincidence that this cowardly act took place at the home of one of the most important officials in Mossadegh's government? There is no proof, of course, that men loyal to the prime minister planned and carried out this evil act, but there can be no doubt that the government's weak policies and close ties to the Communist anarchists contributed to the lawless atmosphere that has allowed such crimes to take place.

Therefore, it is right and just that the good people of Iran lay the blame for this terrible deed at the doorstep of their prime minister, Mohammad Mossadegh.

"Excellent!" Toby crowed. "Did we write that one?"

"No, they did that on their own," Bob said.

"Well, that's a fucking home run if ever there was one." He turned to me. "Didn't I say this'd be big?"

"We got lucky," I said.

Toby finished chewing a mouthful of cereal before answering. "Hey, you saved the day, Jack. No doubt about that. Nice going."

"Yeah, Jack. Good job," Bob echoed. "How's Fatemi doing? We heard he got quite a beating."

"I'm going over to see him later this morning."

"He's gonna live, right?" Toby said. "It wouldn't help us sell the story if he was killed by the guys he's supposed to be in league with. Fortunately, we've been able to keep the fact that he's in the hospital out of the papers."

"Except for *Bakhtar Enrooz,*" Bob interjected. Toby dismissed it with a wave of his hand.

"Nobody reads that piece of shit except for hard-core Mossadegh lovers, and we're never gonna get them."

Toby picked up a copy of the *Tehran Journal,* the only English-language paper in Iran, and except for the crunching of cornflakes, the room fell silent. I poured myself a coffee, but shoved it aside after a couple of sips. I guess I'd gotten too used to the thick shots of Turkish they served in the coffeehouses.

"Where's Afsharti?" I asked after a couple of minutes. Toby looked up from his reading, and paused long enough to decide how he should answer.

"We've got him in a cave, a few miles outside the city."

"Who's watching him?"

"What d'ya mean?"

"Same crew as last night?"

"Yeah. Same guys."

"You feel okay about that?"

He let the paper drop to the table and gave me a "butt out" look. "I appreciate your concern, Jack, but we've got everything under control."

"Like last night?" I said. Toby studied me for a moment, then cleared his throat.

"I can understand why this threw you, but you shouldn't let it get to you. The guy you killed was a nobody. Don't let it upset you."

"I'm not upset," I said. "I'm concerned."

"Well . . ." Toby stretched the word out as he forced a smile. "You shouldn't be. Like I said, it's all under control."

"That's what you said about last night and we ended up almost killing our most important asset."

Toby took a deep, unhappy breath, then leaned forward onto the table, putting all his weight onto his elbows. "I appreciate you coming over so early to give us your thoughts, Jack, but your part in this operation is over now. You did great, but you don't have to worry about it anymore. Really."

Bob stepped in before I had a chance to respond. "What are you concerned about, Jack?" he said, earning a poisonous scowl from Toby.

"Afsharti," I said.

"What about him?"

"That crowd you sent in there wasn't exactly the most professional—"

"They're supposed to be anarchists," Toby growled. "Who the hell did you expect us to use? The local Boy Scout troop?"

"You're putting Afsharti at risk by letting those guys hold on to him," I said.

"Look, Jack . . ." Toby was trying to hold on to his cool, but he was losing the battle. "There are things you don't know about this operation. Things that you don't need to know. So it'd be a whole lot better all around if you spent your time worrying about things that you do know about. Like keeping Fatemi sweet."

I held my tongue. It wasn't easy, but I did. Unloading on Toby might make me feel better, but it would only make matters worse, so I smiled sweetly and swallowed hard.

"Sure," I said, pushing away from the table. I was about to make a quick exit when the sight of Toby's big, fat, supercilious, gloating grin made me reconsider. Diplomacy only goes so far.

"I'll tell you what," I said, pausing at the door. "Since you're either too dumb or too damned arrogant to do anything about it, I'll take care of it myself."

Toby looked a bit stunned, but he recovered quickly. "Stay the hell out of this, Jack," he said darkly. "I mean it. I'll fucking bury you."

"Yeah, well, to tell you the truth, Toby . . . ." I met his angry glare with an easy smile. "That'd be a hell of a lot more scary if you didn't have a wet cornflake hanging off your chin."

Toby didn't move, but I could feel his eyes burning into my back as I headed out the door. I would've paid a lot of money to see the look on his face when he reached up and found that stray piece of cereal.

"Wait up, Jack!"

I was halfway to the car when Bob called after me. I slipped behind my sunglasses as I waited for him to cross the lawn.

"What are you gonna do?" he asked. The truth was that I had absolutely no idea, but I wasn't gonna tell him that.

"Did Toby tell you to ask me that?"

"Christ, Jack," he said, looking a bit crestfallen. "Give me some credit."

"Sorry. What the hell's his problem, anyway?"

"Don't take it personally. Toby's just—"

"An asshole."

He smiled. "Right. But a talented one."

"I'm glad you think so."

Bob rotated his body around slightly so that his back faced the house, and lowered his voice a notch. "Look," he said, "I agree with you about Afsharti."

"You could've said something in there."

"It wouldn't have made any difference. You know how he is. The more you challenge him, the more he digs his heels in."

"Yeah, well, he's digging us a big fucking hole, that's what he's doing. He's already dug me one."

"How do you mean?"

"Yari knows it was a setup."

"Does he know you were involved?"

"He suspects it."

"Damn. Think he'll go to Mossadegh?"

"Not until he's sure. But then he will."

"You've got to keep him from being sure."

"Yeah, I know what I have to do. What about Afsharti?"

"Well . . . We were planning on holding him for a week or two, milk the story for all it's worth, but maybe we should cut it short, stage the rescue in the next couple of days."

"Can you get Toby to go along?"

"I doubt it."

"So . . . ?"

"We'll have to talk to J.L."

"When?"

"The sooner the better, I guess. He plays tennis over at the Turkish embassy every morning, but he's usually back by ten-thirty. Let's say eleven. You, me, and Toby. We'll lay it out for him. Toby won't like it, but what the hell, he doesn't have to like everything."

We shook hands and I headed for the car, feeling a little bit better. Calmer, anyway. Hadi sat up, tossed his newspaper aside, and had the car in gear by the time I sat down.

"To office?" he asked.

"The hospital."

He nodded, pulled away from the curb, did a one-eighty, and sped off. I'd intended to visit Yari later in the day, but I wanted to have a better sense about where we stood before seeing Roosevelt. If Yari was planning to talk to Mossadegh, we'd have to make quick plans.

"You have seen these stories?" Hadi said once we were under way. "It is in the front page of all the newspaper."

"Yeah, big news," I said.

He shook his head in disgust. "It is terrible!"

"What?"

"These Communists! Who in the *hell* do they think they are?"

"You figure it was them, huh?"

"Of course! Who else? They have made revenge. First, they put a bomb in the Soltani mosque, and when they are arrested, they kill the chief of the police!"

"They didn't kill him," I pointed out.

"Yes, but he will be dead." Hadi pointed his finger at the heavens. "You can be certain of it. And this crime will be at the door of Mossadegh himself! He is too weak with these Communists. It needs a strong hand, like of the Shah. I promise you, he will know how to treat with these criminals!"

It was a small room, but neat and clean. Pleasant enough, as hospitals go. A half-open window allowed a hint of warm summer breeze to drift in, providing welcome relief from the stale, antiseptic air that permeated the rest of the building. Yari was dressed and sitting up on the edge of the bed, the left side of his face covered in bandages. He could barely move his head from side to side, but he managed something approaching a smile when I entered.

"Ah! Here is the man who saved my life," he announced to the gathering, which consisted of his wife, his father, Zahra, and two young nurses. Each mumbled a bit of half-hearted praise then the mood sank back into glum.

"I'm going home," Yari said.

"If the doctor allows it," Zahra quickly added.

"He will allow it."

Zahra made a disapproving face, then looked to me. "We are awaiting the X-rays."

"To know if my head is as broken as it feels."

"Well, you look a lot better than you did last night," I said, in a clumsy stab at lighthearted. Yari offered a faint smile then looked around the room.

"Can you excuse us, please?" he said. "Jack and I would like to speak alone for a few moments."

Zahra ushered everyone out and I pulled up the hard wooden chair that Yari's father had vacated.

"You've seen the newspapers?" Yari said, avoiding eye contact.

"Yes," I replied. "I saw enough."

"Quite effective, wouldn't you say?"

"How do you mean?" I said, putting on a puzzled face.

He gave me a scolding look, but I thought I'd better wait to hear what he had to say before attempting any denials. Yari was in no hurry, though. He pulled himself off the bed, went to the window, and stood there, peering out at nothing in particular for what seemed like a very long time before finally turning back to face me.

"You know, Jack," he began, "as I lay here last night, in the dark, I tried very hard to persuade myself that I was wrong about you. That I hadn't heard what I thought I heard.

I was nearly able to do it, too. After all, I told myself, I had been in a state of shock. I could easily have misunderstood or misinterpreted what was said. But the words kept coming back to me, playing over and over in my mind, so very clearly—*'No, not him . . . He cannot be harmed.'* What struck me was the way in which he emphasized the word *him*. This man knew you, or, at the least, he knew who you were."

"Lots of people know who I am."

"Yes, I told myself this, as well. It's a very good argument. You are an important man, and well known in Tehran. It makes perfect sense that those men would know who you are, and it stands to reason that they wouldn't want to involve the United States in their crime. So I decided to dismiss this uneasy feeling I had. But it's not as simple as that, is it? Suspicion is like an unwelcome guest. Once it arrives, it is difficult to make it leave."

Moving a little too suddenly, Yari tried to sit back down again, and winced in pain. He paused to draw a deep breath before continuing.

"I asked myself, how could this have happened? How could these people with guns have entered so easily into my home? Where were General Afsharti's bodyguards? Had they been killed? Had they conspired with the intruders? And who were these men? What did they hope to gain with this act of insanity? All these questions, and many more, filled my head, but I could do nothing. Nothing but lie there, in the dark, and wait for the morning, when I could speak with the police. But, as it turned out, I didn't have to wait for the police. Zahra gave me the answer."

"Zahra?"

"Yes. One innocent comment from her and everything became clear. I didn't know it at the time, but she had refused to leave the hospital. She stayed here last night, all night, sitting on a chair outside my door. I don't even know what time it was when she came in to check on me, but when she found that I was awake, she sat down beside me and we began to talk. You know what it is with women. Nothing important. Just talk.

"I asked her about our guests. I wanted to know if any had been injured." He couldn't help smiling to himself. "She told me, no, that I was the only one foolish enough to argue with armed men who wore hoods over their heads. Then she said that even the bodyguards had been fine—once they woke up. Of course I understood the meaning immediately, and I asked Zahra if there were any police officers nearby. There were two, she told me, just outside the door, so I asked her to bring them into the room.

"I told the officers that they were to go to my house and arrest all the kitchen staff. I wanted all of them—even the cook, who has been with our family for more than thirty years—to be detained.

"Zahra was horrified. She couldn't believe what I was saying. You must understand, Jack, that these people are not like servants. They are as part of our family. I tried to calm her and explain that, although it seemed impossible, there was no other explanation. One of them, or perhaps more than one, had given those bodyguards a drug to make them sleep. At least one of my servants was part of the conspiracy.

" 'It's not true,' she said to me. 'It's impossible. None of them could have been involved. Don't you remember, Yari?' she said. 'It was such a panic, the night before the dinner. In the middle of the preparations, all of the kitchen staff became ill. Have you forgotten?'

"I had forgotten. I suppose the blows to my head had knocked it out of my memory. But I remembered then. They had become ill, all six of them, at the same time. A stomach virus, I thought at the time. Unfortunate, but not suspicious. Now, of course, the significance was unavoidable. I asked Zahra where we found the replacements for our kitchen staff."

Yari paused to study me for a moment. There wasn't so much pain in his expression now, as there was sadness.

"Do you know what she told me?"

"No," I said truthfully. "I don't."

"The girl in your office gave the recommendation," he said. "We got the names from her. I believe her name is Leyla."

TWENTY

Toby. *Fucking Toby!*

I'd known from the moment I saw those snoozing bodyguards that they'd been served something stronger than sugar in their tea, and I'd assumed that Toby had been behind it, but things had been happening so fast that I'd skipped over the how. It was clear now that he'd organized the illness for Yari's kitchen staff, then had Leyla arrange for his crowd to take over.

Goddammit!

I wasn't surprised about Leyla. She'd play for whatever side seemed to be winning. What did surprise me, though—*what pissed me off!*—was that Toby would make such a lamebrained move! His ham-fisted grandstanding was about to blow everything.

"Is there anything you'd like to tell me?" Yari said after laying out the trail of guilt that led to my door. I didn't bother with any protestations of innocence. We were beyond that kind of charade.

"I'm glad you're feeling well enough to go home," I said, standing up. "Naturally, I'll look into all this and let you know what I find out."

"That won't be necessary," Yari responded coolly. "We'll get to the bottom of it soon enough. I'm afraid I've had to ask the police to arrest your secretary."

Poor Leyla, I thought. She'd made her own bed, of course, but I knew what they'd do to her, and she would never be the same. It wouldn't take long to break her, either, and once she talked, Yari would go straight to Mossadegh.

Operation Ajax was about to come unraveled.

"Jack!"

Bob Cotton came running out of the house as we pulled into the driveway. He headed for his black sedan and waved me over.

"Come on! We gotta hurry!"

I told Hadi to wait there, at the safe house, then got out of the car and ran over.

"Jump in!" Bob said, reaching across to open the passenger door. I slid in beside him.

"What's up?"

He didn't answer until he'd gunned the engine and we were barreling down the suburban road at sixty miles an hour.

"We've got problems."

"Afsharti?" I said, holding on to the dashboard as we took a hard corner without brakes.

"He's dead." Bob seemed to think that would surprise me, but it didn't. In fact, it seemed inevitable.

"How?" I asked.

"I'm not sure. Toby got a call and ran out the door. I was waiting for you."

"Christ . . ." was all I could say.

Bob got a little confused with the directions, but after

a couple of wrong turns, he finally found the narrow road that led up into the mountains. After twenty minutes, the cracked asphalt disappeared and we were bouncing along a dry mule path, kicking up a cloud of dust that covered everything, including the back of my throat. About a mile on, we finally swung around to the left, into a long incline. Bob gunned the engine, picking his way around patches of dry brush and large granite boulders as we climbed to the crest of the hill.

A long, dry valley came into view, stretching out into the sun-drenched distance. Bob slipped the car into neutral and we coasted down the gentle slope for a couple of minutes, until we came upon a group of three cars that had been tucked up behind a ten-foot-high ridge.

"Here we are," Bob said, breathing a sigh of relief as he pulled in beside Toby's Ford and killed the engine. "Wasn't sure I had the right spot for a minute there."

As we proceeded along the ravine on foot, the path narrowed, then dipped to the right, where we found the crevice in the rock that served as the cave's entrance. It was quite wide, but less than five feet high, and dark, so we had to crouch down and feel our way along the smooth stone walls. After forty feet or so, the passage opened up into a larger area that was lit by a couple of oil torches. The flames bathed the space with an eerie orange hue, casting us in long, black, flickering shadows that fell across the hard-packed earth, then crept up the walls behind us.

"This way," Bob said. He picked up one of the torches, then disappeared into a tall, dark chasm that I hadn't seen. I followed him down the narrow, rocky grade for some time, stepping carefully along the slippery slope. The air became cool and still as we made our way down into the heart of the cavern, and I became aware of the faint echo of human voices—vague, hollow whisperings that drifted up the channel like wisps of smoke rising in a chimney.

As we came to the end of the passageway, it opened into a long, oval-shaped expanse that rose through sixty feet of rock to the earth's surface. A shaft of soft, natural light fell from a wedge-shaped aperture at the top of the chamber, striking the far side of the grotto, where Toby and a man I didn't know were involved in an intimate conversation. Toby looked up as we approached.

"Just the two of you?"

"Just us," Bob confirmed.

"What'd you tell Lockridge?"

"Nothing. Like you said."

"Good."

I noticed that, a few feet behind them, a corpse was laid out on the ground. It had been covered with an old blanket.

"What the hell happened?" I said.

"He has tried to escape." The unidentified man spoke in heavily accented English, his tone making clear that he didn't actually expect me to believe him, but that it was all I was going to get.

"His hands are still tied," I said, resisting the urge to say what I really wanted to say. The stranger shrugged it off with a condescending smile.

The man had a face that was easy to dislike. Narrow, sloping forehead expanding downward to a set of broad, fleshy jowls; small, snakelike eyes peering out from behind two slots of swollen flesh; a fat, smug lower lip; and a big, bulbous nose that didn't stop dripping. He kept dabbing at it with the silk handkerchief he held in his left hand.

"This is Asad Khasardian, Jack," Bob said before I could continue. "He and his brothers have been very helpful in putting together a number of our actions over the past few weeks."

"Yeah? Did he put this one together?"

"Easy, Jack," Toby warned.

"A pleasure to meet you, Mr. Teller." Khasardian grinned,

making the point that, although I was in the dark about him, he knew all about me. I ignored him and his ego, and crouched down to lift the blanket off the dead man's face.

"There's no need for that," Toby said, placing a hand on my shoulder. He backed off when I shot him a look, and I pulled the cover back. I wasn't prepared for what I saw, and neither was Bob, who whispered, *"Jesus Christ . . ."* and turned away.

Afsharti's face had been plundered. Empty, black holes marked the points where his eyes had been gouged out, and his mouth was frozen in the twisted, silent scream he'd emitted as his tongue was sliced off. The torso was covered in dry brown blood, and the cold stiffness of his flesh told me that he'd been dead for some time. The dry chill of the cave explained why the usual stench of a decomposing body was absent.

"That's enough," Toby said, sounding a bit shaky himself. "Cover him up."

I replaced the blanket and stood up.

"Who in hell did this?" I said, louder than I'd meant to. The question swirled around the chamber, bouncing back and forth between cold, subterranean walls, before coming back to confront me as fading echoes of my own indignation.

"WHO IN HELL DID THIS . . . ? WHO IN HELL DID THIS . . . ? WHO IN HELL DID THIS . . . ?"

As the sound melted away, it left behind a black, ponderous silence. The air was charged with a sense of unsettled scores, and I was overcome with the feeling that we weren't alone, that we were being watched. I caught a fleeting movement out of the corner of my eye. Or perhaps I heard the undertow of someone's breathing. I couldn't be sure what made me turn and peer into the darkness, but there was no mistaking what I saw once I had. There was a group—shadowy figures seated on the ground in a dark corner of the cave. Six or eight men. Maybe more. I couldn't be sure.

One of them rose to his feet, and stood perfectly still, a dark, menacing silhouette against a murky gray background.

"You have asked your question in the wrong way," he said, in hard, guttural English. His voice was oddly thin, lacking in resonance, as if it were somehow being absorbed by the dense surroundings.

"How should I have put it?" I said.

"You asked, 'Who *in hell* did this?' but the question is not correct. It is not the perpetrator who is in hell. It is the victim. I know this because I myself have done it, and as you can see, I am not in hell. It is the opposite. I am in the grace of God."

The sun fell in the sky, allowing the pale light from above to strike the mullah's face. A second wave of revulsion washed over me as I made the connection. The short, dark, scruffy beard growing around bloated features, the white turban and long black robe. But most of all, the twisted smirk that marked the pleasure this man received when he observed the horror that his sick cruelty provoked. There was no sign that he remembered me, but I certainly hadn't forgotten the face that I had first encountered in Qom.

"Why?" Bob blurted out. "Why *in God's name* would you do something like that?!"

The mullah grinned. "The answer is in your own question. It is done in the name of God. It is done in the name of Allah!"

Perhaps the young men who sat in the dark behind this man believed they had carried out the torturous murder in the name of God. Perhaps this mullah had convinced them that it was justice they were meting out, just as he had convinced the mob in Qom that there was justice in stoning that poor young girl to death. But it was clear to me, as it would have been to any sane person, that this man hadn't carried out these vicious acts with some twisted sense of godly justice in mind. No, he hadn't done it because Allah, or any other god, had demanded it. He'd done it because he enjoyed it.

TWENTY-ONE

November 1979

I'd been dreaming of Lenni again, but it was fading quickly. I kept my eyes closed and held on to the images, hoping to commit them to memory before they disappeared into my subconscious, leaving me alone again, with a reality that I was in no hurry to face.

I'd been walking for some time. Up a steep mountain road, with lots of twists and turns, and high grass on either side, making it impossible to see into the distance. It was late in the day, and the light was rapidly fading. I'd meet the occasional person coming down the slope, but the faces were obscured, out of focus, so it was impossible to say whether I knew them or not. The fact that they were ignoring me made me assume they were strangers.

Then, suddenly, Lenni was there, at the side of the

road, kneeling over an upended bicycle. Her hands were greasy, a result of trying to reattach the chain, which had come off. I could tell that she was frustrated and angry, but she was keeping it in check, maintaining her composure as she worked steadily to engage the chain with the gear. Strange that she hasn't seen me, I thought.

I tried to say her name, but nothing came out. There was no wind in my lungs, nothing to push through my vocal cords. I reached down to help her with the chain and in the process my hand brushed against hers. It was a lovely sensation. I looked over to meet her eyes, but she was no longer there. She was on the bike, which had been magically repaired, heading up the side of the mountain, standing on the pedals to get some leverage against the incline. I followed her for a while, still trying to call out, but as she picked up speed it was impossible to keep up, and she soon disappeared around a bend in the road.

I stopped to watch the sun slip down below the horizon. Then I turned and headed down the hill, thinking to myself, So, this is what it feels like to be dead.

A shooting pain brought me rushing back to consciousness. The only remedy was to lie there on the cold concrete floor and be as still as possible until the worst of it melted away. Then I'd pull myself into a sitting position and gently massage the muscles, working down from the calves to the arches. It was probably more psychological than anything else, but it soothed the ache, and that was all that mattered.

I went back to the dream. I'd been having lots of them, and most featured Lenni, in one way or another. But this one had been unique in that sensation of touching her hand. I couldn't recall ever experiencing the sensation of touch in a dream before. It made it all the more vivid. I almost believed that I had seen Lenni.

My feet were purple with bruises, my ankles swollen to twice their size, but nothing was broken—not yet, anyway. As efficient as my torturer was with his rubber hose, I had no doubt that he was capable of inflicting a hell of a lot more damage than he had so far. I hoped that they'd chosen this particular method of torture, which leaves no lasting damage, because they expected to release me at some point. But hope is one thing, believing is another. I felt they were building up to something.

I wasn't sure how long I'd been there. Ten days? Two weeks? I'd tried to keep track at first, but with no light and dark to mark the time, it had all melted into one long, indistinguishable nightmare. I realized that my disorientation was part of the process, but knowing what they were up to wouldn't be much help, not in the long run. Unlike my inept interrogators at the embassy, this crowd knew what they were doing. I'd hold out as long as I could, but in the end, they'd break me. Unless they killed me first, of course.

I hadn't seen the mad mullah since the day at the embassy, when he recognized me as I was being loaded into the van. I think he'd been as surprised to see me as I was to see him. After the initial shock, he'd panicked, and started barking orders to the confused students. They'd been told to turn me over to the Canadian authorities, but this was a mullah, so they'd dutifully trundled me back into the van and sped off under their new instruction. I spent the next few hours lying in the back of the truck, sweating under several layers of heavy wool blankets, while we drove aimlessly around the city (the traffic told me that we hadn't left Tehran). After several phone calls made from pay phones, the students were finally told where they should take me. It wasn't the Canadian embassy.

My world consisted of a windowless room, seven steps long by three steps wide, that was accessed through a heavy wooden door, and lit, twenty-four hours a day, by a single, fifteen-watt fluorescent bulb. The sole furnishing was a small wooden bench, used in the regular beatings I received, and my wardrobe consisted of a pair of worn-out blue cotton pajamas. I'd also been given a moth-eaten combat-green woolen blanket. There was an old toilet and a small sink on the back wall, but they were bone dry. A metal bucket, covered by a warped piece of wood, had been supplied for my personal needs.

Forcing myself onto my feet, I fought the pain that shot up my legs, along the length of my spine, and finally exploded like a burst of red-hot needles ripping through my brain. I leaned up against the damp, crumbling wall and waited for the worst to subside, then took a first tentative step. The routine was to make a hundred clockwise trips—two thousand steps—then to switch directions and go the other way for another two thousand, and so on. As long as I kept a steady pace, my subconscious would count the laps, leaving me free to think, or to concoct elaborate mind games that I hoped would keep me from disappearing into the giant abyss that lay before me. One of my exercises was an attempt to train my mind to interpret pain as pleasure. The idea I concocted was that there is a pain/pleasure continuum in the brain, so if the pain becomes great enough, it will push the needle right around the scale, into the realm of pleasure. It was just a matter of perception, I told myself, and, after all, there were people out there who'd pay a lot of money for the kind of treatment I was getting. I even convinced myself that I was looking forward to the next session so I could test my theory. It turned out to be one of those ideas that looks good on paper.

Most of the time, my mind went off on its own. I followed it into the past, revisiting old places and old faces that I'd stored away in the dark recesses of my memory. I covered a lot of ground, but it always seemed to come back to Lenni. She was my safe port, the calm waters that gave me refuge from the storm. "Don't push your luck, Jack," she'd often say, only half joking, and I'd give my stock answer. "If you don't give it a little push once in a while, it'll forget all about you." Yeah, well, maybe I'd pushed it to the limit this time.

The significance of the mad mullah's panicked reaction at the embassy hadn't sunk in at first, but once I'd given it some thought, it made perfect sense. A history of complicity with the CIA wasn't really something you'd want to have yelled from the rooftops in postrevolutionary Iran, and I was in a position to do some yelling. It was no wonder that he'd had me spirited away. The question was why he'd kept me alive. Clearly, the mullah wanted something from me. What?

My heart skipped a beat when I heard the outer door open, then slam shut. There were only two things it could mean. Either a meal of stale rice, boiled beans, and weak tea was on its way, or it was time for a session with the rubber hose. I knew from the heavy footsteps coming down the stairs that it wasn't the dinner hour.

I drew a sharp breath and waited, listening carefully for the steps along the hallway. As usual, he was in no hurry, taking long deliberate steps, then pausing outside the door to retrieve the set of keys that was clipped to his belt. There was no way to prepare for the beating I was about to receive, except to remind myself to scream. My natural inclination had been to hold back, to deny him the satisfaction, but all that did was make him redouble his efforts, so I'd dropped my inhibitions now. The more screaming the better. In some twisted way, I'd even convinced myself that they were cries of victory.

The key turned in the lock and he appeared, filling the doorway with his massive frame. Six feet tall, with broad, muscular shoulders, massive biceps, and narrow, slightly crossed eyes set into a big, flat, shaved head, my torturer was what you might call the strong, silent type. So silent, in fact, that in the half-dozen sessions I'd endured, I'd yet to hear him utter a single word, let alone string a sentence together. And judging by the relentlessly empty expression that was fixed to his face, I was pretty sure he was incapable of thought, let alone speech. But I guess brainpower doesn't count for much in his line of work, because he was damned good at his job.

"I don't suppose we could reschedule?" I said, trying not to flinch as he stepped through the door. "I've got a pretty hectic day and—"

I stopped short when I noticed that, along with the usual gym bag full of tools that was gripped tightly in his hand, he'd brought a straight-backed wooden chair with him. He carefully placed the seat at one end of the room, and before I could speculate about its purpose, the mad mullah came through the door and planted himself in it. He looked me up and down, then produced a sickly smile.

"It is time for the talk," he said.

"Go to hell."

He gave me a long, venomous look, then, with a wave of his hand, signaled for the show to begin. The privilege of performing before such a great religious figure must have been quite an inspiration for my empty-headed torturer, because he went to work on me with a zeal that had been absent in our previous encounters. I quickly found myself flat on my back, legs elevated, ankles bound to the bench, the battered soles of my feet hanging in midair, exposed and defenseless. I took a couple of deep breaths and steeled myself. This time, I wouldn't scream.

There's no way to adequately describe the pain that comes with a beating like the one I received that day. Everyone has a threshold, a point of no return when, in an act of self-preservation, the mind shuts down. But an experienced assailant, like this one, knows his victim's limits, and will take him to the edge, then step back, allowing the senses to recover before pushing on to the next level of unendurable pain. By the time it was over, I honestly didn't know whether or not they'd succeeded in making me cry out. I was barely holding on to consciousness, aware of my surroundings only as a distant, blurred distortion of reality, and could only hope that the mad mullah's gloomy expression meant that the show hadn't lived up to expectations. I wasn't sure, but my torturer seemed to be hanging his head in shame. Perhaps I had held on, I thought.

The next thing I knew, I was being scraped off the floor, yanked to my feet, and shoved onto my knees before the mullah, who had risen from his seat. He stood there for a moment, perfectly still, looking down at me with cold, stony contempt, then he installed a pair of oversize glasses onto his face. After carefully tucking the earpieces in under his turban, he reached into his pocket and produced a piece of folded paper, which he solemnly opened.

"You are accus-ed of the high crimes against Islamic peoples of Iran," he read slowly, in English. "It has been proven that, without a doubt, you are the CIA instrument of United States, and it is known, with certainty, that you have come in Iran with the purpose of to destroy the Islamic will of the peoples. The facts, which may not be in dispute, have been proven that you make a conspiracy with the godless devils to return the treacherous snake, Reza Pahlavi, to the throne of the Shah."

He lowered the paper and looked down at me.

"It is an act of great kindness that the Grand Ayatollah Seyyed Ruhollah Khomeini makes a generosity to save your life if you make the confession to these facts. It will be done in front of the camera. Will you agree to do so?"

"No," I said once I'd found my voice. "I will not agree to do so."

"Very well," the mullah said, folding the sheet back into

his pocket. "It is decided. You have been found guilty of these charges. The sentence will be death, and it must be carried out immediately."

The mullah took a half step back, giving himself just enough room to fully extend his arm toward me. I felt the cold, hard steel of the barrel against my forehead before I saw the weapon.

"It is now the final chance," the mullah said, his fat finger tugging impatiently at the trigger. "Do you make confession for the camera?"

I took a last deep breath and held it in. I wanted to shut my eyes, conjure up an image of Lenni that would carry me into eternity, but something wouldn't let me. Pride, I guess. I had to meet the mullah's odious gaze, deny him the pleasure, at least, by looking him straight in the eye. I raised my head . . .

And that's when I noticed it. Something etched into the barrel of the pistol. I narrowed my view and these words came into focus:

MODEL OF1911, U.S. ARMY
UNITED STATES PROPERTY

I couldn't help laughing. Not just a little chuckle, either. I actually fell back onto the ground and rolled with spontaneous, uncontrollable laughter. The mad mullah looked at me like I'd lost my mind, and it probably was a case of temporary insanity. But there was a very good reason for my hysteria—I'd just found God.

Though I'd always been open-minded on the question of a Supreme Being, I was sure that if there was a god, He ran the universe not with an iron fist, or with a forgiving compassion, or even with any sense of natural justice. After all, He was all-powerful. If He wanted order, or love and understanding, or fairness, you'd see a lot more of it. No. Those traits that we attributed to God seemed to me to be mere earthly ideals. For me, the most compelling evidence of a God in heaven was His diabolical sense of humor. His sense of irony was everywhere. Even in this desolate torture cell, as I prepared to die, He was ready with a practical joke.

The mad mullah didn't appreciate me spoiling his big moment. He exploded like a spoiled child, kicking me repeatedly in the side, cracking a rib or two in the process. It hurt like hell, but I didn't care. The joke was too good.

The mullah leaned over, placed the gun barrel square on my forehead. "I kill you, I swear it!" he screamed, spitting anger. "You don't believe?!"

I smiled. "Sure I do."

"THEN AT WHAT DO YOU LAUGH? DO YOU LAUGH AT ME?!"

I'd realized as soon as I saw the words etched into the barrel of the pistol. The Colt M1911 was the standard issue sidearm for the U.S. Army. I'd carried one around Europe for three years, which was why I remembered that it was the weapon Donnelly had said was used to execute prisoners at Qasr prison. So I was laughing because, in His infinite wisdom, my Maker had placed me in the exact location that I'd come six thousand miles to be—Qasr prison—but as always, He'd added a little twist. He'd put me at the mercy of a man I hated with more visceral passion than any man I'd ever come across. This mad mullah, who had condemned that poor child in Qom, and who had gouged General Afsharti's eyes out before he killed him, turned out to be none other than the Forty-Five-Caliber Judge.

"You're the man I came looking for," I said.

"What?! What you talking?!" he sputtered, confusion mounting. "Come looking for what?!"

"For you. I came for you."

"Why?! Who has sent you?!"

I grinned up at him. "The Great Satan, of course. Who else? He sent me to kill you."

He looked at me sideways, but I could see that he couldn't quite reject the possibility that there was something to what I was saying. The legend of the great and powerful CIA reached even into this twisted mind.

"Lies!" he cried out.

"No, not at all," I said coolly. "I haven't decided yet how I'll do it. Maybe I'll slice your tongue off and gouge your eyes out, then let you bleed to death, like you did General Afsharti. You told me then that you'd acted in the name of God. Well, however I decide to kill you, I won't need any god to justify it. I'll do it in my own name."

He stood there, holding a gun to my head, his finger on the trigger, yet there was fear in his eyes and a twitch in his cheek. He was scared of me.

"You don't kill me," he said, pressing the steel harder against my flesh. "I kill you."

"Go ahead, then," I said. "Kill me!"

He was sorely tempted, and for a moment I thought he might actually do it, in spite of the consequences. But, in the end, the mad mullah wasn't so mad as to disobey Khomeini. If he'd been given the go-ahead to kill me, I would've been dead already, probably the first day he got his hands on me. Clearly, the Ayatollah had ruled that I was to be kept alive, at least until I made an on-camera confession.

"No," I said. "I guess you don't kill me, after all."

The mullah spent the next few minutes kicking the shit out of me, leaving me lying on the floor, curled up in a fetal ball. I lay there for quite a while then managed to straighten myself out and reflect on what had just happened.

"Very nice," I said to my newly discovered creator. "But what the hell am I supposed to do now?"

No bolt of lightning struck down the door to set me free, and a careful examination of the room revealed that the mullah hadn't conveniently left his weapon behind for me to use in my escape. There were no windows and no hidden doors, and I was in no condition to fight my way out. I'd been put right where I needed to be. Perhaps Yari was yards away, in a similar cell, but I had not even a glimmer of an idea about how I was going to get to him.

I breathed in a lungful of air, hoping to release some of my distress with a long sigh, but it had the opposite effect. A sharp pain made me wince and I cried out. The only thing to do was to lie there, immobile, and try to slip away, into sleep. Maybe I'd have an idea when I woke up.

TWENTY-TWO

I sat up, alert and perfectly still, like some hunted animal trying to locate the source of an approaching danger. Had I dreamed it? Had I even been asleep? I wasn't sure. I couldn't be sure of anything in my present state of mind.

tap TAP taptap . . . TAP tap TAP TAP . . . taptap TAP

No, it was real all right. But faint. So faint that I had to hold my breath in order to hear it. I took in a lungful of stale air and listened.

taptaptap. . . . tap TAP . . . TAP taptap . . . TAP TAP TAP

Morse code? It sure sounded like it. Somebody, somewhere, was sending out a message. But who? And from where? The more I tried to pinpoint the source, the more elusive it became. I stood up too quickly, almost blacked out, and slumped against the wall. Christ, I was weak. Weaker than I'd ever been, but not just physically. As near as I could tell, it had been two weeks since I'd seen the mad mullah. Lacking permission to execute me, he'd apparently decided to let me rot, and it was happening from the inside out.

Hope doesn't flee suddenly, in the full light of day. It slinks away quietly, at night, quitting little by little, thought by dark thought, and by the time you notice it's gone, it's too late, you don't care anymore. Because when hope goes, it doesn't leave much behind. It takes your heart and soul, your very spirit with it. You can walk and talk and eat and shit, but you're not really there anymore, not in any meaningful sense. When you step into that void, the only future available is the inescapable descent into darkness.

TAP tap . . . TAP tap . . . tap . . . tap TAP taptap

I shook my head, tried to come to my senses. That's odd, I thought. The sound seemed to be coming from . . . Yes, it was. I fell to my knees and bent over the cracked, empty toilet bowl that sat in the corner of the cell. Yes, there it was, loud and clear. The latrine was acting like some sort of ceramic auricle, carrying the clandestine missive up from the building's plumbing lines into my cell.

It was easier to make out the pattern now. Whoever the sender, he was as dogged as he was methodical. After carefully tapping out an eleven-letter message, he would pause for exactly ten seconds, presumably to wait for an answer, and when none came, he would start over, repeating the process exactly as he had in the previous transmissions, without the slightest variation in timing or content. I'd picked up a bit of Morse code in the army, but it was pretty rusty, so it took several minutes to decipher even a few isolated letters. It left me with this:

- O - - E - - - - S A

After a few more passes, I'd filled in a couple more letters:

D O - - E L L - - S A

And, finally, the message fell into place:

D O N N E L L Y U S A

Donnelly . . . ? It took me a second, but yes. Yes, of course. Donnelly. Friendly face, fighter pilot, new father. Christ! How long had it been since that Sunday morning when I walked into his office at the American embassy? Three weeks? A month? More? It seemed like a goddamned eternity.

You'd think that reestablishing contact with the world would have had some kind of effect on me. Maybe I should have been filled with great joy. Or, perhaps a more appropriate response would be to feel deeply distressed at the idea that others were suffering the same fate as I was, cast away in some oppressive, dank cell. But the truth of the matter was that I felt neither cheered nor troubled by the revelation. All I felt was numb.

The guy was an optimist, though, you had to give him that. I wondered how many times he'd sent out his message. D*ONNELLY USA* . . . *DONNELLY USA* . . . Over and over. It was more of a plea than a message, really. I'm here, anybody out there? Am I alone? The silence he got back must have been disheartening. Well, for what it was worth, I'd give him an answer.

I went to work with an unexpected burst of energy. I suppose having a mission lifted my spirit. It certainly started my mind turning over. Donnelly couldn't have been tapping out his name for weeks. Even if he had that kind of stamina, I would have noticed it before now. Maybe he'd just arrived. Maybe he'd have news about what was going on in the world. I found myself getting excited, trying to formulate all sorts of questions in simple Morse code.

Detaching the handle from the metal waste bucket that sat in the corner, I doubled it back on itself, took a moment to admire my work, then tested it against the toilet bowl. The sound that came off the cracked ceramic was too dull to carry back to Donnelly's cell, I thought. I'd need to access the pipes themselves. Fortunately, the cement wall behind the latrine was damp and crumbling, and I was able to use the metal tapping tool to dig out the three or four inches needed to expose the empty lead pipe that had once served as the main water line.

I gathered the cement dust into a pile behind the toilet, where it wouldn't be seen, and I couldn't help but smile as I tapped out on the pipe my message for Donnelly:

TELLER007

Adrenaline shot into my system, and my heart pumped with excitement as I awaited the response. Finally, after what seemed like an endless lull, I got this back:

SHAKENORSTIRRED?

I spent half of the next forty-eight hours on my belly, tapping out Morse code on a lead pipe, and the other half on my knees, with my head in the toilet, listening to Donnelly's responses. It was certainly the most unusual communication I'd ever been involved in, but it was probably the most exhilarating, too. We covered a lot of ground, from sports and politics, to books, films, long lost friends, and family history. I guess I must've told Donnelly more about me in those two days than I'd told anyone in my entire lifetime.

It turned out that he had, in fact, arrived just that day, but he knew very little about what had happened to the other hostages. He'd been separated from the rest when, on day six, the Iranians had identified him as a CIA officer, using shredded documents that had been meticulously taped back together by an army of students. He'd been taken to a house somewhere on the outskirts of Tehran, interrogated for two weeks, then moved to his present accommodation. He didn't know until I told him that we were in Qasr.

Donnelly's favorite subject was his hometown of Hope Mills, North Carolina, where he was born and raised. He'd started working with his father at the family's hardware store, on South Main, when he was thirteen. That's where he'd first spotted his future wife, Kathy, but he didn't have the guts to speak to her for three years, when he found himself sitting next to her in Mr. Clark's social studies class. Bill was captain of the football team, Kathy homecoming queen of 1968. When he went off to war, she promised to wait, and she did, in spite of being proposed to by pretty much every boy in Hope Mills. They were married in June of 1974, in the Big Rockfish Presbyterian Church, and after four years of trying, the couple was recently blessed with a baby girl, Jennifer. Donnelly had spent just two months with his daughter when the Company gave him his first field assignment, at the Tehran station. He worried about how his captivity would affect Kathy, but he took comfort in the knowledge that she'd be getting support from the whole town.

Donnelly's America was nothing like the one I knew. His was a wholesome, upstanding, small-town kind of a place, where you go to church, salute the flag, and treat your neighbor as you would have him treat you. It was filled with good, hardworking people who assumed the best about one another, and believed that if you lived right, tomorrow would be an even better day. They liked football and hot dogs, gave regularly to their favorite charity, and sang carols to each other on Christmas Eve. They had faith in God, faith in themselves, and, in spite of recent setbacks, faith in the United States of America.

There was something very appealing about Hope Mills. It was comforting, I guess, in the way a Norman Rockwell painting was, or a Frank Capra movie. It wasn't the place, though, or even the people, that made it so alluring. It was a way of seeing the world. There was a moral certitude, a conviction that doing the right thing was just a matter of doing it. Hope Mills had no place for ambiguity, no gray area between right and wrong. There was a simplicity—a childlike innocence—that can never be retrieved once it's lost.

I don't think I envied Donnelly for having that to go back to, but it did make me think about what I called home. Not the loft on West Broadway. That was just a building. Or New York, either. Sure, the city was as familiar to me as Hope Mills was to Donnelly, but if we ever got out of our shit hole, that wasn't what I would be going back to.

Lenni. That's what I'd be going back to. My long, tapped-out conversations with Donnelly made me realize that, more than any town or city or place, she was my home. If it's true that with hope comes salvation, then I was saved by the idea of seeing Lenni's face again, and sitting down to tell her what I'd been up to all my life.

There would be no more torture sessions, I was sure of that. When the mad mullah came back—*if he came back*—it would be to kill me. My guess was that he wouldn't return, that Ayatollah Khomeini would never allow the summary execution of someone he believed was an official of the United States government. It turned out I was wrong. My heart almost exploded out of my chest when I heard two sets of footsteps coming down the stairs, then along the corridor toward my cell. It wasn't fear that I had to control, though. It was excitement. This was the moment I'd been hoping for. The moment I'd prepared for.

I was ready for the bastards.

My silent torturer was first through the door. He found me in the far corner, lying perfectly still, curled up in the fetal position. The mad mullah followed. As the door slammed shut behind him, I cracked an eyelid to track the men's movements, noting the exact position the mullah took up at the center of the cell. My entire body tensed as I counted the hulking torturer's plodding steps toward me.

One . . . two . . . three . . . Wait, I told myself. Not yet. Don't go too soon . . .

He grunted as he reached down to scrape me off the floor, and that was my cue. Sitting up sharply, I swung my left arm around and, using all my might, flung a fistful of cement dust into his fat face. The giant reeled back onto his heels, hands shooting up to his eyes as he cried out in angry pain.

My plan allowed for five seconds to neutralize the mad mullah before the hulk mounted a counterattack. Shooting to my feet, as I'd practiced, I gripped the twelve-inch length of rusty lead pipe tightly in my right hand and moved swiftly toward the startled imam. I noticed, in the blur of movement, that he already had the execution pistol in his hand, but he was confused by the sudden turn of events, and before he could react, I'd lowered the pipe across his right temple. It landed with a dull *thud,* and so did the mullah. He lay on the concrete floor, not quite out cold, but pretty close.

The pistol slid across the floor, ricocheted off the toilet, and came to rest at the feet of the dazed titan, who was trying to open his teary eyes now. I froze, for no more than a millisecond, but it was enough for him to get a fix on me. He lashed out like a wounded bear, growling and spitting as he blindly advanced on me, arms swinging wildly in my direction. A right hook caught me across the left side of my head and the world was suddenly upside down and spinning, my head ringing with pain.

There was no time to recover—I had to get up now! But my brain was scrambled, I couldn't find my feet.

The hulk reached down, tried to grab hold of me, and his touch brought my senses back. I gripped the lead pipe in both hands and swung it around, striking his chin with enough force that I could feel the jawbone give way. Blood sprayed upward, taking a couple of teeth with it, and this brutal expert in pain let loose a primal scream that must have surpassed even his most abused victim.

He stumbled backward, but kept his footing and came back at me with savage fury. I rolled sideways and, without knowing how, found myself up on my feet, standing just behind him, to his right. Winding up again, I went for a blow to the back of his head, but he turned at the last second, and I scored a direct hit on the center of his face, causing it to cave in on itself, like some collapsing building.

The son of a bitch was still breathing when he hit the ground, struggling to get up. I gathered what was left of my strength and followed up with a quick strike to the top of his head. He fell back to the ground, still and silent. I finished him off with a couple of crushing blows to the skull, leaving his head pretty well demolished. Maybe it was excessive, but I didn't want him unconscious, I wanted him dead.

The mad mullah, who'd been watching the performance as he cowered in the corner of the cell, was shaking uncontrollably. Literally shaking with terror. I think the miserable bastard had peed himself, too. Throwing the pipe aside, I picked up the gun, then removed the set of keys that hung off the dead man's belt. I noticed that my hands were thick with blood and, in fact, so was everything. Pieces of the man's brain clung to the wall like chunks of melted cheese.

"Do you want to live?" I said, my own voice sounding distant and weary. The mullah was too terrified to respond, but he managed to nod his head. "Good," I said. "Then you'll have to do exactly what I tell you to do."

"Yes . . ." he managed. "I will do it . . . You tell . . ."

"Is there anyone else out there?"

"No, no . . ."

"If you're lying I'll kill you, the same way I did him."

"There is no one . . ." he said, oozing fear. "I . . . I swear it!"

I told him to get up, but he was incapable, so I grabbed him by the arm, pulled him onto his feet, and dragged him to the door. Leaning the mullah against the wall, I fumbled with the keys for a moment, then realized that the door was unlocked, and led him out into the hallway, pressing the Colt against the back of his neck, where he could feel the cold metal against his skin.

He'd been telling the truth, anyway. Aside from the rats, who scurried in and out of the dank shadows, the narrow, dimly lit corridor was deserted. We seemed to be in some long-forgotten substructure below the prison, a labyrinth of rusty pipes and loose wiring that fell from the crumbling walls and ceilings.

"Donnelly!" I called out, my voice reverberating through the bleak tableau.

"In here!" came the response.

I found him a few doors down, in a cell similar to mine. Aside from a couple of days' growth on his face, and a suit that was in desperate need of ironing, he was in remarkably good shape. His reaction to me was a bit more dramatic.

"Mother of God, Jack . . ." he whispered. "What in hell did they do to you?"

TWENTY-THREE

August 1953

"We need to be together on this, Jack."

Toby wasn't looking where he was going as he left the cave and stumbled over a rock. I was in no mood to make it easy for him, so I picked up my pace. He scrambled to catch up.

"It won't do anybody any good if we go to J.L. pointing fingers at each other," he said. "Afsharti's dead. There's nothing we can do about that. Let's try and put it in a positive light."

I came to a stop and swung around on him. "You wanna explain how we present a complete fucking disaster in a positive light?"

"Come on, Jack. For God's sake, I mean, take a deep breath, will you? Okay, things didn't exactly go as planned, but there's no point in going over a cliff about it. We can fix this, but we've got to speak with one voice."

The midafternoon sun was white hot, bleaching out what little color there was in the parched mountain landscape. I watched the beads of sweat that were forming on Toby's forehead roll down the side of his face and neck, then slip under his collar. My own shirt was drenched with sweat, too.

Looking back toward the cave's entrance, I saw Bob emerge, followed by Khasardian. They spotted us and marched up the ravine toward where we stood, halfway to the cars. Toby gave me a sideways glance as we waited.

"Jack and I were just talking about the best way to handle things," he said as they joined us.

"He can just disappear." Khasardian wiped the sweat off his brow with his snotty handkerchief. "The body will never be found, and the episode will soon be forgotten."

"Sure, that's one way to go," Toby said. "But I was thinking, maybe we can do better. Turn it to our advantage."

"How the hell do we do that?" Bob spoke up.

"Well . . ." Toby shifted his weight and glanced up at the sky, for no particular reason. "What if we stuck with the original idea? A police rescue. But instead of Afsharti coming out the hero, he comes out the victim. The kidnappers panic when they see the police, he gets shot and killed in the confusion."

Bob shook his head. "I don't know, Toby. You saw what he looks like."

"So he gets shot in the face. We can play that up, even say they tortured him. You know—'Barbaric Bolsheviks,' that kind of shit. What do you think, Asad?"

"Yes, it can work," Khasardian agreed. "Why not? I have a doctor who can perform the autopsy."

"Great." Toby smiled and turned to Bob. "It'll make great copy. In some ways, it'd be even better than we planned."

Bob nodded his head. He clearly didn't like it, but it was enough for Toby, who turned to me.

"What do you say, Jack? You with us?"

I gave him a long look. "Jesus Christ!"

"We're all on board, Jack. Don't be difficult."

"What the hell were you thinking?! Do you even know who those fanatics are?!"

"They call themselves the 'Warriors of Islam,'" Khasardian said. "Fanatics? Yes, of course. But they can be controlled."

"Controlled?! Is that what you call this?!" I turned back to Toby. "Have you had anything to do with the planning of this fucked-up operation, or did you just hand the whole thing over to this jackass?!"

"Slow down there, Jack. This won't accomplish anything . . ."

Khasardian took a step toward me. "If he calls me a jackass again, I swear, he will be sorry!"

"You're a jackass," I shot back, stepping forward to give him a clear target, if he wanted it. He huffed and puffed a couple of times, shook an angry finger at me, but that was as far as he was gonna take it.

"Knock it off, Jack," Toby said. "This isn't the goddamned third grade. What do you want? You want me to take responsibility? Okay. I take responsibility. But we are where we are, and we have to make the best of it. Now, I think this idea of a botched rescue attempt is the way to go, but if you've got a better idea, go ahead and spit it out!"

I gave myself a moment to calm down. "Afsharti is the least of our worries," I said.

"What do you mean?"

"I mean that it doesn't matter how we handle this if we don't clean up the mess that was made of the kidnapping."

"You mean Fatemi? Okay, so he's in the hospital, but I don't see how that—"

"Jesus Christ, Toby, shut up. You don't see because you don't fucking listen! You rush into this stuff without thinking it through!"

"What the hell are you talking about?"

"Fatemi's not in the hospital. He checked himself out this morning so he could go to Mossadegh and tell him that I was involved in the kidnapping. The whole operation's blown, because you and this jackass here were dumb enough to use my secretary to place your people in Yari's kitchen. What were you thinking? That Yari was too stupid to make the connection?!"

Toby gave Khasardian a look. The Iranian didn't have to say anything. His sheepish look said it all. Toby turned back to me.

"Has he talked to Mossadegh yet?"

"Not as far as I know. He'll wait for Leyla's confession."

"Leyla's been arrested?" Bob piped in.

"This morning."

"Shit." Toby frowned. "She won't last long. And she'll implicate us all." He looked to Khasardian. "You *are* a jackass!"

"You told me to take care of the bodyguards, and I did so." He wiped his hands back and forth, absolving himself of any guilt in the matter. Toby shook his head and turned back to me.

"We've got to get to Fatemi before he goes to Mossadegh. Now, if you stick with me on this, Jack, I've got an idea how you can—"

"Forget it." I turned and headed for the car.

Toby called after me. "What are you gonna do?"

"I don't know!" I called back. "But I'm sure as hell not gonna cover your ass!"

He was breathless by the time he caught up with me. "If you take this to J.L. before we clean it up, it'll fuck everybody, not just me. They'll close the whole operation down and we'll each have a big fat zero sitting at the top of our file."

I ignored him and kept walking.

"Jack!" He grabbed my arm. I only meant to sweep his hand away, but I must've caught him off balance. As I spun around, he held on, and went tumbling backward, landing square on his back. We shared a momentary look, each of us as shocked as the other, then I stepped forward and offered him a hand. He ignored it and pulled himself to his feet as Bob and Khasardian arrived on the scene. Toby dusted himself down and turned to Bob.

"Take Jack back to the house," he said. "He's got some things to say to J.L."

Bob got lost again on our way back, but not as convincingly as he had the first time around. At any rate, by the time we walked onto Roosevelt's terrace, Toby was already sitting there, looking very self-satisfied. I noticed that he had a manila envelope in his hand.

"Have a seat, guys," Roosevelt said, very businesslike as he motioned us toward the two empty places around the glass coffee table. "Toby was just filling me in."

I shot Bob a look, which he studiously avoided. He chose the last seat in the shade, leaving me with the only one exposed to the late-afternoon sunlight.

"I don't want to spend time apportioning blame," Roosevelt began, staring straight at me. "There will be ample time for that should things fall apart, and ultimately, I will take full responsibility for a failure. Which is precisely why that is not an acceptable outcome. We will do whatever is necessary to salvage the situation. Are we all agreed on that as a basis to go forward?"

He paused, waiting for a response from each one of us. Toby said, "Agreed," Bob mumbled, "Right," and I was silent. Roosevelt allowed a moment to pass before prompting me.

"Jack?"

I looked from Roosevelt to Toby, then to Bob, and back to Roosevelt. "I guess I'd like to hear what you have in mind."

"Not exactly the team spirit we were looking for," Toby

hastened to say. Roosevelt placed a hand in the air to silence him.

"No, no, that's a fair response," he said. "In fact, I respect your honesty, Jack. After all, you're the one with the relationship, so you'll be handling the damage control. Show him, Toby."

Toby tossed the envelope onto the table. He could've handed it to me, but I guess he thought that was a more dramatic method of delivery. I eyed the package for a moment, then reached over and picked it up. It was one of those reusable interoffice envelopes, the kind that has two columns of blank lines on the front, where the last recipient's name is crossed off the list and the next is written in. This was a new envelope, with no names on it.

I unwound the string that held the flap closed and removed a stack of eight-by-ten black-and-white photographs. The top picture was dark and grainy, taken at night with a very long lens. At the center of the shot was the shadowy image of a black sedan, parked on a deserted street in front of a modest suburban house. A man, emerging from the far side of the car, was looking down, his face hidden by the brim of his hat.

The next shot, taken just a few seconds later, was a closer angle, and revealed that there was a woman seated in the car, on the near passenger side. The man had come around to open the door for her, but neither his nor his companion's face was visible. In the third frame, the couple was captured as they passed beneath a streetlamp. While the man's face was still in shadow, the woman's face was clearly illuminated. My heart sank when I recognized Zahra.

There was one more street shot, as the pair entered the house, then the quality of the photos deteriorated. Taken from a new angle, with an even longer lens and using extremely fast film, the first of these photos seemed to hold no more than a mass of light and dark pixels. But as I studied it more closely, the image of an empty room, as seen through an exterior window, emerged. There followed a series of shots, taken in rapid succession, as the lovers came into view, embracing and kissing passionately as they undressed each other. The most damaging shot—the one that Toby would make sure was on the desk of every newspaper editor in Tehran and every political rival Yari had—was a ruinously clear shot of Zahra, mostly undressed, being held from behind by her still-unidentified lover, whose face was buried in her neck as he fondled a breast.

I looked at Toby. I'm sure the disgust I felt in the pit of my stomach was clearly visible on my face.

"There's one more," he said.

The final shot caught Zahra's lover at the window as he belatedly pulled the drapes closed. It took me a moment to place his dark, angular face.

"Know him?" Toby asked.

"I've met him a couple of times," I replied. "His name is Azari. Ali Ashraf Azari. He's an army officer. A lieutenant, I think."

"And a Commie."

"We have reliable reports that he's a member of the Tudeh Party," Roosevelt explained. "We'd been watching him when we came across her."

I could feel Roosevelt's penetrating stare as I replaced the photos in the envelope. I looked up to meet it. "These are for me?"

"Yes."

"We have copies," Toby said, and Roosevelt shot him a look.

"Jack is aware of that," he said, then turned back to me. "Are you happy to make the move with Fatemi?"

"I'm not sure *happy* is the right way to put it."

"Look, Jack," Roosevelt said in a sincere-sounding voice, "I don't like using these sorts of tactics, either, but the situation doesn't give us any choice. We need him on our side now."

"Can I promise him the negatives?"

"You can promise that the negatives will be destroyed on the day Mossadegh is arrested. And if he gives us full cooperation, he'll be given a job in the new government."

"Right," I said as I stood up. "I guess I'd better get to him before he gets to Mossadegh."

"Hey, Jack!" Toby stood up and followed me to the door.

"Yeah?"

"No hard feelings, huh?"

I wasn't sure if he meant that he had no hard feelings toward me, or that I should have none toward him, but whatever he was trying to say, it didn't change anything, and I wished that he'd just kept his mouth shut.

"Sure," I said. "No hard feelings."

TWENTY-FOUR

The envelope lay beside me, on the backseat of the car. If I'd placed it there in an effort to disassociate myself from its contents, it wasn't going to work. It was mine now. And as much as I hated it—as dirty and base as it made me feel—I knew I would have to use it.

The uneasy feeling in the pit of my stomach condensed to form a painful knot. I was about to deliver a devastating blow to Yari, his family, and, above all, to Zahra. In love with the wrong man, she had turned to me because she had no place else to go. I'd been sympathetic to her pleas—at least I'd pretended to be—but I'd ignored them, dismissing her distress as nothing more than the fleeting woes of a teenage girl. What would happen to Zahra now? I wondered. Would she be ostracized? Sent away perhaps, banished from home, family, and friends. Or quickly wedded off to the undertaker before rumors made her an unacceptable candidate for marriage.

A casualty of war, I tried to tell myself. But what the hell kind of war were we engaged in? Had the defense of democracy really come down to skulking around bedroom windows, photographing people in their most intimate moments, like some sleazy Hollywood private eye? I'd seen war up close, and I'd experienced a full range of human emotions during my three years of combat, from bitter repulsion to sorrowful reverence, but the one thing I'd never felt was cheap. I did now.

Hadi made the turn onto Yari's street and I steeled myself for what was to come. I thought about my first visit to the Fatemi home, three months earlier, for Zahra's sister's wedding. It occurred to me that I'd seen Azari there. Yes, I'd interrupted a conversation with Viktor Kerensky, who Sam had later told me ran the KGB station in Tehran. Then I recalled giving Azari's name to Sam. That's right. I'd phoned Sam that night. He'd asked me whom I'd seen with Kerensky, and I'd told him about Azari.

For Christ's sake! Was that how they'd decided he was a Communist?! Was that why they'd arranged for him to be followed? Because I'd seen him talking with Kerensky? I wanted to believe they had more to go on than that, but having seen now how Toby operated, it seemed unlikely. Azari was probably as much a Communist as he was a Buddhist. Not that it mattered what he was. He wasn't the issue. He was the wedge.

And what about Kerensky? Where had the KGB chief been all these months? Where had any Russian agent been, for that matter? Had they been playing some insidious game behind the scenes, manipulating events in order to install a government more sympathetic to their regime? There was no evidence of that. In fact, there was no sign that they were doing anything in Iran. No, it seemed that the only crowd manipulating events from behind the scenes was us. And we didn't seem to be doing a very good job at it.

* * *

A plainclothes policeman greeted me at the door. I handed him my business card and was told to wait in the vestibule with his partner while he checked to see if I would be seen. The better part of twenty minutes passed before the detective reappeared and indicated for me to follow. The house was eerily quiet as we climbed the stairs, then walked along the narrow, carpeted hallway toward Yari's bedroom. Gripping the blue folder that held the manila envelope tightly in my hand, I realized that my mouth and throat had dried up. I tried to lick my lips, but there was nothing there.

I found Yari standing at the window, fully dressed, looking out onto the empty courtyard. The hastily made-up bed told me that he'd gotten out of it to receive me.

"I'm surprised to see you," he said, turning to face me.

"I thought we should talk."

"Your secretary has already provided a great deal of information about you and your company."

"I'm here to tell you the rest."

Yari gave me a long, studious look. The bandages that covered the left side of his face made him hard to read, but I had the sense that, though skeptical, he was ready to listen. No doors had been closed, which meant that he hadn't yet spoken with Mossadegh.

"The Americo Oil Company doesn't exist," I began. "At least, not as an oil company. It's the creation of the United States government. Specifically the Central Intelligence Agency."

"Go on," he said, taking an unplanned step toward me.

"It was created as part of a plan to remove the present government of Iran and replace it with one that will be less vulnerable to interference from the Soviet Union. My role has been to win your confidence in order to gather information about the government's strengths and weaknesses. Through my efforts, we've been able to identify and recruit a number of military officers to our cause, including some generals."

Yari wasn't hard to read now. His initial expression of incredulity gave way to one of contempt. I knew it would get worse, but I also knew that I had to put my feelings aside, just as he would have to put his aside when he understood what was at stake.

"In order to win public support for the change," I continued, "we've been running a campaign to undermine Mossadegh. Much of what you've seen in the newspapers over the past three months has been initiated by us. The idea is to discredit the government by tying it to the Tudeh Party, which we've been portraying as a bunch of out-of-control anarchists."

Yari found his voice. "So you had Afsharti kidnapped from my house in order to make it look as though I had conspired with the Communists."

"Yes," I said flatly, doing my best to sound callous about it.

"I see. And the general?"

"He knew nothing about it," I said. There was no point in telling him about Afsharti's fate. That could wait.

Yari took a deep breath and furrowed his brow. The bitterness in his eyes was softened with a trace of sadness. "What is the reason for the confession, Jack? Why are you telling me all of this?"

"Because I want you to join us."

He looked at me like I was insane. I think he might even have laughed if he hadn't found my suggestion so arrogantly grievous. Then a wave of anger overtook him.

"I should have you arrested right now!"

"You can't . . ."

My heart raced as I reached for the envelope. It was in my hand when the door flew open, startling us both. Zahra entered, carrying a tray of food.

"Yari!" she cried, stopping in midstep. "What are you doing?! Why are you out of bed?!" She looked to me for support. "The doctor told him to stay in the bed! He could start bleeding inside the head when he stands!"

"Not now, Zahra," Yari said. "It's not a good time—"

"You're right! It's not a good time! Go away, Jack!" She placed the tray on a table and shooed me away, like a pesky fly. "Yari needs to rest. Business will have to wait."

"Zahra, please," Yari pleaded as she took him by the arm and started pulling him toward the bed.

"You must be in bed."

Yari yanked his arm free and stood his ground. He spoke quietly, but firmly. "I'll go to bed after I've talked with Jack."

His sister looked back and forth between us. If she picked up any sign of the tension that hung in the air, she dismissed it, concerned only with her brother's well-being.

"Jack can stay if you get into bed," she decided. "Otherwise, I will stay, too."

She crossed her arms and planted herself on the bed, a no-nonsense version of her usually capricious pout cemented onto her face. Yari stood there, in the middle of the room, powerless in the face of her tenacity. He looked somewhat embarrassed.

"All right," he finally said with a sigh of defeat. "I'll lie on the bed." He sat on the bed and started to ease himself down onto the pillow, but Zahra wasn't going to let him off that easily.

"In the bed," she stressed. "And in your pajamas."

"Zahra . . ."

She stood up, snatched a pair of black silk pajamas off the dressing screen that stood in the corner of the room, and held them out at arm's length for Yari. There was another standoff.

"Help me, Jack," she said after a moment. "He'll listen to you."

"You're doing fine."

I couldn't help smiling, and I think Yari might've betrayed one, too, as he surrendered to the inevitable. He wearily accepted the pajamas and disappeared behind the screen. Zahra beamed triumphantly as he slipped in between the sheets, but she wasn't ready to declare victory yet.

"Now you must eat something," she said, reaching for the tray.

"Later, Zahra," Yari said, in a way that told her it was time to quit. She replaced the tray on the table, turned, and flitted toward the door.

"Don't stay long, Jack," she said, leaving behind a last over-the-shoulder look of satisfaction. An awkward silence fell over the room and we avoided looking at each other.

"She's . . . She's taking good care of you," I finally ventured. Yari couldn't suppress a smile.

"She is a good girl," he said proudly.

Yes, I thought. She is a good girl.

"So . . . ?"

Toby had been pacing back and forth like a caged animal, ready to pounce the moment I came through the door. Al Keating was seated at a table, engrossed in a book, and Bob was lying peacefully on the floor in front of the phonograph, eyes closed, listening to a Perry Como LP. He pulled himself up onto one elbow as I entered.

"We still in business?" he asked.

I nodded. "Everything's under control."

Bob pulled himself to his feet. "We should brief J.L."

"It'd be better if Jack filled us in first," Toby said, but it was too late because Roosevelt was standing in the doorway. He paused to relight the pipe clenched between his teeth, then eyed me through the cloud of smoke he'd created.

"You showed him the photos?"

"Yes."

"How did he take it?"

I shrugged. "He'll cooperate."

"Good."

Roosevelt hesitated, then, with nothing more to add, he turned and disappeared back up the stairway. I'd expected more of a grilling, so had spent the trip back to the safe house writing and rehearsing the scene in my head, the way it might've happened if I'd gone through with it. But it seemed that even Toby was going to take me at my word.

"It's a dirty business," he said, patting me on the back as he left the room. Bob followed him out, leaving me with Al, who gave me a look, then went back to his book.

I wasn't sure if it had been weakness or strength that made me put the photos back in the folder. I guess it depends on your point of view. At any rate, Zahra's timely interruption had changed my mind. I just didn't have it in me to use her like that. When she'd gone, Yari had pulled himself up in the bed and eyed me with what I thought was a fair amount of reticence. Enough to make me think there was a chance I could bluff it out.

"After what you've told me, I can't simply let you leave," he'd said unconvincingly. "And since you hold no diplomatic immunity, there is nothing to prevent me from having you arrested."

"Sure," I said, pulling up a seat. "You can arrest me. But you'd better think it through first. Think it through all the way, taking into account how this is likely to play out. Because what you decide now isn't going to affect just you. It will affect your entire family, for the rest of their lives."

He didn't respond, but I could see that I had his attention, so I continued.

"What if I told you that I'm so important that all you have to do is arrest me and the entire operation to replace Mossadegh will come crashing down? I don't think you'd believe me, and you'd be right. There are powerful forces that want a new prime minister, Yari. The government of the United States of America, for one, but they're not alone. Most of the generals in your own army want a change, and so does the Shah. So do a majority of the people of Iran."

"They've been told lies."

"And they will continue to be told lies, regardless of what you do with me. It's time to be a realist, Yari. With all those forces working together, with one aim in mind—to get rid of Mossadegh—what do you think his chances are? Come on, what do you think?"

"Now that we know the truth, Mossadegh will act quickly. He can—"

"Even if he expels every last diplomat in the American embassy, he won't touch our people. This is the CIA, Yari. They're everywhere. In your police, your military, inside your own government. Mossadegh can't win. He's finished, regardless of what you do. Why not be on the winning side? If not for your sake, for your family's."

I paused a moment, to let it sink in. Yari sat there, staring straight ahead, at the wall. I couldn't read his mind, but his silence told me I'd struck a chord, so I pressed on.

"You don't have to give up your principles," I said. "Just your man. Nobody wants to take away your democracy. They want to strengthen it. Look what America did in Europe, after the war. You can play a big part in that, Yari. I promise you that you will have an important position in the new government."

He turned sharply to face me. "Who the hell are you to offer me a position in the government of my own country?!"

"I'm your friend."

"My friend?" He laughed bitterly and shook his head. "Tell me then, my friend. What would you say if our roles were reversed?"

"I'd say that it's unfair, and unjust. That I have no right to interfere in your country's affairs. And my first reaction would be to fight it in any way I could, even if I knew it was a losing battle. But I hope I'd come to my senses before it was too late, and realize that the better way—for me, my country, and my family—would be to accept the inevitable. I wish things were different, but they aren't. Neither one of us can change it. Work with us and I promise that you'll stay in a position of influence, and the United States will do everything it can to help you build a better, stronger democracy for Iran. Work against us, and, well . . . Before you decide what to do, Yari, I hope you'll think about how much you have to lose."

What didn't occur to me, of course—what I could never have anticipated—was how much we all had to lose.

TWENTY-FIVE

"Damn!" Toby let a soft whistle escape through his bottom teeth. "Now that's what I call a shitload of money."

Bob Cotton leaned over to run his fingers across the stacks of used fifty-dollar bills. "How much is it?"

"A couple of million," Roosevelt said offhandedly. "There's another three in that one." He nodded toward the corner of his office, where a second valise, slightly larger than the first, was sitting unopened.

"About that raise . . ." Bob quipped. But Roosevelt was in no mood for jokes that morning. It was the fifteenth of August 1953. D-day in Tehran.

"All payouts will be made in two installments," he said, grabbing two bundles of bills, one in each hand. "Half today, with the balance payable tomorrow, once Mossadegh is safely under arrest. That goes for everyone—military, police, political, media, whatever. This will be a cash-on-delivery coup."

It was unusual for Roosevelt to hold a meeting in his office. He loved the heat and preferred to sit on the terrace, or by the pool, but I guess flashing that kind of money around would make anybody nervous. Today, he was taking no chances. He'd even drawn the venetian blinds.

Sitting on the desk, beside the cash-laden suitcase, was a stack of manila envelopes and a piece of lined writing paper. A list of names was scribbled down the right-hand side of the sheet, each one with a dollar figure beside it. Roosevelt started at the top.

"Colonel Nasiri, twenty thousand."

He placed four bundles of bills in one of the envelopes, sealed it with a small, damp sponge, then handed it to Toby. Once he'd crossed all the names off his list, passing out a dozen packages of various sizes, he turned to me.

"You didn't put in a request for Fatemi, Jack."

"He hasn't asked for money," I said.

"Did you offer?"

"No."

Roosevelt paused, furrowed his brow. "Is this man reliable?"

"No less reliable than if he wanted money."

Toby couldn't help jumping in. "He's seen the pictures, right?"

"Yes," I lied. "He's seen them."

Three weeks had passed since I'd secured Yari's cooperation without having to resort to blackmail. Toby, always suspicious, had pressed me on several occasions for details, but in the end, I was pretty sure he believed me. If he hadn't, the photos would've found their way to Yari through some other route.

I was surprised at how compliant Yari had been since I laid out the facts for him. I guess he was smart enough to see the writing on the wall, and enough of a politician to heed the message. But unlike most, if not all our recruits, he wasn't motivated by personal gain. He was still driven by his ideals. Maybe that sounds corny, or a bit starry-eyed, and it probably was, but it didn't make it any less true. Yari was a romantic, who dreamed of a country that was based on the principles of social justice, as proclaimed by Cyrus the Great, two and a half thousand years earlier. But it turned out that he was enough of a realist to understand that his dream could never be realized with the active opposition of the most powerful country on the planet. He didn't like or agree with the idea that Mossadegh had to be replaced, but, he reasoned, if he had to go, it didn't mean that his hopes for Iran had to go with him. That was how I was reading him anyway, and why I hadn't offered him money.

"Maybe you'd better give him this," Roosevelt said, stuffing thirty grand into an envelope. "I don't think it can do any harm."

I nodded and took the money, though I wasn't sure what I'd do with it. I'd take it with me, I decided, and play it by ear.

We went through the day's activities one last time, even though there wasn't much more we could do at this point. Things had been in place for some time, delayed only by the Shah's reluctance to sign the *firman,* or royal decree, that we'd drafted for him. Without it, there would be no legal basis for the arrest of the prime minister, but more to the point, none of the royalist military officers we'd lined up would make a move without it. So, for the past two weeks Roosevelt had been making midnight trips to the palace, trying to cajole the skittish monarch into joining the plot. In the end, he'd used pretty much the same tactic I'd used on Yari, saying the coup would go ahead with him or without him, and making clear that if he wanted to keep his throne, it was time to sign on the dotted line.

The plan was simple enough. Shortly before midnight, Colonel Nasiri would lead a convoy of officers and soldiers from the imperial guard onto the streets of Tehran. Their first stop would be at the home of General Taqi Riahi, the army chief of staff, who was an unshakable Mossadegh ally.

Once he was taken into custody, the caravan would proceed to Mossadegh's home, where the prime minister would be shown the *firman* that dissolved the government and dismissed him from office. If he made any protest—which, of course, he would—he would be placed under arrest, as well, and both men would be transported to Qasr prison. Government lawyers, under the supervision of Al Keating, had already drawn up legal papers, charging the prime minister with treason.

Once Mossadegh was in custody, shortly after midnight, a group of midlevel army officers, all on the payroll, would fan out across the city, taking control of the telephone and telegraph exchanges, as well as Radio Tehran. Another group would go to the homes of cabinet members, government officials, and party leaders, rouse them from their beds, and drag them off to join the former prime minister behind bars. Yari would be the one senior member of the government to avoid that fate.

The following morning, at 6 A.M., the new prime minister, General Fazlollah Zahedi, would address the country on national radio. The speech—drafted by Bob Cotton and approved in London and Washington—would announce the change in government, and pledge a new era of well-being for the Iranian people. There would be new roads, new schools, and free health care for all. More jobs would be available, with higher wages, and there would be lower prices at the markets. Order would be restored, bringing an end to the anarchy and crime that had become all too common on the streets of Tehran. Your new government, he would conclude, will give the children of Iran a modern country that is strong, free, secure, and prosperous.

Who could argue with that?

My apprehension grew as I approached the front door. I hadn't been to Yari's home since the day he left the hospital, and though I knew I'd be received politely, I also knew that

I wouldn't be welcome. But it was Saturday, so I had no choice but to make the house call.

Up until now, the only thing I'd asked of Yari was his silence, but today I needed more than that. Mossadegh was a notoriously unpredictable man, and had been known to disappear without warning, often for days at a time. He'd sometimes hole up in the bedroom of his boyhood home, about an hour outside Tehran, or check himself into a hospital, where he would fret about some imagined disease until he was coaxed back into the world. Yari was among the small circle of people who'd be kept informed of his whereabouts, and I wanted to be sure that he'd let me in on any last-minute changes to the schedule. It wouldn't be much of a coup if we couldn't find the prime minister.

A grim-faced housekeeper had me wait on the doorstep while she checked to see if Mr. Fatemi would see me. It was a punishingly hot day, the kind that makes you feel that you can't draw a real breath, so I slipped out of my jacket, hung it over my arm, and used my panama hat as a fan. The effort just made me hotter, and by the time the lady returned, I was dripping with sweat.

I was led to the end of a high corridor, where a pair of arched doors opened onto a formal sitting room. It was a part of the house that I hadn't seen before, and it had that lifeless quality that you find in a room reserved for solemn, usually unhappy affairs. I could imagine it being a place to mourn a family member, or perhaps to pray for a sick one.

The housekeeper left without a word, but I caught the suspicious glance she threw my way as she pulled the door shut behind her. I threw my coat and hat on a white silk armchair, lit a Lucky Strike, and took a turn around the room. There was a sense of quiet impregnability about the place, a womblike security that made me feel anxious, like an intruder in a house full of sleeping people. Exhaling a lungful of smoke, I watched it drift lazily upward into a shaft of sunlight that had found its way through the heavy satin drapes that covered the windows. Was their purpose to block the light from entering, or were they there to prevent passersby from looking in? Well, whatever the intent, the many layers of heavy material accomplished both.

Something drew my eyes toward the far side of the room, where a piece of art was displayed on a shoulder-high stand. A stone sculpture, unilluminated, seemingly forgotten in the dark corner. As I approached, it took on the shape of a man's head. An older man, it seemed, but that might've been an effect of the long, rectangular beard that cascaded off his chin, neatly organized in several dozen rows of tightly wound curls. His large, pear-shaped eyes were empty—perhaps they'd been painted at one time—but still managed to convey the expression of a man who met the world with both authority and compassion. His full lips seemed poised to speak, and when they did, the words would be deliberate, and full of conviction.

"He died in battle."

Yari hit a wall switch, flooding the stone image with crisp, clean, white light. He'd come in silently, or perhaps I'd been too engrossed in my face-to-face with King Cyrus to be aware of his entrance. Anyway, it took me by surprise.

"That's how legends are made," I said, but Yari shrugged it off for the silly comment that it was. He crossed the room, stood beside me, and stared into Cyrus's face.

"History has given us many conquerors," he said softly. "Greatness can come only from what is done with the victory."

"First you have to win," I said.

He turned to meet my look head-on. "Yes. There is that. But . . ." He hesitated, unsure if he should proceed, then decided that he would. "Men matter, Jack. It matters which men we choose as our leaders. Great ones don't come along very often. When they do, we dispose of them at our own peril."

"Like Mossadegh?"

Yari smiled, allowing the bitterness to show through. "Yes. I believe he had the potential to be one of those men who shape events. But don't worry." He sighed and turned his gaze back toward the stone. "I'm not like him. I have no intention of trying to turn the tide of history."

I stashed the envelope containing the thirty grand in the glove compartment. Offering it to Yari would've been like rubbing salt in the wound, or adding insult to injury, or whatever cheap cliché you care to use. He'd agreed to keep me informed about Mossadegh's movements, and that was it. I tried to say something about him doing the right thing, and that once the new government was in place, we could work together toward a better future for Iran, but it sounded hollow, even to my own ears. Yari just smiled courteously and said he hoped I was right.

I don't want to give you the impression that I'd lost faith in what we were doing. Sure, I was unhappy about the tactics—the photos were a cheap shot and the Afsharti operation had been just plain stupid—but nothing had changed my underlying belief that Mossadegh had to go. Sure, the Soviets were in disarray while they figured out who was going to fill Stalin's shoes, but that wouldn't last long. As soon as the power vacuum was filled, there could be little doubt that the Kremlin's eyes would turn south, toward Iran. Yes, now was the time to act, and, I rationalized, there was no reason why Iran, under the protective umbrella of the United States, couldn't flourish into a strong, modern democracy, as Western Europe had after the war. Anyway, that's what was going through my mind as I turned the ignition and started to pull away from the house.

"Jack!"

Zahra ran up to the car and leaned into the window. "I didn't know you were here! Have you been with Yari?"

"Yes, I . . . I just left him."

"I hope you cheered him up! He's been very . . ." She

didn't have the word at hand, so made a grumpy face to illustrate her brother's mood.

"He has a lot on his mind," I said, which she dismissed with a shrug.

"You weren't going to leave without seeing me, were you?" She pouted. "I have something to tell you, and I won't let you slip away this time!"

I put up no resistance as she opened the door, took hold of my arm, and pulled me out from behind the wheel. Seemingly oblivious to the effects of the heat, Zahra chatted amiably as she escorted me, arm in arm, through the courtyard, then into the garden and down the slope toward the water. She seemed to know where she was going, and after a few minutes, we arrived at an out-of-the-way spot at the edge of the stream.

"Come," she said, pulling me closer. "We'll go in the water."

"In the water?"

"You'll feel better!"

She plopped herself down on the bank, kicked off her shoes, and unashamedly rolled down her nylons. Tossing a mischievous look over her shoulder, she held her skirt up and waded in.

"Come in, Jack!" She beckoned. "Don't be shy!"

What the hell, I thought, and sat down to untie my shoes. I had one of them off when Zahra suddenly called out.

"Jack! Help me! I . . . I can't move!"

There was a look of genuine panic on her face, and she was reaching out to me with both arms, like a frightened child would. The next thing I knew, I was splashing through the water, with one shoe on and one shoe off. Zahra had waded out too far, into deeper waters, where she found the stream's muddy bottom.

"I'm sinking," she said, almost matter-of-factly, but in a small, frightened voice.

I couldn't see much through the sullied water, but it

seemed that Zahra was buried up to her knees, and the more she struggled to pull herself out, the deeper she was getting.

"Don't move," I instructed her. "Stay perfectly still."

"Can you pull me out?"

"Put your arms on my shoulder."

She did.

"Okay. I want you to lean forward and put all your weight on me . . . That's it. Now—" I hesitated.

"What?"

"I'm stuck, too."

"No . . ."

"Yes."

We gave each other one of those "what the hell do we do now?" looks, then there was nothing to do but laugh. We stood there, stuck in the mud, Zahra's arms around my shoulders, laughing uncontrollably for a good few minutes before we finally got hold of ourselves.

"What can we do?" Zahra said.

I took a deep breath and gathered my thoughts. "Swim," I said.

"Swim?"

"If we lie down, it'll take the weight off and we'll be able to pull ourselves free." I was skeptical, but it was the only idea I had, so I made it sound like a sure thing.

"Ready?" I said.

She nodded, and we dropped down together into the cool fresh waters. With a little maneuvering, I was able to worm my way out of the mud (leaving my shoe behind) but Zahra was in a bit deeper and couldn't get free. In the end, I had to lie back, almost flat on my back and—trying to keep my head above water—slowly twist her loose, extracting her from the mire like a cork from a bottle.

We crawled back onto the bank, soaked through and through, and fell into fits of laughter again. Zahra had a full, throaty, uninhibited laugh that was infectious, and I gave myself over to it, forgetting for the moment about all the stuff that was supposed to be so goddamned important. We lay there on our backs, coughing and sputtering and laughing until there was nothing left. Then Zahra turned on her side and just looked at me. I wasn't sure what the significance of the look was. There probably wasn't any. I was just projecting my own feelings onto her expression.

"I'm sorry," I said.

"For what?"

"I haven't really been much help to you, have I?"

She smiled. "No, you haven't. Aside from saving me from drowning in two feet of water, that is."

I wanted to offer to help her now, to talk to Yari on her behalf, but it was too late for that, of course. She sat up, pulled her knees up, and wrapped her arms around her legs, as if she'd suddenly felt a chill.

"It's all right, Jack," she said, sounding suddenly serious, and much older. "I had no right to ask for your help. It put you in a difficult position. I was afraid to do it myself, but I shouldn't have been. It's my life. It's up to me to say how I want to live it." She lowered her head onto her knees and looked over at me.

"This is what I wanted to tell you, Jack. I've decided to talk with Yari and my father. I'll say that I won't marry the man they have chosen for me. I'll marry the man I have chosen. The man that I love with all my heart."

Hadi sat up behind the wheel and gave me a cockeyed look. Something to do with the fact that I was soaking wet, shoeless, and covered in mud from head to toe. I decided to let him wonder, and slipped silently into the backseat as if nothing had happened. He gave it up with a shrug and keyed the engine.

"Hotel?" he asked, eyeing me in the mirror.

The round-trip to the Iranshahr would've been well over an hour, and the safe house was just ten minutes away, so

I told him to take me straight there. It was pushing five o'clock already, when we were supposed to gather for a last briefing before Roosevelt gave the coup its final go-ahead. I could get cleaned up while Hadi went on to the hotel to fetch me a change of clothes.

As we pulled away from the curb, another car came to a stop in front of the house. We were already moving so I couldn't be sure, but I thought the man who stepped out onto the road was none other than Lieutenant Azari. It struck me as odd that Zahra's lover would be visiting her at home when she was betrothed to another man, but I didn't give it more than a passing thought. I was glad she'd decided to make a declaration of independence. She deserved a shot at happiness.

In fact, I was feeling more upbeat about everything. While Yari was understandably disgruntled about Mossadegh's fate, he seemed resigned to it, and his bitterness would surely fade with time, particularly once he learned about the cabinet-level post I'd arranged for him in the new government. Perhaps we'd even be able to reestablish some version of the friendship that had started to develop between us.

That was my hope anyway as I sat back and took in the rich warmth of the day's last sunlight. I thought about the changes that darkness would bring, and the lives that would be affected, and for one brief, passing moment, I panicked. At the time, I chalked it up to a case of pregame jitters, but maybe there was more to it than that. Maybe, deep down, I knew my optimism was just another deception.

TWENTY-SIX

"What the hell'd'ya do, Jack? Get baptized?" Toby greeted me with a shit-eating grin on his face and a bottle of Russian vodka in his hand.

"Something like that."

"Christian, I hope!"

"I forgot to ask."

He laughed. "Well, join the party! You're about three drinks behind!"

The party consisted of Toby, Bob Cotton, Al Keating, and a couple of guys I hadn't seen before, sitting around the living room of the safe house, drinking and telling tales of their own exceptional exploits. Roosevelt, I learned, hadn't yet returned from the American embassy, where he was briefing the ambassador on the coming events.

I poured myself a large scotch on the rocks, escaped upstairs, and ran a hot bath. I must've dozed off in the tub because by the time I got out, it was dark and there was a change of clothes hanging on the inside of the door. I found somebody's razor in the cabinet, used it to shave, then dressed and headed downstairs.

The festivities were in full swing, with smoke and sweat filling the air, and the phonograph blaring out Broadway show tunes at full volume. It occurred to me that it might be a bit premature for a victory celebration, but even Roosevelt was letting his hair down.

"Jack!" He greeted me like a long-lost son, placing his arm around my shoulder as he ushered me into the room. "Now the gang's complete, I can make my toast!"

He called for silence, which was ignored until Bob Cotton backed him up, shouting out, "Shut the hell up! J.L. wants to talk!"

Somebody lunged for the phonograph, fumbled the arm, and scraped the needle across "There Is Nothing Like a Dame" from *South Pacific*. It made an awful noise, but it quieted the room. I was handed a tall vodka, neat, and Roosevelt took center stage.

"Gentlemen!" he called out, raising his glass. "To you! For tonight you will make history!"

A drunken cheer went up. Glasses were emptied and refilled, then there was silence again as we waited for Roosevelt to continue. He took a moment, his wrinkled brow signaling that he had something important on his mind.

"I'm proud of you men," he finally said, in a hushed tone, deadly serious. "Proud of each and every one of you. Because should this operation succeed tonight—and there is every reason to believe that it will—you will have accomplished something of great importance. More important than you perhaps realize."

He cast his eye around the room. Not wanting to break the spell, no one spoke, or even moved.

"The world can no longer afford an all-out war." He reverted to his usual, more professorial manner. "The consequences are simply unimaginable. Yet, we find ourselves facing an enemy who is bent on expansion, and we've learned the hard lesson of the price that must be paid when that is allowed to go unchecked. So, we must find a third way. A path between war and appeasement.

"Tonight, we will show the way. We'll show that the choice is not between a suicidal war, on the one hand, and, on the other, folding our tent and leaving the world to communism. We're going to show that we can beat the enemy at his own game.

"The stakes are high, gentlemen. If we can contain the Soviet Union, I believe it will die its own death, strangled by its own authoritarian system. Allow it to flourish and, eventually, there will come a day when we will have to face the unimaginable."

He raised his voice and his glass again.

"So I drink to you, gentlemen! To my small band of covert warriors, who will lead the way to peace and security in our time! All we ask is for a little luck!"

Bob Cotton hit his cue and lowered the needle onto the soundtrack from *Guys and Dolls*. A great cheer went up, and a chorus of drunken voices joined Robert Alda in a rousing rendition of "Luck Be a Lady." Singing was never my strong suit, so I hovered in the background, enjoying the revelry. Up to a point, anyway. On the fourth or fifth go-round, I slipped out, to the quiet peace of the back garden. Drawn to the soft lights of the swimming pool, I found a sun lounger, stretched out, and got lost in the starry sky.

"I guess you're not much of a party guy."

Toby had been hoping to take me by surprise, but he was too drunk or too clumsy to pull it off. I'd heard the clinking of the ice in his glass as he tried to sneak up behind me.

"Depends on the party," I said, without bothering to turn around.

"Yeah, well . . ." He pulled a second lounger even with mine, sat down on its edge. "I guess we're not gonna win any singing contests in the near future."

"That's a safe bet," I said.

He looked out across the darkness, breathed in a lungful of air, and slowly exhaled. "You know," he said, "believe it or not, this could almost remind me of home."

"What?"

"This. The night. Something about it. The stillness of the air maybe. The weight of it. The sweetness." He shook his head and allowed himself a chuckle. "There hasn't been a whole hell of a lot about this place that remotely reminds me of East Tennessee, but something about this night does." He let it linger for a moment, then looked over at me. "Ever been?"

"No. Just passing through."

"That's what most people do. Unless you're a fisherman, that is. The fly-fishing brings 'em in from all over the place. Nothing like it."

"I'm not much of a fisherman, either."

"Too bad for you." He knocked back what was left of his vodka, then watched me out of the corner of his eye. "Whatever else you think of me, Jack, I'm a real, honest-to-goodness, flag-waving patriot. I believe in all that shit. I believe in it with all my heart."

"I never doubted it."

"And what about you?"

"What about me?"

"What do you believe in with all your heart?"

"What makes you think I've got a heart?"

Toby shook his head, started to raise his glass to his lips, then remembered it was empty. "I know more about you than you think I do," he said.

"Is that right?"

"For instance . . . I know where you were on the morning of June the sixth, 1944."

He'd managed to ambush me this time. "What about it?" I said, managing to sound indifferent.

" 'Showed unyielding determination and extraordinary

heroism in the face of ruthless enemy resistance.' That sound at all familiar?"

"You shouldn't believe everything you read," I said, firing up a smoke. Toby squinted his eyes at me and frowned.

"I just don't get you, Jack."

"Does it matter?"

"Let me tell you something . . ." There was frustration creeping into his voice now. "I went to Roosevelt a few weeks ago, after the Afsharti business. To complain about you. I told him that I thought you weren't fully committed to what we were doing, and that, to be frank, I didn't trust you. I said that I wasn't sure you had the intestinal fortitude for this kind of work. That's when he showed me your file. Naturally, I felt like a complete asshole."

"Naturally."

He gave me a look, but didn't bite. "I had to concede that whatever you were lacking, it wasn't guts. Roosevelt then made it abundantly clear that he was backing you, one hundred percent, and he expected me to do the same. So I have. But I wasn't wrong, was I, Jack? You do have questions about all this."

"What do you want me to say, Toby? That I get a lump in my throat when I see the Stars and Stripes?" I didn't want to let him get to me, but he was.

"Tell me something, Jack." He leaned in and lowered his voice. "When you hit that beach in Normandy, you didn't have any questions then, did you? Of course you didn't. You couldn't afford to. There was no time to think, 'Are we doing the right thing?' or 'Is this really necessary?' It was kill or be killed, right? Win or lose. Well, it's no different here."

I gave him a look.

"Okay, there are no machine-gun nests to storm, but we're performing exactly the same task as you were nine years ago in France. We're protecting freedom. Protecting those Stars and Stripes, which incidentally, do give me a lump in my throat, every time I see them. We're fighting 'em here, so we don't have to fight 'em back home.

"I'm not questioning your patriotism, Jack, or your guts. You've proved yourself on both those counts. But this is just the first battle in a long, dirty war, and I, for one, intend to be playing a big part in it. All I'm saying is, if you plan to stick around for the next act, you better get your head sorted out."

He sighed, and pulled himself to his feet. "Now I'm gonna go inside, and get my glass filled up again. You're welcome to join us anytime."

I sat there in the dark for quite a while, thinking about Toby. He was arrogant and ambitious, and while intelligent, he was too goddamned gung ho to think things through, as proved in the Afsharti disaster. But he wasn't wrong, not in this case. It was a dirty little war we had on our hands, but, as Roosevelt said, it was the only one we could afford. If I was going to fight it—and it looked like I was—there was no choice but to jump in with both feet. I just wished it was as simple as storming a beach.

Khasardian showed up around 3 A.M., looking like he'd seen a ghost. His own.

"It is disaster!" he exclaimed as we all gathered around him and the two henchmen who accompanied him. "Truly, it is complete disaster!"

"Tell me exactly what happened," Roosevelt said, his voice injecting a note of calm into the situation. Khasardian took a breath.

"They have been awaiting us . . ."

"Who?"

"The army . . . Some commanders . . . They were hiding near Mossadegh's home, waiting for Nasiri to come. They knew about it. They knew he was coming. They were ready with soldiers and tanks . . ."

"Where is Colonel Nasiri now?" Roosevelt asked.

"They have arrested him. And many others. We have just managed to escape, so we have come directly here to tell you what had happened. It is the worst disaster, as bad as it can be!"

"All right," Roosevelt said, clearly annoyed by his agent's panicked reaction. "I want everybody to hit the phones. Talk to all your assets, and anyone else who might know something . . . But don't tell them anything. I don't want this to become a self-fulfilling prophecy. I'm going over to the embassy. Toby, you be ready with a full telephone briefing as soon as I get there. I want to know just how bad it is before I send any cables off to Washington."

Khasardian nominated one of his guys to drive Roosevelt, and as soon as they disappeared out the door, the house burst into action. All five telephone lines were buzzing with frantic calls, everyone trying to figure out what the guy on the other end knew, without giving anything away. Each and every one of the calls to military contacts went unanswered.

I found Khasardian on the kitchen phone. He was yelling down the line in Farsi when I came in, something about arranging a private airplane to take him out of the country. I walked over, grabbed the handset, and replaced it in the cradle.

"What the hell you have done?" he spat at me. "This was very important man!"

"I need to know something."

"You can wait!"

He picked up the handset again and started to dial. I wasn't in the mood, so I wrapped the wire around my fist and ripped it out of the wall.

"I need to know now," I said, taking a step toward him.

"Okay, okay!" He surrendered, actually raising his hands as he took a step backward. "What is so important you must know now?"

"Who was the officer-in-charge at Mossadegh's house?"

"Who was officer-in-charge?"

"Right."

"I . . . I don't know . . . I don't remember . . ."

"Try," I said.

Khasardian frowned, then turned to his remaining henchman—a young guy, built like a tank, who'd been watching the back door. He queried the guy in Farsi, they had a bit of back-and-forth, came to an agreement, then Khasardian turned back to me.

"Yes, it's right. It was a young lieutenant who was in charge. In fact, he was the one who personally placed Colonel Nasiri under arrest."

"Do you have a name?"

"Yes. It is Ali Ashraf Azari."

Bob was on the phone in Roosevelt's office, trying to stay cool as he spoke with some newspaper editor about the early edition. He looked up when I entered and held up his index finger, signaling for me to wait a second.

"Wait one hour, that's all I'm saying," he said into the receiver. "Believe me, you don't want to get this one wrong . . ."

He paused to listen.

"That's what they're saying, but you don't know if . . . Look, just wait. Better to be a couple of hours late than to print something you'll regret later . . . If you . . . Right. Okay. Good. Yes, I promise I'll phone you in an hour."

He hung up and shook his head. "It doesn't look good. Mossadegh's press office has already been in touch with all the papers. They're saying there's been a failed coup by the military, with the support of 'foreign elements.'"

"I need your car," I said.

"What for?"

"I have to see somebody."

"I don't think that's such a good idea, Jack. They've got tanks on the street and they're stopping everyone. Use the phone."

"I have to see this guy in person," I said.

Bob sat back and fixed me with a long look. "I can't, Jack," he said. "No. If you get picked up, we're screwed."

I was considering my options when a smooth, baritone voice spoke up from over my shoulder. "We're already screwed."

I spun around, found Toby's big frame filling the doorway. He gave me a sideways look, shook his head, then spoke to Bob. "Give him the key."

Bob shrugged his shoulders, reached into his pocket, and tossed me a set of keys. I turned to go, but Toby stayed where he was, staring me down as I waited to exit.

"Get it now, Jack?" he said.

"You're blocking my way," I replied, and, after holding his ground for a moment, he stepped aside.

The streets weren't safe. I'd already slipped by one patrol, and I was hearing the occasional rattle of automatic gunfire in the distance. Sticking to the back roads, I drove cautiously, stopping at each intersection to listen for the low rumble of approaching tanks.

The area around the hotel was particularly tricky. I had to park several blocks away and make my way on foot, using the maze of back alleys to avoid the many checkpoints that had been set up in the downtown area. I used the building's trade entrance, ringing the bell over and over until Shamil finally appeared, rubbing the sleep out of his eyes. He was unaware of what was happening outside, so I sent him back to bed and headed up to my room, choosing the stairs over the old, plodding elevator. Ten minutes later, I was back in the car, winding my way north, with the manila envelope, which had been buried under my shirts in the dresser drawer, on the seat beside me.

I was angry. No, I was more than that. I was incensed. Not because I'd been betrayed. Double-crossed, deceived, and deluded, yes, but not betrayed. How could I be betrayed when there had never been any trust to betray? My relationship with Yari had, from the very beginning, been based on lies. At least on my part. No, my anger was a lot less noble than that. I was pissed off because I'd lost. I'd been outplayed.

I'd been sucked in and strung along and played for a *fucking jerk*! It wasn't Yari I was angry with, though. I was angry with *myself*! For Christ's sake, I'd held all the cards, but I'd been too goddamned soft to play them! Toby was right. This game was played in the sewer, and if you weren't prepared to swim in shit, you'd better find something else to do. Well, I wasn't about to quit. I was ready to do what I should have done three weeks earlier. I liked Zahra, but I wasn't about to lose Iran in order to save her dignity.

I should've known better than to believe Yari could be bought off with the promise of a new job. Maybe, in my heart of hearts, I had known. I certainly knew the moment I heard what had happened at Mossadegh's house. The fact that Azari had been the officer-in-charge just confirmed it. Hell, I'd even seen him at the house that afternoon, not an hour after I'd told Yari what was to happen! How could I have missed it? How could I have been *so damned stupid*?

I got myself so worked up that I made a sharp left turn and almost ran straight into a British-made Mk III Crusader tank. It was a mistake that provided a $30,000 windfall to one lucky young sergeant. I wondered as I pulled away if his unit would see any of the action.

Yari answered the bell himself, dressed in a business suit. "You've heard the news?" he said as I entered. I gave him a look. He knew damn well I'd heard the news.

"Well . . ." He shrugged. "These things are bound to be unpredictable."

"Let's not play games," I said.

"Oh?" He shot me a look. "But I thought you enjoyed games. You play them so well."

"You're smarter than this, Yari. We had an understanding."

"The understanding was based on the idea that you would win. That doesn't seem to be the case."

"It's not over."

"Yes, Jack," he said quietly. "It is over, and you have lost." We faced each other across the tile floor. "Why did you come here?" he finally said.

"To tell you what you have to do to make this right."

He shook his head. "You're no different than the rest of them," he said. "I had hopes—"

"I don't give a damn about your hopes," I said flatly, surprised at how empty my own voice sounded. Yari made no attempt to disguise his contempt.

"Well, then. It seems that you've made a dangerous trip for no reason."

"No," I said. "I have a reason."

I held the manila envelope out for him to take. Yari couldn't have known what was inside, but he seemed to understand that, whatever it was, it would change things. He looked up at me and I suddenly felt sick to my stomach. It didn't help that I hadn't eaten or slept in I don't know how many hours, but I wasn't gonna kid myself. I knew where the pain in my gut was coming from.

"I'm sorry," I said, breaking the promise I'd made to myself. "But you've given me no choice."

He hesitated, then stepped forward, and was about to take the envelope when Zahra's voice called out from somewhere inside the house.

"Yari! Yari, where are you?"

She stopped short when she saw me, and ducked back behind the door. Shy about being seen in her dressing gown and slippers, she stuck her head out and smiled charmingly.

"Jack? Why are you here so early?" Her face dropped when she saw our expressions. "What's happened?"

"Nothing," Yari said. "Everything is fine. Go back inside."

"I can see that something has happened," she persisted. "What is it?"

Yari sighed. "There's been an attempt to overthrow the government." Zahra gasped, and he quickly continued. "A small group of army officers tried to arrest Mossadegh, but they were unsuccessful. They've been arrested themselves."

"Thank God," she said, then looked to me. "The British are behind it, aren't they?"

I hesitated, but she waited for a response. "Hard to say," I mumbled.

"When will they understand that those days are over?" She was prepared to continue, but Yari cut her off.

"Go inside now," he said sternly. "Turn on the radio. Mossadegh will speak soon. I'll be there in a moment. Jack and I have things we must discuss."

Zahra nodded, then turned to me and smiled as she withdrew back into the house. It was no more than an innocent parting glance, of no particular significance, but it was enough to sink my heart.

Yari took the envelope, slowly opened it, and removed the contents. He stood there, perfectly still, for what seemed like an eternity, staring at the first grainy image. Then he looked at the second photograph, and the third. When he came to the final shot, he gasped, then rocked back on his heels and slumped against the wall. His face had gone as white as a sheet.

The reaction was predictable, of course, and I'd prepared myself for it. But what I hadn't anticipated was my own response. The anger was gone, but so was everything else. I felt nothing as I stood there watching Yari's pain, his growing distress. It was as if something had gone *click* inside me and switched off all my humanity. There was no sympathy, no shame, no guilt, and no regret. If I felt anything at all, it was contempt. Contempt for the raw hatred that I saw in Yari's eyes when he looked up at me. After all, I told myself, he'd brought it on himself. He'd tried to outplay me and he'd lost.

Yari pulled himself off the wall, straightened his shoulders, and looked me in the eye. "What kind of a man are you?" he said quietly.

TWENTY-SEVEN

November 1979

"Holy Christ, Jack. Are you okay?"

Donnelly couldn't quite get over his shock at my blood-soaked appearance. He stood there, in the middle of his cell, a slightly stunned look fixed to his face.

"I'm all right," I assured him. "You?"

"Yeah, yeah, I'm good." He looked at the mad mullah, who was cowering beside me, then back at me. "I guess you—"

I confirmed it with a nod. Donnelly knew about what I'd been planning for the mullah and my torturer. If they had gone into his cell, he would've been ready with the same reception.

"Think he can get us out of here?" Donnelly asked.

I placed the barrel of the Colt up against the imam's temple. "Let's ask him."

"Yes, yes!" the cleric quickly exclaimed. "I can show to you the way! It is a hidden door! No one will see you!"

"Us," I corrected him. "No one will see *us* . . ."

I was starting to fade, depleted by the murderous rush of adrenaline that had flooded my system a few moments earlier. Donnelly saw it and took over.

"Where exactly is this exit?" he inquired. "How far from here?"

Having committed no violent killings, Donnelly apparently didn't merit the respect I was being afforded. The mullah simply ignored the question. Donnelly scooped up a pebble-size piece of concrete off the floor, and used it to scratch an *X* in the wall.

"If that's where we are, show me the exit," he said, offering the improvised piece of chalk to the mullah, who shrugged his shoulders, as if he didn't understand. That was the extent of Donnelly's patience. He closed his fist around the chunk of concrete, reared back, and delivered an old-fashioned punch in the nose. The cleric went down hard, and lay on the floor, covering his face and whimpering like a wounded puppy, until Donnelly grabbed him by the arm and scooped him up.

"We're here," Donnelly reiterated as he shoved the mullah in front of his map. "Show us where the exit is."

The imam complied, drawing a line going left from Donnelly's *X,* to the end of the corridor, then right, with a little jig to the left, where he made another *X.*

"It is here." He sniffed back the trickle of blood. "It takes only one minute. Maybe two."

"Is anyone guarding it?" Donnelly asked.

"No."

"Why not?"

"It is a part of the prison that is not used."

"What's outside?"

The mullah shrugged. "An alleyway. From there you can make a good escape."

Donnelly grabbed him from behind, spun him around, and shoved him up against the wall. He cocked his arm, threatening another fist in the face. "If you're lying," he said, "or if you give us any trouble, anything at all, my friend won't hesitate to kill you. You believe that, don't you?"

"Yes, yes," he said flatly. "I believe."

Donnelly pushed the imam into a corner, then turned to me.

"Sure you're okay, Jack?" he said quietly.

"I'm fine," I said.

"You don't look fine."

I insisted that I was, even though I was feeling pretty far from fine.

"Are you okay with the gun?"

It felt like I was holding a couple of tons of steel in my hand, but I said, "Sure," anyway. Donnelly took me at my word.

"Okay. I'll walk on his left side and hold on to him. You stay behind us, with the Colt to his head. Ready?"

"I can't," I said.

"What do you mean? Can't what?"

"I . . . I can't leave." A quizzical look came over Donnelly's face. "I . . . I came here for a reason," I said. "I've got to see it through. I want to, anyway."

"Your friend."

"Look, I know it's nuts," I said. "But one way or another, I've ended up here, in the same goddamned prison. There's no way I can walk away. I'm either gonna get him out, or—"

"Die trying?"

I shrugged.

"I don't expect you to come along," I said. "It's nothing to do with—"

"Jack . . ." Donnelly frowned.

"Yeah?"

"You know what a wingman is, don't you?"

"Yeah. I know what a wingman is."

"Good. Because you just got yourself one." He patted me on the back. "Let's find your friend and get the hell out of this hole."

Seeing the abject fear in the mad mullah's eyes was enough to reinvigorate me. Of course, if he'd been thinking straight, he would've realized that we needed him too much to kill him, but logic tends to go out the window when you have the barrel of a Colt .45 halfway down your throat.

"Shall I take it out?" I said.

He nodded.

"Will you tell me the truth this time?"

He nodded again, so I removed the pistol and took a step back to give him some breathing room. The gun-in-the-mouth routine was a bit melodramatic, but, as always, it had a wonderfully therapeutic effect on the mad mullah's foggy memory.

"Yari Fatemi . . ." he said as he found his voice. "Yes . . . Yes. I know him."

"And where to find him?"

"Yes, I know."

"Good, because you're going to take us there."

"Yes. I take you."

Donnelly stepped forward. "And no funny stuff."

Confused by the remark, the mullah tried to smile, but came up short.

"No problems," I interpreted.

"Yes, of course," he said. "With me, no one is give you problem."

Naturally, the mullah wanted to underscore just how much more valuable he'd be as a hostage than as a corpse, but there was no need. It was clearly and uncomfortably obvious that he was our one and only shot at getting out of there in one piece. Even with him, the odds had to be pretty low, but without him, well, you'd have to put our chances somewhere in the neighborhood of zero.

Funny, then, that I'd be feeling so upbeat. In fact, it was more a feeling of intoxication. A sensation that I hadn't experienced in many years, probably going back to Vietnam. It's a strange thing, facing death, and even stranger when you choose to do so. It's not something any sane person wants to do. We spend most of our time trying to avoid that particular confrontation, because it's not one we'll often win. All sorts of precautions are taken as we try to evade and outsmart death, unaware that it's always right there, on our heels, stealing a little piece here and a little piece there. Then, finally, one day, we turn around and there he is. The Grim Reaper. He takes us by surprise, when we're least expecting it, or when we're too weak to fight back, and more often than not, we're so worn out or damaged that we just take his hand and slip away, to follow him into eternity. And that's why it's so exhilarating—so damned heartening—to be able to look the bastard square in the eye and say, "Fuck you! This is what I'm doing! If you don't like it, here I am! Come and get me, you ugly son of a bitch!"

Cracking the heavy iron door that led up from the building's substructure, I was hit by a blinding afternoon light. I looked away, giving my eyes a chance to adjust, then peered down a long, narrow passageway, at the end of which, about fifty yards away, two uniformed men lounged in the shadow of an old, crumbling archway. Each had an M-16 rifle slung over his shoulder. Okay, I thought. So far, so good. It was exactly how the mullah had said it would be. I turned to Donnelly and nodded. He nodded back, and we went into action.

Pulling the unsuspecting mullah into a rear choke hold, Donnelly had him out the door before he knew what was happening. I followed quickly, staying behind and to the right, holding the Colt a few inches from the cleric's head, making sure it was fully visible. My heart was pumping and my mind racing as we moved swiftly up the hallway, doing our best to take the guards by surprise. At thirty yards, one looked up from his cigarette and watched us for a moment, not yet taking in what he was seeing. The Colt was fully loaded, with seven rounds in the magazine and one on the chamber. If they started shooting, I wouldn't waste one on the mullah. I'd hit the floor and return fire. But slow and easy, I told myself. Don't get rattled. Make it count.

A sudden, wincing pain shot up the inside of my leg, and hit me like a steel hammer in the groin.

Jesus Christ!

I pulled up and doubled over in agony, unable to breathe, barely able to stay upright. I must've blacked out for a fraction of a second, too, because the next thing I knew I was looking up at Donnelly, who'd spun around to see what the hell had happened. He said something—I had no idea what—but it didn't matter because behind him the guards were tossing their smokes aside and spinning into action, sliding their weapons around and zeroing in on us.

I don't know how I did it—I guess the prospect of going down in a hail of gunfire was enough incentive—but one way or another I sucked in a lungful of air, yanked myself upright, and pointed the Colt in the direction of our terrified hostage.

"We have your mullah!" I called out, somehow finding the Farsi in the depths of my brain. *"If you shoot, I'll kill your mullah!"*

Nothing happened. Nobody spoke, nobody moved, nobody even breathed. The two guards stood there, like statues, rifles trained on us, deciding what to do next. I was about to break the deadlock and take my chances with the Colt, when the mullah managed to squeeze a sound out of his vocal cords, in spite of Donnelly's iron grip on them. He sounded more like a love-struck duck than a feared imam, but whatever he said, it worked. The two soldiers hesitated, looked at each other, then took a step back and let their weapons drop to the floor.

I turned the pistol on them as Donnelly released the cleric and ran forward. He scooped up their rifles then turned back to me with an expression of mixed euphoria and alarm.

"Jesus, Jack," he said.

The old archway fed into a dark, domed tunnel that connected the prison's fifty-year-old annex, where we'd been housed, with the main structure, a once grand castle dating back to the late eighteenth century. Here, the broken tiles and institutional gray of the twentieth century gave way to an ocher-colored brick walkway surrounded by the rich chiaroscuro of timeworn stone. There was an eerie emptiness to the place, the only sound a low, almost inaudible moan that was probably just the wind whistling through the old walls, but could just as well have been the anguished chorus of the many poor souls who'd suffered and died in the obscurity of these shadows. It sent a chill up my spine.

We were venturing into the very heart of the institution, where Yari awaited trial, conviction, and inevitable execution. His would-be judge, the mad mullah, was our guide, leading us through the seemingly endless maze of forgotten back passages and dark stairways that he said only he knew. Beside him walked the two guards, one dressed in Donnelly's wrinkled white shirt and khaki trousers, the other in my bloodstained pajamas. We followed behind, wearing their uniforms, carrying their rifles.

Passing through several dark twists and turns, no one spoke, not even a whisper. There was no telling what slumbering souls it might disturb.

After several minutes—though I couldn't really trust my sense of time—we came upon a row of cells. Two dozen iron-barred doors, twelve on each side of the corridor, with no more than six feet separating each one. A line of twenty-watt bulbs, hanging from frayed wires, provided the only lighting on the block, which could be accessed from only one side, the way we came in. At the bottom was a dead end.

The unit was watched over by a homely, bearded man with a broad face, a crooked nose, and a small conical hat atop a mop of long curls. He hastily discarded the magazine he'd been ogling and leaped to attention when the mullah appeared at the door of his tiny office. After some bowing and scraping, he realized that something was amiss, but was canny enough to pretend that he didn't. He clasped his hands together at his chest and asked how he could serve His Eminence.

"Fatemi," the mullah said, offering no embellishments.

The jailer jumped to it, fumbling around among the many keys that hung on the wall, finally turning back to the mullah to await further instructions.

"What is your name?" I asked, stepping forward.

"I am Kharon," he answered, surprised to be asked.

"Take me to Fatemi, Kharon," I said.

Looking to the mullah for approval, he got nothing, so he stepped into the corridor and, with a compliant bow of the head, signaled for me to follow. At first, the darkened cells along the way seemed to be vacant, but, of course, they weren't. The condemned had shrunk back into the shadows, averting their eyes as we passed, praying to God that it wasn't their turn, that it wasn't them I was coming for. As miserable as their lives had become, as hopeless their situation, none was ready for release. No one wanted the kind of freedom the mad mullah was doling out.

The jailer stopped at the very last door. He looked to me for an instruction, but I looked past him, into the cell, where a man was stretched out, faceup, on a small cot. Aside from a faint shaft of light that fell across his forehead, he lay in shadow. His only movement—the only sign that he was alive—was the shallow rise and fall of his chest as he breathed in and out. He might have been asleep, but I didn't think so.

My hands were shaking uncontrollably, and I was having trouble breathing. I hadn't anticipated anything like this. It wasn't like me to react with so much emotion. Christ, I'd had friends, good friends, die in my arms, and nothing like this had ever happened. I'd met presidents and kings and it hadn't shaken me. Why now? Why did facing Yari Fatemi fill me with such . . . what was it? Fear? No. Not fear. It was a much deeper disquiet that enveloped me.

I gave the jailer a sharp nod, and he slipped the key into the lock. Pulling the door open, he stepped aside to let me enter alone.

Yari didn't move at first, didn't even open his eyes. I sensed that he was aware of me standing over him, but I suppose he saw no good reason to acknowledge my presence. He'd recognized the sound of the boots approaching, the clatter of the rifle. His heart probably jumped when it was his cell door that was opened. He was probably wondering why he hadn't been pulled off his bed and dragged away yet.

It was an odd sensation looking down on him. I felt that I could see all the years that had gone by, all the battles, all the struggles, and, ultimately, all the disappointment Yari felt, in both the world and in himself. He had aged, certainly. The hair was thinner, the eyes deeper set, the lips less confident without the dashing mustache. But the natural elegance that I remembered was still present, undiminished by the hard lines that life had etched into his face. If anything, it had been enhanced. Through all the weariness, the resignation, perhaps even the acceptance of his fate, I saw in Yari what I'd seen in him on the day we met. A quiet, graceful dignity.

When, after several minutes, neither of us had moved, I quietly said his name. There was a long pause then he opened his eyes. But it was too dark.

"Go there . . ." he said, gesturing toward the cell door. "Go into the light, where I can see you."

I stepped back, into what faint illumination there was. I removed the guard's cap that was on my head, and waited. With a long sigh, Yari swung his legs over the side of the cot, pulled himself into a sitting position. Lowering his head into his hands, he massaged his forehead, as if trying to relieve a permanent ache.

"Do you recognize me?" I said.

He looked up at me, but didn't answer.

"Jack Teller," I said.

"So it has happened," he said, more to himself than to me.

"What?"

"I have lost my mind. I thought it might happen, but I suppose I didn't expect to know that it had happened." He smiled unexpectedly. "What a funny thing. Very strange indeed."

"You haven't lost your mind, Yari. As impossible as it seems, I'm really here."

He stood up and took a step closer. "You seem real."

"I am. I'm here to get you out of here."

He laughed. "Now I know you aren't real!"

"Come on. I'll show you."

I reached for him, tried to lead him out the door, but he froze up. He didn't want to step outside the safety of his cell. Who knows what was going through his mind. Month after month, alone in the dark, speaking to no one, having only your thoughts. Yari had probably been flirting with the edge of reason for some time, holding on by sheer force of will, and now, the only rational explanation for my sudden appearance was that he had lost all sense of reason. He was at an impossible impasse, and I saw the struggle in the disturbing disquiet of his eyes. I didn't know how to assuage him.

"Zahra sent me," I said.

Her name was like a shot to his heart. A long, soul-wrenching sigh erupted from somewhere deep inside, and it was as though a gate had been opened, releasing a flood of welled-up emotion, overtaking all the little strength he had left. He hunched over, holding his gut, and tried to hold back his cries. I reached out to pull him up into an embrace. I held him tightly, and patted him on the back, as a mother would an injured child.

"She told me to come get you out of here," I whispered in his ear. "And we both know, your sister isn't a lady who takes no for an answer."

A sudden burst of laughter exploded from his gut, then he pulled away and looked at me through tear-filled eyes.

"How can it be?" he asked plaintively. "I . . . I don't understand."

"Neither do I, Yari. Neither do I."

TWENTY-EIGHT

August 1953

"Excuse me a moment."

Roosevelt got up to answer the phone that was ringing on his desk, leaving Toby, Bob Cotton, and myself slumped into the wicker chairs on the terrace. It was 7:30 A.M. on Sunday—the morning after our failed coup—and none of us had had any sleep. It showed.

"Yes?" Roosevelt's voice drifted out through the open doors. "I see . . . Are we sure about that . . . ? Right. Yes, it does . . . All right. Well, keep me informed."

He reappeared, looking even gloomier than he had before, and took his seat again. "The Shah's fled the country," he said flatly. "He flew himself and the empress to Baghdad early this morning."

"He's got the backbone of a snail," Toby grumbled.

"I'm not sure I blame him," Roosevelt responded, sounding an uncharacteristically defeatist note.

"They'll use it as proof of his guilt," Bob said.

"Yes." Roosevelt sighed. "And I wouldn't be surprised if Mossadegh declares a People's Republic of Iran before the week is out." He removed his glasses and pinched the bridge of his nose.

"What does Washington say?" Toby asked.

Roosevelt replaced his eyeglasses, reached into his shirt pocket, and removed a thin sheet of paper, which he unfolded and read:

TP-AJAX TERMINATED. NO FURTHER ACTION REQUIRED. ADVISE YOU AND YOUR TEAM. LEAVE COUNTRY ASAP.

He returned the cable to his pocket and leaned back. "Failure's not in my blood," he said.

Toby shifted uncomfortably in his chair. "I don't think putting it in those terms will do anybody any good. Clearly, we've not had the kind of success we were hoping for, but let's not forget that we've done some good here. We've established a solid network of people. We're miles ahead of the Soviets."

Roosevelt looked at him like he was a glass of sour milk. "That's not going to get you very far."

"I'm certainly not suggesting that we call it a success," Toby backtracked. "I'm just saying that there's nothing to be gained by calling it a total failure."

"It's too soon to call it anything," I said.

They all looked at me.

"What's that supposed to mean?" asked Bob.

"It means that it's not over yet. Maybe it will turn out to be too late to turn things around, but it's also too early to throw in the towel."

"Nobody wants to give up, Jack," Bob protested. "But we're looking at a pretty dire set of facts here. Every single one of our army officers is either under arrest or in hiding, my editors aren't even returning my calls, and now it looks like the Shah has called it quits."

"He'll come back if there's a reason to," I said. Roosevelt sat forward wearily, rested his hands on his knees.

"Have you got something in mind?"

"Yari Fatemi."

"What about him?"

"He's Mossadegh's most trusted aide. And he's still with us."

"Are you sure about that?"

"I just left him," I said. "And, yes, I'm sure."

"Okay, then," Roosevelt said. "Continue."

"He placed a call to Mossadegh this morning. I was in the room."

"And?"

"He reported that all the conspirators had been arrested and that he'd been able to determine with absolute certainty that they'd acted alone, without any outside assistance or interference."

Roosevelt looked disappointed. "That's fine, in terms of damage control, but you said it's not over yet."

"There's more."

"Go on."

"He recommended that all police and military units be taken off the streets." Roosevelt narrowed his eyes at me, then reached into his pocket and removed a pipe and tobacco pouch.

"What was Mossadegh's response?"

"He agreed."

Bob jumped in at that point. "Mossadegh agreed to remove all security from the streets of Tehran on the morning after an attempted coup?"

"Yes."

"Why would he do that?" Roosevelt asked.

"It was pointed out to him that when people woke up

to news of the failed coup, they'd come out onto the street to celebrate. And since these would be Mossadegh's own supporters, it would be best to allow the celebrations to go ahead without interference from the police or military."

"That's nuts," Bob said.

I smiled. "Mossadegh didn't see it that way."

"Hmm." Roosevelt sat back and packed his pipe.

"Even if he's foolish enough to follow through," Bob persevered, "how does it help us? Like I said, all our people are either under arrest or in hiding."

I looked to Roosevelt. "You still have that suitcase full of money?"

"Yes," he said. "Of course I do."

"If there's one thing we've learned in Iran, it's that you can buy any kind of crowd you want. You can buy a pro crowd or an anti crowd, or . . . "

"Yes . . ." I could see the wheels turning in Roosevelt's head.

"With enough money, you can buy both."

Roosevelt paused long enough to light his pipe. "Why not?" he mused. "Why the hell not? We've got nothing to lose, do we?"

"Not a thing."

"I'm lost," Bob complained. "What are we talking about?"

Roosevelt ignored the query, and turned to Toby. "Are you in touch with Khasardian?"

"I know how to reach him."

"Good. Get him over here."

"I'm not sure he's gonna want to—"

"If he's here before noon, I'll personally hand him fifty thousand dollars in cash. If he chooses not to come, inform him that I'll make sure the government of the United States of America will make it a priority to track him down and kill him, along with his entire family."

Toby looked a bit taken aback, but quickly warmed to the assignment. "Right," he said, unable to suppress a smile.

"Can one of you please tell me what the hell you have in mind?" Bob said, practically pleading. Roosevelt smiled cagily and looked to me.

"Tell him, Jack."

I shrugged. "Why settle for a coup when you can afford a revolution?"

The atmosphere was electric, the noise deafening. A feeling of unfettered euphoria filled the air as the crowd surged forward, making its way through the narrow streets and alleys of Tehran's grand bazaar. They carried banners and photos and chanted *"Death to Mossadegh! Long Live the Shah!"*

I'd arrived in the early hours of Wednesday morning, three days after Plan B went into effect, as a small crowd began to congregate outside the Shah Mosque, located at the southern edge of the city. By noon, the rally had grown to several thousand, and now, egged on by Khasardian's agents, the assemblage emerged onto Khordad Avenue, swelling the street as it headed west. Their destination—whether they knew it or not—was Ferdosi Square, where they would meet up with other groups that had been gathering around the city's mosques and parks. The horde would then march north, to converge on Mossadegh's house, to demand his resignation and the return of the Shah.

It was most likely the oddest political rally ever assembled. A three-ring circus—literally. In the lead was a contingent of Iran's traditional weight lifters, known as Zurkaneh. Hulking giants of men, they sported preposterous mustaches, and paraded up the street in no more than a pair of sandals and a loincloth, juggling giant pins and hefting massive barbells into the air as they sauntered forward. Then came the acrobats, twisting and tumbling, and the dancers, spinning up the street like a troupe of whirling dervishes. Buzzing around the fringes of the strange collection, men passed out ten-rial notes to observers, who happily pocketed the cash and joined in the chorus of *"Death to Mossadegh!"*

Tehran had been under siege by a very different kind of crowd over the previous forty-eight hours. Like today's group, the participants had been provided by Khasardian, and funded out of Roosevelt's suitcase, but the difference couldn't have been more striking. That crowd, drawn from criminal gangs and thugs from the capital's southern slums, had marauded, unchecked, through the streets, throwing stones through windows, setting fires, and looting shops as they chanted *"Long Live Mossadegh!"* and *"Death to the Shah!"* The riots climaxed when the mob descended on the parliament building, where, using saws and chains, they pulled the statue of the Shah's father from its pedestal. As the bronze came crashing to the ground, the city seemed to be teetering on the edge of anarchy.

On Tuesday evening, Mossadegh met with his top advisors. Yari, the lone voice of dissent, had managed to carry the argument, convincing the prime minister to allow the demonstration to burn itself out. These were, after all, the prime minister's own supporters, he'd argued. It would be a mistake to allow the police to intervene and risk turning the crowd against the government. Mossadegh's real mistake, of course, was in placing such unqualified trust in Yari. It was the final nail in his coffin. By allowing the rioters to run rampant, Mossadegh turned the police against him, as well as many previously loyal army commanders.

Hanging back, I watched the crowd from a distance until the last stragglers had disappeared up Ferdosi Street, leaving behind an eerie silence. After phoning my report in to Roosevelt, who'd been anxiously awaiting news back at the safe house, I had a few hours to kill before my rendezvous with Toby and Bob. We'd arranged to meet a couple of blocks from Mossadegh's residence, in Pahlavi Square, to watch events unfold, and, more important, to push things along, if necessary. There would be no vodka shots and show tunes this time around.

I hadn't had a real meal in days, and now, suddenly, my appetite came rushing back. I felt like walking, so I entered the bazaar, which was uncharacteristically still. Most of the stalls were closed, and aside from a couple of solitary beggars and a few stray cats, I had the place to myself. I don't think I realized until I was on the doorstep that I'd been heading for Café Naderi. It, too, was strangely subdued, the usually rousing games of *takhte-nard* cast with a distinctly melancholy tone. The faces were unfamiliar, as well. I didn't recognize any of the players.

"Salam . . ." I greeted Naderi, who was propped up against the bar, waiting for something to do.

"Ah! Salam! Salam alaykum!" The proprietor recalled the face, but not the name.

"Where is everyone?" I said.

"They have gone in the protest."

"Even Saleh, the Champion of Tehran?"

Naderi's face fell. "Ah. Allah, in his wisdom, has taken our friend. He has died just one month ago."

"Oh . . ." I took a moment to absorb the news, which hit me harder than it probably should have. "I'm sorry to hear that. I truly am."

Naderi nodded and neither of us seemed to know what else to say, so we stood there, silently facing each other for a long moment. We couldn't end it like that, so I spoke up.

"I guess he had a good life."

"Yes. We pray that Allah will forgive his sins."

"I doubt that Saleh had many sins," I said. Naderi paused, as if he was really thinking about it. After a moment he looked up at me, his eyes full of sincerity.

"None of us is without sin."

Pahlavi Square was inaccessible, blocked by the dense crowds that now ruled the streets, so I left Hadi with the car again and walked north, picking my way through the crush, toward the far end of the square, where Toby and I had agreed to meet. The mob had grown beyond our wildest expectations. Even Roosevelt, who'd spent the last seventy-two hours handing out tens of thousands of dollars to anyone he thought could deliver anything resembling a crowd, hadn't counted on this. It seemed that all of Tehran had come out to demand the return of their Shah. Cries of *"Death to Mossadegh!"* filled the air, and as the last light faded, the distant crackle of machine-gun fire and soft bursts of exploding mortars punctuated the night. Our revolution had taken on a life of its own.

"Jack! Over here!"

A half dozen of Khasardian's goons had set up a perimeter to keep the crowd away from the phone booth that was our meeting place. I slipped through the net to find Toby and Bob, both grinning from ear to ear.

"How do you like it?" Toby beamed, as if he'd laid on the whole affair for my benefit.

"What do we hear?" I asked.

"It's in the bag!"

"Not quite," Bob corrected him. "But close. The crowd has the house surrounded, but Mossadegh has a small contingent of troops in the compound. They've got machine-gun fortifications and Sherman tanks, but we think we have some friendly units on the way."

"Everybody loves a winner," Toby said with a wink.

The phone rang and Bob leaped to pick it up. Toby couldn't stop smiling and even patted me on the back. "Look around you, buddy! We're making history! And you know what? It's just the beginning!"

"Maybe."

His smile gave way to a frown. "Come on, Jack. You can smile now. Look what we've done here. This is big."

"I don't know what we've done here," I said. "And neither do you. Maybe we'll know in ten or twenty years."

"Bullshit!" He took a step toward me. "I'll tell you right now what we did. We won. There's nothing complicated about it. We won. And I'll tell you something else. It beats the hell out of losing, and that's the only other choice we've got. But the bullshit part of it is that you know that as well as I do. Why do you have to make it more complicated than it needs to be?"

"I don't," I said.

Toby stepped back and gave me a long, sideways look. Then he said, "It was Fatemi, wasn't it?"

"What do you mean?"

"You know what I mean. He fucked us over. That first night, he was the one who betrayed us to Mossadegh. He had no reason not to because you didn't use those pictures. At least not until you realized what he'd done."

He paused to get my response, but I didn't have one, so we just looked across the darkness at each other for a moment.

"You don't have to answer, Jack," he finally said. "We both know it's true. But look, I'm not out to get you. We're on the same side of this thing. It's a new game for both of us, and the truth is we've both made mistakes. What do you say we work together? We can help each other."

Bob came off the phone and gave us the thumbs-up.

"Mossadegh called out some army units to come to his rescue, but they decided to switch sides. They brought tanks and artillery up, started blasting away at the house. There's some confusion about whether Mossadegh's in custody or if he slipped away, but, either way, he's finished."

Toby reacted to the news with surprising reserve. He shook hands with Bob, who got quickly back on the phone, then he turned back to me.

"This is for you," he said, handing me an envelope.

"What is it?"

"An airline ticket."

"Where to?"

"First to Nice. Take a week, lie in the sun, get yourself fucked by a French girl. The second leg is to Guatemala."

"What's in Guatemala?"

"Bananas."

"Bananas?"

Toby shrugged. "I'll explain when we get down there. The point is that we're just getting started. We've shown the bureaucrats in Washington what we can do, but this was just one battle. This is gonna be a long, tough war and I want you on my team."

"I don't know, Toby," I said. "I don't know if—"

He put his hands up. "Don't answer now. Have that week in the sun. See how you feel after that."

I looked up to see Khasardian charging toward us, arms opened wide. He ignored me, walked straight into an awkward embrace with Toby.

"Come," he said once they'd disentangled. "I have brought some friends to meet you."

I watched as he pulled Toby through the crowd, to a spot about thirty yards away, where something was creating a lot of excitement. People were pressing forward from all sides, reaching and calling out, hoping to get close to whoever was behind the wall of armed young men who guarded him. When Khasardian appeared with Toby, the human chain opened up long enough to allow them through, and I caught a glimpse of two bearded men—both imams, in long, dark robes and black turbans. Toby bowed deferentially as he was introduced, then the group disappeared into the sea of people.

"Who was that?" I asked Bob as he rejoined me.

"Ayatollah Kashani," he said. "Half the people here came out because he said they should. Probably more than half." He gave me a look. "He got one of J.L.'s envelopes, too."

"Who's the other one?"

"His second in command. Name's Khomeini, I think."

I was about to turn away when I caught sight of a familiar face in the crowd—one of the Ayatollah's bodyguards. He'd already spotted me, and was staring back with what I can only call viral hatred in his eyes. He had reason to look at me like that, of course. I'd killed his brother, snapped his neck in two. But I felt there was more to it, that his contempt for me ran deeper and was more fundamental than that. After all, he was a devoted Warrior of Islam. Where would he be without hatred?

"Gonna come back to the house for a glass of champagne?" Bob asked.

"No," I said. "I think I'll get some sleep."

"Don't blame you. Well. See you around, then."

"Right," I said. "See you."

Bob headed off to find Toby. I stood there a moment, taking it all in. It was quite a sight, all right. Then, remembering the airline ticket I was holding in my hand, I tossed it on the ground and started to walk away. It only took a couple of steps to have second thoughts. I stopped, turned around, picked up the envelope, and slipped it into my pocket. What the hell, I thought. I'll decide tomorrow.

Two days later, I paid another early morning visit on Yari. I was on my way to the airport, and though I knew he wouldn't shed any tears over my departure, I didn't feel right leaving without seeing him. Rather than let me through the door, he came out and we stood in the grass.

"I'd be a liar if I wished you well," he said when I told him I was leaving.

"Sure," I said. "I don't expect you to. But I . . . I guess I wanted to wish you well."

"Is that all?"

"Look, Yari, I know I'm the last person you want to take advice from, but forget about me. And forget Mossadegh. What's done is done. You have an opportunity here, an opportunity to make Iran great again. I know that you've been offered a job in the cabinet, and I hope you take it. You'll have the full support of the United States now, to build a real democracy, with real benefits for real people."

Yari looked straight into my eyes and, for a moment, I thought he might have softened. But I'd misread him again.

"I think you always saw me as some sort of starry-eyed romantic, pursuing an impossible dream in a world that I didn't understand." He shook his head and smiled, with a bitterness that hadn't been there before. "But isn't it funny? It turns out that, in fact, I am the realist and you are the starry-eyed romantic."

Hadi accompanied me out onto the tarmac. I don't know if he really wanted to see me off, or if he felt obliged to. Maybe he thought someone should. Anyway, whatever the reason, I appreciated it. I shook his hand, thanked him for everything, and handed him the envelope containing five grand that I'd been saving for him. He was surprised and appreciative.

"Tell me something, Hadi."

"Yes?"

"What do you think about what's happened over the past few days?"

He shook his head. "I am just a driver. I don't know about these kinds of things."

"Tell me what you think."

He shrugged. "Mossadegh was a good man, but the Shah is the Shah. And for me, I am happy with the one who has the power. Only a fool will say otherwise." He paused, gave me a look, and decided he could continue. "I have not an education, but perhaps I am not a fool, too. I know that what is brought by the wind, will be carried away by the wind."

TWENTY-NINE

November 1979

Yari was acting strange. It wasn't just that he hadn't said a word since I led him out of his prison cell. He seemed distant, uninvolved in what was happening. He just stood there, frowning, as if pondering some imponderable, searching for an answer to a question that had no answer.

"Yari?" I said.

He looked at me, but didn't respond.

"Are you all right?"

"Yes . . . Yes, I'm fine."

"You'll have to wear these," I said, holding out a set of handcuffs.

He made no protest, compliantly holding out his wrists for me to snap the cuffs into place. But he was still preoccupied. He kept looking back toward his cell. I thought at first that he was watching Donnelly tie and gag the jailer and the two guards before he locked them inside Yari's cell, but

Donnelly had completed the task and returned to the top of the block, and Yari was still staring down the block.

I should explain what's going to happen, I thought. Maybe it will bring him into the moment. "We're going to walk out the front gate, Yari," I said. "You, me, and Donnelly. They won't challenge us because we have the mullah with us. They'll do what he tells them to do, and he'll do what I tell him. Do you understand?"

He nodded.

"Good. All you have to do is be quiet and keep your head down. Don't say anything and don't look at anyone." I didn't want any stray looks of hope to give our game away. "Do you understand?"

He looked up at me and softly, almost inaudibly, said, "I can't."

"What do you mean?" I said. "You can't what?"

"I can't go."

"What are you talking about, Yari?"

"It's not right."

"Not right? Of course it's right!"

"No. I can't leave them. I won't."

"Leave who?"

"Them . . ." He gestured, arms locked together, toward the row of cells along the corridor.

"Who?" I said. "Who can't you leave?"

"Them."

"Do you mean *all* of them?"

"Yes." He nodded. "All of them."

Looking along the corridor, I noticed for the first time that the condemned men were no longer hiding in the shadows. Each stood at his cell door, peering out from behind the bars, eyes fixed on the unfolding events. They watched with caution, not yet prepared to allow themselves the hope that had long been abandoned.

"No," I said flatly. "It's impossible."

"Why? If they let one go, they will let us all."

"Yari . . . Listen to me . . . It could never work. None of us would get out alive."

He nodded. "Yes, I understand. You are probably right. So I will stay, as well."

"You can't stay!"

He gave me a long, slightly bemused look, then frowned. "I was ready to die. Perhaps it's best that way. Better, anyway, than stealing a few years at the expense of others."

"It's not at their expense!" I argued. "They were never meant to be saved!"

"How do you know what is meant to be?"

I drew a breath, but held my tongue. I glanced over at Donnelly, who was looking more than a little concerned.

"If there were one or two of them," I said, trying to find some middle ground. "Men that you know—"

"I know none of them," Yari replied. "But why does this matter? Should innocent men be left to die simply because I don't know them?"

"If you don't know them, how do you know they're innocent?"

"They are innocent until proven guilty. Or does that great ideal apply only to citizens of the United States?"

It was as though all the grand injustice of the world—all the wrongs Yari had seen, or felt, or suffered—had come down to this one defining moment, and by taking a stand here, he could erase all the unholy bargains, all the sordid compromise that had slowly eaten away at his core. But was I any different? Hadn't I come to erase my own sins? I'd been arrogant enough to think that removing Yari from within the walls of a building would set him free, and give him a second chance at life, but, like all of us, the prison he inhabited was one he'd constructed himself. The only men who do no time in these prisons built of necessity, or neglect, or even weakness of spirit, are those who die young, and the only escape is to find your own way out. Yari had found his way. Now I would have to find mine.

* * *

"A bus?"

Donnelly stared at me, incredulous. I'd pulled him aside to sound him out on the idea, and wasn't surprised that his initial reaction was less than enthusiastic.

"That just might be the craziest idea I've ever heard," he said.

"I think it can work."

"A bus?"

"Look, our friend over there doesn't just run this place." I nodded toward the mad mullah. "He's the word of God. Literally. Whatever he says, no matter how nuts, they have to go along. Nobody can question him."

Donnelly still looked skeptical.

"There's a phone in that office, right?"

"Right . . ."

"Okay. What if we get the mullah on the line with whoever's in charge of logistics? He tells him that the Ayatollah Khomeini wants to have a group of prisoners brought down to his headquarters, in Qom . . ."

"What for?"

"No one will ask, but if somebody does, we'll say it's for a press conference."

"A press conference?"

"Right. They're going to confess their sins and ask the Ayatollah's forgiveness in front of the cameras. They love that sort of thing."

Donnelly didn't argue the point, so I continued.

"Anyway, the mullah instructs him to have a bus waiting at the front gate, fueled and ready to go—"

"And we just waltz out the door with a couple of dozen prisoners, under the noses of who knows how many armed guards."

"I can't say it's not risky."

"It's suicidal, Jack. You know it is. At least I hope you do!"

"It's my only way out."

He gave me a long, lugubrious look. "What are you saying?"

"I'm saying that I can't leave without Fatemi, and he won't leave without the rest of them."

Donnelly shook his head. "Terrific. Why don't we just spring the whole goddamned prison? What's a few thousand more?"

"Look," I said. "You're right. It's a long shot, and I wouldn't blame you if you said no. In fact, you should say no. You've got a wife and baby to think about."

"And if I do say no?"

"You go out with the mullah. I'll wish you luck and have no hard feelings."

"Jesus Christ, Jack. Would you really stay behind?"

I shrugged. "No choice, I'm afraid. I wish there was, but there isn't."

Donnelly looked away. He took in a lungful of air, slowly blew it out, then turned back to face me.

"Shit," he said. "Looks like we're all stuck in the same damned boat."

8 . . . 4 . . . 3 . . .

I watched carefully as the mullah dialed the warden's extension. We'd checked the number on a list the jailer kept in his top drawer, and just to be sure the cleric didn't try anything, Yari was bent over the desk, listening in on the receiver. I stood opposite, my hand on the cradle, ready to cut the call off if there was the slightest deviation from the script. In the end, the conversation lasted no more than a few seconds. The mullah, spitting orders down the line, must have been convincing because when he hung up, Yari nodded his head, indicating we were all set.

"How long?" I asked.

"He will ring back when the bus is ready," he said. "Perhaps twenty minutes."

I checked the wall clock—4:12—then looked over at Donnelly, who was standing at the door, just outside the office. Having already gathered up the keys that hung on the far wall, he nodded, and slipped away, to start releasing prisoners and getting them into some kind of order.

A weighty silence descended on the room. Yari, the mad mullah, and me, caught up in that tiny space, each of us staring straight ahead, with nothing to say and no need to pretend. The clock ticked slowly by, the atmosphere growing more oppressive with each excruciating minute. Then, out of nowhere, Yari started laughing.

"What's funny?" I said.

"We."

"We?"

"Yes. You and I. And especially him."

The mullah, not sharing the joke, just sat there, glaring at us.

"Look at him," Yari said, staring back. "What do you see? An ignorant fool, that's what. No more than that. An evil, ignorant fool. Yet, he won. He outsmarted both of us. So what does it make us? Even bigger fools, I think, because we allowed him to win. Between your arrogance and my weakness, we made him what he is. We gave the people nowhere else to turn, so they turned to him. And now look at us. The best we can do is escape, you to the safety of your home and me to find sanctuary. All we can do is run from this pitiful clown and hope that he doesn't follow."

With that, Yari fell back into silence. Then the phone rang.

Beyond the twelve-foot-high iron gate lay salvation, in the form of a green-and-white city bus. Unfortunately, between it and us stood a contingent of eight armed guards, along with a very officious-looking official, whom I took to be the warden.

Our procession was made up of two rows of twelve

prisoners. Led by the mad mullah, I trailed close behind, with Donnelly bringing up the rear, and Yari somewhere in between. There hadn't been enough handcuffs to go around, so we'd told the men in the back to hold their hands together at the crotch, as if they were manacled, and everyone had been instructed to keep their eyes lowered, fixed to the floor in front of their feet.

At thirty yards, I saw trouble. The warden was jumpy, and the guards, lined up like a firing squad across the exit, were tense, ready for action.

"Be careful," I whispered in the mullah's ear, and he nodded.

Signaling for the prisoners to stop, I stepped forward with the imam as he prepared to confront the nervous administrator. Both men were trembling, and the guards were on edge. You could feel in the air the potential for violence.

"Why is this gate closed?!" the mullah demanded to know. *"I order you to open it immediately!"*

"Yes, Excellency, of course." The warden equivocated: *"I . . . I would like to open the gate, but . . . but I have been told I must await—"*

"OPEN IT!" The mullah exploded into a spitting rage. *"OPEN THE GATE THIS MOMENT! IF YOU DISOBEY ME, I WILL HOLD YOU PERSONALLY RESPONSIBLE AND I WILL SEE THAT YOU SUFFER THE CONSEQUENCES!"*

The man clearly knew what this madman was capable of. He shrank back, but he didn't fold. As he cast a nervous glance in my direction, it was clear that he knew exactly what was happening. He knew what was at stake, too, but to drive the point home, I stepped forward and, without saying a word, made certain he understood that his life was on the line. He drew a shaky breath and turned back to the mullah.

"Forgive me, Excellency, but . . ." He held out a clipboard

with a sheet of paper attached to it. "*I . . . I must ask that you sign the order . . .*"

The mullah fixed him with a long, withering glare. The poor guy turned gray with fear, his hand trembled uncontrollably, and he could hardly breathe. But he didn't back down. The cleric curled his lip in an expression of utter contempt.

I saw that the warden was ready with a fountain pen. Reaching across, I grabbed it from him and offered it to the mullah. He transferred his contempt to me, then angrily grabbed the pen and scratched his name across the bottom of the document.

I escorted the mullah onto the coach, handcuffed him to a back-row seat, then went back onto the sidewalk, to push the prisoners along as, one by one, they filed up the steps. The guards had gathered outside the gate to smoke cigarettes and watch our exodus. They knew full well that something wasn't right, but none was foolish enough to interfere. If the warden and the mullah were in agreement, why would they step in?

It was a slow process—painfully slow—but when half our party had boarded, and Yari stepped into the bus, I allowed myself to think that maybe, just maybe, we were gonna make it.

A black sedan appeared out of nowhere and came to a screeching halt on the street beside us. A youngish man, dressed in dark pants and an army jacket, flew out of the backseat and went straight at the warden, gesticulating madly and screaming at the top of his lungs. The warden tried to offer up his clipboard, but the man just brushed it away and raised the pitch of his voice. The guards tossed their cigarettes aside and stood up, swinging their M-16s around, at the ready.

I shot Donnelly a look, but he had his eyes on the man,

who was approaching him, spewing the same diatribe he'd afforded the warden. When the man reached into his pocket and came out with a handgun, Donnelly didn't wait to see what his intentions were. He unloaded several rounds into the guy's chest. Before anyone knew what had happened, the man was splayed out on the sidewalk, the last tremors of life pulsing through his body. There was a split second of shocked silence . . .

Then all hell broke loose.

All eight guards started blasting away, indiscriminately spraying the area with an unholy barrage of firepower. The warden was the first to go down, his body pummeled from top to bottom with friendly fire as he tried desperately to get out of the way. A half dozen prisoners fell, too, and lay dead or dying on the sidewalk as the others dove to the ground, clinging to the pavement as they said an urgent prayer.

Donnelly spun around on the guards, taking two out with his opening burst. I went into a crouch position and started firing back toward the building, hitting two myself, and earning a volley of return fire that forced me back behind the bus. The four guards still standing made a dash for the prison gate, laying down fire as they went. Donnelly got one in the back, I hit another, and the last two made it inside.

"Go! Go! Go!"

Donnelly used the lull to start pulling the surviving prisoners off the sidewalk and shoving them toward the bus. I came out, and was starting to push them up the steps, when out of the corner of my eye, I saw one of the guards step out from behind the gate and start firing, wild-eyed, spraying bullets everywhere, hoping he'd connect with something, anything.

He did.

It felt like a sledgehammer had come crashing down on my back, knocking me off my feet with the force of a moving freight train. I hit the ground hard and lost track of everything but the excruciating pain. I saw some movement—

Donnelly firing into my assailant—then I lost everything. There was nothing but black. Cold, black, empty space.

Then a voice. Calm and soothing.

"Put your arms around me," it said.

I tried to say something, but it must have come out as no more than a groan. I opened my eyes and caught a glimpse of Yari leaning over me. But I was in and out of consciousness, and the next thing I knew, I was being moved. Yari on my left, Donnelly on my right, dragging me up the steps, to the safety of the bus.

I must have passed out again. The next thing I remembered, the bus was on the move and Yari was wrapping my shoulder in a makeshift bandage. I watched him work, and at a certain point, he realized that my eyes were open. He didn't say anything, but there was something in his expression that reminded me of the first time I'd seen him, when he'd followed Zahra over to my table at the Café Pars. He had that same sparkle in his eye.

"Wasn't I supposed to be saving you?" I said.

He didn't respond for a moment, then he looked up at me and smiled. "It seems that we have saved each other."

THIRTY

There was one last piece of unfinished business.

Whether through the incompetence of the Iranian authorities, or plain dumb luck, we made it through the center of Tehran, and onto the Mehrabad Airport runway, with unimpeded ease. Donnelly organized an assault team of five, who shot the lock off a service gate, drove the bus right up to the steps of an Olympic Airlines F-28, and took the aircraft with no resistance.

I was still in pain—a lot of pain—but I was thinking clearly now, and I could walk. Yari tried to help me off the bus, but I told him to wait for me on the tarmac. I think he knew why. Anyway, he didn't object.

I just sat there for a moment, preparing myself. I didn't feel particularly emotional about it, one way or another, but, still, it's not something you do without some kind of preparation. It was painful to stand up, and I had to use the seats for support, moving from one to the other as I struggled down the aisle to the rear of the bus, where the mad mullah sat, his eyes fixed warily on me.

When I stood over him, he tried very hard to smile. He tugged at his handcuffs.

"You . . . You make me free now?"

Yes," I said quietly. "I make you free."

He froze when he saw that it wasn't a key that I took from my pocket, but the Colt. He must have known it was a possibility, but I suppose he was hoping for mercy. Maybe he was counting on it.

I raised the gun and pointed it at his head. I don't know why I didn't pull the trigger right away, but for some reason, I didn't. I watched a drop of sweat fall from under his turban, roll across his brow, and finally mix with the tears that were forming in his eyes.

"Why?" he asked pitifully, his voice quivering in terror. "Why you do this? I . . . I have done what you ask. I have helped you . . ."

I hadn't planned on saying anything, but now it seemed somehow appropriate. I drew a breath. "There was a young girl," I said. "Many years ago, in Qom."

"What . . . ? I . . . I don't know what—"

"No, you won't remember her. But I do. I remember how she struggled to get free, and the way she cried out in pain. And I remember you. Your face, as you watched her die, slowly and painfully, covered in her own blood. Do you know what you did as she pleaded for mercy?"

"I . . . I . . ."

"You laughed," I said. "You laughed."

"I don't know what—"

A stabbing pain shot down from my neck and enveloped my chest, making it hard to breathe. I straightened my back and stiffened my arm, knowing that the backlash from the shot would make it worse. When I spoke, the voice seemed far away, as if my mouth was moving, but someone else, deep inside, was speaking.

"You are accused of the cold-blooded murder of a child. An innocent girl who was guilty of nothing but being born in the wrong place. How do you plead?"

"But—"

"How do you plead?" I repeated.

"I . . . I am innocent . . ."

"No. You're not."

"I beg you," he sobbed. "Please . . . I beg for my life!"

It's a difficult thing, to kill a defenseless man while he's looking you in the eye, even one as repulsive as the mad mullah. Maybe it's even a sin. I don't know. I suppose some would say that an act of forgiveness would have been the Christian thing to do, that it would have somehow brought me closer to God. Maybe that's true. But I wasn't looking for God. I was looking for justice.

The bullet struck the mullah in the middle of the forehead, killing him instantly. I didn't feel in any way good or righteous about it. In fact, I felt physically sick.

Yari's attention was fixed out the window, on the lights of Tehran as they faded into the darkness of the eastern sky. I don't pretend to know what was going through his mind, but perhaps, along with the inevitable regrets, and the sadness at seeing his country fade from view, he felt some hope, as well. Hope that the dreams he once held for his country—for the people of Iran—might someday be realized.

He sensed my gaze and turned to meet my eyes across the aisle. We were too distant to speak, but I don't think there was much that could've been said, anyway. He held my look for some time, though, and then, before turning back to the window, he gave me a little nod. Nothing more. Just a nod.

I never saw him again. I looked for him after leaving the hospital at the Rhine-Main base, where I'd spent a week recuperating and being debriefed, but he had disappeared. I hoped that, wherever he ended up, he would find and make peace with Zahra. But, of course, that was between them.

THIRTY-ONE

The road was slippery, and visibility close to zero, but I was determined to make it to Stockbridge before the end of the day. Lenni had no idea I was coming—she had no idea about anything—and the image of the look on her face when I showed up on the doorstep was enough to make me smile as I pushed on through the driving snow.

I'd flown in to New York that morning, on an overnight C-130 from Germany. Donnelly had already headed back to his family, but he'd come in to say good-bye before he left. He gave me a hearty handshake, wished me a Happy New Year, and said if I ever needed a wingman again, to give him a call. We've remained friends, and get together whenever we can.

Lenni had left a note on the kitchen table in the loft:

Jack –

As I write this, I have no idea where in the world you are. If you're reading it, you must be standing in the loft and you might (I hope) be wondering where in the world I am. I've gone up to the Berkshires to spend Christmas with Mom. I'll be back on the 2nd or 3rd and you can be sure that, in the meantime, I'll be thinking of you. I hope you're okay. Where in hell are you?!

L

I was running on empty somewhere around New Paltz, so I pulled into a rest stop to fill up. Picking up the last copy of the day-old Sunday *Times,* I headed into the cafeteria, ordered black coffee and toast, and slipped into a booth by the window.

The lead article went like this:

CARTER TELLS SOVIETS TO PULL TROOPS OUT OF AFGHANISTAN

He Warns of "Consequences"

Washington, Dec. 29—President Carter, in the harshest diplomatic exchange of his presidency, has warned the Soviet Union to withdraw its forces from Afghanistan or face "serious consequences." The President has received intelligence reports that an additional 15,000 to 20,000 Soviet troops have crossed into Afghanistan in the last 24 hours. The reinforcements were reported heading to Kabul, where a Moscow-backed coup on Thursday led to the overthrow and execution of President Hafizullah Amin.

Mr. Carter outlined his views of the developments in Afghanistan and Iran at a White House luncheon with a small group of reporters. In his remarks, Mr. Carter made it clear that he regarded the Soviet intervention as a provocative act that could threaten other nations in the area. He said that this should have a sobering effect on the decisions of Iran's Revolutionary Council that has been ruling the country since the deposing of Shah Mohammed Reza Pahlevi.

The President seemed to be hoping that the Soviet action would scare Khomeini into a friendlier attitude toward the Great Satan, but, of course, that just showed how poorly he understood what America was facing. I scanned down the article for more on the hostages, and found this sentence: "The President stated that he was aware of the country's growing impatience with the hostage situation in Iran, and noted he was in regular contact with Secretary of State Cyrus Vance, who had been negotiating with members of the Security Council about the next move in the crisis."

My heart sank as I thought about the faces I'd seen at the embassy that day. Their government was settling in for the long haul.

The most interesting item came near the end of the article:

> Mr. Carter noted that about 300,000 Afghan rebels have crossed into the isolated regions of northern Pakistan, where they will be able to move easily back and forth across the frontier. Direct American assistance to these rebels, he said, is under active consideration.

The Company had probably already delivered its first shipment of arms. And it made sense. We certainly couldn't go to war with the Soviet Union over their Afghan coup, so we'd have to fall back on the tried-and-true method of surrogate warfare. Well, tried, anyway. You couldn't fault the policy, though, because there weren't any other options, unless you thought doing nothing was an option. Still, I couldn't help thinking about "The Warriors of Islam."

Browsing through the rest of the paper, I was startled to find Toby Walters staring out at me from the obituary page. It was an official photograph, probably taken ten years earlier, and didn't match up with either the ambitious field agent I'd known in Iran, or the burned-out, old bureaucrat I found reading spy novels and drinking cognac in Virginia. He met the camera head-on in the photo, like he met the world, with a no-nonsense, "I'm in charge" kind of expression fixed to his face. The kind of face you'd want keeping an eye on a dangerous world.

Of course I saw Toby in a different light. He was, more than anything, a consummate Company man. A true believer who understood the game, and who knew that you couldn't fight a dirty little war without getting a little bit dirty. His methods went way too far, and more often than not, they backfired. But in the end, he was just a man who, like all of us, did what he thought he had to do. I never saw him as a friend, but for better or worse, we'd made some history together, and his passing made me sad.

The streetlamps sparkled like little jewels of light, set in a veil of clean white snow. I left the car on the main road and trudged through three blocks of unplowed drifts before I finally approached the big, clapboard house at the end of Bramble Lane. A handsome gray-haired woman in her seventies answered the door. She was curious, but not the slightest bit concerned about a knock on her door at eleven o'clock on New Year's Eve. She probably thought one of the neighbors was stopping by with a pie and best wishes.

"Mrs. Summers?"

"Yes . . ."

"I'm Jack."

"Jack . . . ?" It took her a moment to make the connection. "Oh! Jack! My word! Come in! Come in!"

Lenni had been in the kitchen, so hadn't heard my knock. The look on her face when she found me standing in the living room, warming myself by the fire, lived up to all my expectations.

"Well, that really is something!" her mother exclaimed.

"I believe this is the first time I've ever known Lenni to come up speechless!"

I woke early the next morning, and slipped out of bed to stand on the back porch and watch the sun rise over the frozen lake at the back of the house. There was a stillness, a timeless beauty to the scene that, usually, I would've found unsettling. But it had the opposite effect on me that morning. I was happy to take it for what it was.

Lenni was in the living room, building a fire, when I came in. I gave her a hand.

"You've lost weight," she said.

"I'll tell you about it sometime. Not now, though."

She nodded and threw another log on the fire. "It's good to have you back."

"It's good to be back."

We didn't speak for a moment, but the crackle of the fire as it came to life between us filled the space.

"You must've had a wonderful childhood," I said. "It's a beautiful place."

"You should see it in the summer."

"I could see spending some time up here. You're always saying how you'd love to do that."

She smiled. "And you always say how the quiet would drive you crazy."

"Maybe I'm ready for some quiet."

She stole a glance at me, decided I sounded serious enough to pursue it. "What would you do?"

"I don't know." I shrugged. "Write a book maybe."

Now she laughed out loud. "Well, I'd certainly read it!"

She went off to the kitchen to make coffee, and I browsed through a collection of old books that were lined up on the mantel. For some reason, I pulled down a volume of poems by W. B. Yeats. It was strange, because I never got much out of poetry, but as I turned to a random page, there were some lines that caught my eye.

It went like this:

Turning and turning in a widening gyre
The falcon cannot hear the falconer;
Things fall apart; the centre cannot hold;
Mere anarchy is loosed upon the world,
The blood-dimmed tide is loosed, and everywhere
The ceremony of innocence is drowned;
The best lack all conviction, while the worst
Are full of passionate intensity.

Surely, some revelation is at hand . . .

I was distracted by a heavenly scent coming from the kitchen. Lenni must have had something good in the oven.

ACKNOWLEDGMENTS

I would be remiss if I didn't mention some of the people who contributed their time, insight, and support to this undertaking. My friend Frank Viviano has been a great sounding board and an invaluable source of information and ideas. I always came away from our weekly cappuccino sessions with something to think about, and much of it found its way into the book. I don't know how many drafts of the manuscript my sister, Francie Gabbay, read, but each time she gave me sound advice and much appreciated moral support. Others who read *The Tehran Conviction* at various stages, and provided valuable feedback, were Jim Glass, Zara Light, Carol Sirkus, Andy Sirkus, and Kerry Bell.

Though I've never met or spoken with him, I must also thank Stephen Kinzer, whose wonderful book, *All the Shah's Men,* tells the compelling true story of the 1953 overthrow of the Iranian government. I recommend it to anyone with an interest in the history of America and Iran's stormy relationship—and we should all be interested.

As always, my wife, Julia, deserves a special thanks for providing support and tolerance that often goes beyond the call of duty.

EXPLOSIVE THRILLERS FROM

TOM GABBAY

THE BERLIN CONSPIRACY

978-0-06-078788-2

After the Bay of Pigs fiasco, ex-agent Jack Teller is through with the CIA—until the Berlin station is contacted by a Colonel in the East German Stasi just days before President John F. Kennedy's scheduled visit to the Wall. The informant claims a plot is brewing at the highest levels of the U.S. government to assassinate the American president in Germany.

THE LISBON CROSSING

978-0-06-118844-2

With Europe in the iron grip of Hitler's war machine, Jack Teller arrives in neutral Lisbon with international screen legend Lili Sterne. The German-born actress wants Jack to find her childhood friend who escaped Berlin one step ahead of the Nazi terror. A shattering discovery leads him to the perilous boulevards of occupied Paris, where his actions could change the course of the war.

THE TEHRAN CONVICTION

978-0-06-118860-2

Twenty-six years after helping to topple a fledgling democracy, Agent Jack Teller returns to Iran, where he must risk everything to save one man from Islamic justice—a man he once called his friend.

Visit www.AuthorTracker.com for exclusive information on your favorite HarperCollins authors.

Available wherever books are sold or please call 1-800-331-3761 to order.

TG 0110

Edge-of-your-seat thrillers from
New York Times bestselling author

JAMES ROLLINS

THE JUDAS STRAIN

978-0-06-076538-5

A horrific plague has arisen from the depths of the Indian Ocean to devastate humankind.

BLACK ORDER

978-0-06-076537-8

Buried in the past, an ancient conspiracy now rises to threaten all life.

MAP OF BONES

978-0-06-076524-8

There are those with dark plans for stolen sacred remains that will alter the future of mankind.

SANDSTORM

978-0-06-058067-4

Twenty years ago, a wealthy British financier disappeared near Ubar, the fabled city buried beneath the sands of Oman. Now the terrifying secrets of his disappearance are revealed.

ICE HUNT

978-0-06-052160-8

Danger lives at the top of the world . . . where nothing can survive except fear.

Visit www.AuthorTracker.com for exclusive information on your favorite HarperCollins authors.

JR 0308

Available wherever books are sold or please call 1-800-331-3761 to order.

 # 1 *NEW YORK TIMES* BESTSELLING AUTHOR

MICHAEL CRICHTON

NEXT

978-0-06-087316-5

Welcome to our genetic world. Fast, furious and out of control. This is not the world of the future—it's the world right now.

STATE OF FEAR

978-0-06-178266-4

In Tokyo, in Los Angeles, in Antarctica, in the Solomon Islands . . . an intelligence agent races to put all the pieces of a worldwide puzzle together to prevent a global catastrophe.

PREY

978-0-06-170308-9

In the Nevada desert, an experiment has gone horribly wrong. A cloud of nanoparticles—micro-robots—has escaped from the laboratory. It has been programmed as a predator and every attempt to destroy it has failed. And we are the prey.

Visit www.AuthorTracker.com for exclusive information on your favorite HarperCollins authors.

Available wherever books are sold or please call 1-800-331-3761 to order.

MC1 0209

NEED SOMETHING NEW TO READ?

Download it Now!

Visit www.harpercollinsebooks.com to choose from thousands of titles you can easily download to your computer or PDA.

Save 20% off the printed book price. Ordering is easy and secure.

HarperCollins e-books

Download to your laptop, PDA, or phone for convenient, immediate, or on-the-go reading. Visit www.harpercollinsebooks.com or other online e-book retailers.

Visit www.AuthorTracker.com for exclusive information on your favorite HarperCollins authors.

Available wherever books are sold or please call 1-800-331-3761 to order.

HRE 0307